Alligator Alley

Volume 2 of the continuing adventures of
Glen Wilson...

Other books by Ken Coffman

Fiction

Steel Waters, by Ken Coffman
Twisted Shadow, by Ken Coffman with Mark Bothum
Glen Wilson's Bad Medicine
Hartz String Theory

Nonfiction
Real World FPGA Design with Verilog

The Armchair Adventurer
www.ArmchairAdventurer.net

Books can be ordered from:

www.bytechservices.com
1500A East College Way #554
Mount Vernon, WA 98273

Alligator Alley

Volume 2 of the continuing adventures of
Glen Wilson…

Ken Coffman

and

Mark Bothum

ISBN 0-975-43140-4

Published by:

The Armchair Adventurer
1500A East College Way #554
Mount Vernon, WA 98273

Dedication

Ken: For my friend Craig S. Ranta. Of all the good folks I know, there are a few I'd confess (under duress) that are smarter than me. Entrepreneur, engineer, applied researcher, musician, concert promoter, race car driver and retired parachutist. How can your humble novelist top all that? At least I wasn't beat at tic-tac-toe by a chicken...

For literary inspiration, I thank Edward Abbey, RIP.

Mark: To my family for loving support...

We wish to thank our editorial board for encouragement, guidance, proofreading and commentary.

Judy Coffman
Stacy Kennedy
Ken Lomax
Dock Brown
Gary Croft
Dale Edwards
Kathy Kennedy

Author notes on the Armchair Adventurer edition of Alligator Alley

The genesis of Alligator Alley came in the early 1990's. I was working for an aerospace company and someone cancelled out of a trip to DAC (Design Automation Conference) in Orlando. So, late on Thursday, my boss asked me if I wanted to go and I said sure.

He said fine, your flight is on Saturday. Surprise! I flew to Orlando and had Sunday all to myself, just me and my little Japanese rental car with unlimited mileage. I looked at a map and on a whim decided to drive to Key Largo (probably because of the Humphrey Bogart movie). I vividly remember a few things about that trip beyond the fact that it's a long-ass drive with the round trip taking something like 14 hours. I drove through Kissimmee, Haines City, Okeechobee, Belle Glade, Key Largo (of course), Fort Myers and back up Highway 17 to Orlando. I stopped briefly and had a piece of Key Lime pie in Key Largo and then drove back, drafting behind a semi truck at 90 MPH through a tremendous tropical storm with lightning bolts attacking the landscape. Very intense.

Prior to Alligator Alley, I'd started several novels, but they never went anywhere. I'd write 10,000 words or so and they'd fizzle out. In the meantime, I'd switched jobs and worked for a bar code company. I was idly surfing around the company intranet looking for something and I traversed through some obscure links into a directory innocently titled "Parts Lists". In this directory, I stumbled across some very odd rambling, a sort of blog, but this is before blogs existed. A collection of bizarre vignettes about highly-unlikely things that happened over the weekend. I was quite struck by the writing; it was extreme and hallucinatory. I was reminded of things I'd read by Hunter Thompson and William S. Burroughs. Trained as an engineer, I immediately tried to figure out what could be done with this talent. To this day, I believe I discovered a unique and important writing voice. I gathered my thoughts (and my courage), tracked down this author and suggested we work together on a novel. Rather too quickly I think, he agreed. Now, what should we write about? I remembered my business trip to Orlando and suggested that we work on the adventure of a rather blandly named oddball: Glen Wilson.

Working with a partner was interesting. For this collaboration, Mark was an instant audience; I could spend a few hours writing and get instant feedback and encouragement. I could sit back and wait for exciting and stimulating work to pour out of Mark's overheated imagination. This arrangement kept me motivated and the project actually got completed. A miracle! I think our styles and habits fit together well. I removed a lot of his ellipses … (leaving plenty, believe me) and battered at things until we had something that fit together.

When Alligator Alley was done, I felt a lingering loss. Partially because this project, that had eaten all my spare time for over a year, was complete. I experienced a sort of post-partum depression because the characters had become very good friends (I'm aware this is nuts) and I missed interacting with them. There were more stories to be told. There are now four Glen Wilson novels and there are four more planned. The central theme in my mind is the real character of Glen, is he a positive or negative force in the universe? I have an idea, but you'll have to wait until the last novel to find out. Until then, Glen Wilson lives!

KLC – April 2005

You can email me at kcoffman@sos.net if you have questions or comments. As always, online reviews, good or bad, are greatly appreciated.

LEONARD

Leonard Allen Mullins was the most devout and regular Sunday School attendee in Southern Florida. From the age of five until he reached puberty, on every Sunday, there was Leonard, brushed, scrubbed and bearing his cleanest jeans. Not that anyone paid attention. Only the Cosmos kept track of these matters. It wasn't a great love of God that made Leonard go. Church gave him escape from the farm: the listing single-wide trailer parked where the axle gave out, the weedy yard decorated with his father's coiled copper tubing, the fermenting sugar beets, and the flies that swarmed around the racks of tanning hides. His father didn't go to church, so church was sanctuary. His mother did attend, but only to pray for his father's soul.

As a child, Leonard had a diminutive frame that earned him the nickname 'Monkey Boy', which had gradually evolved to 'Lenny', as in 'Lenny the Monkey Boy'. Leonard could not decide which name he liked least, but he knew that he really hated both names together. After puberty, Leonard sprouted to over six feet, but the names stuck.

Leonard's faithful Sunday School attendance had acquainted him with Job, and sometimes Leonard figured that maybe Job had gotten off easy. Maybe Satan had been just practicing until now, waiting until his nails were sharpened just right for embedding them deep into Leonard's hairy little monkey butt.

"Leonard! Get out here! Customer's waiting."

Clemson Bremmer turned his head and spit a yellow stream which splattered a scraggly yellowish cur nosing an empty trash can.

"What you looking for, Dog? Ain't nuthin in there."

Dog lowered his head. Without looking at Clem he slunk around the corner. Only Clem and Leonard knew Dog used to be white.

"Leonard!"

Damn him. Clem was sure Leonard was daydreaming or jerking off in the bathroom. He heaved forward, grunting a little from the strain. The front legs of his chair thudded onto the old porch with the full impact of Clem's 350-plus pounds. Clem chose his chairs with great care.

The locals knew Clem doctored his gas and the tourist trade had dropped since the highway bypass opened, leaving Clem only the biologists, poachers, and underage beer buyers. Leonard once tried

1

thinning the oil in the 55 gallon drums too with used motor oil, this story was still told in the bars around Carnestown.

Clem swayed towards the pumps, cruising on his second six-pack of the morning. He estimated the sale: '72 Chevy Custom/10, dual tanks. Full fill-up could be 40 gallons, maybe a pack of Marlboros and a half rack of Bud. Clem liked to estimate the sale. When he was wrong he blamed Leonard.

He dug up a gap-toothed smile as he reached the truck. Could be some good ol' boys from upstate. Maybe some college kids. Could mean a full rack of Bud.

"What else can I do ya'll for today?" Clem said to the driver who wore the Marine jarhead haircut that was back in fashion after the September 11 attacks on the World Trade Center. Jarhead was pumping Clem's diluted gasoline on the far side and he didn't look up when Clem spoke. The truck door on Clem's side opened and a girl stepped out. Clem stared. *Leonard, you missed out on this one!* She was tall, mostly legs and breasts in denim cutoffs a size and a half too small and filling out a skimpy halter-top that the day's humidity helped to make more revealing. She had short blond hair in mousse spikes. Her dazzling smile illuminated Clem, who managed to return a broken-toothed and tobacco-stained leer. She stepped closer.

Sumthin' wrong with her eye? She reached behind her back. *Yup, quite the shiner.* She came up with an old Army Colt. *Just where'd she have room for THAT?* was Clem's last thought as a 45 slug blew a three inch hole out the back of his head.

Leonard jerked and dropped his People magazine to the urine-soaked floor. Brad and Jennifer lay face down in the pee. *What was that? Backfire? Did we have a customer?*

He'd heard Clem bellowing at him earlier but figured it would just be "Leonard, do... Whatever! And where were you?" The things that Clem bellowed could wait. *Just hold your gators, you fat cow.* Leonard would never really say that, but it was a guilty pleasure to think it again and again all day.

He picked up the soggy magazine and heaved it into the trash. He heard the cash register bell as he pulled up his overalls and slipped the straps over his narrow shoulders. He pushed up a sleeve and reached into the toilet tank to pull the stopper. Clem would be harping at him to fix that soon. He watched the water swirl away and heard a door slam. He sighed and struggled with the stubborn door latch. An engine fired up. Glass packs roared, it was an American V-8. From the engine sound he could tell it had a fouled plug and a couple of valves that needed adjusting. He kicked the bottom of the door and it sprung open as tires spun in the roadside gravel. Clem would probably make him sweep that gravel up. *Eat mud, you buffalo.* He shuffled into the 'office'.

The cash drawer was open. Sure. *Now if I'd done that…* He started to push it closed and stopped. It was barren except for a handful of pennies. He stared blankly. He glanced around the room and back at the drawer. It was still empty. All the cigarettes and some of Clem's black rocks were missing. This was—this was very bad. Clem would… He didn't know. Yes, he did. Clem would think he took the money. Clem would call the Sheriff. That stuck-up Deputy Rawlins would come out, look down at Leonard through his mirrored glasses, and remind Clem how he'd bullied Leonard since they were kids. Then Deputy Rawlins would bring up the time Leonard walked out of Ed's Grocery with a forgotten fruit pie in his shirt pocket. An honest mistake that had cost his job stocking shelves. Leonard hated Deputy Rawlins. Then, without warning, came inspiration. He brightened and reached for the phone. He'd call the State Police himself, before Clem found out! Wherever Clem was, probably passed out on the porch. No Deputy Rawlins, and they would hardly expect the culprit to call in the report! The number (911) was penciled under the receiver. However, the phone was dead.

Leonard stared at the useless handset. This was another Bad Thing. On some kind of roll here. He dropped it to the floor, leaned over the oily plywood shelf that Clem called his desk, and tugged on the dangling cord. It wouldn't budge. He bent to look under the desk but the corner of the open cash drawer surprised him with a painful slice over his left eyebrow. "Shit…" He glanced skyward. "Oops, I meant…" He pulled his hand away, glanced at it. Another head wound and lots of blood. Leonard lost it. "I meant SHIT! Why can't I ever get a decent break? This is a bad day. I MEANT FUCKIN' SHIT!" It hadn't been much of a week either. "SHIT SHIT SHIT!!!" Burning in eternal hell wouldn't be much worse.

He crashed through the screen door with both hands on his face.

"Clem, where are you hiding, damn you!"

He slowly edged around the gas pump and then tripped over Clem's dead body. Clem used to say: 'Cheer up Leonard, things could get worse.' And sure enough, things always got worse.

ELKE

Elke Rittenauer dropped her suitcase and garment bag by the door. She checked again to make sure the plane ticket to Orlando was in her bag. She mentally walked through the apartment to make sure the faucets and appliances were all turned off. Everything was quiet; the curtains were pulled tight and room was outlined in gray by the dim light filtering through. Dust covers were thrown over the couch and her reading chair. The cat was outside. The damn thing could eat moles and sparrows for a week. Elke felt tired and depressed, the usual lately. She didn't care about the apartment. The whole place could burn, with her in it, and it would be no big loss. She checked the hem of her checked wool skirt in the mirror to make sure it was straight. She brushed her short hair back from her face and scrubbed a little of her peach lipstick off a front tooth.

The airport van was outside. As she locked the door she had a sudden vision of her jet hurtling into a Florida swamp, then alligators tearing at the bodies of the dead passengers. She pictured her ex-husband coming out of the woodwork to try to cash in an insurance policy— otherwise, no one would even notice. Even the alligators would probably spit her out and search for something younger and less dried out. She stood straight and tottered on her high heels down the sidewalk to the van. Maybe I'll put an alligator handbag on my credit card when I'm down there, she thought. Other than that, she couldn't see a single other reason for living.

WEBSTER

FBI agent-in-training Orrin Webster leaned over the counter with his silk tie hanging loosely around his neck. He wore a beige silk suit from Hong Kong, no socks, and leather moccasins. The dress code had eased up a lot since Hoover died. He was watching Lisa Boonton rummage through some files. She was about 23, blond, and her skin was evenly tanned. She had a purple stripe in her hair and her ears were pierced in four places on each side. She was single but wore a wedding band to keep the creeps at bay. She was the day clerk at the St. Louis FBI weapons crib.

"Hey dude, what are you after?" she asked.

"I can't decide if I want a Glock 23 or a Heckler and Koch P-7," Webster replied.

"Bullshit, you'll take a Smith and Wesson Thirty-Eight Special just like all the other boys."

"No, I'm serious, I've got my paperwork right here."

He handed over a manila folder. She slid her glasses on and looked through the bundle.

"Where's your checkout for semiautomatics?" she asked.

He pulled a slip of paper from his wallet.

"Right here."

"Damn it. I hate giving you cowboys the real thing. Did you know that between 1980 and 1990, if an officer went down, he was shot with his own gun twenty-two percent of the time?"

"Where did you read that?"

"I didn't read it, I just made it up. I'll bet I'm close, though. You're just going to get your smart butt shot off. A big gun doesn't make you any stronger or smarter. If 6 rounds don't do the job, 17 more aren't going to save your butt. Okay, look, I have a Glock 19 that already has some scratches, you can take that. What do you need it for anyway?"

"I'm going to Orlando and put the hurt on an asshole named Wilson."

"Who's babysitting you, Everson? Thomas?"

"No one is babysitting me," Webster pouted. "The boss is sending me down by myself. I have to coordinate with the Smokies down there, that's all. To go with the Glock I'll take twenty rounds of Black Talon and an Astra A-75 for backup. And how about a kiss for luck?"

"You bring back the Glock without scratching it up any more than it already is, then you'll get your kiss. Forget the Astra and use your cellular phone for backup. Now sign here, here, and here," she said, handing him a clipboard. "And that Black Talon is just hyped-up crap, just bullshit," she said, leaning over the counter to look down the hallway. No one was coming.

"I've got some stuff my brother cooked up. He calls it White Rhino."

She fumbled through her purse and handed him a plastic clip of stubby gray cartridges.

Webster put the gray bullets in his pocket without looking at them.

"Let me know how those work for you, will ya?" Lisa said.

"Yeah, whatever," Webster said remotely. He hefted the sleek Glock and pointed it at the wall. "Is this thing loaded?"

"All guns are loaded, honey. If you don't know that then you'd ought to go back to that management gig at Burger King."

"Gimme a break, Lisa. Besides, these days, you need a gun to survive at Burger King too."

He took off his jacket and wriggled into the shoulder holster. He put his jacket back on. He whipped out the Glock and pointed it at the wall.

"Okay Wilson, I'm the heat and you're busted. Don't move a muscle or I'll ventilate your sorry backside."

"Lord help us all," Lisa muttered.

MURPHY

Captain Margaret Murphy stood at attention with her back straight and her hands clenched stiffly at her sides. Her dark hair was pulled back neatly into a bun except for a few strands that had worked free and were drifting in the air pushed around the room by a ceiling fan. She stared through a gauzy curtain at a spot across the State Patrol parking lot between a Florida National Bank building and a WalMart store. She focused on a dusty and sick-looking palm tree. Her supervisor, Major Rogers Smythe, sat on the corner of his desk and waved a one-inch sheaf of paper.

"The investigating team concluded that you used unnecessary force," Smythe lectured. "You're suspended for a week without pay and a disciplinary action has been recorded in your personnel file. That will close the matter."

Smythe stared at Murphy. Her face was blank and unreadable.

"Okay, that's all the stuff for the record," Smythe said. "At ease, Murphy."

Murphy unclenched her hands and relaxed her posture slightly.

"Now for the part that's off the record," Smythe continued. "I added a recommendation for commendation to your file and we'll burn a week of comp time so you won't lose any money. I hate to second-guess you guys out in the field. Still, it would have been better if you'd just shot the guy once. Okay, Murphy?"

"Sure, boss," Murphy said flatly.

Smythe sighed. "You're the best cop we have in the field. I don't want to lose you. Try not to shoot anybody for a week or two—would that be all right with you, Murphy?"

She nodded. Smythe patted her arm in a fatherly manner.

"Fine." He handed over her badge and gun. "Just sign these papers."

She didn't look at them, just scribbled her name wherever Smythe had scrawled an X in red ink.

"Now get back to work, dammit."

Murphy nodded and left the room. A small crowd had gathered in the hallway outside Smythe's office. They smiled and slapped her on the back as she maneuvered her way through.

"Welcome back, Murphy," someone said. The internal affairs case was supposedly confidential but the rumor mill was well-developed and usually accurate.

"Speech," one of the patrolmen called out. Smythe leaned against his office doorway and watched. Murphy stopped and gestured with the badge and revolver she clutched in her hand.

"Here's the way it is, guys," she said quietly while staring at a spot high on the wall. "Murphy shoots bad guy. Murphy gets her hands slapped. Murphy gets back to work. End of story."

She pushed through and walked upstairs to her desk. There was a smattering of applause.

"Murphy for president!" a trooper shouted.

"Right on," someone seconded.

"Gentlemen, break it up before I call the riot squad," Smythe said.

"We are the riot squad," a patrolman called out.

Smythe laughed as he pushed his door shut.

GLEN

Glen Wilson rubbed a scar on his left hand where the little finger was missing. He was sitting in the International Controls Corporation lunchroom. The girl he was talking with, Bonnie Periera, looked sixteen but she was actually an innocent twenty-two years old. Glen gestured at her with a half-eaten blueberry muffin.

"I had a little misunderstanding with a guy down in Bolivia and lost my poor little pinkie a long time ago; the damn thing still itches. Got it in a cigar box back home. You know how they say the hair and fingernails keep growing after you're dead? I gotta get that finger out every month and trim the nail." He laughed at the expression on

Bonnie's face. "Ha, just kidding, got you on that one, didn't I? The scar does itch though, like when the weather's changing or something."

Bonnie was a software engineering student, an intern taking the semester off to get some industry experience. She was fresh meat because she hadn't heard any of Glen's stories yet.

"How exactly did you lose it?" she asked.

Glen took a sip of coffee.

"I was arguing with a business associate. You know how hotheaded the Latin Americans can be. He flipped out and hacked off my finger with a machete before I could make him see reason."

"Your business associate had a machete? What kind of business was that?" Bonnie asked with a puzzled look on her face.

"Never mind. I ended our disagreement by pushing him over the side of a bridge. It was far enough to the river that he had a few seconds to really regret messing with me."

Dean Grayson, Glen's boss, walked up and heard the end of Glen's story.

"Wilson, you're full of bullshit. I read your insurance claim. You had an infected nail and a doctor amputated your pinkie."

"Well, that makes kind of a dull story, doesn't it?"

"How do you expect people to believe your crap if you're always changing your stories around?" Grayson asked.

"I don't care if anyone believes me or not. If your pedestrian mind insists that truth always aligns with fact, then I'm sorry. That's your problem, not mine. Now beat it, I'm talking here."

"I can see you're teaching Bonnie some of your bad habits," Grayson said dryly. He looked pointedly at his watch. "I hate to interrupt your busy schedule, but Sue Burns ate a bad seafood salad and can't go to the trade show in Orlando. No one else can go so you're going in her place."

"Great," Glen said, getting up and brushing muffin crumbs off his trousers.

Grayson handed him some airline tickets. He held out the company's platinum American Express card. Glen grabbed it but Grayson would not let it go.

"No bullshit this time," Grayson said, "Parker is still pissed off about your last expense report."

"Hey, I get the message. I'm a changed man. A company man. A frugal man. A careful and thrifty man," Glen said, trying to tug the card out of Grayson's grip.

"I can't believe we're doing this," Grayson said with his eyes clinched closed and a sour look on his face.

"I'll travel on the cheap this time," Glen promised, "I'll eat at McDonald's and ride the shuttle buses. I'll drink tap water and skip all desserts."

Glen pulled hard and got the card. He turned and waved it at Bonnie, who was watching the exchange with wonder.

"It's party time," he said in a stage whisper, flourishing the card and grinning broadly. "When I come back I'll teach you how to write a creative expense report."

"Damn it," Grayson said bitterly, "this is a big mistake."

Alligator Alley

PART ONE

A few of us now know from the closed-system experts that the golden rule doesn't work. Those few of us who are rich and who really have the figures know that it is worse than one chance in one hundred that you can survive your allotted days in any comfort. It is not you or the other fellow; it is you or one hundred others. And if you are going to survive... you're going to have to do it at the expense of others. So, do it as neatly and cleanly and politely as you know how and your conscience will allow.

- Advice from an "uncle" to R. Buckminster Fuller in 1913 as related in Utopia or Oblivion

I had a conscience once, but it cost me money so I gave it up.

- Glen Wilson

CHAPTER 1

Sunday Evening, May 18

LEONARD

Leonard Allen Mullins lay sprawled in the gravel of the two-bit gas station thinking *I coulda been an astronaut and Clem has a big hole in the back of his head.* Leonard's father had always laughed at the dream of Space Ranger Mullins.

"Boy, you can't even pee right," he often said.

His old man had a twisted sense of humor and enjoyed tormenting Leonard. The determined Leonard had practiced faithfully, holding a straining bladder for hours after drinking a bucket of well water. His father's criteria always outpaced his urinary accomplishments.

The old man had finally ended his cruel sport by issuing the final challenge: "Son, an astronaut must hold it for two weeks sometimes and then piss over a ten-foot-wall."

Crushed, Leonard lowered his sights, knowing he could never meet the stringent standards of the Astronaut Picking People because of a defective pisser. *Maybe I could have been a fighter pilot instead and Clem's brains are spread out on the gravel.* His mother had finally explained The Way It Really Is.

"Leonard, you're very—special."

His mother had been attractive enough, almost pretty to others, intensely beautiful to Leonard, with soft brown eyes and wavy brown hair just starting to show a bit of gray. Too frail for life on the Dixie Farm among the old boats, the diesel barrels, and the rusty engine blocks.

"People like us—well, you didn't get much of a head start, Leonard. Not from me, or your dad, or from the Good Lord." Her eyes had brimmed with tears as she'd held him close. "Maybe someday you could have a fruit stand or something like that. Wouldn't that be okay? Meeting lots of people? Folks from all over would come to your stand

and when they got home they'd tell all their friends about Leonard Allen Mullins and his wonderful fruit. Wouldn't that be fine?"

Leonard had allowed that would be a right fine thing, but he mentally changed the fruit stand into a gator farm. Gators were righteous.

I'll have me a BIG ol' gator farm someday and Clem's been blown right out of his canvas shoes.

He rolled up onto one elbow.

"Clem?"

Clem's body. Definitely dead. Leonard poked him in the shoulder. A fat black fly buzzed in for a landing at the edge of the sticky pool of blood.

Leonard sat up. Some of his own blood dripped off his chin, splashed, and mixed with Clem's. He shut his eyes, gripped his knees, and rocked back and forth for a while. He had to tell somebody. Clem was shot dead while Leonard sat on the toilet reading about the rise and fall of Britney Spears. He had to tell someone. He opened his eyes. The Ochopee Tavern was just down the road. He'd use their pay phone to call the State Police or maybe even the Sheriff. Somehow he didn't care about Deputy Rawlins any more. He got to his feet and walked on trembling legs towards his old truck, a rusty bare metal and primer '54 Dodge with bald tires and sagging springs. He kept his keys chained to a strap on his overalls. He clambered in, inserted the key with a shaky hand, and pressed the starter button with his foot. <Click-click-click> He'd left the lights on again. *Good Lord, doesn't Leonard Mullins ever get a break?*

It was a long walk in the steaming heat to Ochopee, but Leonard got there and made the call.

GLEN

Sunday Evening

From the audio diary of Glen Wilson

The stub of my little finger had been itching something fierce for a few days, so I was ready for action from the moment the plane rolled to a stop. Here I am in good old Orlando. Delightful Orlando. The puckery brown center of Butthole, USA. The trade rags had been hinting that this computer equipment trade show would define industry leaders in several areas or I wouldn't be here. You don't send a punk with an MBA and cute smile into a roiling whirlpool of desperation, hunger, and under-the-booth blow jobs like the Orlando show and expect to make your quarterly bonus. No, you send someone that's brought the ship home before, someone who's felt the subtle shifts in the tide and nailed the main channel, someone who's gaffed the big ones and chopped the little ones into bait. You send me, Glen Wilson.

The baggage claim crowd looked like an audition for a Geritol commercial. I pushed through without any trouble. Some old nag started yipping so I flashed her my wallet and monotoned "FBI ma'am, and we're in a hurry." I grabbed my bags and overheard a mournful "Wasn't that just a Triple-A card?" Too late, I was already moving.

I'm in one of those cutesy airport lounges with the walls covered with cutesy flyboy junk. The whores were drinking cutesy pineapple drinks in cutesy fluted glasses with cutesy umbrellas. I could blow chunks, it was so sickening. I snagged a corner table and started sizing things up. Mostly tourists in loud shirts and white shoes (a few full Clevelands: white shoes, polyester pants AND white belts), but the counter sported a couple of local heroes loudly and arrogantly discussing 'cells' and 'windshear' while glancing around to see who they were impressing. Not me. They were obviously a couple of dummies. I wasn't impressed by the local talent either; not a hooker in the place worth looking at twice. I'd do better downtown. Expense reports have an 'entertainment' column and I planned to 'entertain' the hell out of things. Starting ASAP. But first, what to do with these lame pilots? I don't mind arrogance if it's backed by talent or experience. Otherwise, it sets me off. I riffled through the collection of credentials I kept in my briefcase, this called for more than an expired Triple-A card. I always carried some official-looking papers and a badge or two in case of need.

"Buy you guys a drink?"

The flyboys eyed me in the mirror as I approached. The younger one swiveled around with his elbow on the bar.

"You ain't some kinda faggot, are you?"

I visualized driving my shotglass deep into his face, but I stretched my grin another tooth or so and clapped him on the shoulder.

"No, son, I'm sorry. Got a lot of butt pirates around here, do you?"

I caught the bartender's eye and circled my finger for a round.

I continued. "No, I'm just the FAA." I flashed an impressive green ID card that I'd printed on a color printer and laminated at Kinko's. "I'd like to ask you and your friend here a few questions. That all right with you?"

From the way the blood drained out of his face I knew I'd hit paydirt. The bartender slapped a couple bottles of Hefeweizen on the counter and took my twenty.

"Well, now! That's fine beer you lads are drinking! I'm from Seattle, so I know my beer. Flying tourists around must be paying better than it did in my day! That's good, I like to see hard work paying off, especially for fine, young, honest pilots."

The older one, had to be almost thirty, found enough grit to start casual, but went downhill fast.

"Well... Uh, what's this. What are you, I mean... Just what is this all about?"

I coughed and looked at him pointedly.

"Sir," he added.

He went through three pockets until he found his cigarettes and through three matches to get it lit. I took a long pull off my beer and waited until he started to say something else, then I jumped in.

"Hell, nothing for you boys to worry about, at least I don't think so. Your pilot logs are up to date, aren't they? Nothing in those logs about flying under the radar over the Glades at night, is there? Christ no, hell's bells, everyone knows the kinda trouble you could get into doing that kind of stuff. Trophy hunters, drug dealers, illegal aliens et cetera, and so on, ad infinitum."

I pulled out a twenty-nine cent notepad from my jacket pocket, flipped a few pages, and wetted the tip of my pencil with my tongue.

"I'm sure you boys know about not drinking before you fly, but are you aware that there is a new regulation? FAR 1177-3 if I'm not mistaken and I'm sure I'm not. This regulation states that pilots and crew will do no drinking for eight hours after a job. You see what I'm getting at here?"

Mr. Casual looked at his pal, then back at me. He couldn't quite bring himself to look me in the eye.

"That's bullshit."

"Well son, suppose there was a problem on a flight and we wanted to see if there was an intoxicated pilot? See how that works? We can check you out for eight hours afterwards and make sure there's no problem. Really, it's for your benefit. Could prove you're just a bad driver, not drunk, you see?"

"Christ man, we didn't know. We just stopped in for a quick one, that's all."

Bingo!

"Well boys, I'm not here to ruin your lives, I think we can avoid all the paperwork if you gentlemen would just make a little donation to the FAA retirement fund. Then everybody goes home friends. Maybe in the future you boys do your drinking closer to home instead of the airport bar. Got me?"

* * *

"Gordon, it's not the heat, it's the humidity!"

Some schoolteacher-type was whining to her husband-boyfriend-mealticket and fanning herself with a half-dozen travel brochures. Her face was flushed to such a remarkable shade of hot-pink that she looked to be only minutes away from needing an autopsy. I considered offering the services of Doctor Wilson, but I was in a rather mellow mood with the money in my pocket those pussy flyboys had coughed up. I had places to go, people to see, so as I walked past I simply offered some friendly advice.

"Tell her to fuck off, Gordon."

Gordo jerked a little and looked around, but I was already curbside, scanning for taxis and kicking myself for not grabbing a rental car. Not a cabbie in sight. I turned back to the sidewalk where it surely looked like a Nine-One-One call was imminent for Mrs. Gordo. Well, what the hell. I have no excuse, sometimes tourists make me crazy. I walked over and gave Gordon a stiff-arm to the chest and peered into the startled eyes of Mrs. 'I Wanna See ALL of Central Florida in One Sweltering Afternoon'.

"Good Lord," I shouted, "this poor woman should be in a hospital!"

I grabbed Gordo's arm without looking, waited a split second, then spun to face him. "You have insurance, of course? Never mind, that's not important now."

I turned back to the woman and planted a hand firmly over her left breast.

"My God! A myocardial fumarole!"

I rotated back to Gordon.

"Do you have a car nearby?"

Squeeze-squeeze. He stared at my hand massaging his wife's breast. The look on his face was priceless.

15

"No, uh no, we're tourists, a group tour thing, but... Can't we call for an ambulance, or something?" He paused, still staring. "You're a doctor?"

Damn it, no car. Well, it was worth a try.

"Of course I'm a doctor, you blockhead!" I waved my loose arm in an extravagant gesture. "Run! Find a phone booth! Call 911! Tell them to hurry! There is no time to waste! Use my name!"

He did the right thing, of course, dashing off without knowing my name, while his wife slapped feebly at my groping hand with her damp brochures. I peered into her eyes again and promised, "This won't hurt." I glanced at the small but gathering crowd. I was going leave it at that but I got a glimpse of the old Gore/Streisand '04 button on her hemp bag before she slammed my head with it.

An Earth-shoe Greenpeace liberal. I think there is still a hundred dollar bounty on this type in Wyoming. I whispered to her, "Well, actually this is going to hurt quite a bit."

"Here comes the ambulance," I shouted.

Everybody looked, even Miz Gordo, so no one saw the punch except the old crone from the baggage claim line. She pointed an accusing finger at me and said something like "For shame, you dirty creep."

I was ashamed and very sorry. Also, I was happy to grab the cab that pulled up and escape before the crowd could get nasty.

Orlando was muggy-hot and Carlos (I read his name off the taxi license), my Cuban cabbie, couldn't seem to understand "air conditioner, you sonuvabitch," so I sweated buckets all the way into town. I tossed ten bucks over the seat, grabbed my bags from the trunk, and walked past the cabbie's outstretched hand (I'll give you a tip, amigo) and entered the hotel with a flurry of angry Spanish behind me. Not the first time, but it was generally a female voice doing the cursing. I used to get around in Spanish pretty good when I was running dope, but these days I'm more or less limited to the stuff that's useful on Rainier Avenue in Seattle like "How much for a quickie?" and "Do you have a younger sister?" I dropped my bags and walked back to the cabbie. He didn't know what was coming down and I saw him reach for the Taurus snubnose he kept in his belt. I got right up close, close enough to smell the beer and pepperoni on his stale breath. I pulled a hundred dollar bill from my back pocket, waved it in his face, then dropped it in his dirty hand. "You got a card, amigo?" He handed me a damp and dog-eared card which I stuck in my pocket.

"Next time, air conditioner?" I asked.

"You got it, boss. Call me day or night. I'm your limo man."

Amazing how they speak English just fine when there's a c-note in it for them.

ICC was too cheap to rent me a decent room and the desk clerk flipped me some shit about being full-up so I hung around the lobby reading brochures on the fascinating history and incredible sight-seeing opportunities of Orlando until a greasy punk in a bellboy monkey suit slunk out of an elevator, looking like he needed a few bucks, a shave, a few good meals, a girlfriend, and probably a high school diploma. I caught his eye on the way over and for a second he froze like a fawn in my highbeams. He obviously assumed I was someone else. I thought he was going to make a break, he definitely thought about it, but he slumped his shoulders, took a deep breath, and while staring me straight in the eye said all in one breath, "Dude, like I know I owe Manny, I ain't got it yet but I'll have it tomorrow just cut me some slack this one time and I'll make it up to you, swear to God, I've got a deal going down tonight so first thing in the morning or tonight if you wanna hang around or come back or I could drop by your place or we could meet somewhere later if you want 'cause like Manny don't need to know how much you pick up and hell, everybody gets off..."

About this point I grabbed him by the lapels and pulled him closer. I read his nametag. I wasn't exactly sure what this kid's problem was, but I thought I'd go with the flow.

"Tonight—right Raymond?"

He didn't even blink. The little fucker had balls, little mousy ones, but balls just the same.

"Sure, man, like I said."

I wasn't sure I could win a stare-down with this guy. He'd had practice. At least a year in the joint, I'd say. It upset me, so I let him go, got a grip on the sparkling stud in his left ear, and ripped it free.

"Jesus, man! Whatcha doing? Jesus Christ!"

He pulled a hand from his ear and looked at the bloody smear, then quickly glanced around. The passersby were pointedly paying us no attention.

"You're a crazy man..."

He looked back up at me and warily took a step back. Like that would help.

"Let's call it collateral."

I held my booty up to the light and whistled.

"Nice. Must be a month's pay. Better not be a goddam CZ."

I looked back at my new friend and smiled. I was feeling much better.

"Okay bud. Looks like we've got a deal, except..." I waved the earring in the general direction of the front desk and sighed. "Except it seems somebody messed up my reservations, got me flying coach when I KNOW there's gotta be a first class berth left in this dive somewhere." I plucked his cigarettes from his shirt pocket and shook one out. "You work here, right?"

Either that or he wore the stupid pillbox hat for fun.

His eyes flicked over to the large 'NO SMOKING' sign in four languages. He took another step back.

"I only been here a couple months. I can't do that kind of shit."

I pocketed the earring and lit up. I tossed him back the pack.

"Then you'd better call in a couple of favors bud, there's my luggage."

I was halfway to the front door when I turned and saw him staring vacantly at my bags. I pulled a banana from a fruit basket by the door and lobbed it at his head. "Glen Wilson is the name. Leave the room number with the desk clerk."

The dumb banana struck me as funny, so I grabbed another one and stuck it in my pocket. Never can tell when a banana might come in handy when you are in Orlando. At the door I turned, waved, and shouted. "And send one of these fruit baskets up. Vaya con Diablo!"

Choto... My Spanish was starting to come back quite nicely.

Late that night, when I got back to the hotel, I could see Raymond-the-bellboy had really come through. The adjoining suites must've cost him ALL his favors, meaning that he must owe this Manny character a small fortune and that he probably didn't have the money. Not that it mattered to me, although it might be good for a few chuckles if he bothered to show his face again.

After splashing some cold water on my face I was ready to face the hotel bar. It was still early but things were ramping up nicely. Some of the convention crowd had already arrived and found the bar well stocked. Alcohol loosens tongues like nothing short of sodium pentothal, which I reserved for emergency purposes only. Information is power, my friends, but sometimes disinformation will just have to do. I still had a truckload of gray-market microprocessors to unload, and they were getting colder by the minute. I noticed a couple of stuffed suits that were hitting it early and often. They looked like 5,000-dollar, single-signature, no-questions-asked types. And I just happened to have a pen....

LEONARD

Leonard sat in the back of Deputy Rawlins' patrol car. The windows were open but the air was still and the temperature was nearly unbearable; his overalls and shirt were sopping. To give his sweaty feet some circulation, Leonard took off his boots and tossed them out the window. The afternoon hours passed slowly. He watched the coroner take photographs. He watched Clem's body get loaded in the back of a black Lincoln hearse. Occasionally the radio would squawk but Leonard couldn't understand anything that it said.

From time to time the coroner, the funeral director, or the police beat reporter from the East Naples Weekly would point at Leonard, but none approached. Leonard recognized the reporter because Clem lined Dog's house with the paper that he got from a free stand at the market. The reporter had a grainy picture and byline for his column, "The Heat Beat." Leonard simply sat, watched, and waited.

Carl Bremmer, the only lawyer in Everglades City, pulled up in his Buick Roadmaster station wagon. Carl was about average height, but skeleton thin, and had a burnt-toast tan adorned with black flecks of skin cancer. He stank of the black Cuban cigarillos he was never without. Clem's ex-wife, Sarah, moved in with Carl after Clem threw her out. Clem hated both of them, but Carl still did whatever legal work Clem needed done. He was, after all, Clem's stepbrother.

Leonard cringed and sank down in the seat when he saw Sarah leave the car and waddle around the gas pumps, but she didn't come in his direction. He wondered what would become of the station. It was the only home he knew. What would happen to Dog? Who would water the worm tub? Who would beat on the air compressor with an adjustable wrench when it pooped out? Leonard knew of a half-dozen rotting relics on the highway to Miami. Clem's Place would probably join them.

Clem had carried a chunk of shrapnel in his shoulder from a land mine in Korea. Leonard remembered Clem saying about a million times: "An inch to the right, and I'm pushing up daisies. When your number's up boy, then your fucking number's up, no sense getting your boxers in a twist about it." Leonard could still see him speaking the words with teeth clenched around a cigarette. *Dear Clem. Why did your number come up today? What angel of God put a bullet through your head? What was special about today? Why you and not me? What am I going to do? Where am I going to go?*

Leonard started when Deputy Rawlins rapped on the roof.

"Okay Monk, let's go over this again," Rawlins said. *Monk!* Leonard throttled back his anger. "You were playing with your pecker in the can and you didn't see the car?" Rawlins asked.

"I didn't see the car."

"You were wanking off in the shitter and you didn't see who blew Clem's brains out," Rawlins said with his eyebrows wiggling above his mirror sunglasses.

"I didn't see no one."

"You were too busy pounding your pud to help Clem with a customer?"

"All I know is that they drove an American car, maybe a pickup, and it had a big-block V-8, probably a GM of some type."

"Well great, I'm glad we got that valuable information. Won't be no trouble at all to solve this case now. Well M-B, I guess I've got everything I need for my report. Why don't you take off, go home and do whatever it is you do."

Leonard opened the door and slipped his boots back on.

"And Monkey-boy," Rawlins said.

Leonard concentrated on pulling the leather laces tight.

"You keep whacking off and your little wiener is going to fall clean off."

Rawlins' laughter trailed Leonard as he walked toward his little house. He walked around the back side of the station to avoid having to speak to Carl and Sarah. Dog fell into step beside him. *Dog, why can't Leonard get a break? Is there anyone in the world who needs one more?*

In his house, Leonard sat at his old dinette and fed Dog a handful of peanuts. He opened a can of Campbell's pork and beans. He speared the little piece of pork fat and examined it. *This is the pork?* He fed it to Dog. He wiped the fork on his overalls to get rid of the dog germs and squirted some mustard into the can. He morosely ate his cold beans slowly while staring out the window.

Later, while laying in bed, Leonard tried not to think of everything that happened that day. There was just enough light from the Goofy night light that he could watch the bugs beating on the window above his bed. He stared at a mildewy patch in the corner of the ceiling where the plaster sagged. Someday, Leonard would have to climb on the roof with some sheet metal and Blackjack and do some repair work. Someday. Leonard's whole body was heavy and sodden with sweat. Someday. He drifted off to sleep and dreamed of running his own service station. He knew he'd do well. So well, he might get one of those awards on TV.

Leonard stood in the spotlight accepting the award, a miniature golden gas pump. Above his head a TV screen pulsed: Leonard Allen Mullins, Gas Station Owner of the Year.

"Thank you all, I just don't know what else to say." He pulled a slip of paper from his tuxedo pocket. "I'd just like to thank my mother, and Dog, and above all, Clem who taught me almost everything."

A picture of his sparkling clean service station appeared on the monitor.

"I owe my success to some fresh ideas in promotion."

The screen switched to a picture of Dog sitting beside a hand-lettered sign. The sign said: Free Red Vines with Fil-up.

"If I could get my wife to help me? Come up, honey."

There was a thunderous wave of applause and a few wolf whistles. A beautiful young girl in a skintight silver gown stood and walked up the stairs. She was blond and wore bright red lipstick. The gown was slit up one leg was so tight that her, her, her... Oh! She had dark hair and wore a brown wool skirt. Her jacket covered her chest quite properly so her naughties were not at all visible. She wore sensible shoes. Her teeth gleamed. She smiled as she handed Leonard the envelope. He held the envelope over his head and slipped his other arm around her. He pressed her to him, squashing her soft, her... He held her hand.

She wore a giant dazzling diamond that he brought to his lips and kissed.

"It wouldn't be right if I did not share my good luck with others. I hold in my hand a check made out to the Teddy Bear Museum of Naples, for... One Million Dollars!"

The crowd erupted. The director of the museum looked a lot like Clem's stepbrother, the lawyer Carl Bremmer. He accepted the check with trembling fingers. He sank to his knees and started kissing Leonard's hand.

"Oh, it's nothing," Leonard said modestly. "It's the least I can do."

His wife pulled his head down and kissed him long and hard. The crowd roared. Everyone was standing, hooting, and clapping. His wife cupped his head and he kissed down her neck and across her breastbone. She pulled his head down and, with his teeth, he pulled off her buttons and spit them out. He tore her blouse down around her shoulders and ran his tongue down the cleft of her chest. The hall filled with wild cheering and the hot heavy air smelled of.... What?

21

Alligator Alley

Leonard sat up in his bed. Dog, sleeping in the corner, farted again. Darn it. Leonard buried his head in the covers. Gotta stop feeding Dog those peanuts, he thought as he drifted back to sleep.

THERE'S A LITTLE SNAKE INSIDE OF ME
BRED INTO ME FOR GENERATIONS, PART OF THE FAMILY
AND HE TELLS ME THINGS THAT I DON'T WANNA HEAR
ABOUT GRABBING ALL THE MONEY
AND MAKING PEOPLE FEAR ME
SSSSSS

- FRANCIS DUNNERY

Little Snake from the album Tall Blonde Helecopter

CHAPTER 2

Monday Morning, May 19

GLEN

Glen rinsed toothpaste from his mouth and spit into the sink. He checked the alignment of his tie in the bathroom mirror. Tired from the flight and a little depressed, he bent close to the glass. If you get close enough you can see inside the eyes and the years fall away.

Everyone has a defining moment. For Glen, it was this: from the age of eight to eleven, he was terrorized by a boy a year older. Andy Morton, twenty pounds heavier, four inches taller, and one-hundred percent meaner. His specialty: a weekly dose of split lips, Indian rubs, and Charlie-horses. Then came the showdown on Birch Street. The end of Glen's life. Lying on his stomach and bleeding into the dirt, Glen had an epiphany; a vision of living the rest of his life in fear. He could see the words carved on his tombstone:

Glen "the Loser" Wilson, 1950-1961
Ate dirt and ran away

Glen decided to simply do what was needed. He picked himself out of the dust and buried a right fist in Andy's big surprised belly. He grabbed Andy's collar, twisted it like a noose, and shook his dirty fist in Andy's face. *You touch me again and you're going to have to kill me because I won't rest until I've wrung out your dying breath with these two hands! Today is as fine a day as any to die. So... Bring it on.*

The mature words did not scare Andy but the shocking intensity did. This marked the end and the beginning of Glen's life.

Yes, bring it on. Glen smoothed his oily hair. It's time to face the crowd and sell or be sold. Eat or be eaten. *Bring it on.*

The Orlando/Orange County Convention Center was filled with banners and posters of the computer industry big hitters and heavy breathers. Hewlett-Packard, Microsoft, Red Hat, Dell, IBM, and Apple. Each company advertised the latest computer hardware, accessories, and software. Glen pushed through the crowd, grabbing freebies from the displays as he passed; he collected a pocket-full of miniature flashlights, screwdrivers, key chains, mechanical pencils, and plastic rulers.

Glen caught a glimpse of himself reflected in a window. Six feet three inches tall, sporting a gray Seattle suntan, and twenty pounds overweight. He tucked his shirt into his elastic-waisted slacks and smoothed his hair. After an hour of power-smoozing and kibitzing, he found himself talking to Elke Rittenauer, a representative of the huge Korean company, Goldbright International.

"Remember that fire at the epoxy plant in Malaysia?" Glen asked. "A small fire in an AC power switch vault a few years back? The price of DRAMs have still never recovered from that. Did you ever wonder how that fire got started?"

Elke was about 40, thin as a greyhound, and was wearing a careworn face. Glen watched her carefully, knowing that a Deutschlander her age, working for a Korean semiconductor company, would be dangerous to turn your back on. Besides, he thought she was cute with her bobbed blond hair and tweezer-shaped eyebrows.

A soft spot resided in Glen's heart for women whose eyebrows were a very different shade than the artificial color on top of their heads.

"Artificial shortages," he continued, "I'm telling you, that's the way to make real money. Buy commodity futures and stock puts, hire someone to start a fire across the world in an epoxy plant, then just sit back and watch the money roll in. For example, suppose there was a software error in Final Test at Hitachi and all their SRAMs are hung up. All of them at zero yield."

"They'd work three shifts to find the problem and fix it in a few days," she said.

"That's all it takes. A rumor on the net and the stock blips down. You buy like crazy. Then the problem is solved, the stock blips up, maybe overshoots a bit, and you sell. Make a ton of money in a few days."

"Glen, you are a genuinely evil man."

"Everywhere I go, people think that ambition and moxie are evil things. No one understands me. I'm really just a pussycat deep inside."

"Way, way down deep inside. What does it cost to buy into one of your schemes?"

"Ah, good question. Shall we discuss it over lunch?"

Elke looked at her watch.

"Hell yes," she said.

* * *

Glen looked at Elke over his Caesar salad. They were sitting near the fountain at the Convention Center restaurant.

"I have a feeling about you, Elke. I like you."

"Look Glen, let's not fool around. I'm forty years old, I make sixty-two thousand bucks a year, plus whatever I can weasel out in my expense reports. I have a crappy apartment in New Jersey. I'm paying eleven thousand a year to my ex for child support for children from his first marriage that he talked me into adopting. I have a fifteen hundred dollar CD in the bank earning three and a half percent interest, a five-year-old Ford, and a refrigerator that is empty except two bottles of Dunkelweis and some cheese that isn't supposed to be green, but is. Life better deal me a fucking break soon or I'm going to end up a drooling dimwit watching Oprah in a rest home with a bunch of incontinent bridge-playing old ladies. I'm doing all right at Goldbright, but there is a fresh crop of young and ambitious Harvard studs and Vassar babes in short skirts with silicon tits ready to fuck anything that moves to slime their way up the corporate food chain. It's time to make a move and I have the feeling you're the man with a plan. Now drink your wine and tell me some things no one else knows." Elke flushed, took a deep breath, and sipped some ice water. "I'm sorry. I don't know where that came from," she said.

"No, it's okay Elke, I don't mind, that was cute." He looked at her as if he expected her to continue.

"You talk," she insisted.

"Okay. I went to the University of Washington, I studied electrical engineering. It turned out that the professors didn't teach and the teaching assistants who did teach were a bunch of morons. I dropped out. I was making good money selling answers to the exams and brokering thesis papers so I was too busy to study anyway. I was drafted and spent sixteen months really going to school in Saigon. I worked for a master sergeant at a supply depot. He taught me damn near everything I know about logistics. If you needed medical supplies, toilet paper, or wanted to trade cigarettes for heroin, you talked to Sergeant Stephens.

Black guy, about 6-3, kickboxer. Believe me, nobody fucked around with Steve Stephens. We would have won that war if Steve could have figured out a percentage on it. I came back with an old leather suitcase stuffed with a little over a million dollars in unmarked twenties. Remember, this was back when a million was worth something. Those were some days."

Glen gestured to the waitress to have his wine glass refilled.

"I must be out of my mind, why am I telling you this stuff?" he said.

"Because I'm the only one handy. What happened to all that money?"

"It spent a couple of years gathering dust under my bed. When the Fed went off the gold standard in the early 70's it became obvious I needed to invest in something, but that was later. I spent some time trying to make a llama and chinchilla ranch in southern Oregon pay. That wasted a couple of years. After a short career importing raw materials from Bolivia, I took a nine-to-five with HP in Corvallis, buying keypads and LCDs. That about bored me to death. That place was so straight I couldn't even slice off a point on the side. I gave that up. I did better selling IBM mainframes and software to the Feds who were in the middle of fighting the war on poverty. Nothing like a good war to turn a buck. What are we in now? A war on terrorism, right?"

"Just tell me what happened to that suitcase full of money. Is it still under your bed?"

"No, just hang on. Remember that game, Pong? After the success of that retarded game, I backed some eggheads in a venture to create a new game called Warp Factor 9. Like Star Trek with some graphics, right? Well, it was a good idea but we wrote it for CPM and had to create our own graphics language running on Z-80's. Two years later the money was gone and I had a building full of Nova and CPM computers, altogether worth about seventy-five cents, and a product still a year away from production. I fired the engineers, declared Chapter 11, hired a local contractor to set fire to the building and collected ten cents on the dollar from the insurance company. They weren't happy about it but they couldn't prove anything and they eventually paid up. That was my quick way of turning a million into about 50K and change. I muled a couple more loads of snow in from Bolivia and built up my nut again. After my last freelance trip, I was flush again, although I made a few enemies along the way. Tough way to make a buck."

He gestured at the stub of his finger and continued.

"Real tough. After that, I spent a couple of years underground in Silicon Valley, living in a van and selling pirated copies of Visicalc and

Lotus 1-2-3. When things cooled off—well, what really happened was that most of my enemies died. Anyway, I took this job with ICC. Now I just run a few ventures on the side to keep things interesting."

"And you still keep a suitcase of greenbacks under your bed?"

"Sleep over some night and I'll show you. Just make sure I know you're coming, okay? I'm running out of room in my backyard for burying unannounced visitors. Besides, I don't keep many greenbacks anymore as most of my mad money is in Krugerands and Hong Kong dollars now."

"What are you saving it for? Early retirement?"

"I'll retire when the backhoe has buried my coffin and tamped the dirt down good. Can I tell you a secret? Can you keep your mouth shut?"

"Sure, tell me."

"I'm saving the money for a run at Congress. That's where the real action is. Now tell me a little about yourself."

"I went to school in Karlsruhe and earned a Masters in Technical School diploma. I graduated number 1 in a class of 640. After that...."

Glen looked at his watch.

"Sorry babe, I gotta get in one more run before the show closes." He bent over and kissed her cheek. "Catch the bill for me, will ya? I'll get the next one."

He winked, cinched up his tie, and walked briskly out of the restaurant.

LEONARD

Leonard opened his eyes and noticed the late morning sunlight climbing the wall. *Oh, no*, he thought, *I'm late. Clem will kick my butt.* He wiggled into his overalls and pulled on his boots without bothering to tie the laces. Something nagged him, some unpleasant half-formed thought. He ran to the kitchen and made a couple of peanut butter and raisin sandwiches. He put on his Skoal hat and ran to the front door. On the little porch he stopped. The memory of the previous day flooded into his mind. He collapsed on the stair, sat down, and cried. His despair slowly morphed into anger.

"You dirty creep!" Leonard shouted to the sky. He threw his lunch bag into the air as high as he could. "I'm Leonard Allen Mullins and I'm tired of you pooping on me. I say my prayers and I try not to use bad words. What do you expect of me? Damn you."

Realizing what he had just said, he was instantly terrified. He stood trembling, waiting for a lightning bolt to flash down from the sky. Dog came up and licked his hand. The sky was a typical washed-out Florida blue. There was no sign of any lightning. Leonard bent down and Dog lapped his face.

"What are we going to do, Dog? We can't stand around here all day."

With his head hung low, Leonard walked over and picked up his lunch. The sandwiches were a little smashed but would be all right. He thought about going back into his house but decided to go to the gas station and see what nightmare God could dream up for him next.

Leonard sat in Clem's chair on the porch with his lunch on his lap, stroking Dog's head, and staring into space. A dusty blue Pontiac Sunbird rental car pulled up. Leonard pointed to the closed sign, then thought again.

"Closed? Why are we closed?"

He unlocked the office door and flipped on the pumps. He walked to the car, leaned in the window, and smiled.

"Fill her up with unleaded?"

The sunburned driver nodded. "Got anything cold to drink?"

"Yup, pop machine's inside," Leonard replied. "Mountain Dew, Pepsi, might even be some iced tea left."

When the tank was full the pump read $19.33. The driver proffered a twenty. Leonard panicked, it was Clem's job to make sure there was change in the till.

"It's okay," the driver said, toasting with his Pepsi. "Keep the change."

"Wow," Leonard replied.

Around noon, a Volkswagen bus pulled in and a half-dozen college students piled out. Leonard ran out front wiping his hands with an oily shop cloth.

"Hi guys, can I help you?"

They reeked of dope and loaded up on gasoline, fried fruit pies, and Baby Ruths. He sold his peanut butter and raisin sandwiches for a buck each to a stoned slacker with dark glasses and dreads. They even bought a package of Red Vines. When they pulled out in a cloud of blue smoke (most of it from the van's engine) Leonard counted the money. It was a 28 dollar sale.

"Wow," Leonard said.

GLEN

Glen was wandering the central aisle in the convention center when he grabbed the arm of a guy passing by.

"Hey, Charlie Parker, what's shaking?" Glen said.

Charlie did a double-take.

"Christ, Glen, when did you get out of jail?"

They took full measure of each other. Charlie was a tall Texan with thinning red hair and a bulbous red nose. He was a purchasing manager for a semiconductor company near Dallas. Glen had served with him in Vietnam.

"They couldn't make their case, so I never went to jail, thanks for asking. Hit Seattle PD for sixty tax-free big ones. Wrongful arrest, lost wages and benefits, mental distress. That will teach those goddam Fascists, eh? But, never mind all that. I'm having a business meeting in my room tonight. Some booze and some babes. What do you say?"

Charlie shook his head. "No, I'm still hung over from your party three years ago. I'm married and have a kid now. I need to stay out of trouble. Thanks for the invite."

He pulled away brushing at the sleeve of his jacket. Glen followed him a few steps.

"I got a line on some graymarket Octium 4 point 5's, ought-four date code, absolutely untraceable. No FDIV problems, good prices."

"Gotta run Glen, I'll catch you later."

"Just thirty percent of Intel's list and you can have a couple thousand. I can ship them UPS red and have them on your dock by Friday? Or, how about some .5 nanosecond 6400M DRAMs?"

"See you around."

Glen continued walking the show floor. He grabbed a free peppermint from a bowl and popped it in his mouth. He rolled his eyes when he saw a scrawny punk he knew named David Foster. David was about 30, with matted oily hair and a very bad complexion. He sported a fish belly white CRT tan and appeared to be jittery from a near overdose of Jolt colas.

"Glen, Glen, Glen. Hang on. I hear you have some of Microsoft's Tribeca beta-test source-code."

"Any moron can get that stuff from the Golden Arcade in Hong Kong, don't bother me with this petty crap."

Foster hustled to keep up. "I'm serious, Glen. How about a hundred bucks?"

"Okay, show me your money."

Foster pulled a wrinkled bill from his pocket and Glen grabbed it out of his hand.

"Gimme your e-mail address," Glen said.

Foster pulled a business card from his shirt pocket. Glen glanced at it.

"Software Guru, give me a fucking break," Glen said, rolling his eyes.

"The UU-encoded source will be in your mailbox sometime late tomorrow. It takes that much time to route through the blind drop addresses in Europe."

"Thanks, Glen. Thanks a lot."

Glen waved him off and continued his rounds of the convention displays. Through a glass door, he saw a group of smokers standing around outside the vendor hospitality area. He walked out to join them. He leaned against the wall next to a sandy-haired California surfer-type. His hair was cut short in the back and long on the sides. It curled around his face and he was constantly rocking his head back to keep the hair out of his eyes. The face was familiar—Monterey perhaps? Maybe Vegas? Glen didn't remember much about the Vegas trip. Glen motioned for a cigarette and the surfer reluctantly shook out a Marlboro for him.

"I don't carry because I'm trying to quit. Thanks, man," Glen said, fumbling in his pocket for a light. "Soon it will be illegal to smoke anywhere," Glen continued. "Goddam PC cops will arrest you in your house if you smoke when kids if kids are within 1,000 feet."

"It's discrimination, sure as hell," Surfer-boy replied.

The others nodded and sucked smoke deep into their lungs. He read the surfer's name from his nametag.

"Warren, glad to meet you, my name's Glen Wilson and I'm with International Controls Corporation, out of Redmond, Washington."

Warren snapped to attention.

"I hear you guys are bidding out for some Sun Workstations and CAE software..." he said breathlessly.

"That's a fact. We're going to buy a few seats. Related to that order, maybe you can help me. I'm following up a rumor. I hear there is some shady business going on, some kickbacks. You know anything about that?" Glen said.

"No, I can't think of anything I've heard. There was some stuff about Specialty Automation on the net, but nothing about ICC," Warren replied.

"Some yahoo was taking a two percent cut," Glen said as he blew smoke into the air. "If a one point cash payment was left in a mailbox, an order for equipment and software would magically get placed soon after. Then, once the order was delivered, another one percent went in the box. Slimy bastards. Slick, but slimy."

"You're right, that's pretty rotten. I hope you catch those dickheads."

"Well, here's my biz card." Glen rummaged around in his coat pocket and produced one. "If you hear anything, go ahead and contact me at this address. I keep my own personal box at one of those mailbox places for security reasons, you know what I mean?"

"Sure, you're kind of undercover, right?" Warren asked.

"You can say that. By the way, I'm having a party tonight over at the Marriott, stop by if you feel like it."

The guy nodded and stuck Glen's card in his wallet. He had a puzzled look, as if he were thinking about something. He nodded absently at Glen, stubbed out his cigarette, and pulled open the door to go back inside.

"Good meeting you and thanks for the smoke," Glen called out, waving the cigarette. Following the herd instinct, the other smokers also went inside.

Glen leaned against the wall and rummaged around in his pockets, cataloging his loot. He pulled out his voice recorder. He punched the record button: *"My, that's a lovely dress you have on today, Missus Cleaver. Missus fucking meat Cleaver, ha!"*

He pushed REPLAY and listened to his words. They made him giggle hysterically. Wiping tears from his eyes, he smoked his cigarette for a moment, then pressed record again. The words poured out.

He pushed stop and stared at the little recorder for a minute. He was sweating lightly and felt dizzy. Christ, what a rush, like a hit of amyl nitrate. Finally, a place where the truth could come out. Well, maybe not the truth, but closest real life comes to it. His veins felt as if they were roaring with methedrine. He collected some curious looks as he passed a fresh batch of smokers going on break as he went back inside. He quickly got back into trolling the crowd but the recorder weighed down his pocket, it felt like it was on fire.

On the outskirts of the main floor, he found a booth for Info Highway Inc. It looked threadbare. An overeager twenty-some slacker was sitting at a PC looking uncomfortable in a suit and tie. He weighed at least 200 pounds and his rear end oozed over the edge of his seat. His name tag said Timmy Olson and his title was Knowledge Asset. Without getting up, he reached over his shoulder and offered Glen a limp handshake.

"Check this out, I'm controlling a robot-arm at MIT. I'm sending the commands through the Internet. The Information Superhighway."

The screen had a low-resolution 3-D image of a robot arm. With the mouse, Timmy moved the arm and picked up a child's alphabet block and brought it closer to the screen.

Christ, Glen thought, *this was old news back in the 90's*.

Timmy continued. "Cool, eh? Want to see if there is any Mountain Dew in the MIT pop machine?"

"I have an idea, my man. There's not much happening around. How about I watch the display for you so you can take a little break?"

"I don't know," the kid said, looking around.

"They have free muffins at the Apple Power PC display over on aisle two."

"Free muffins? That's great," he said, licking his lips. "If you're sure you'll be okay? Just hang on to anyone if they ask about our service, I'll be right back."

"No problem, dude."

As soon as Timmy disappeared, Glen exited the robot-arm program, logged into a wireless LAN, and signed into his e-mail account. He typed in his password and read subject lines for a couple of dull messages from his boss, some requests for his Octium chips, and some crap from the ICC corporate accountants which he quickly deleted. He didn't see what he was looking for, so he tapped the instant messenger icon and typed out a message to Floyd Rosen in Denver.

I'm looking for a transaction number and I'm not seeing it, he typed.

Floyd's reply scrolled slowly across the screen.

Sorry Glen, I just need a few more days. I'll clear a check and the money will be there. No bullshit, give me a little more time.

I have bills to pay. What's the chance that the money will transfer in the next 10 minutes?

No can do. I swear you'll have it by Friday, latest.

No. Net 30 means net 30. Good-bye, Floyd.

End of Thursday's business day, Pacific Standard Time, it's there. Slip me a break this time.

Good-bye Floyd.

Glen exited the phone utility and brought up his Netscape browser. He looked around to make sure no one was looking and typed in his password. He double-clicked an icon labeled 'Surprise Package' and the screen filled with a picture of a bundle of dynamite and a fuse. Glen tapped the left mouse button and the fuse flared. At this moment, Timmy returned wiping his face with a napkin. He had muffin crumbs on his tie. They watched the fuse burn down. The dynamite exploded. The image was high resolution with digitally sampled sound. Timmy jumped and dropped his napkin.

"Oh, tres cool, which game is this?"

"I call it 'Net 30 means Net 30'," Glen said. He pressed the computer reset button and rebooted. "Thanks," he said as he walked out of the display cubicle.

Timmy called after him, "Is that an open-source package?"

Glen ignored him.

Later, Glen was chatting with Patrick Clark, who was manning the Computational Dynamics RISC PC display. His name tag identified him as the VP of Engineering.

"Remember that FDIV fiasco with the Pentium? What did that end up costing Intel, $475 million, give or take change?" Glen asked.

"Yes, they sure bungled that one. That mathematician, the one who turned that up? Where was he from? West Virginia or something?"

"A guy named Nicely from Lynchburg, Virginia. Well, I've come across something similar. I have a team of Computer Science grad students in Bombay that has been testing your CD 603 processor. Seems there is a bug in the 775 megahertz version."

Patrick did a double-take.

"I don't know what you are talking about."

"Oh, I think you do. There is a range of floating point numbers between 7 and 7.2 million that result in errors in your multiply-accumulate microprogram. I don't think it is a big deal, but probably a problem for your stock if this information leaked onto the Internet somehow. Maybe you guys could use this code to help debug your design?"

"I guess you're suggesting some sort of exclusive license for the code?"

"You've read my mind. I think we could do each other some good here. I'm thinking of a number around, say, seventy-five thousand in tax-free cash, if you get my drift."

"That is a lot of frigging Tandori rice, you prick. Wait a minute. I've heard of you. Glen Wilson, I knew that name was familiar. You did a number on Centurion Computer."

"That wasn't my fault. They bounced a check. I didn't get to where I am by eating rubber checks. Gotta keep up my Subaru payments."

"One of these days someone is going to reformat your hard drive."

"Well, until that day, you and I are going to be in business together. So, how soon can you spring the dough?"

"If I have to pay a penny more than 50K I have to go back to venture capital for another round or unload some stock options. It'll take a couple of weeks."

"Okay, make it fifty thousand. To show what a straight shooter I am, I'll give you six weeks. Here's my card, which shows my account numbers. It's been very pleasant doing business with you. Oh, I'm having a little party in my room, we'll celebrate our mutual good fortune."

"Prick," Patrick replied.

"Yeah," Glen said. He slipped back into the trade show crowd.

"Hey Wilson," someone hissed.

Glen turned and faced a nervous looking man. He was about thirty and wore a rumpled suit, worn-out cowboy boots, and a string tie.

"Do I know you?" Glen asked.

"No, but I know you. I'm Martin. We need to talk."

He grabbed Glen's arm and pulled him to the end of the aisle. They stood by a fire extinguisher.

"I have a client that is desperate for some silicon. I hear you have a line on some one-hundred-gig DRAM sticks?"

"Yeah, I've got a couple hundred. E-mail me a ship-to address and we'll cut a deal. Buy fifty and get a twenty percent discount. Ten percent finder's fee to you, my man," Glen said, grinning.

"The client doesn't do cash."

"Fine, what are you trading?"

Martin glanced around to make sure no one was listening.

"We have some weapons. Mines, grenades, and a couple of Dragon missiles."

"You gotta be kidding. I'm in silicon. I don't need no heavy metal."

Martin leaned close and whispered.

"We can get you a suitcase nuke in case you are into real-man fireworks."

"I appreciate the offer, I really do, but that stuff ain't my thing. Sell the stuff, get a pocket full of cash, then give me a call."

"Look, you need some fire power, you call me, okay?" Martin said, sticking a biz card in Glen's coat pocket.

"I don't think I will, but if I do…"

"Right."

Martin disappeared into the crowd.

"Hey Glen? Glen?"

Glen was at the America Online display stuffing demonstration FLASH disks in his pocket. He looked up to see Mike Stephens with an older man he did not know.

"Glen, I want you to meet my friend Charlie, he's an editor with the magazine."

It was widely known that Mike was the mysterious rumor columnist for a national trade magazine.

"Howdy Mike, nice to meet you, Charlie. Look, I'm having a party in my room tonight if you guys want to cut loose a bit. Here, have a card, my room number is on the back. I'm staying at the Marriott."

"I'm trying to stay out of trouble now," Mike said. "Thanks anyway. Look Glen, have you heard about anything big going down?"

"Yes, Philippe Kahn, Steve Jobs, and Paul Allen are starting a rock band called Byte Me. They have a weekly Wednesday night gig back in Walnut Creek."

"I'm serious Glen, this show's been slow so far," Mike pleaded.

"Tell me about it." Glen thought for a moment. "Okay, come to my little party tonight and I'll give you the inside scoop on the Sony/Microsoft buyout."

"What? Bull," Mike said with wonder. "Who is buying whom?"

"That's what I'll tell you. I hacked a 256-bit encrypted e-mail from Chairman Bill himself that I'll show you," Glen said.

"Double bull, no one has broken AES-256. That would be news."

"Straight up, brother. See you tonight." Glen disappeared into the crowd.

Charlie looked a little shaken.

"He was just joking, right? The big banks have a couple of trillion on the web encrypted with AES-256. He's talking treason, mayhem, and global chaos."

Mike watched Glen disappear into the crowd. He spoke quietly.

"Well, with Glen you can never tell. Last year he sold me a Superbowl winner in December. Cost me five thousand dollars."

"Fine, you fell for a scam," Charlie said with relief. "You blew five thousand. Now you know he's full of bologna. It's nothing to be ashamed of, I bought a Chevy Cavalier once."

"No, Charlie, you don't get it. They won. I cleaned up in Vegas, cleared seventy-five K."

"Christ on a crutch," Charlie said.

ELKE

Elke finished the carafe of Chablis left over from her lunch with Glen. FBI Special Agent Orrin Webster sat down with her.

"Ms. Rittenauer? I'm Agent Webster with the FBI, can I speak with you for just a moment?" He showed her his badge and gave her a business card. "It's very important."

"What do you want?"

"It's about that man you had lunch with, Glen Wilson."

"Which man was that?"

Webster waved to a man standing nearby wearing a black suit and sunglasses. He was handed a large envelope. He pulled some eight by ten black and white photographs from the envelope and laid them on the table one-by-one. Taken minutes earlier, they clearly showed Elke having lunch with Glen Wilson.

"You guys are shooting me from the wrong side," she said. "My left side shows the acne scars better."

Elke looked closely at the photographs.

"Your contrast sucks," she said pointing at the pictures with her fork. "You guys need to buy some decent equipment. Okay, I had a Caesar salad with a guy, is that illegal now?"

"No, ma'am, Caesar salads are still legal. I'm just curious about what you two talked about. Did Mr. Wilson say anything about the AES-256?"

"I don't suppose you're offering me a job, say as a consultant? My hourly rate for everything just short of sex is two-hundred an hour. I get paid time and a half for sex."

Webster flushed deep red.

"You're adorable," Elke continued, "maybe we can waive the overtime premium, sweetie."

Webster flushed even redder. He glowed like a stoplight.

"No, no, we don't have anything like that kind of money to work with," he exclaimed.

"Well, when your Chief bumps up your allowance, I'm sure you'll know where to find me." She stood up and tossed her napkin on her plate. "I'm not under arrest, is that correct?"

"No ma'am, you're not under arrest," Webster sputtered. "Not yet. I just want to have a friendly chat with you."

"Then be a good boy and pick up the bill, will you?" She patted his hand. "Stop by and see me when you are ready to get serious. Ta."

She gathered up her handbag, took one of the photographs, slowly folded it, and stuck it in her jacket pocket. *Well*, she thought as she walked back to the trade show, *now things are getting vaguely interesting, aren't they?*

LEONARD

Leonard was mopping the bathroom floor when he heard a car pull up.

"Come on, Dog, we got another customer," he said.

The car turned out to be Carl Bremmer's station wagon. Leonard's face fell. Carl and Sarah got out and walked up to Leonard, who couldn't seem to move.

"I'm sorry, I was just trying to help. All the money is in the cash register." He turned out his pockets. "See, I didn't take nothin'."

"What are you talking about?" Carl asked. He tossed his cigarillo stub into the gravel. Sarah came around the car with her arms spread to give Leonard a hug. She was about five feet tall and wore one of those frizzy old-lady hair styles. Her pale blue eyes swam in a sea of gin. Her face was pleasant and grandmotherly, though she was only in her mid-forties. She wore a flowery muumuu, heavy black shoes, and tan stockings. She would fit well in any third world country, even southern Florida.

"Listen honey, we need to talk," Sarah said.

"If you'll get in the car I'll take you to my office. There is some paperwork we need to take care of," Carl added.

Leonard wriggled out of Sarah's grasp, walked back, and flipped the OPEN sign to CLOSED. He made sure the door was locked.

"Okay. What paper?" Leonard asked.

Sarah wrapped herself around his arm.

He pulled his arm away.

"What is going on!" Leonard cried.

"I'd rather we talk at the office."

"We can talk now, what is this all about?" Leonard said firmly.

"Come on, honeypie…"

"Now."

"Look Len—nard, Clem thought of you as his son," Carl said.

"He did?" Leonard asked shrilly.

"Yes, and he wanted you to have the station."

"Wha—?"

Sarah grabbed his arm again.

"We're going to make some real money," she said with her eyes glowing wetly. "I've got some ideas, maybe sell expresso, some crafts, get rid of the bait tank and the worm tub, paint everything up nice."

"The station is mine, Clem left me the station?" Leonard asked.

When they both nodded his knees gave way and he collapsed into the gravel.

Leonard regained consciousness in Clem's chair. Sarah was patting his cheeks with a wet napkin.

"Ah, Leonard. Very good. You're awake. There are just a few papers to sign. We can do it here if you want." Carl pushed the papers forward and proffered a pen. "Just sign at the bottom."

"Was I dreaming or did Clem really leave me the station?" Leonard asked.

"Yes—I mean no. Forget it, just sign the papers."

"All to me, all mine?"

"Yes, Leonard. Now, please, sign right here."

"I can't believe it."

Leonard got up and started pacing. He noticed the CLOSED sign and flipped it back to OPEN. Carl and Sarah looked blankly at each other.

"Honey, sit down here and sign the papers and everything will be taken care of," Sarah implored.

"Oh man, oh man." Leonard hovered over Sarah. "I can do everything my way?"

"Yes, we can. As soon as you sign."

Leonard started pacing again. He stopped.

"I can change the name?"

"You can do whatever you want as soon as you sign these papers."

"Leonard's Grub and Gas. Leonard and Dog's Place. Oh, man. I can't...."

"Leonard! Stop pacing! Sit down here and sign these papers."

"Okay, okay. Geez, give a guy a chance, will you?"

He sat at the desk. As he pulled the papers toward him, he saw an envelope with his name on it. It was in Clem's handwriting. He dropped the pen.

"What's this?"

"You get that after you've signed," Carl said.

"Wow, Clem left me a note from beyond the grave. I thought Clem hated me. I've got to read this."

He walked off the porch holding the envelope in front of his face. A rusted out Yugo pulled up to the pumps. Leonard stuffed the envelope in his back pocket and pumped two bucks worth for the kid behind the wheel who looked to be about twelve-years-old.

"Shit-fire," Carl whispered.

"Grub and Gas. Damned moron," Sarah said as she pulled a pint bottle of gin from her purse. She took a long pull and drained the bottle. She looked at it longingly, then tossed the empty into an oil barrel that served as a garbage can.

"What if he doesn't sign?" she said.

"He's an idiot, he'll sign. He just has to, that's all."

A stake-bed truck pulled in with dual 30 gallon tanks and an outboard motor tank in the back. The driver was trying to trade some fresh shrimp for gas. Leonard couldn't decide how much shrimp he could eat.

"Shit, this is going to take all day," Sarah said. "Let's come back tomorrow, right now I need a drink."

Carl walked to the gas pump and stuffed the papers in Leonard's pocket.

"We need to take off, so we'll be back to pick these up later. Please sign them tonight and we'll get on with things. Okay, Leonard?" Leonard nodded vacantly as he watched the number wheels ratchet on the pump.

"Don't forget," Carl continued, speaking slowly, as if to a two-year-old. "Clem's funeral is on Wednesday. Ten o'clock."

Chapter 3

Monday Afternoon, May 19

Glen

Glen walked out the front of the convention center. The air was as thick as hot syrup and the sky was dark. It was nearly time for the afternoon thunderstorm. Glen spotted Carlos, his driver from the previous evening, in the middle of the taxi line. He walked past the other drivers and jumped into Carlos's cab. The other drivers honked their horns and made obscene gestures but Glen ignored them.

"Hello Carlos, how they hanging?"

"Hey boss, I hope you're in better mood today."

"We'll see how it goes." Glen scraped a kitchen match on the No Smoking sign and lit a cigarette. "I need some girls for a party tonight. Do you know where to go?"

"Yeah, I'll take care of you."

"Fine. I get bored easily and I don't want to see the same scenery more than once, if you catch my drift. Let's get out of here."

"Okay, boss."

Glen leaned back in the seat, watched the city flow past his window, and played with his voice recorder.

"Here we are, boss."

Glen shook his head and pushed stop on the recorder. Outside the window it was dusk and the few street lights that were not shattered were working overtime.

What happened to the afternoon? he thought.

"Where are we?" he asked.

"This is Altamonte Springs. You'll find some conchitas in one of these bars along the street," Carlos replied.

It was a shoddy part of town with pickup trucks and low-riders parked haphazardly. A Harley-Davidson rumbled by.

"Okay, Carlos, meet me back here at eight?" Glen said, waving a fifty-dollar bill.

"You got it, boss."

The cab rolled off in a cloud of blue smoke.

Glen scanned the street to get his bearings. He was standing in front of a bar called 'The Town Pump' but he didn't like the look of it. It was a cheap place for working men to get drunk. Boring. Depressing. Down the block and across the street some neon signs flickered. He could just barely read the sign: "The Sportsman's Club." That one looked better, there was even a bouncer and a few people lined up waiting at the door. Perfect. He crossed over and walked down the sidewalk. Two rather rough looking guys came out of an alley and bumped into him. The taller was white and wore an old olive drab army coat. He was about six feet tall with his long dark hair pulled back in a ponytail. The shorter man was black, five foot eight, and stocky. Shorty had a wispy beard, a thin mustache, and dreads visible under a colorful woven hat. They were both in their early twenties.

"Watch where the fuck you're going, man," Ponytail said.

"Yeah, watch it."

"Sorry guys, didn't see you come out of the dark," Glen said.

"Well, he's sorry, Willie, how do you like that," Ponytail said.

"He's sorry, all right. A real sorry turd."

They both thought that was amusing.

Glen tried to maneuver around them but they split up and blocked his path.

"Going somewhere, shithead?"

"Hello," Glen said, "I recognize you from my eighth grade English class. Mister William, how are you doing? Good to see you, my friend."

Glen grabbed Willie's hand and started shaking it.

"Wha?" was all Willie could manage.

"Goddam it Willie, you didn't even go to the eighth grade, this guy is screwing with you."

"Hey, that's right. What the fuck, man?"

Glen mentally shrugged. *This doesn't always work, but it was worth a shot. Let's try Act Two.*

"Sorry guys, my mistake," Glen apologized.

"Yeah, your mistake. Now let's have your wallet and your watch."

They pulled out knives that gleamed wickedly in the dim street light. Glen watched them closely. They were hesitant and shaky. A couple of rookies.

"Wallet, asshole," Willie repeated.

Now what? Most people are afraid of crazy, the unknown. Let's see how they like it when the script goes random on them.

"Hallelujah, brothers, the Lord has thrown a blazing fire into my path. Twin Lucifers to test my mettle," Glen shouted forcefully.

Glen started jerking and doing little half dance steps. "And I sayeth unto you, that the Lord of the green pastures will beat a path to your door, and will smite you with fire, smoke, and locusts. Take heed, take heed, take heed."

What do you know, this did rattle them. Glen could see their hands really start to shake.

"Look mister, just hand over the wallet, and you're on your way," Ponytail said nervously.

He clearly did not like this unexpected turn of events.

"Ho-dee-doe, and though I walk through the ravine of revenge, I shall smite thee upon thy heads with brass and granite stars!"

"Just cut him, Willie. Make him shut up." Willie took a hesitant step forward and raised his knife. Glen's shoved his hand dived into his pocket and whipped out the banana. He waved it menacingly. Willie chopped the banana in half with a swipe of his knife. *Damn, the banana thing worked well in San Antonio,* Glen thought. *The only thing left was to try a spastic seizure.* He fell back in the dirty alley and twitched violently while contorting his face and grunting. That did it, the would-be muggers looked at each other, then took off down the street. Glen got up and brushed the trash off his suit. Acting like a spaz was a little degrading but Glen was not one to argue with results.

The bouncer at the Sportsman's Club curiously watched the pair run by. Glen walked toward the club peeling his banana stub. He took one bite, then tossed it in the gutter. *I don't even like bananas.*

There were a half-dozen college kids lined up and waiting to enter the club. The bouncer waved Glen to the front of the line.

"What was that all about?" the bouncer asked, jerking his thumb down the street at the fleeing boys.

"Oh, just a couple of knuckleheads, nothing to get excited about."

"If you say so," he said as he opened the door and ushered Glen through.

"Thank you, my man," Glen said, pressing a bill into the bouncer's palm.

Just inside, Glen had to buy a ticket for ten dollars, good for two drinks. He requested a receipt for his expense report. The cashier gave him a sour look but coughed one up from a ragged receipt book. The place was packed with tourists, drug dealers, drunken yuppies, defrocked priests, slumming teachers, and off-duty cops. Through the smoke and flashing lights Glen could see a nearly-nude dancer writhing on a small stage like one of those obligatory scenes in a cheap Hollywood movie script. He lit a cigarette and grinned. *Honey, I'm home.* He ordered a beer and the bartender scribbled on the drink ticket. Glen leaned against the bar and studied the crowd.

WEBSTER

FBI Agent Webster was talking on his cell phone in his hotel room when a message spewed from his portable FAX machine. He said good-bye and took the single sheet from the machine. There was a report from the contractor that was following Glen Wilson.

GW caught taxi #045 at the convention center at 5:40 PM. It was the same driver as last night. We should explore the possible connection. Traffic was heavy so it took a long time to arrive downtown. GW left the taxi at 6:35 PM.

Two muggers attacked him. He entered the Sportsman's Club at 6:45 PM.

Surveillance continues.

Webster read the FAX twice and it still didn't make sense.

GLEN

In the Sportsman's Club, a slight man with thinning hair and a bushy gray beard sidled up to Glen.

"You ever heard of Brownian motion?" the bearded-one asked.

His beard and the tips of his fingers were stained yellow and he had a well-chewed cigar in his mouth. He picked at his scalp nervously. He was wearing a houndstooth jacket with leather patches on the elbows. Glen had noticed him earlier and had pegged him as a junior college instructor or something similar.

"Yes, the random motion of atoms caused by thermal energy, what about it?" Glen replied.

"Ah, clearly an educated man, very good. Notice how the crowd mixes and swirls? I think it is very Brownian."

"Very good, Mr. Einstein. You don't mind if I call you Einstein, do you?"

"Actually, my name is Rogers. Gary Rogers. You can call me whatever you like, I guess. I like to study crowds and apply the laws of physics to their actions. Are you familiar with chaos and fractal theory?"

"I've looked at it a bit. Look Einstein, I'll tell you one of my theories, are you ready?" Rogers nodded hesitantly. "My theory is that theory is good most of the time, but sometimes theory is full of shit."

"Well, I suppose that is somewhat profound."

"Yeah, now fuck off, I'm busy."

Glen noticed that the girls were paying a lot of attention to a silk-shirted, slick-haired, alligator-booted, gold-chained, UV-tanned, and mirror-sunglassed punk. He was a walking disco cliche. According to the bartender, the guy's name was Pablo. The crowd did a slow orbit around the table where Pablo held court. He was very drunk, slouched down in his chair and moving slowly. In contrast, the ape with the gun sitting next to him was plenty alert. The ape didn't need the gun. He was so ugly he could stick out a finger, say bang, and half the room would fall down dead.

Glen walked up, stuck out his hand and introduced himself.

"Glen Wilson is the name and I'm glad to make your acquaintance, Mr. Pablo, sir."

Pablo looked at the outstretched hand as if it were a cockroach at a banquet. Glen decided to cut to the chase. He took a wad of c-notes from his back pocket, slowly counted out 20 of them, flattened them out, and laid them on the table.

"Please ask Mister Kong to cut these puppies right down the middle, right here." Glen motioned with a finger.

Pablo waved a hand at the bills and a straight razor appeared in Kong's ham fist. Very smooth, Glen was impressed. Kong sliced the bills as precisely as a surgeon and the razor evaporated. Glen stuck half the bills back in his pocket and pushed the other half toward Pablo. He threw down a business card with his room number scribbled on it. He had about one-half of Pablo's full attention.

"A couple of clean and friendly girls, a boom box, and no chaperone?"

Pablo thought for a microsecond, then gave a slight nod. Kong gathered up the bills. Glen caught the Ape's eye.

"Sorry fella, I didn't catch your name."

"Manny. And Wilson?"

"Yes, sir?"

"Mark up the girls and the price goes up. Way up."

So, they take care of their inventory. Glen could respect that. He had good instinct about people. Manny looked dumb, but his speech was precise, his clothes fit perfectly, and his attention did not waver. Glen had a sudden vision of Pablo laid out in a fine wooden box clutching a bouquet of lilies. Glen really hoped that the kid back at the hotel was doing business with a different and much less dangerous Manny. Glen nodded and gave a little salute with his finger.

OK, a done deal. He looked at his watch. There remained forty minutes before Carlos would come by again. Time for another beer. His mouth was very dry.

He rolled out of the club twenty minutes early and stood under the neon lights scoping the street. The line at the door had grown. Carlos parked the cab at the end of the block and Glen could see a figure leaning in the window chatting with the driver. He was not one-hundred-percent sure, but it looked like one of his pals from the alley. Interesting, the cab lets tourists out by the alley and the dumb punks in the alley shake them down. The bouncer nodded at Glen in greeting.

"Have you ever wondered why the cabbie drops his ride down the block when it's clear the action is down here?" Glen asked.

"That question has crossed my mind, sir."

"Isn't it bad for Pablo's business?"

"Not if Pablo takes a cut either way."

Ah, yes, there's always that.

He liked the bouncer and slipped him a fifty, just Glen's way of making friends and influencing people.

"What do they call you?"

"Robert."

The cab cruised down and was idling at the curb. Carlos was grinning but looked sweatier than usual. He pushed open the back door from the inside. Glen could hear the air conditioner roaring. He could not read Robert's expression as they rolled away. Glen and Carlos didn't speak on the way back to the hotel.

Glen got back to his hotel room about nine o'clock. David Foster, the pimply kid who bought the Tribeca software earlier that day, was waiting by the door with a guy Glen didn't know though the dude looked vaguely familiar. Glen wondered if he had seen him at the convention. David seemed more wired than usual, like he'd been munching chocolate covered espresso beans.

"Glen! Cool to see you, man." David stood directly in front of the door.

"Well, if you get out of the way, I'll let you in." *He didn't remember inviting David, but OK.* "I hope you weren't waiting long?"

The room looked good. It was decorated with the flowers, booze, and snacks he'd ordered. Glen went to the bedroom and unloaded his wallet, keyrings, digital camera, cellular phone, PDA, calculator, notebook, voice recorder and all his random souvenirs from the trade show.

"Geez, great room, this place has been sold out for weeks, how'd you swing this double?", David said, talking around the cheese and crackers he was stuffing in his mouth as he wandered through the suite. "Oh, Glen, I want you to meet my friend, Oscar Jones."

Glen pulled two beers from a tub of ice, tossed one to Oscar, then flopped down on the sofa. Oscar looked surprised, then set the beer on the table without opening it.

"Lovely to meet you, Oscar." Glen grabbed a card from a stack on the end table and passed it over. "You got a card?"

Oscar pawed through his vinyl wallet.

"Aw man, I don't believe it! I've got more back at the room, okay if I swing 'em by tomorrow morning?" He paused and looked around.

Antsy little guy.

"Look, Glen," 'Mister Jones' continued. "Can I call you Glen? David said maybe you could help me out of a pickle. We have a new product line coming out and—shoot, how can I say this. You know. What with the development costs and all. Those darn engineers. DX-880's. We need enough DX-880's to fill a pilot run and a few months of production, but we're a little late in our account with Intel, and paying list for the dog-gone things..." He sighed. "We're still a startup, you know that."

Oh, really? I thought you were from I-B fucking M. No card at a convention party? A real purchasing agent would forget his pants first. Add to that a cheap vinyl wallet and no drinking. A three-year-old would notice something wrong with this picture. Oscar Jones, my ass. I wonder what his real name is?

"Well, Mr. Jones, you drop off a card tomorrow and I'll see if I can't do something for you."

"I was thinking we could do some business now, I have money."

'Jones' pulled out an envelope and offered it.

Saved by a knock at the door! Glen walked to the door and stood with his hand on the knob. He turned and looked at Oscar.

"Tomorrow," Glen said firmly as he pulled the door open.

The girls had arrived. Glen counted three lovelies loaded down with a huge Sony boombox, some insulated flasks, and about four pounds of eye makeup.

"I'm Lila," the lead girl said, "and this is Lou and DeeDee."

She peered around Glen into the room.

"Is it just going to be you three? I thought this was going to be a party."

"It's still early," Glen replied, "Come in, ladies."

LEONARD

Leonard sat on the old porch of the gas station enjoying a canned ice tea and pondering Special Relativity. *I wonder why all my relatives are so special? Ha Dog, Leonard's funny, eh?* Dog lay in the dust with his head on his paws watching Leonard. He did not respond. Leonard was trying to figure out a name for his station. *I love you, Clem, but we need a better name than Clem's Place to bring in the customers. Leonard's Food and Fuel? No, too plain. Mullin's Gas and Go. Better. Leonard's Lunch-N-Lube? Yeah!* Leonard jumped up and did a little dance. *That's it, Lunch-N-Lube.*

A powerful and mean-looking thunderhead piled up to the southeast and Leonard could see jittery flashes of lightning reflected from its underbelly. He stood and watched in awe for the next few minutes as the big nimbus generated a tremendous updraft and flattened as it smacked into the stratosphere. Leonard grinned with delight until a gust took his hat and the first huge drops of rain started spotting the dust and hot pavement. Maybe he'd go inside and see what could be done to improve things. He retrieved his hat just before it blew around the corner by the worm tub. He hurried through the door and the wind slammed it shut behind him.

Inside, he stopped and surveyed Clem's kingdom. To the left a plywood 'desk' perched on gray concrete bricks. The window above it was decorated with dirty cobwebs and accessorized with dead flies. The vintage cash register rested precariously on one end of the desk. The most commonly-used keys were stained black with motor oil. Directly across from the front door the cracked glass of the beer and frozen bait cooler was patched with a flapping strip of tattered duct tape.

Leonard sighed. *Sure is a lot of improving to do.* A single rack of shelves divided the room. One side was populated with oil, washer fluid, engine additives, and miscellaneous "For Your Auto Care Needs." The other side had the cigarettes, chewing tobacco, candy, and knickknacks. The knickknack business had really fallen off as of late. The seashells and driftwood carvings were downright dusty. The far end of the room was dimly lit by a single bare bulb that swung overhead. Drafts from the approaching storm created an eerie play of shadows along the walls. Leonard didn't mind, as he had no fear of the haunts like some. He had a quick flash of Clem bleeding in the gravel. He shook his head to clear the vision.

There were two doors set into the far wall; one to the aromatic bathroom and the other to the garage. There were lots of things that could be done such as installing a real door instead of a padlocked chickenwire gate or, perhaps, buying one of them power lift jobs like the big Chevron station in Naples. A lightning bolt lit the room for an instant, and was directly followed by a tremendous crack of thunder.

The light bulb flickered and dimmed, then brightened again. The door to the garage flew open and a yellow blur streaked across the room and disappeared under the desk. Leonard leaned over and sniggled (not to be taken too lightly, he was the only person in Florida capable of sniggling) at Dog. He kneeled and grabbed Dog's collar.

"The improvements at the Lunch-N-Lube are going to start with you getting a bath," he said.

Leonard was certainly breaking the law. Somebody, somewhere just had to have passed a law against chaining a dog to a chickenwire garage door in the middle of a thunderstorm and hosing him down with a pressure washer. Dog was sure of it. He howled for the authorities, any authority to rescue him from the madman with the pressure washer who didn't realize they were sure to be killed at any moment by the dog-eating demons that lived in the sky. A nearby FLASH and CRACK prompted a change in tactics. Dog decided he'd just lay low and maybe the demons would just take the idiot and leave the poor long-suffering animal alone.

Leonard was doing a little jig as he laughed at the storm and Dog and everyone who had ever called him Lenny the Monkey Boy as the rain swirled in great sheets through a darkening sky and rinsed the last of the chaw from Dog's hide and the blight from Leonard Mullin's soul.

A grey Plymouth slowed. Doctor Pinder hoped to wait out the worst of the storm at the gas station. He rubbed his tired eyes and peered through the windshield. The wipers fought a pointless battle with the downpour. The Doctor was not sure, but it looked like a man in saturated overalls was stomping circles around a cowering dog, spraying a pressure washer into the storm with aimless abandon, and screaming "LEONARD! CALL ME LEONARD! HAH HA!"

Doctor Pinder tapped his gas gauge and made a quick decision. He pulled back onto the blacktop. The storm wasn't that bad and he probably had enough gas to make it to Miles City.

CHAPTER 4

Monday Evening, May 19

GLEN

"It's early yet, make yourselves comfortable," Glen said as he waved the girls into the room with a grand gesture.

"Cool," Lila said as she slipped by and set her boom-box on an end table.

Lou and DeeDee split up to survey the suite.

"Bitchin' room," Lou said, obviously impressed. The twinkly lights of Disneyworld sparkled through the open curtains.

"You're the host?"

"That," he said as he admired her from head to toe, "is correct."

She was clinging to the wrong side of thirty but was still solid party material. All of her parts were complete and accounted for. Maybe thirty-five years-old and five-feet-nothing including the three-inch heels. A hundred pounds of blonde-hair with dark roots and brown-skinned Caribbean T-and-A.

"And these guys are probably leaving, right, guys?" Glen said pointedly.

David and his pimple farm were staring at DeeDee with his eyes locked-in like targeting radar. She scraped a fingernail over the signature on a painting.

"This is a print."

She seemed disappointed.

"You know about art?" David said, tripping over an invisible obstacle as he approached her.

"I'm fascinated by this type of art, it's such an abstract medium these days; both surreal and impressionistic. I took a semester of art at Florida State."

David's eyes were bonded to the oscillating hem of her miniskirt.

"I thought you were leaving." DeeDee moved to the bar and tapped a decanter. "Hey! I think this is real crystal."

"No shit?" Lou had been attempting small talk with a red-faced 'Mister Jones', but broke it off in mid-inanity to examine the room service crystal.

Lila adjusted knobs on her stereo. The room filled with someone singing about winding roads, windy afternoons, and a failed corn crop. A string section sawed on the theme.

"Can't you get a different station?" Glen had standards. Lila rated about a seven on the critical Wilson Scale and it took at least a nine to get away with playing bad music.

"You're a critic?" Lila dug in her bag. "I've got a party CD in here somewhere, you'll love it."

Glen cracked a beer and surveyed Lila. Probably 25, looked 30. Built like a first-string Las Vegas all-nighter; thin and wiry. Brought her own mood music. Two-to-one it would be somebody named Michael. The CD cover showed a buff guy wearing a tux jacket and no shirt or shoes. He was singing passionately into a microphone that did not have a cable and it wasn't the wireless kind.

"Check this out, 'Thirty-two Greatest Hits of the Eighties'. Cool, huh? Don't you just love the oldies?"

Oldies. In Glen's world, Johnny Mathis sang the oldies. In Lila's it was Led Zeppelin. Strange. Her lipstick was lopsided and smeared a bit. Glen's heart throbbed. Well, something was throbbing. He felt himself falling in love yet again.

"That's great, babe. What's in here?" he asked, pointing at their insulated bottles.

He handed Lila his beer, grabbed one of the insulated bottles, and walked over to the bar. Lila followed him. The top on the Thermos was too tight for him to remove. Embarrassing. She reached around and took it from him, pleasing his nose with her imported cologne. Probably imported from Newark. She hiked up her skirt, stuck the Thermos between her thighs, and deftly twisted the top loose with both hands. She handed it back.

He grinned at her.

"Impressive."

"I can crack coconuts with these." She patted her thighs.

"You'll have to show me that one sometime. We could make a great exercise video."

He flipped a glass and filled it with what looked like a Bloody Mary. The smell of Tabasco and V-8 juice tickled his nose. He offered the glass to Lila.

She raised her hands and waved him away.

"Oh, no. I'm a beer drinker."

She wore a white knit top. The loose weave clearly revealed a black brassiere. She lifted her top and turned sideways.

"See? Beer belly."

All Glen saw was the flat stomach of a woman who claimed she could crack coconuts with her thighs. Interesting. He patted her tummy as he passed her by and walked over to Lou. Lou was holding a glass up to the light and tapping it with a swizzle stick.

"The stirring sticks are leaded crystal too," she said with wonder.

He took the stick from her and replaced it with the Bloody Mary. She stared at it for a second and placed it on a coaster.

"I don't think so, sweetie." She said as she wrapped her arms around his neck.

"I just like the hard stuff, y'know?" She stepped closer and pressed against him. "Um, and I don't think you're there yet, major dude."

She pulled away and picked up the drink as she headed back towards Jones, smiling over her shoulder.

"You just let me know when," she teased.

Glen went back to the sink and sniffed at the Thermos. There was a faint chemical smell hovering over the Tabasco. Two strikes was an out in this game.

Glen leaned against the counter and watched Jones guzzle his drink. Lou was sitting on his lap. She dabbed the crimson spots at the corners of his mouth with a napkin. She caught Glen's eye for an instant. She shrugged, then buried her face in Jones's neck.

Glen, tired of answering the door, propped it open with an empty champagne bottle. This allowed the nuns from down the hall to get an eyeful of what they were missing. A constant stream of guys entered. Glen knew most of them. Word spread quickly when Glen announced a party. He squinted around a cigarette and made sure everyone's glasses stayed filled.

DeeDee was dancing with Paul, one of the marketing guys Glen had met in the bar the night before. His tie was loose and his shirt half unbuttoned. Glen watched him slyly spill some of his drink down the front of her blouse.

"Oops! Lemme get that."

Paul dropped his drink and buried his face between her small breasts. She laughed and pushed him away. She waved her arms like a belly dancer, then smoothly lifted her top over her head and tossed it into the corner. She started dancing again with her bare breasts jiggling. They would have been jouncing but Glen didn't think that word was discovered yet.

Lou was on the couch between a couple of hotshots from a Denver disk drive company. It looked as if a three-way grope was going on. Peculiar, only two guys and six hands. Lou saw DeeDee's act, jumped up, and joined in.

"We're Go-Go girls!"

She climbed onto the coffee table in her high heels and started shimmying. The appreciative whoops got Glen's attention. He watched for a minute, then went behind her and pulled down the zipper of her skirt. It started to slip.

"Whoa!" She grabbed at it and glared at Glen. Then her lips twitched upward. She shrugged, let the skirt go, and kicked it away.

"Okay," she said gamely as she went back to her shimmying.

The music had been getting steadily louder. Nobody seemed to mind that it was the same CD over and over. Glen exchanged the party disk with an old Van Halen but three songs in Lila gave David Lee Roth the boot and put in a Latin hiphop disk. *Whatever.* Glen pulled a beer out of the ice that filled the kitchenette sink. He noticed Jones snoring on the couch with an empty glass tipped over beside him. Glen looked around for Lila and noticed the bedroom door was closed. He eased it open to be greeted by the sight of David Foster's pockmarked rear end as he pulled up his pants.

"Great party, thanks Glen," David said over his shoulder, grinning sloppily. Lila wiped her hands on the bedspread and stuffed a bill down the front of her dress. Glen walked over and snagged it.

"Fifty bucks? What am I paying Pablo for?"

"That's my tip, cowboy." She snatched the money back. She looked him over. "I'd say fifty is more of me than you could handle, old man."

Old man?

"So show me," Glen said.

She knelt and reached for his zipper. Glen caught her hand.

"I don't think so."

He pulled her up and steered her towards the bed.

"Let's try the real thing," he said.

Lila shrugged her dress off her shoulders in one practiced move.

"Whatever you say, old timer."

"Go wash your hands first, will you? And I need to see your HIV card."

"Sure, sugar. I'll show you mine and you show me yours," she said over her shoulder as she walked to the bathroom.

Later, Glen lifted off her and shook his head.

"Maybe I am getting old."

Lila kept her legs wrapped around him.

"I dunno there, Mr. Businessman," she said squeezing him with her thighs. "That wasn't half bad." She tried to pull him back. "Sloppy seconds, maybe?"

Glen laughed. "Later." He pried her arms away. "Besides, I don't want DeeDee to get lonely out there."

"That bitch and her little-girl tits." Lila scowled. She crossed her arms and cupped her breasts. "I thought guys only liked big ones. I spent a lot of money on these damn things."

"They're perfect." He kissed each one gently.

He pulled on his pants. Lila sat up and grabbed her dress off the floor. She slipped into it just as smoothly as she'd slipped out of it.

"I'm almost tempted to let you ride without the tip," she said.

"Great, baby. It was good for me too."

"I said almost, party-boy," she said with her hand out.

Glen found his wallet and handed over a hundred. They left the bedroom together hand-in-hand.

The party had evolved, or devolved, or something. The lights were dim. The smokers had the room looking as if the smoke alarm should be screeching, but someone had removed the batteries and yanked the wires. Glen could smell pot mixed with the tobacco smoke. The mirror from behind the bar was lying on the coffee table and one of the Denver boys was chopping up some cocaine on it with a razor blade. Lila made a beeline towards it. Glen faked a sneeze and the guy snapped a hand over his precious pile to shield it. He raised the razor blade.

"Watch it," he said.

"Sorry. Allergies," Glen replied.

Some people have no sense of humor.

"You want a hit?"

"No, my body is a temple. I don't like to poison the temple."

The guy pointed at Glen's beer.

"Right," Glen said, "health food. Liquid bread. Exactly my point."

"You're full of crap."

"So?" Glen replied as he headed to the bar. Lou was dancing on a different table, wearing just her high heels, orange panties, and a drunken smile. The shimmy had slowed to a sway. The other Denver boy was running his hands over her ass.

In the kitchenette DeeDee was bent over two barstools with the marketing VP on top of her. Glen dumped his warm beer in the sink.

"You guys take that to the bedroom."

"Uh." The VP rotated his head slowly. His eyes didn't quite focus. "Uh."

He fell into a heap on the floor.

"Or you could stay right here, I guess." Glen patted DeeDee on the butt. "I think he's done." She didn't say anything. Glen leaned over and looked in her face. Sound asleep. "Well, at least you'll have the fond memories."

Lila wandered in, flipped DeeDee's skirt down, gently smoothed it out, and handed Glen a glass of cold champagne.

"Your parties always go like this?" she asked.

"No. Sometimes they turn into filthy disgusting drunken orgies."

He took a swig of the champagne. He stared through the doorway and watched Lou dance. After a few minutes, the Denver guy's knees crumbled. Lou let him slip softly to the floor. Glen drained his glass and noticed that all the guys were unconscious and that Lila and Lou were looking at him expectantly. *Okay*, he thought. He pushed away from the counter. *I guess that just leaves me to do a man's job.* He took one step but the floor appeared to be made of sponge. Or Jello. It tilted and swayed. He stopped and sniffed at his champagne glass. That same chemical that he smelled in the Thermos. *Oh shit.* He looped the glass toward the sink and missed. His arms stretched like rubber bands toward the floor. The carpet flipped up in front of his face. Remarkable. *I'm standing straight up with my face pressed into the carpet.* His eyes focused on a handmade cigarette stub smoldering in front of his face. Someone dribbled champagne on the butt. *Oh shit,* he thought again as the world drifted away.

PART TWO

I used to believe that the universe was either random or that the Supreme Being had a very warped sense of humor. Now I am convinced that everything happens for a reason, but we'll never know what that reason is.

- Glen Wilson

CHAPTER 5

Tuesday Morning, May 20

GLEN

Glen woke up on the floor with his head throbbing which was odd, since he did not drink that much. He sat up slowly and looked around at the wreckage of the room. It looked more like a plundering than a party. *What the fuck?* There were at least eight unconscious bodies in view, strewn across the couch and on the main room floor. An older guy in a rumpled suit was sleeping in the tub. There was no sign of the girls. He noticed the white stripe on the wrist of the tub guy. His watch was missing. *Oh hell.* Glen remembered the champagne. Glen couldn't believe that he had fallen for a scam that was at least 2,000 years old. *Stupid, stupid, stupid.* Glen went through the pile in the master bedroom. All of his electronic toys were still there but his cash and wallet were gone. The fools left thousands of dollars in electronics, but took all the watches and rings. Glen shook his head, but slowly to keep it from flying off.

Mister Jones's unconscious and shirtless body was sprawled on the couch. His pants were bunched around his ankles. Glen dragged him onto the floor and arranged David and Mister Jones so their bodies intertwined, face to pimply face. He got his Polaroid instant camera from the bedroom and took a couple of pictures. The digital camera took much better pictures, but the Polaroids were nearly impossible to fake. No one believed a digital camera anymore. *Might as well have some fun if I'm going to be fucked over,* he thought. The pictures came out fine.

Moving gingerly, Glen got dressed and refilled his coat pockets with his stuff. He got a bottle of aspirin from his shaving kit, popped five, and washed them down with hot water that he drank straight from the faucet. He caught a glimpse of himself in the mirror. His eyes were bloodshot and his hair was standing up straight.

Magnificent, he thought. He raised his palms to his temples and pressed as hard as he could. He stood for a moment and watched himself disintegrate.

I taste blood and I don't know why. It's a rich and salty taste. My finger stub burns with an unknown fierceness. A blazing, flaming, and devouring pain.

Something very weird is coming my way, something wicked. Ha! "Something Wicked This Way Comes!" Who was that, Bradbury? I think so.... Hey, Ray! Ever mistakenly hire the divorce lawyer that's sleeping with your soon-to-be ex-wife? At odd times I wonder if he's used to his customized wheelchair and typing out depositions with his nose. Now that's truly Something Wicked.

The best laid plans. This was supposed to be an in-and-out. A quickie—Take What You Can, Keep Tabs on the Competition, Party Like a Fiend, Pad the Expense Report, and survive the Long Crawl Home. The Glen Wilson Standard. This feels more like a long ago white-knuckle ride through the desert from LAX to Phoenix in a stolen '65 Mustang convertible, carrying enough rock to light up Hollywood, and hurling empty beer bottles at the moon. Kid stuff. Am I getting old? Is that what this is about? Once, a year ago, I woke in the night, unable to move with a fight-or-flight adrenaline rush screaming at the reptile. A snapshot of Hell, wallet-size, and I still carry the scars. It didn't kill me so I emerged stronger. Doubt is for the weak.

And hesitation is for the foolish. Fear is a set of blinders for those who stay between the lines, under the limit, with a ten-car-length following distance. Scanning for trouble. Scared to death of the unexpected detour. Am I losing The Edge? Would I know? Does the cutlass have to be buried to the hilt in my ribs? Then and only then will I see the obvious? Yes—Yes, a rut would form slowly! Unnoticed at first, until every turn is uphill. But now I am aware. A danger known is feared the less and I know where the danger lies. Not in God or the Devil. Not in heaven or hell. In me. The danger lives and breathes liquid fire in me.

The man in the mirror went through regret, despair, helplessness, and then came through the other side. Glen watched himself getting genuinely pissed-off, head-to-toe, left-to-right, to the farthest corner of his blackened soul. Then the mask settled slowly over his face. He leaned close to the mirror and, with sweet and exaggerated politeness, with innocence oozing from his pores, said mildly "Excuse me, might I have my wallet back, please?"

After a few minutes wondering the hotel hallways, Glen found Raymond the bellhop on the third floor helping an elderly couple with their bags. Ray looked startled and he clearly considered taking off down the hall. The murderous look in Glen's eyes warned him against running.

"You and I are going to have a conversation," Glen said tersely.

"I can't, man, I'm on until three o'clock."

"It's break time," Glen replied.

They took a table near a corner in the employee break room. The room was empty except for a couple of maids yammering in Spanish. Glen bought two cups of bad coffee that spit out of a wheezing vending machine and choked down two more aspirins. Ray was nervous and kept watching the door and checking his watch.

"You look like shit, man. That must have been some party. We had to move the newlyweds next door, got complaints all down the hall."

"Yeah, yeah, so sue me."

"You don't know Manny at all, do you?" Raymond asked.

"Big guy, dresses well, about six-foot-two inches tall, six-foot-three inches wide, who works for a wise-ass punk named Pablo?"

Glen held his breath, hoping he had guessed right.

"Yes," Raymond said thoughtfully, "that's Manny. I thought he was a friend of yours?"

"No, not today. What's your beef with Manny?"

"It's a long story, but..."

"Forget the story, just tell me how much."

Ray looked ashamed. "Seven thou and change. Plus the damn interest of course," he said, tracing the design on the laminated tabletop with a fingertip.

"Tell me where I might find our buddy Pablo."

"He has a condo on Division Street, the 3400 block. You'll know he's there if you see his pink Jaguar."

"Look Ray, you came through with the room," Glen said as sincerely as he could. "I owe you one for that. I'm going to look up Mr. Pablo and persuade him to cut you a deal, say three K cash, and you guys part as friends. What do you say?"

"How do I..." Raymond began.

"You don't."

"What if you...

"I won't," Glen said flatly.

They stared at each other for a minute.

"It will take ten minutes to get the money."

"The clock is ticking."

When Raymond left the room, Glen pulled out his cellular phone and dialed Carlos' cell phone. Yes, Carlos could be outside the Marriott in fifteen minutes.

When Raymond returned, Glen took the wad of money and stuck it in his pocket without looking at it. He snatched a yellow pencil out of Ray's pocket.

"And your watch, please."

"Ah, man," Ray said, but he did remove it.

Glen examined it. It was a cheap Casio digital.

"Hardly worth stealing," Glen commented as he strapped it on.

"Then just give it back."

"Don't start with me, boy," Glen warned over his shoulder as he walked out of the breakroom.

Glen trotted down the front steps of the Marriott and jumped into the taxi. He gave Carlos the address on Division Street. There was a flicker of recognition in Carlos's eyes. He didn't look happy about it, but said "Okay, chief." He pulled the car out into traffic.

"And lose the tail, will you?"

Carlos watched the rearview mirror. A nondescript four-door sedan lingered a few cars back. Carlos lost them by taking a right turn around a bus and scattering pedestrians in the crosswalk. Glen stewed over events of the evening, the muggers, Manny, the hookers, his wallet. *Maybe it's true*, he thought. *Maybe nice guys like me always do finish last.*

When they arrived at the address, Glen told Carlos to circle the block. Everything looked quiet. The pink Jaguar was parked on the street. Pablo must pull some weight, the hood ornament was still in place and all the windows were intact. The condo was covered in gray stucco. The fronds of a palm tree whispered in the gentle suburban breeze. English Ivy grew around the windows. It was too refined a neighborhood for a creep like Pablo. Glen ordered Carlos to wait and gave him a look that said "Or else." Carlos nodded and unfolded an Orlando Sentinel. Glen strode up the sidewalk. He pressed the doorbell button and pounded on the door. There was no answer. He looked in the window but couldn't see anything moving inside. A radio blasted from inside somewhere. Glen tried the front door and found it unlocked. He patted his pockets for a weapon and pulled out the yellow pencil he had taken from Raymond. It was dull. *Better than nothing*, he thought.

He stuck his head in the door and hollered "Yoo-hoo, anybody home?"

There was no answer. He looked up and down the street, then slipped in and pulled the door shut behind him. The air conditioning whispered quietly. The place was cool and comfortable after the morning heat. Glen started exploring.

He walked down a hallway, listened, then knocked on the door. The radio was blasting Salsa from behind it. No answer. He pushed the door open and saw Pablo duct taped to a chair. His throat was slashed. About 105 gallons of blood decorated the hardwood floor.

"Oh my, Mr. Pablo, you don't look well at all."

It didn't bother Glen that Pablo did not answer. He stepped around the bloody trail and stooped down in front of Pablo. He turned the radio down to a whisper. He lifted an arm to check for rigor mortis. The body was cold but still flexible. There were deep cuts on the face that looked like they'd been made by a razor. What did they want? He tilted the head back and looked into the corpse's eyes.

"I guess you won't tell me where my wallet is?"

He let the head flop down and performed a quick search of the room. He didn't find anything interesting. He punched the button on the telephone answering machine and listened to the message. The voice sounded like Lila from the party.

"Hi Pablo, everything went down smooth. We got the wallets and some jewelry. Listen, lover, are we going to get together later? Manny says he's taking some time off, he's taking DeeDee for a little vacation. Are we going too? I hope so. I miss you baby, kiss, kiss." That was the only message.

"I don't think so, sweetie," Glen replied.

Glen noticed a safe open on the wall.

"Gave up the combination, did you?"

The safe was empty except for some old Mexican Pesos. He checked the usual hiding places; under the mattress, the backs of the closets, the freezer. Nothing, the place had been tossed by some pros. Glen went out the front door, whistled at Carlos, and motioned for him to enter.

"Pablo wants to speak with you."

Carlos did not look near nervous enough. Perhaps he's one of Pablo's friends from the old country. When Carlos entered the living room, Glen reached under Carlos's shirt and pulled out the snub nose 38. He tripped him over a chair. Carlos scrabbled across the floor and turned so his back was against the wall. Glen flipped the cylinder out and dumped the bullets out in his hand. The ends had been drilled out roughly; they were homemade hollowpoints. *Nasty*. Glen kneeled. He seemed to have Carlos's undivided attention.

"Listen carefully. I'm not pleased about your deal with the dumb kids in the alley. You take my money and then pull shit like that." Glen shook his head sadly. "I'll give you one more chance. Tell me where to find Manny and we will go our separate ways as friends."

"Fuck off." Carlos replied.

"Last chance, partner."

"Eat me, gringo." At that, Carlos's hand darted into his shirt and he whipped out a thin knife. He was fast, but not fast enough. Glen buried the pencil in his thigh and slapped the knife from his hand. Carlos's bulging eyes could see what had happened but his body had not telegraphed the complete message yet. He sat, staring at the pencil with unbelieving eyes.

Looked to me like Pablo's operation had been a bit top-heavy and Manny did some re-organization. Too bad Manny couldn't re-engineer corporate America, looks like he's a natural at making staff cuts. Manny crunches the numbers dealing with productivity and profit, and a layer of management gets the axe. Or in this case, the razor. A very sharp razor judging from the new look Pablo was sporting. An interesting policy I'd like to introduce at ICC. "Don't be stupid, bossMAN... Next time the staff cuts are going to be a little deeper."

Seems I'd missed the retirement party. No gold watch for Pablo? No golden parachute? I choke back the tears. These corporate realignments can be tiring, so Manny takes a sabbatical, a little holiday while the situation cools. Maybe he needs some time to practice the intricate "across-the-eyebrows-slash." Or the delicate "firing-three-bullets-to-the-head-after-knife-in-the-kidney-stab."

All that is fine with me. The quest for perfection is something I admire, but the fucker still has my wallet and a little of my pride.

Even with my quick lesson about how the pencil can be more powerful than the blade, Carlos wasn't going to cooperate. To be expected, as Manny is one big and ugly dude. Not suave and sophisticated like Yours Truly. However, if you take the hard road, you should be ready for the bumps. That's why it's called the Hard Road. Jerk me around? I didn't feel too guilty about breaking one of Pablo's polo clubs across Carlos's head. He saw it coming and clamped his eyes shut, probably expecting worse. He should have. I flecked some paint from the pencil and stuck the flecks under one of Pablo's fingernails. I rubbed Carlos's knife in the blood. I dragged his two-timing butt across the room and rolled him around in the gore a bit. The way I left him, he

*would have some difficulty explaining things when the cops showed up.
I'm modest but have to admit it was a beautiful scene. Suitable for
framing. The work of natural genius if I must say so myself.*

*I considered wiping my fingerprints, but decided not to bother.
The FeeBees switched to a Cray supercomputer database system a few
years back, and it was accessible via a very secure network by the more
important of the world's enforcement agencies. Do you get it? I'm
connected over the big pond through the Net. Protected by firewalls and
RSA-ensured security. Too bad, but the temptation of scanning the net
for alt.anarchists or cruising some Jolly Roger's home page has left the
backdoor cracked for anyone with enough insight to break a few locks. I
don't want to make it sound too easy because I have the advantage of a
post-grad crew in Bombay and some 'retired' KGB crypto-hackers. All
are delighted to take my greenbacks. Add to the formula my willingness
to employ some friendly extortion to fill in the blanks. The result? My
service and arrest record prints were no longer indexed correctly, and
never would be. The Feds would be clueless and left puzzling over
Carlos's laughable story.*

*Rubbing my aching neck, I checked the fridge on the way out and
grabbed a bottle of some local brew. I popped the top and sang one of
my theme songs:*

*"WELLLL... I woke up this morning and I got myself a
BEEEER..." Rest in peace, Jimmy. I gagged and spit the beer in the sink.
They drink alligator piss down here? Damn it, I should have known
about Pablo's taste when I saw the pink Jag.*

The cab was still idling at the curb. Glen felt the immense weight
of unfinished business strobing in time with the pounding in his temples.
He felt a little better after smashing the lamp on the taxi roof with the
broken handle of the polo club he found still in his hand. He tossed the
handle onto the hood of the gaudy Jag and slipped behind the wheel of
the cab. The meter read 26 dollars and change. He whistled a bar of
"Free Ride" by the Edgar Winter Group, then flipped off the meter.

Glen parked the cab by the familiar alley up the street from the
Sportsman. He rooted around in his suitcase and pulled out some clothes
line rope. He knotted a big loop with one of his Boy Scout knots. He
walked slowly by the alley where his friends were waiting.

"Look, it's the Banana-Man." They looked as if fortified with
chemical courage; jittery and mean. Ponytail seemed to vibrate in his
army jacket.

They backed him into the darkness of the alley.

"Oh, hi boys. Sorry, but I'm out of bananas right now."

Glen pulled the hammer back on Carlos's .38 Special as he drew it from his coat pocket. He pointed it at the center of Willie's head.

"Okay man, take it easy." The boys dropped their blades and raised their hands slowly. Glen backed them against the wall.

"Willie, listen to me, man. There ain't no bullets in that gun."

Glen laughed. He swung the gun into Ponytail's face.

"Just because the chambers you can see are empty doesn't mean the one under the hammer is empty. Does it? Correct me if I'm wrong about that, fellas. That's the one we care about? The one under the hammer? Am I the kind of guy to come here with an empty gun? Come on, tough guy, let's find out what kind of oatmeal you have between your ears."

Ponytail employed his frazzled brain cells for a moment then produced a lame and sickly smile.

"We're just kidding around, Banana-Man. Aren't we, Tim? Yeah. Put the gun down and we'll go get a beer or something."

So, Ponytail's name is Tim. Who cares?

"I'm not in the mood, boys. Turn so you are facing each other and give yourselves a big friendly hug."

They shuffled their feet and followed the order. Glen passed the nylon loop over their heads, worked it around their chests, and jerked the loop tight. He kicked them over and they fell into the refuse. He pitched the gun to the ground, retrieved the knives, and checked to see which one was the sharpest. He pulled off their grubby tennis shoes. He slit all 4 dirty socks and gingerly tossed them aside.

"You guys should invest in a washing machine. This is disgusting."

"What are you doing, man?" Willie's shaky voice revealed that he still did not like Glen's random scripts.

"I'm trying to find Manny and I sure could use your help." He calmly started cutting their jackets, ripped them free, and searched the pockets. He tossed the trash away; a cheap plastic lighter, some keys, a plastic bag with a few grams of crystal, a packet of condoms. Willie had an X-Men comic rolled up in his inside pocket.

"You surprise me, Willie, I wouldn't take you for a patron of literature."

He tapped Willie on the nose with the comic book.

"You know what causes the most fights in the big house? Huh?" He poked Tim with the comic. "Which cartoon to watch on Saturday morning. No kidding."

He flipped the comic into the growing pile of trash. He dropped the jackets and started cutting their shirts.

"Manny has left town for a while. That's all we know."

"I believe you." He pulled a pack of cigarettes out of a pocket.

"Menthol," he said with contempt as he tossed them away.

They were wriggling, so Glen put his shoe on Willie and pulled the strap tighter. They couldn't move much but they really started squirming when Glen started slicing their pant leg seams.

"Man, we've told you everything!" Ponytail shouted.

"Are you queer or something?" Willie asked. "Faggot!"

"No, my man. I don't swing that way. Is that a big problem in this town or what? Get a lot of visitors from Key West?" They did not seem to have an answer. "Just a rhetorical question," he said as he went through their pants pockets.

He looked through the wallets and pocketed the bills. They had about sixty bucks between them. Their driver's licenses read Timothy Allen Davis and William Francis Washington. He tossed the wallets, the pocket change, and a penknife onto the pile. Willie was wearing red bikini briefs and Tim wore yellow boxers.

"You two make a very charming couple." He slipped the blade under the elastic of Willie's shorts and made a sawing motion. "Do you guys really want to be found here with your wieners hanging out?"

Willie made a decision.

"Talk to Robert, the man at the door down the street. He can find Manny."

"I already figured that," Glen replied. "Tell me something I don't know."

"That's it. There ain't no more."

"Okay, gentlemen. Let me give you some advice. Do I have your undivided attention?" He paused. "You guys sure look snug."

"You going to cut us loose, or what?" Willie said.

"Sorry, my friends. I want you to have some time for a conversation and to think things out. I suggest you guys cut out this crap. Get some straight jobs, get your GEDs, go to junior college. Try to hang out with a better class of people. Because, frankly…" He pricked both of their arms and little puddles of blood welled up. "You boys are just baby ducks on the freeway." With that he stabbed the knife into the wall.

"Fuck off, banana-man," Willie said with his eyes fixed on the crimson streak running down his arm.

"Ciao," Glen said as he left the alley.

Robert, the bouncer, was back at the Sportsman's door chewing on a toothpick. He was standing with the bartender. They watched Glen emerge from the alley. The bartender's face darkened. He cursed and slapped a bill into Robert's hand, then went inside.

"How did you do?" Glen asked.

"Fifty big ones." Robert pulled the bill from his pocket, kissed it, then stuck it back. "Easy money."

"It's never too hard for a clever man to make a few bucks," Glen replied.

He leaned against the wall with Robert. In silence they watched cars drive by for a while.

"Been some people asking about you. They looked like Feds to me. I played dumb. I think they bought it."

Glen fished in his pockets and found his Polaroids of David Foster and Mister Jones.

"Was this the guy?"

Robert eyed the picture and nodded his head yes. He wanted to ask about the picture, but didn't.

"He looked pretty hung over, like you."

"Had a little party last night. Lila's special recipe for Bloody Marys packs a punch, I think."

"That's what I've heard."

"Well, so it goes. I don't mind paying some dues, but I'd like to get my wallet back."

"Just go buy another one and save yourself a lot of misery."

"Sure, easy for you to say. First, you let someone steal your wallet. Then it's your girl, your balls, and your soul. You end up sitting in your filthy boxers, scratching your flabby ass, watching Donahue on that mind-sucking box and wondering where your manhood went. It's a slippery slope and a man has to be eternally vigilant."

"You're one crazy Yankee, aren't you?"

"Whatever." Glen pulled Raymond's bankroll out of his jacket and counted out five hundred. "I think if I could just explain the situation to Manny, we could work stuff out."

Robert looked both ways down the street, then smoothly palmed the bills. He handed Glen a folded square of paper. Glen unfolded a photocopy of a calendar page with a series of phone numbers scribbled on the dates. Glen pulled out his cellular phone and dialed the first number. It was for the Haines City Holiday Inn. "What is Manny's last name?" he whispered as the call was routed.

"Rodriguez," Robert replied.

"Could I speak to Mr. Manuel Rodriguez, please?"

"Mr. Rodriguez has left instructions that he does not want to be disturbed. Can I take a message, please?"

"Sure, this is Pablo. I'm going to take a nap now. Tell him that I will call back after my little rest."

"Yes, sir, is that all?" She sounded a little puzzled.

"Yes, he'll know what this is about. Thank you much," he said as he punched the disconnect button.

"What's the story on the driver?" Robert gestured at the cab.

"In my world there are a few simple rules. One, if you don't want to sell, then fine, you're a civilian. However, if you sell, you stay sold. The law of the urban jungle. That reminds me. You can send the Feds over to Pablo's if you wish. They'll find the driver there. He'll be nursing a stinker of a headache, I'm afraid."

"For those guys in the alley? Should I call an ambulance or the meat wagon?"

"They're fine, give them a couple of hours, then you can cut them loose. Give them a little time to ponder the error of their ways." Glen gave a two finger salute. "Been good doing business with you."

He rambled toward the cab.

"Hey," Robert called out after him. "What do they call you?"

Glen turned, waved, and shouted back, "Call me the Banana-Man."

LEONARD

Leonard was counting the money in the till. He had about three hundred dollars and he wasn't quite sure what to do with it. Clem had handled all the deposits, such as they were, at the bank in East Naples. Sarah Bremmer pulled up in the station wagon. She waved and raised her fat arms to give Leonard a big hug, but Leonard ducked out. He walked to the road and looked up and down. It was quiet. Sarah followed and gave him a suffocating hug. She was short. She pulled his head to her bosom.

"Ow, you're gonna break my neck," Leonard cried.

"Let's sit down, Leonard. I mixed you up some pink lemonade from the can just the way you like it, with extra sugar."

She went to the car and pulled out a Atlas Mason quart jar filled with lemonade and melting ice cubes. The drink was sweet and sticky.

Sarah was drinking iced tea with a very visible thick band of gin on top. She sat in Clem's chair.

"Did you sign the papers that Carl left for you?"

"Oh man, I forgot."

He got up, went in the office, and retrieved the legal papers. He suddenly remembered the letter that Clem had left. It was still in the back pocket of his overalls. He brought that out too.

He rotated the letter in his hands.

"This is just like a voice from the grave, like one of those TV reruns." He raised his hands and made a scary face at Sarah. "Do not adjust your set, we control the, the—"

"The vertical, the horizontal." She slapped at his hands. "Now stop it."

She picked up the papers. "You haven't signed them, Leonard. You said you'd sign them." There was sticky pink stuff on them. "What have you done, is this strawberry jam? Yuck!"

Leonard hung his head. "Sorry, Sarah."

"Never mind. I have a pen, go ahead and sign them now."

Leonard was distracted by the letter. He slipped a blackened fingernail under the seal.

"Forget the letter for a minute, sign the papers, then you can read the letter. Please Leonard, for me." He was unconscious, looking with wonder at the letter. "Okay Leonard, you win. Look, how about if I read you the letter. Would that make you happy?"

"Yes, please."

Leonard handed her the letter. He was grinning broadly.

She roughly tore the letter from his grasp and ripped it open. The envelope held a single sheet of tablet paper. Leonard could see that Clem had written in large clear letters. Sarah pulled her reading glasses from her purse, settled them on her nose, and cleared her throat.

"Dear Leonard. I think of you as my son, the son that Sarah never—Uh, the son I wish that Sarah and I could have had. Sarah has always had a special place for you in her heart. Now that I'm gone, Sarah is your best friend. If Sarah has some papers, I want you to sign them right away, right now. Quit messing around. I'll see you in heaven soon, signed Clem."

"I can't get over it, Clem talking to me from heaven," Leonard said with awe. "I guess I'd better sign these papers."

Sarah breathed a huge sigh of relief. The instant the pen touched the paper a yellow Mustang convertible slid to a stop on the gravel.

"Hang on Sarah, I got a customer!"

"Balls," she said. She drained her tea.

By the time Leonard came back to the porch Sarah had nodded off. Leonard eased Clem's letter from under her Mason jar and he shook off the excess moisture.

Dear Leonard:

I think of you as my son, the son that Sarah never wanted to have. Worried about her figure, can you believe it? You know about my will now, that's good.

If anything happens to me, the place is yours but I think Sarah and that shitheel lawyer Carl will try to steal it from you. Don't sign anything they give you.

PS: The roof over the lady's can leaks, get it fixed before the next heavy rain.

PPS: Brush your teeth every now and then or you'll scare the customers away. You're a good boy.

Clem

The third time Leonard read it, he had the general idea. The thought of losing the Lunch-N-Lube filled him with white-hot anger. He grabbed a broom from the office and started hitting Sarah. She woke with a start and knocked over her Mason jar. Dog didn't like the look of the situation and disappeared around the side of the building.

Leonard was crying. "This is my dream, nobody is going to take my dream away."

"Leonard, stop it." She covered her head with her flabby arms. He drove her to the car with the broom. She was sobbing and walking as fast as she could. Every ounce of her fat was quivering and jiggling.

"You'll be sorry, you Mongoloid idiot."

"And don't come back here no more," Leonard yelled.

She got the car started and spun the tires in the gravel before she raced away. Leonard threw the broom after her. After a while, Dog decided it was safe to come back and lay on his burlap bag. He kept a close eye on Leonard. There was far too much excitement around here for Dog's taste.

CHAPTER 6

Tuesday, Around Noon, May 20

MURPHY AND WEBSTER

FBI Special Agent Orrin Webster pulled his rental car to the curb in front of the Pablo Estevez place. He counted four black and white police units parked with their lights flashing. He noted the officers interviewing neighbors and dusting the Jaguar for fingerprints. He also noted the yellow crime scene tape draped around the palm trees. An ambulance pulled away with no siren. He adjusted his tie and brushed off his shoulders in case some dandruff had settled there, picked up a leather zipper case, and climbed out of his car. He lifted the yellow tape and walked across the grass toward the front door.

A police sergeant waved down Webster.

"Excuse me, this is a crime scene."

Webster flashed his badge.

"FBI. Who's in charge here?"

"Captain Murphy is inside. Please try not to touch anything, we're dusting for prints."

Well, duh, Webster thought. "Of course," he said. "I was number three in my class at Quantico. Okay?"

The sergeant raised his eyebrows in curiosity. "Sorry, Number Three, just watch yourself."

The sergeant opened the front door and ushered Webster through. As Webster entered the house he could see the strobe lights flashing as the photographers documented a room down the hall.

"Murphy, where are you, Murphy?" the sergeant called out.

Murphy was medium-height and slightly-built. She was a plain-looking woman with freckles on her wide face. She looked like a Midwest farm girl, but she dressed business-suave in a tan cashmere jacket, floppy silk tie, brown wool skirt, and white stockings. Her shoes were polished brown mirrors. Her dark hair was pulled back into a bun

71

and she had rimless glasses hanging from a chain around her neck. Another chain held her identification. She was about 35, neat, with light makeup. Not a hair was out of place.

"I'm Murphy. What the fuck, over?"

"This is Number Three," the sergeant said.

"Orrin Webster," he said with irritation as he handed over his ID card.

Murphy looked his card over carefully, twisting it under the light to see the hologram.

"What's this Number Three stuff?" Murphy asked the sergeant.

"He said he was Number Three at Quantico."

"Is that right?" Murphy said quizzically.

"Yes," Webster said proudly, "I was third out of a class of one hundred and thirty."

"No, I meant, did you really tell him that? And why? Oh, never mind. What has attracted the FBI's interest in this case?"

She passed back his ID.

"Somebody called in a tip. Can you show me around?"

"Okay, we found an unconscious man here." She gestured at some chalk marks on the floor. "What was his name?"

The sergeant flipped the pages of his notebook.

"Carlos Villareal, a cab driver."

"He had a lump on his head apparently caused by a polo club. The handle was found outside. He had a pencil stabbed in his thigh, possibly stuck there by the deceased."

They brushed by a technician who was vacuuming the carpeting as they walked down the hall to the bedroom.

"The stiff was taped into the chair there." Murphy said, gesturing. "A well-known local character, Pablo Estevez. Throat cut, that explains the blood. The safe was open, so it may be a burglary. There were at least two, the neighbors saw two men arrive in a cab, then one drove off after smashing the light off the top. Threw a temper tantrum or something."

They walked through the house. Webster froze when they entered the kitchen.

"Somebody had a beer!" Webster said, excited.

"Yes. It was still cold when we arrived."

Webster bent down and stuck his nose two inches away from the bottle. He unzipped his case, pulled out a four inch magnifying glass, and examined the bottle carefully.

"Hot damn, I think I've got him." He looked in the sink and pointed.

"Look, somebody spit. Did you guys spit?"

"No, Number Three, I don't spit at a crime scene. What about you, Sarge? You spit at a scene?"

The sergeant shrugged. She raised her voice. "Anybody spit in the sink here? Huh?"

The photographers and technicians paused and looked up, then went back to their work.

"I guess that does it, there's no spitting on my crew. You don't have to be a third runner-up at FeeBee school to know that."

"We got him, we got him. Get this bottle into an evidence bag immediately. Collect as much of that saliva as possible. Send it via Fed Ex to our lab in Virginia. We'll match the DNA pattern in a few hours and nail this sucker. Yes! Murder one, and Wilson gets twenty years in the slammer for sure."

Webster raised his fist like he'd scored a hat trick in an NHL final. He walked out the door with a spring to his step.

"Who's this Wilson? Hold on, Webster, do you have some information that you should share with Florida SPD?"

Without turning, Webster said, "I'll be in touch."

The cops watched Webster jump in his car and drive away.

"That Number Three is the excitable type, eh?"

"Those guys just love showing off their expensive lab gear." Murphy shrugged. "Let's get back to work."

GLEN

Glen stopped the cab at a 7-11. The clerk behind the counter was a washed-out looking bottle-blond with dark brown roots.

"I need a phone card," Glen said.

"What shall I program it for?"

The clerk's name tag said Yvonne.

Glen brought out his wad of bills and counted out a thousand.

"Let's make it an even thousand," he said as he threw some pepperoni sticks on the counter. "I want a lottery ticket too."

"Great," Yvonne said. "You going for the twenty-one million?"

"No, it's too hard to keep a low profile if you win the big one. Just the match game is fine."

"Okay, mister."

Glen drove around until he found a phone booth with a high speed data port that wasn't smashed. He slid the phone card though the sensor, then hooked a long cord to his laptop computer. He uncoiled the wire, sat on the hood of the cab, and logged into the Net. He transferred the source code that he had sold and checked his e-mail. He posted a message to his boss that all was well and that he was on the trail of a big sale. He transferred his lottery ticket numbers to Bombay so the crew could work on them.

"Mister, hey mister?"

Glen looked up to see a scrawny black youth of about five pulling on his pants leg. He was dressed in a bigger person's jeans, neatly patched, clean, but at least ten years and two generations old.

"What's up kiddo?"

"Are you logged in?"

"Yes."

"Can we play Barney Doom 2010 for a while?"

He was going to tell the boy to fuck off, but he was bored so he said "Okay" instead.

He handed the kid a joystick. They played until the afternoon rain started. The youngster was good and racked up seven Barneys to Glen's three. After Glen put the laptop away and rolled up the phone cord, he handed the kid a business card.

"What's your name, kid?"

He stood up straight and looked up at Glen. He was about three and a half feet tall.

"Benjamin Franklin Jackson," he said proudly.

"Okay Bennie, you call me when you get serious," Glen said.

The kid solemnly put the card in his pocket and skipped away. Glen felt better, blowing up Barney and his friends was good therapy. The throbbing in his head had retreated, saving its strength to fight another day. He pointed the car toward Haines City and cruised through the lightning and thunder. The radio would not stop squawking so he ripped it out and threw it out the window at a stoplight. He was glad, 20 minutes later, to see Orlando in his rearview mirror.

MURPHY

At the State Patrol headquarters, Webster, Murphy, and Murphy's boss, Major Smythe, were having a heated conversation. Webster's supervisor, Tom Baker, was shouting over the speakerphone.

"Webster, you will cooperate with the troopers or your ass will be packed in the baggage compartment of the next plane home. You got me?"

"I don't need a deadweight partner holding me back in my investigation!"

"We've been through this, cowboy. You're going to need help from the local authorities. If they want to assign you and Murphy to work together, that is fine with God, it's fine with the Director, it's fine with me, and it's perfectly fine with you."

"I want to go on record with a protest."

"Fine, noted. Now get your ass back to work. Is there anything else, Captain Murphy and Major Smythe?"

"If we could get the lab results faxed to us here, that would be good," Murphy said.

"No problem. Anything else you need, you holler. Webster will give his full cooperation. Catch you later."

The connection was broken. They listened to the static for a moment before Smythe switched off the speakerphone.

"Can Murphy and I have a few moments alone?" Webster asked.

"Sure, I've got real work to do anyway," Major Smythe said as he left the room. He eased the door shut behind him.

Webster hovered over Captain Murphy. She stood up and they were eye-to-eye.

"I don't want any misunderstanding. This is my operation, and I'm going to run things my way. Got it?"

"Of course, no problem, Number Three."

Webster's face discolored as he leaned close. "Am I going to have trouble with you?"

"None."

His face loomed before her like a full moon.

"If I say jump, you're going to say 'How high, sir.'"

"Yes."

He leaned even closer. Murphy did not move a muscle. He raised his hands as if he was going to grasp her shoulders. There was a loud ratcheting click in the quiet room. Webster froze with his hands in the air. Murphy's face was completely blank.

He lowered his hands slowly.

"As long as we have everything straight." Webster stepped back.

"No question, sir." Murphy pulled her handbag from behind her back, brought out her Rossi Model 971, a stainless steel .357 Magnum with a 2-inch barrel and rubber hand grip. With the gun pointed at the floor she eased the hammer back. She dropped the revolver back in her bag, snapped the bag shut, and placed the bag on the table.

"Everything is crystal clear," she added.

"Good," Webster said.

A clerk poked his head in the door. He looked at them with curiosity. They were sitting silently and looking at opposite walls. The clerk placed a manila folder on the table and quietly shut the door. Webster grabbed the folder.

"Great, it's the lab results from the DNA testing. Hot dog!"

He riffled through the fax papers and read the last page carefully. His face drained of color. He dropped the bundle. He was so angry he was shaking as he stormed out of the room. Murphy read all the pages slowly and methodically.

Major Smythe poked his head in the door just as Murphy finished reading the last sheet. Smythe looked at her with question marks in his eyes. The normally staid Murphy was wiping tears from the corners of her eyes, trying her hardest not to laugh out loud.

"Is everything okay, Murphy?"

"I'm just looking at the lab results from the saliva samples and the beer bottle we took at the Estevez place."

"Did they come up with a cross?"

"Yes."

"Come on, Murphy, don't mess around. What does it say?"

"Well, I'm sure the FBI never screws up."

"So?"

"So, our first job will be to figure out how Richard Milhous Nixon rose from the grave and had a beer at the Pablo Estevez place."

Later that afternoon, Webster and Murphy were interrogating Elke in the Convention Center coffee shop. Webster was angry with Elke; so upset that his hands were shaking. Coffee surged out of his cup onto the plastic tabletop. He mopped it up with a paper napkin.

"Do you need to look at these pictures again?" He waved a sheaf of photographs an inch thick. "You had lunch with this guy. Your lips were moving, that means you were talking about something, and I want to know about it."

Murphy held up her hands, palms together, like she was praying.

"Look, Number Three, why don't you give us a few minutes."

Webster leaned back in his chair.

"Take all the time you want," he said.

"I mean, excuse us. You know, go take a leak or something," Murphy urged.

"Okay. Okay." He pushed his chair back and stood over the two ladies. "But when I come back...." he said over his shoulder as he stomped away.

"Sorry," Murphy said quietly when she was sure Webster couldn't hear her. "This is our takeoff on the Good Cop, Bad Cop interrogation technique. I call it Smart Cop, Dumb Cop."

Elke giggled, then finally spoke.

"I met Wilson at my booth. He seemed interesting and we had lunch. Salads."

"I know about the salads, they were well documented in Number Three's report," Murphy said.

"We talked about the semiconductor business and about the show. That's all. Shop talk."

"Did you make any arrangement to meet later or anything?"

"No, but I wouldn't mind."

"Number Three sure has a hard-on for this guy. He may be dangerous," Murphy warned.

"Well, my life could use some danger. I'm tired of guys who are brainless north of their beltline. Know what I mean?"

"Yes, unfortunately I do," Murphy shook her head. "Will you call me if you get in a bind?" She handed over a card.

"Sure." Elke slid the card into her handbag. "Tell me, what's the deal with this Number Three stuff?"

"He graduated number three in his FBI training class."

"Oh," Elke replied.

GLEN

Glen, heeding some pressure on his bladder, pulled the cab into a rest stop on Highway 92 just south of Kissimmee. Something in the parking lot did not look right. There was a rusty old Cadillac conch-cruiser idling across from some picnic tables that was belching clouds of blue smoke. Some figures were hunched behind a dumpster. Suddenly, everything popped into focus. Glen saw a tall youth in a silver and black Raiders T-shirt strike a tourist with a silver baseball bat. The tourist fell. A woman was screaming. There was a Chevy rental car parked in the lot. Beside that, no one was around. Glen popped the latches on his suitcase and pawed through it looking for something, anything.

Ah, this should do the trick. I found a little plastic sample bottle, it contained a new super glue made in the Philippines, like a cyanoacrylate ester (super-glue) adhesive, only more penetrating and about 200 times stronger. I squirted a glob on each of the Cadillac's door handles, then walked toward the struggling figures. The two muggers looked like twins with razor-cut hair, baggy blue jeans, and fancy high-top basketball shoes with the laces unraveled. One wore red shoes and the other wore black. As I approached, they ran around me. Black shoes waved the bat and warned, "Back off, old man, unless you want a taste of this." I just raised my hands, smiled my sweetest smile, and shook my head no.

Old man. There's that again. Fuck. I watched them reach their door handles at the same time. Nearly wrenching their arms from their sockets, the way that Cadillac was built, they were NOT going anywhere. Their hands would rend from their arms before that glue would release. Something to do with the surface area and texture of skin. The harder they pulled, the harder it would grip. Genuinely nasty stuff in the wrong hands.

"What the hell, man?" Black shoes was a little wild-eyed. I ambled closer to the car.

"What did you do to us, asshole?" Red shoes was a lot wild-eyed.

I stepped close enough that Black shoes tried a furious left-handed cut with the bat. An admirable try. I grinned as the bat plowed into the windshield and embedded itself in the safety glass. He couldn't wrench it free before I snatched it from his hand. An aluminum Louisville Slugger. I weighed it in my hands and admired the balance.

"Wish we had bats like this when I was a boy. Bet you can clear the fence every time."

I caught Red Shoe's eyes across the hood of the car and nodded.

"Hey Dude, check this action."

I slammed the handle of the bat into his buddy's left kidney. The punk collapsed with a silent scream with his mouth contracting in spasms. I bent over to look him in the face and frowned.

"This is not good. Once had a pet fish that looked like you and I had to freeze it."

Red shoes was shouting something incoherent, jerking on the door handle with enough force to rock that Detroit heavy iron. I shook my head.

"Yes, I agree completely. But listen, that's supposed to be the kindest way, the fish goes numb and doesn't feel a thing."

The lady tourist slowly approached the car. I went around the other side and took a few practice swings. Red shoes squirmed and did his best to rip off the door handle. I don't think he was impressed with the pure form of my swing.

"You're right, I'm an old man, you should have seen me ten years ago. I could whack hooligans like you all day and not break a sweat."

I extended the bat and sighted down its length at the flat horizon.

"You ever seen 'Jeopardy'?" I asked.

Red shoes was bug-eyed and silent.

"The Bambino?" I asked.

Red shoes stared. Lights on, nobody home.

I lowered the bat. "How about the Yankee Clipper?" Still nothing. I sighed. "The Iron Horse?"

Red shoes brightened. Sensing a ray of hope, he offered *"Mickey Mantle?"*

I scratched at my nose, got a good grip, pawed the ground, and spit.

"That wasn't in the form of a question."

I hammered him in the ribs, but not too hard. Give him a body cast and six months, he'll heal. He yelped, crouched lower, and raised his free arm in defense.

"And incorrect, sir, sorry," I said.

For that I thumped him a good one, CRACK. I put the bat behind my neck and swiveled my hips back and forth to stretch my back muscles. I was still a little tight from the drive.

A quiet "Thank you, sir," announced the tourist's arrival. Tears streamed down her face. "They would have killed us. They already had Dieter's wallet. They did not need to beat him."

She had a German accent which I placed from around Stuttgart.

"No problem, ma'am, I know all about losing a wallet. Here, take a shot at him."

I offered her the bat. She looked at me with disbelief.

"What? No, thank you please, I couldn't."

"Really, you'll feel a whole lot better… Look at your husband."

He was slumped against the dumpster with blood coursing down his head.

"Take it!" I commanded. She took the bat gingerly, hesitantly. I glared at her. "You want to spend the next ten years in therapy? Doctor Wilson says end it here!"

She looked at me for a few seconds with her liquid brown eyes, then tightened her grip and inched forward. She glanced back at her husband, then stepped up to the plate and took a small swing at Red shoes, a tap on the knee that he partially deflected. She looked back one more time, then hit him again a little harder.

"Jesus lady, stop it!" Red shoes whined.

She shifted her grip and started smacking him in earnest. She had a nice approach to the swing coming all the way from her toes. Red shoes was bleating like a lamb facing the gelding pliers. On the tenth stroke I grabbed the bat on the backswing.

"Hold on, lady. Save some for the dummkopf on the other side."

I held her hand and led her around the car where she whacked on Black shoes for a while.

Out of breath, she gawked with wonder at the silver bat. I reached down and lifted a wallet from Black shoe's pocket. I passed it to her and eased the bat from her hand.

"Dieter's?" I asked.

She nodded and said, "I don't know how I can ever thank you."

"Well, a hundred bucks sounds about right to me," I replied, holding out my hand.

She paid up without any argument. I liked the bat so I tossed it in the front seat of the taxi. I helped Dieter into his car, then headed to the rest room. I still needed to drain Big Ed. Standing at the urinal, I rolled my head on my shoulders. I didn't feel too bad, my eyes were grainy but the headache had retreated to a dull heaviness at the back of my skull. I recommend a taste of Burgess's ultraviolence as medicine for all your injury and pain. Pissing into the chewing gum and cigarette butts, I enjoyed that pause that refreshes.

CHAPTER 7

Tuesday Afternoon, May 20

MURPHY

Webster had reserved a suite at the Marriott and had rented furniture which included a large oak desk. Murphy sat at a kitchen table with papers scattered on it. Webster sat in a high-backed leather chair with his feet up on the desk.

"Who do we have next?" Webster asked Murphy.

"Patrick Clark, he's with Computational Dynamics, Vice President of Engineering. He had a short and apparently heated conversation with Glen."

"I could be a vice president for one of these computer companies. Heck yes, expense accounts, company car, private secretary. Sitting on my rear end counting my money."

There was a knock at the door.

"Come in," Webster hollered.

When Patrick entered, Webster gestured for him to sit at a kitchen chair placed in front of his desk. Patrick looked tired. He rolled his head on his shoulders and rubbed his eyes.

"What's the deal?" he asked.

"The deal is, I'll ask the questions and you'll answer them. Okay? You were talking to Glen Wilson yesterday. What did you talk about?"

"Glen Wilson? Who's that?"

"I'm asking the questions."

Webster dropped his feet from the desktop, swiveled around, and leaned his elbows on the desk.

"Show him the pictures, Murphy."

Murphy got up and handed Patrick some photographs. She made eye contact with him and shrugged her shoulders.

"I remember this guy. Some dweeby geek asking about Power PC workstations. I don't know him. Why are you interested in him?"

"This is the last time I'm reminding you! I ask the questions, you shut your face and answer them."

"Which is it?"

"What?"

"Do I shut my face or answer your questions? Oh, I forgot, you're asking the questions."

Webster addressed Murphy. "Looks like we have a tough guy here. Am I going to have to kick his butt?"

Murphy tossed down her pencil and rubbed her eyes.

Patrick stood. "Look assbite, you ask me to come here, unofficial, just a friendly visit, then you start pulling my dick. Go screw yourself, FBI-man. If you have a charge or some paperwork then let's see it. No? Then excuse me, I've got work to do."

Patrick slammed the door on his way out.

"Nice job, Number Three."

"No one respects the law any more. Anyway, it was obvious that he knows nothing." Webster changed the subject. "What were we talking about?"

"A computer show here in Orlando," Murphy said flatly. "A computer database shows Richard Nixon drinking beer up in Altamonte Springs? This guy Wilson seems to know a lot about computers. This is awfully bizarre."

"Computers? Who understands them? Guys with pocket protectors, tape on their glasses, and high water pants. Dilberts."

"Okay then, what's with AES-256? More computer stuff, right?"

Webster stood up and started pacing.

"That's different," he said. "The security of the United States is at risk. My boss explained the whole thing to me. Social Security, IRS records, voting machines, nuclear weapons research, all protected with the AES security algorithm. Unbreakable. Impervious. Impenetrable."

"Then what are you afraid of?"

"Nothing." He took a sip of bottled water. "I'm afraid of nothing. Who's up next?"

Murphy sighed and looked at the schedule. "David Foster, your friend from the party."

Foster knocked on the door right on schedule.

"Sit down, Foster," Webster said, gesturing at the chair with a rolled up newspaper. "I'm interviewing everyone that has crossed paths with Glen Wilson. He's a very slippery fellow. How long have you known him?"

"I met him a few years ago, I see him at trade shows. Man, that was some party, wasn't it? Beautiful girls, eh? Wish I could remember more of it."

"Shut up. Just answer the questions." Webster checked to see if Murphy was paying any attention. She appeared immersed in her paperwork. "How did you meet him?"

"I just told you. I met him at a trade show in Las Vegas. Man, you must have a cool job. How do you get to be an FBI agent?"

"The job chooses you, you don't choose the job. Most people wash out of the Academy. I graduated number three in my class."

"Number three! That's cool. Is that your class ring? Can I see it?"

Webster waved him over.

"Class of ought-3. Too radical. Can you just buy the ring or do you have to go to the Academy to get one?"

"You can't even get one if you go, you have to graduate. I've even got the Honor's ruby, see?"

"Wow. I'll bet the babes fall all over you."

Webster leaned over the desk and spoke quietly. "Yes, I get more than my share, I must say. It's almost too easy. Sometimes it isn't sporting, if you get what I mean." He was beaming with pride.

"Do you have a gun?"

"You bet, a Glock 19, I've got a Glock 23 at home but I don't need that much firepower for a numb-nut like Wilson. I won't even need the gun, I'll just pop him with some of the martial arts moves I learned at the Academy, I'll squash him like a bug."

David looked a little nervous. "Well, you might want to be a little careful—"

"I'll break his neck, I'll kick his ass, I'll fake him, snake him, and break him. He'll wish he hadn't crossed swords with Orrin Webster of the FBI."

"Okay," David said hesitantly. "Well, Glen may be a crook but he sure throws a great party. Last thing I remember was you dancing with that hooker with her hands down your pants."

Webster stole a look at Murphy and shook his head. "Okay, Foster, I think we've covered enough ground here." He pointed his newspaper at him. "Don't leave town until I tell you. Got me?"

"Yes sir."

Murphy looked up after David shut the door.

"That was a masterful job of interrogation, Number Three," Murphy said. "Do I understand the plan? You're going to break Wilson's neck, then kick his ass?"

"You just stick to your job, Miss smart-pants Murphy, and I'll take care of the questioning. I don't expect a State Bull like you to understand my advanced technique."

"I'm impressed by how you dragged information out of him. What did we learn? You're going to squash Wilson like a bug? You like a whore to stick her hand down your pants?"

"You think you can do a better job? Fine, you do the next interview and I'll sit back, watch, and learn. Would that be all right Miz I'm-so-dang-smart Murphy?"

"That would be fine, Number Three."

There was a quiet knock on the door.

"Come in, Mister Parker," Murphy called out.

The Texan came hesitantly into the room. Webster sat at the table making a mess of the paperwork.

"Can I call you Charlie?" Murphy asked.

Charlie nodded.

"Fine, I'm Murphy and he's Agent Webster of the FBI. Care for a cup of coffee?"

Charlie nodded again and Murphy poured him a steaming cup of the oily brew. "We're talking to everyone who knows Glen Wilson," Murphy continued, "He's got the feds in a bit of a tizzy about some hacked security codes."

"Knowing Glen, that doesn't surprise me," Charlie said. He grimaced at the bitter coffee. He placed the cup on the floor next to the chair.

"How long have you known Glen?"

"I first met him in Saigon where we worked at a warehouse together."

"Would you describe you and he as friends?"

"Not really friends, I don't think Glen has many friends. Glen's a strange bird. I'm sure you already know that."

"We don't know much of anything. There have been some odd things happening."

"That Glen, he's a real spark plug. I'll tell you how we met, maybe that will give you a clue. I was drinking heavy back then. Everyone was. There was a Marine sergeant named Spivey, Tom Spivey, I think. He was a big guy, like a rabid coyote, mean, unpredictable, psychotic. Glen was playing cards in a bar with a girl on his lap. Spivey didn't like Glen and was always flipping him guff. Glen mostly just ignored him and tried to stay out of his way. Then Spivey said something about Glen's mom, just some bullshit insult—

The place was filled with smoke. A ceiling fan turned slowly, not doing any good. Light poured into the dark room through slats in the bamboo blinds. Glen had one hand up the skirt of his whore, while the other held a cigarette, poured whiskey, and handled his cards. Glen was flushed, sweating, and very drunk; it was at least 110 degrees in the room. A couple of GI's passed around an opium pipe. Spivey was playing with his Colt 45, ratcheting back the slide, pointing, and shooting it at Glen's girl. Glen didn't care, but his girl was nervous. Spivey kept putting in a cartridge, jacking it out, then firing. You could never tell if— accidentally or not—a shell might be under the hammer when he pulled the trigger. Spivey had a round face and red piggy eyes buried in fat and flesh. Now and then he would say "bang" when he pulled the trigger.

"Hey Wilson?"

Glen slid out two cards and was dealt replacements.

"Did I ever tell you what a good cocksucker your mama is?"

Glen lifted an edge of his cards. He had a pair of sevens. He raised a dollar and watched the reaction from the other players.

"Yeah, Wilson, she sucked me off then licked my crack for dessert. What do you think of that?"

Click, ratchet, click. Glen called. The Japanese player, Matsuda, folded. Glen lost the hand to two kings. A new hand was dealt.

"All ten inches, all the way to the hilt. If she missed a drop she'd get down on all fours and lap it off the floor like a dog. Face like a dog, on her knees like a dog."

Glen kept a jack and asked for four new cards.

"Feed me, baby, she'd always say. I fed her all right. Fed her good."

Glen was dealt two more jacks and raised five dollars. Everyone dropped out but Matsuda. He raised another five.

"Then she'd lick the crack of my ass for dessert." Click.

"You're repeating yourself, Spivey," Glen said, looking out over the table.

"I fed her good."

Glen beat Matsuda's pair of aces and raked in the pot. He gently lifted his girl onto her feet and unsteadily walked to the bar to face Spivey.

"You're getting dull."

Spivey jacked the cartridge in and stuck the pistol in Glen's face.

"You want some dessert, too?" Spivey asked.

Glen grabbed Spivey's belt, pulled out the waistband, and stuck a grenade down his pants. The pin was already pulled. He pulled the lever and shoved Spivey out the door. It was a long count with Spivey stumbling in circles with his .45 in one hand and the other scrabbling in his pants for the grenade. He erupted into a crimson cloud.

Charlie shook his head and he sipped his coffee. His hand was shaking slightly.

"Seems like yesterday," he said. "By the time the MPs got there, Glen was back to playing poker. No one would say a word. I'm just saying Glen was cool, didn't get upset or laugh much, either. Maybe he's mellowed out, I don't know, but like a rattlesnake sleeping on a rock, you might be better off leaving him alone. The MPs didn't like Spivey either and it was written up as a Claymore accident."

"How about more recently? What has he been up to?"

"He disappeared for a few years in the seventies but since then I come across him now and then. I quit drinking a couple of years ago. I have a wife and a kid so we don't have much in common any more. I hear he's doing some business on the side, gray market chips and stuff. Beyond that, I couldn't say."

"Is it possible he's hacked databases? For example, he has apparently corrupted an FBI computer system."

"Well, Glen isn't technically trained. He's no engineer, but he has friends and people around the world who work for him and help him out. With Glen, you never know what he may be into."

"Thank you, Charlie. Here's my card. Please give a call if anything comes to you that might be useful."

Charlie walked to the door, stood for a moment with his hand on the knob.

"If you do come across Glen—?"

"Yes, Charlie."

"He may seem like a clown, but he can be dangerous. Very dangerous."

Murphy nodded solemnly. Charlie nodded back and pulled the door quietly shut behind him.

"I suppose you're pleased with yourself?" Webster said sarcastically. He was flipping his pencil in the air and catching it.

"I thought that went well enough," Murphy said.

"Oh, sure. Don't repeat yourself or you'll get a hand grenade down your panties. Watch out for the 'dangerous' man. That will look real good in the report. What's next?"

Murphy looked at her watch. "That was it, but I think we have time to go interview that cab driver," she said.

LEONARD

Leonard was looking over the shoulder of Andy, the guy who refilled the candy machine.

"Why do you put in so many peanut M&M's? Nobody likes M&M's," Leonard said.

Andy was very patient.

"No Leonard, you don't like M&M's. Everyone else likes them and we sell lots of them. See how that works? You put in the stuff that people will buy and sometimes people buy stuff that you won't eat. I hate Rollos, but tourists buy them, so I put them in. See," he said as he stuffed a column with Rollos.

"I think people like Red Vines. Put in more Red Vines." Leonard was eating his second package and his lips were stained pink.

"Damn it, Leonard. I only sell three packs of Red Vines a week on the whole route."

"That's because you don't put enough in. Fill up those two slots."

"It doesn't matter how many you put in if people won't buy them. Oh, forget it." He threw up his hands. "Okay Leonard, okay," Andy said as he went back to the van for more Red Vines. "What happened to the other dog, the yellow one?"

"I just gave him a bath. That's the same old Dog."

At his name, Dog perked up his ears. He looked at Leonard suspiciously. Leonard did not move toward the power washer hose, so Dog relaxed.

"Can I get a machine filled up with only Red Vines?"

"No," Andy said firmly, "you can't."

"Oh," Leonard said. He wore a woeful look. "Okay."

MURPHY

Murphy lifted the chart from the hook on the end of the hospital bed and leafed through it. Webster pulled up a stool and leaned over. Carlos's eyes flicked between them suspiciously from beneath the turban-like bandages.

"Slight concussion, contusions. Eighteen stitches on the head, another seven on the thigh. Who beat the crap out of you, Mister Villareal?" Murphy asked.

Carlos plucked at his hospital gown. He tried to see the television behind Murphy. She turned around and switched it off.

"TV turns your brain to mush," she muttered. "Please read him the charge."

Webster pulled some papers out of a manila envelope.

"Carlos Villareal, you are under arrest for first-degree murder of one Pablo S. Estevez…"

"I didn't kill him."

"Oh, that's interesting. I guess we're done here, Webster. He didn't do it. Just happened to choose the wrong place to take a little nap. Pablo's blood under his fingernails is just a coincidence. Ditto the pencil shaving under Pablo's fingernails. Damn, we're going to have to do some real policework now."

Webster looked at her with disgust. He ignored her sarcasm and turned to Carlos.

"Okay fine, Carlos. It would be greatly appreciated if you could help us find the real killer," Webster said.

He held out a water glass with a straw for Carlos to sip.

"Don't know," he said when he was done drinking.

"What can you tell us about the guy you drove to Pablo's place?" he asked.

"What guy?"

Webster pulled some photographs from the folder. They were profile shots that clearly showed Glen entering Carlos's cab.

Carlos glanced at the pictures.

"Never seen him before, you got the wrong Mexican."

Murphy sat on the bed and started massaging Carlos's knee.

"Come on Carlos. Don't be stubborn. We're on your side but you have to give us a little help," she said. She slid her hand up an inch. Carlos licked his lips and gauged the distance between her hand and the bandage on his thigh. She moved her hand another inch while firmly kneading his flesh.

"You're tight, you need to relax," she commented. "We know you're clean, we just want to know about your friend, Glen Wilson."

"Don't know him."

Her hand was just below the bandage and she stroked lightly across it."

"Damn it. That goddam hijo de puta cocksucker bastard asshole fuckhead turd-eating pendejo prick."

"Oh, so you know him after all," Murphy smiled. "In that case, would you mind telling us how exactly you met our Mister Wilson?"

GLEN

Glen rapped out a drumbeat on the Holiday Inn check-in counter. The kid behind the counter wore his hair in an Army Ranger special: white sidewalls with an eighth inch of blond hair on top. It looked good with his pirate hoop earring. Yuppie grunge. His name tag said Roger.

"How can I help you, Mister?" Roger said as he slid a clipboard and pencil across the counter.

"Glen Wilson here and I'm here to see my friend Manuel Rodriguez," Glen replied.

"Sorry, sir, I'm pretty sure Mr. Rodriguez has checked out." He pecked at a computer terminal. "Yes, he left an hour ago."

"Shitty-damn." Glen took the folded calendar out of his pocket. The next stop was Belle Glade: another hundred miles or so.

Glen took a mental inventory. A couple of hours of sleep last night before and a full day spent violating virgins and saving dragons. Or something like that. Glen's mind felt fuzzy. Time to suck down a few beers, get a solid horizontal nine, and hit it again hard in the morning.

"Well, I guess I'll spend the night, give me a room away from the highway, will you." He scribbled his name on the rental form and made up a license number and address.

"Can I imprint your credit card for the billing?"

Glen actually reached halfway around for his wallet. *Damn.*

"You guys still take cash?"

Roger did not look pleased. "Yes sir, Euros at par, greenbacks at zero point nine. A hundred dollar deposit if you want the minibar unlocked."

Glen tossed some bills on the counter. "I remember when—Oh, forget it," he said. He slipped the cardkey into his pocket. "Can you overnight express this for me?" He slid an envelope over the counter. It was addressed to Elke at the hotel back in Orlando. The clerk nodded yes. "Okay then, my bag's in the car, pull it around for me. Make sure the bed is turned down. I'll be in the bar." As he strolled away, he said over his shoulder, "I need my medicine."

The bar was all dim light, hushed voices, muted clinking glasses, plastic ferns, and mirrors. A hazy fog of pipe and cigar smoke seemed to ooze from the walls. As Glen slipped onto a bar stool he caught a glimpse of a woman sitting at a booth nursing a pink drink in a tall fluted glass. *Damn it.* Glen would never have survived in sales without being able to instantly link a name with a face. *Which one? Not Lou. DeeDee. No question, it's DeeDee from the party.*

Hmmmm.

Glen was not impressed with the draft selections: Lone Star, Bud light and Miller High Life, so he ordered a bottle of Michelob Dark.

"Is this chair taken?"

Glen turned and looked at her. *Does a gator crap in the swamp?* She had short black hair and she looked a little like Meg Ryan. She wore white Keds, no socks, faded blue jeans, a pale tan line in place of a watch, no ring, and a V-neck tank top that showed her black bra straps. Meg Ryan with a seductive inch of tanned cleavage, heavy blush and eyeliner, and red lipstick. Thirty years old and a hundred and five pounds.

"No, please have a seat, DeeDee."

She looked surprised as she settled on the barstool.

"I would have bet a hundred you wouldn't recognize me."

"Well, you'd have lost that one." Glen gestured a small toast with his beer and took a drink. "Not very polite the way you girls suckered me last night."

"Well, sorry. Manny sets things up and we do what we're told. Never mind that, the prick left me here, now I'm not sure what I'm going to do."

Pointless for her to practice a speech for the Golden Globe award. There was more truth in a Democrat's stump speech than her claim of abandonment.

"Perhaps you could put me up for the night? Maybe I can figure out a way to pay you back for last night?" She smiled but it was a little forced and Glen read the hint of tension in her eyes. Just following orders again.

Glen nodded, drained his beer. "If we put our heads together, do some serious thinking, I'll bet we can come up with something."

They found the room on the first floor in back. Glen fumbled with the cardkey, opened the door, flipped on the lights and looked around. Nineties chic; TV bolted to the wall and steel bars on the windows. He headed straight for the minibar and did a quick inventory, came out with some Baileys Irish Cream and some plastic glasses. As he turned around, DeeDee pulled a chrome pistol from her drawstring bag. *I guess it's true, Americans are truly crazy about their guns,* Glen thought.

"Why not have a drink before you kill me?"

"Shut up. Who are you and why are you chasing Manny?"

The bore on the gun looked like a freight train tunnel. Glen recognized it as a Smith and Wesson Sigma, 9mm, 15 in the clip, and one in the chamber. It was a high tech number with polymer frame and nickel coating. Glen could see that the trigger safety was off.

"Let's not screw around. If you're going to shoot me, then just do it."

Glen took a slow step forward.

"Just give me a second to say my prayers," he added.

He closed his eyes and whispered. *Lord have mercy on those without a fucking clue.* He reached up slowly and took the gun from her hand and handed her a plastic cup. He eased back the Sigma's hammer and released the clip. He opened the door and tossed the clip into the bushes. He ejected the bullet from the chamber and looked at it. A subsonic Delrin-cased bullet; quiet and expensive. He waved the cartridge at her.

"You could put out someone's eye with this," he scolded.

He jammed the cartridge back into the gun. As he poured her liqueur, he lectured.

"There are a couple ways this can go. You can finish your drink, then take off, no harm done."

She sat on the bed and sipped her drink.

"Care for some ice for that?"

She shook her head no.

"Or, we can—" Using the pistol he slid the shoulder strap of her tank top onto her arm. "Settle in here," caressing her face with the barrel, "and get cozy. Hold on a second."

He went into the bathroom and ran warm water onto a washcloth. He gently scrubbed the eyeliner, blush, and lipstick from her face. He tossed the cloth into the corner.

"That's much better, I can see you now. Do you have your HIV card?"

She nodded, dug around in her handbag, and pulled the card from her wallet. Glen made sure the card was up to date.

"You'll have to trust me, my card is in the wallet you girls made off with," Glen said.

DeeDee nodded and lifted her arms. Glen worked her shirt off, then unhooked her bra. With his tongue, he traced the red impressions the bra made on her sides.

Nothing like the prospect of imminent death to get a guy good and hard. I'm sure some dome-headed freak with a psych degree has spent a million dollars and a lifetime trying to figure that one out. 'And so, Mister Brown, how did you FEEL when we dropped the elevator?' Should have just asked me. It was the hormones screaming: 'Ach! We're all gonna die! Pay attention, quick like a bunny! Breed somebody! Anybody!' One shouldn't ignore instinct. Like there's a choice. Whatever the reason, a woman with a gun and a wild-mad look gets me every time. If it's a guy, I'm thinking about how to get that gun, shove it under his chin, and blast his brains into the next world. If it's a girl, I want to whip out Big Ed and see how close we can come to finding paradise lost.

DeeDee was a good-looking woman and in a bit of a lather; her eyes were steamy and damp. She was my kind of girl, the kind with breasts. I worked her yellow panties over her narrow hips and tossed them aside. Her pubic hair was shaved in bikini fashion: a dark arrowhead in the dim room light. I stood over her and pressed the cold-steel Sigma into the palm of her hand. She looked from the gun up to me, then from the gun down at me. I leaned her back onto the bed and hovered. She pressed the barrel into the rib over my heart. She was breathing faster. I parted her legs and adjusted her hips, looked into her eyes and slowly started working my way in with my hands making light circles around her breasts. I ran my fingers down her armpit, across her sides, and around her groin. She closed her eyes and cocked the pistol. She made a little sound and grasped the gun with both hands, digging it hard into my chest. I pushed back against it and began moving, slowly at first, then picking up the tempo to pace her little gasps. She closed her eyes and wrapped her arms around my neck with the gun still in her hand. She pulled me down hard and spasmed, shuddering. I joined her, a quivering mass of raw nerve and melting flesh. The gun went off behind my head with the bullet smashing into the television set. That subsonic Delrin was definitely a quiet round, I was impressed; no screams from next door and no rude pounding on the wall.

The second time was even better, a lot longer, and I made her do some of the work. The gun was a forgotten prop on the floor. Once again I proved the adage to DeeDee. Nice guys like me do finish last.

Afterwards, they lay sleeping peacefully with the gun gleaming in the shattered glass from the television.

CHAPTER 8

Wednesday Morning, May 21

GLEN

Glen brushed his teeth and surveyed the room. He could hear a maid upstairs running a vacuum cleaner. He spit in the sink, leaned over, and rinsed out his mouth with water from the faucet.

"Watch the broken glass, DeeDee. I feel like a goddam rock star. The only thing missing is the cocaine and the needles."

DeeDee was sitting on the edge of the bed in her yellow panties with her short hair sticking up in spikes. She leaned down and picked up the pistol. After rummaging around in her handbag she found another clip. She rammed the clip home and dropped the gun into the bag. She pushed her hair back from her face.

"What's that thing you were talking to?"

"It's digital voice recorder."

"Let me see it."

Glen passed it to her. She pressed the REWIND and PLAY.

"The gun was a forgotten prop on the floor. Once again I proved the adage to DeeDee. Nice guys like me do finish last."

She made a sour face at Glen and pressed RECORD.

"He came in two minutes, farted, rolled over, and went to sleep. His breath smelled like dog shit and he has a two-inch dick."

"Hey!" Glen grabbed the recorder back. "Don't screw around with that, it's not a toy, dammit."

As she brushed by Glen on her way to the bathroom he gave her a friendly swat on the butt. He opened his laptop computer, placed it on the desk, and switched on the lamp. He unplugged the phone and plugged in his modem. He logged into his homepage. He started building a database agent. He started with the name, Manuel Rodriguez.

"DeeDee? Do you know when or where Manny was born?"

"No. He's one of the Marielita's from the Eighties."

He's about 40, Glen guessed. He probably applied for a Social Security card in the Miami area, so Glen assumed a couple of probable SSN prefixes.

"Any brothers or sisters?"

"No, I haven't heard of any." DeeDee stuck her towel-wrapped head out of the bathroom. "What are you doing?"

"Just trying to pull together a database on Manny." The screen showed more than 11,000 hits so far. There were too many Rodriguezes in southern Florida, he had a long way to go. "How about a middle name or initial?"

"X, Xavier, I think."

Aha, that cuts us down to 237 hits.

"Do you know which banks he does business with?"

DeeDee looked over his shoulder. "I spent a lot of time in the car waiting for him to come out of First Florida."

Glen linked in the IRS database for transactions over $10,000 that are logged on Federal Form 8300. He set the agent loose and logged out.

"This will take at least a couple of hours," he said as he unplugged and folded up the computer.

"You can get information on him this way?" DeeDee asked.

"Probably. I doubt that Manny has been careful."

"Are you a secret agent or something?"

"No, just a guy who can afford to subscribe to the KnowX, the Equifax Credit reporting service, and a few others. This is no big deal. Wait until we tap into the IRS mainframe, then you'll be impressed."

"Is that legal?" she asked.

"What fun would it be if it were legal? Do you know where Manny is staying in Belle Glade?"

DeeDee answered from the bathroom.

"His cousin has a place on Okeechobee. They're going fishing this afternoon."

"I'm going to need you to help me find the place."

"Yeah, whatever," she replied as she flushed the toilet.

Glen buttoned his last shirt button and snapped his suitcase shut. He put a fifty-dollar bill under the pillow.

"What did you do that for?"

"I always tip the maids, they have a lousy job. They have to clean up this mess," he waved at the room. "Besides, leave a big tip and they don't count the towels." He laughed. "When you're dressed, meet me in the restaurant," he said as he walked out the door.

Glen irrigated his scrambled eggs with Tabasco sauce. The early morning sun poured in the restaurant windows.

"Are you going to kill Manny?" DeeDee said as she picked at her sausage and tried to appear casual.

"I have no particular beef with Manny, he's hustling just like we all are. I just want my wallet back."

DeeDee leaned over the table and whispered. "You're going to have to kill him, I think."

"So much melodrama for such a little lady. You going to eat your toast?"

"What's your plan?"

"There is no plan. Christ, you're a real pain in the rear, aren't you? We find Manny in Belle Glade, I explain the situation to him, he gives my wallet back, and I get back to my life. Okay?"

She sat back and pouted. She fingered her necklace and stared out the window. "I just thought we could go into business together."

"I rub out Manny and his goons and we set up shop together. We take over Pablo's operation in Orlando? Fifty-fifty, I do the heavy lifting and you count the money?"

DeeDee flicked her eyes at him to see if he was serious. He stroked her hand with his greasy fork.

"Look DeeDee, I live by some basic rules. One is to never seek complications because plenty of them occur naturally. I like to keep things simple."

"I thought you were a real man but you're just a fucking worm, a bug which is going to get squashed."

"Maybe so." He stood. "You got any cash to pay for breakfast?" he said as he tossed his napkin on the table and walked out the door. "I'll meet you outside in the car."

The ride south on Highway 27 was a quiet one.

A RANDOM NOTE

The Silicon Graphics 20110 was the fastest computer in the world and had been for the last five months. It would stay the fastest until the Thomson Concorde 35 fired up in Paris the following year. The engineers got their kicks by running a thousand simultaneous Symantec

System Index programs. Each ran at about 25,000 times the speed of the old 4.77 Megahertz IBM PC. That is, they ran at 25,000 unless....

Harold Evans peered into his monitor. He was drinking a Snapple and scratching his bearded chin with a mechanical pencil.

"What, what, what," he grumbled.

The system was losing clock cycles at a rate of 14 trillion per hour. This was enough computing horsepower to calculate pi to 26 thousand digits, to predict the trajectory of a complete Space Shuttle mission to within 0.01% accuracy, or to win 125 grandmaster level games of chess simultaneously. All in ten minutes.

"Do we have a virus? Are we being hacked? What, what, what?" he grumbled.

The system diagnostics turned up the same thing they always did: exactly nothing. There were rumors about a team from Bombay hacking DOD supercomputers but Harold didn't know whether to believe them or not. After 93 minutes the system was released. Harold checked his watch. His boss had gone home. Harold shrugged and invoked Everquest and promptly forgot about the problem.

HOLLY

Holly pushed into the hock shop and the bells chained to the door jingled. Her blond hair was spiked and she wore purple makeup around her eyes to hide the shiner. She was jittery and strung out. She carried a box of junk that she had collected over the last year or so. The box contained a couple of car stereos, some rings and necklaces, and other miscellaneous junk. The guy behind the counter was tall and black and carried scars on his face like Seal. He spoke with a slight Creole accent.

"What have you for me, sweetie?" he asked as he pulled the box across the counter.

"Some good stuff in here, good stuff," she said.

"Selling or hocking?"

"Selling."

He took the jewelry out piece by piece and peered at each with a loupe.

"Shit," he said tossing a ring aside. "Shit, shit, this is okay."

He set a ring aside carefully and continued the sorting.

"Shit, shit, this is okay."

He glanced at the tape decks and pawed through the other stuff.

"Okay girlie, since I'm in a good mood, I give you a hundred for the whole box."

"Bullshit, this stuff is worth five hundred, easy."

"A hundred bucks is what it's worth to me. Take it or buzz off, babe."

"Okay, sorry. Take another look, please. I need more than a hundred."

He pursed his lips and halfheartedly looked again. A black rock caught his eye. He hefted it. It was surprisingly heavy. A bit of the paint flecked off to reveal a dull golden glow underneath.

"Tell you what honey-pie. I like you. Come to the back room, give me a quick blow and I'll give you two hundred for this box of shit."

In the urban jungle you must be alert to survive. Holly was headachy, frazzled, and hung over, but she sensed something in the clerk's voice.

"A blow job will be another hundred, three total, and if you got warts on your dick, I'm not sucking it for no amount of no money."

She pulled the box back and looked through the contents herself. A couple of cheap watches, a couple of credit cards, and some random junk. Then the black rock caught her eye too.

"Okay," the clerk said, "three hundred and no blow job. Deal?"

"What's this?" she asked.

She pulled out the rock. The clerk cursed in French under his breath.

As she pulled a pocket knife from her purse the clerk caught a glimpse of the pearl grips on her old Colt 45. She scraped paint from the rock and uncovered more gold. A gold nugget.

"Okay," she said, "are you ready to quit fucking around?"

He sighed and pulled a scale from under the counter. He placed the rock on the scale. It weighed in at slightly more than twenty troy ounces.

"All right, I'll give you six thousand cash, and that includes the blow job."

"Seven and you blow yourself."

"That's a fair price, three hundred an ounce."

"Gold's going for over six bills an ounce."

"Not for cash with no paperwork it ain't. That's twenty bucks more than you'll get anywhere else in town. Take my offer or take it down the street."

"No blow job," she said firmly.

"No blow job," he agreed.

They shook on it. She placed the nugget on the center of the counter. He walked around the counter and locked the front door.

"I need to get the money from the safe," he said pointing at a security camera. "You stay put, I'll be watching."

He left the room for about ninety seconds, which seemed like an eternity to Holly.

He brought out a bundle of rubber-banded hundred dollar bills and counted them out on the counter. She counted them herself and slipped the wad into her purse.

"Nice doing business with you," she said as he unlocked the front door.

"You find anymore of them rocks, you bring them to me and I'll pay three-twenty an ounce."

She had a vision in her head of a shelf with a lot more of these rocks but she couldn't picture where she'd seen them.

"There are a lot more where that came from," she said to him. *But where was that?* she said to herself as the door eased itself shut.

LEONARD

Leonard pulled the bill of his Skoal hat down around his eyes. It was too bright and hot to be standing in this field. He was a sight in his dirty tennis shoes, faded blue jeans, white shirt, string tie, and the sports jacket his mother bought at the Salvation Army store. Across the field a backhoe motor rumbled. The grave diggers were smoking cigarettes and waiting for their turn.

The minister droned on from Numbers 19. "And it shall be a perpetual statute unto them, that he that sprinkleth the water of separation shall wash his clothes; and he that toucheth the water of separation shall be unclean until even. And whatsoever the unclean person toucheth shall be unclean; and the soul that toucheth it shall be unclean until even."

Leonard didn't have any idea what Reverend O'Toole was talking about but he did know that the good Reverend had a fetish about staying clean and washed his hands 40 to 50 times a day.

The sun was low in the eastern sky. The group standing around the hole fidgeted and slapped the occasional gnat or sand fly. There were six standing at the grave: Deputy Rawlins; the Reverend and his wife; Carl Bremmer, the lawyer; Sarah Bremmer, Clem's ex-wife; and Leonard. Sarah wore a cotton print dress with large sweat stains under the arms. She reeked of gin. She clutched Leonard's arm to her ample breast.

The Reverend closed his book and recited some verses from Genesis 34 from memory. "And Jacob said to Simeon and Levi, Ye have troubled me to make me stink among the inhabitants of the land, among the Canaanites and the Perizzites: and I being few in number, they shall gather themselves together against me, and slay me; and I shall be destroyed, I and my house. And they said, Should he deal with our sister as with a harlot?"

The Reverend paused and looked solemnly at each person with his hands clasped behind his back.

"So we bid our friend farewell, may his spirit rest in eternal peace. Amen."

The amen chorus echoed quietly around the grave. Each gathered a handful of limestone gravel and tossed it in the hole. Leonard gazed into the hole lost in his thoughts. Everyone went to their cars except Leonard, Carl, and Sarah.

Leonard tried to pull his arm free, but Sarah gripped him tightly.

"We're so sorry, Lenny. Oh, I mean Leonard. Please listen a minute, Leonard."

Carl Bremmer mopped his forehead with a handkerchief.

"Beautiful sermon, wasn't it? That Reverend is crazier than a one-legged 'gator and gets worse every year," Carl said. "Listen, we need to talk, I'm wondering if we could meet in my office later today. We still have that paperwork we need to take care of."

Leonard jerked his arm loose.

"Here's what I think of your papers." He pulled the bundle out of his pocket, tore them up, and tossed them into the grave. "Now, you guys stay away from me."

Sarah was crying as Carl took her arm and led her to the car.

"This is not the end, you idiot!" Carl yelled as he climbed into his Buick.

Leonard stood alone at the edge of the grave with tears running down his face.

"Good-bye, Clemson," he said quietly. "Too bad you can't tell me where you hid the plunger for the toilet. Somebody tried to flush a roll of paper and made a huge mess."

MURPHY

Elke waved at Captain Murphy across the hotel lobby, nodded politely at Webster and sat on the padded bench. They studied the silk flowers and fake oriental vases. They watched the bellhops haul luggage into the elevator. Webster fidgeted and plucked lint from his slacks.

"Missus Rittenauer, you called us for some reason, could we get down to it?" he said with an irritated tone.

Elke sat quietly, apparently fascinated by the pattern in the carpet.

"Okay, fine. Captain Murphy, if you'll excuse me, I'm going to get some decaf from the coffee shop. Anybody want anything?"

There was no response. Webster turned in disgust and walked to the coffee shop.

When Webster was out of sight, Elke dug a business-sized envelope from her purse.

"I received this an hour ago," Elke said.

Murphy looked it over on both sides and carefully examined the date stamp.

"May I?" she asked.

Elke nodded yes.

The envelope contained a Florida lottery ticket and a short note written on a 'Snakes of Florida' postcard.

Dear Elke:

I'm writing from the parking lot at the Holiday Inn at Haines City. A nice place if you like plastic flamingoes and postcards from the Gator Jumparoo. There is a separate section in the parking lot for golf carts!

I'm going to be on the road for a day or two longer, please cash in the enclosed ticket, pay the taxes, we'll split the remainder 50-50. I know, I know, I'm too kind.

Catch you later.

GW

Murphy looked carefully at the lottery ticket.

"Hold on here," she said.

She pawed through her handbag and pulled out three lottery tickets. They were tickets for the same game and identical except for the lottery numbers. She held them side by side.

"What the hell is he talking about?" She examined them for a full minute; front and back. "Thank you for showing me this, Miz Rittenauer. Do you mind if I keep it?"

"Yes, I do mind." Elke gently pulled her ticket out of Murphy's grasp. "I think I'd better hang onto it. You can keep the postcard. By the way, you can call me Elke if you like."

"Great. I'm Margaret but everyone calls me Murphy."

They shook hands as if meeting for the first time.

"What exactly is your interest in Wilson? Number Three said something about the encryption software—"

"I don't know anything about that except that Webster has his Jockeys in a twist about it. National security, data encryption, net pirates, blah, blah, blah. I don't understand any of it. A man matching Glen's description was seen leaving the murder scene of a sorry lowlife named Pablo Estevez."

"Sounds very circumstantial to me. Was there some physical evidence tying Glen to the murder?"

Murphy stifled a grin as she thought of Tricky-Dick Nixon...

"Nothing we can use," she said.

She placed her hand on Elke's arm.

"I've been straight with you and told you more than I should. Can you tell me what your connection with Wilson is, please?"

Elke looked up at the ceiling.

"I can't explain what is going on. Change of life, mid-life crisis, something. I've been depressed, bored, desperate for something, anything to happen. Glen has an energy, a vibe... I've felt something missing and I sensed Glen might fill me. He's an asshole, but worth trying. That's what I think, that Glen may be worth trying. Like a new drug, or hairstyle, or therapy. Whether that makes sense or not, that's it and that's all."

Murphy pondered for a moment. "It makes too much sense for my own comfort, I'm afraid."

She noticed her hand was still on Elke's arm. She pulled it back.

"Well," Murphy took a deep breath, "you'll call if anything...?"

"Sure," Elke said as she stood and smoothed out her navy skirt. She checked her hair in the mirror on the wall and wiped a little moisture from the corners of her eyes. She nodded at Murphy and walked stiffly toward the elevators. Webster walked from the coffee shop blowing into a steaming paper cup. Murphy handed him the postcard. Webster set down his coffee and looked it over.

"What's the deal with the lottery ticket?" he asked.

"I'm not sure, but I've got a feeling." She handed him her three tickets. "The ticket was just like these. The numbers aren't drawn until tomorrow afternoon. The prize is one hundred and fifty thousand dollars."

"Well that's it, then. The guy is playing a dumb joke or is insane."

"I wonder. I guess we pack our gear and go check out Haines City. Webster, I think we need to recruit Elke. She obviously has some rapport going with this guy. She should come down with us. She can help us."

"Bullshit. She wants two hundred bucks an hour. I say we go visit this Holiday Inn at Haines City, pick up this turd, shove the lottery ticket up his butt, and throw him in the slammer for a few years."

He handed her back the tickets. She held them for a moment, then crumpled them and tossed them in the ashtray.

"Hey, those could be worth one hundred and fifty grand." He reached over her, picked them out of the litter and straightened them out.

"I don't think so," she replied.

She massaged her temples with the heels of her hands.

"Well, I'll take them," Webster said as he stuck them in his jacket pocket. "Dumb broad," he muttered.

He stood.

"I'll get the car," he said. "You call down and see if Wilson is still there. If not, make sure they don't clean the room so we can collect some more evidence. There's no more time to waste, dang it."

"Yes, sir."

CHAPTER 9

Early Wednesday Afternoon, May 21

MURPHY

Murphy rapped sharply on the door. "State Police, open up!" she said in a loud and firm voice. Webster looked pained.

"The desk clerk said Wilson checked out over an hour ago," he said.

"Look Webster, the book says to knock and announce yourself," Murphy lectured. "Okay?"

Murphy turned the key in the lock. Webster pushed the door open and brushed by her. Something shiny in the bushes caught her eye. She leaned over and carefully picked up the pistol clip. Webster froze in the doorway. She tapped him on the shoulder.

"This was in the bush."

Webster looked at it for a second. "Funny looking bullets. Don't stand around with your thumb up your hiney. Bag it and tag it."

"Okay, Number Three."

She peeked around Webster. The room was a bit of a mess with wet towels on the floor and bedsheets tangled and wadded on the bed. Glittering glass from the television sparkled everywhere. The door of the minibar was hanging open and empty mini-bottles were scattered around.

"Some party." She picked up the plastic drink cups and bagged them. "We better ship these off to forensics as soon as possible."

"That won't be necessary." Webster looked as if he was struggling with bad bowels. He glanced under the bed and checked the bathroom, tiptoeing around the broken glass.

Murphy leaned over the bed. "I'd say that Glen didn't sleep alone last night."

"Why do you say that?"

"You mean besides the two plastic cups, the tangled sheets, and the washcloth covered with lipstick?" She lifted the damp cloth from the

103

corner. "I can smell it, that's why. I smell raw hammering sex. Not a lonely guy playing with his dick in a ratty motel room. This is pure animal passion, the place reeks of it."

"So what, Doctor Ruth? What does it tell you that will help catch this guy?"

"Forget it," she said as she tossed the washcloth back into the corner. "I just think we're going to have trouble with this guy."

She smoothed the sheet and sat on the bed. "I need to go back to Orlando for a couple of hours."

"What for? The clerk said he saw them traveling south."

"It's personal business."

"I get it, a manicure appointment? Going to get your roots re-tinted?"

"Right, something like that. You can page me if something comes up."

"Fine," Webster replied.

Murphy saw the corner of a bill sticking out under a pillow. She drew it out.

"Huh," Webster said. "What kind of jerk leaves fifty bucks for the maid?"

"A guy who is used to leaving a mess behind, I suppose."

She slipped it back under the pillow.

"Make sure she gets it, will you?"

"Sure Murphy, whatever you say."

Two technicians from the Polk County Police team rapped on the door. Webster waved them in.

"I want a complete sweep, how many, what they had for dinner, who was on top. Okay?" Webster said.

The technicians nodded. Murphy handed them the evidence bags she had collected. They started taking pictures as she walked out into the blinding sunshine.

HOLLY

Holly unlocked the door of the apartment and strolled in. Jimmy, barefoot and barechested, was stirring some chocolate pudding on the gas stove.

"Where's Tanya and Paul?" Holly asked.

"They went to the park to see if they can find some roofie or X or smack or something. How'd we do, baby?" he asked.

"We got two hundred bucks," she said. "He wanted a BJ but I told him I'm saving myself for you."

She lit a thick joint, reached around his chest, and placed it between his lips. He took a deep drag. She put the joint in her mouth and ran her hands slowly down his chest and into his jeans. His jeans were a little large and hung loosely on his hips. He wasn't wearing underpants. She stroked his penis and cupped his balls.

"Baby, you're feeling frisky, eh?" he said, laughing.

"Oh yeah, I'm hot for you," she said.

He turned his head toward her and she directed a thick stream of smoke in his face. He breathed deeply. She tugged him toward the bedroom and he stumbled along willingly. She pushed him down on the bed, pulled his jeans down around his ankles, and straddled him. He came in about two minutes. She stroked his chest.

"Baby," she said quietly.

"Yeah, sugar?"

"Where did I pick up that black rock that was in the box? I think it was out in the swamp somewhere, but I can't remember."

"I don't know. Who cares?"

"No big deal, the pawnshop guy was curious, is all."

"I don't have the foggiest idea," he said.

"Sometimes I can almost picture where we were. I shot a fat guy or you did. I can't quite grasp it."

They smelled something.

"Shit," she cried.

She jumped off him and ran to the kitchen where black smoke was erupting from the pudding pan. She threw it in the sink and ran in some water. Jimmy put his arms around her from the back.

"No big deal," he said. "With the two hundred we can buy another pan and some more pudding, right, baby?"

"Right," she said in an irritated tone, pushing him away.

She walked to the bathroom, pulled the door shut, and locked the door. Jimmy flopped on the couch and turned on the television. He was happy to find a Three Stooges show. The Stooges went well with the marijuana and his mellow afterglow.

GLEN

Glen rubbed his eyes and rolled his head on his shoulders to loosen the kinks. After passing Sebring, the scenery was dreary, all flat green fields and the highway a straight line to the horizon. There was no AM radio in the taxi. Glen grew tired of whistling "Knights in White Satin." DeeDee had taken some Halcyon and was leaning groggily against the door. Glen poked her and tried to strike up a conversation, but she was out cold.

I should have stopped in Sebring when I noticed the fuel gauge was getting low. Gas stations were something else for the endangered species list around here. Wherever the hell "here" is. I still had a trace of hangover from whatever Lila spiked her punch with. I'd only managed three roadkills so far. The first two turtles had been Lila and DeeDee, and a larger rodent that I couldn't identify had been the other one, What's-Her-Name. I still needed a Manny. I'd stop and back over that one a few times if I didn't run out of gas first. I started looking for a place to ditch the cab before it ended up sitting in plain sight on the shoulder.

I spotted a small cottage set back from the road with a pickup truck and old boat sitting in the driveway. My finely tuned ears could hear the whispering "—use me Glen, oh baby use me up and throw me away—" I eased up behind the slutty little boat and got out. I left the engine running. Nobody in sight. I reached in the back of the boat, snapped the fuel line off the motor and heaved the whole gas tank over the side, set it on the floor of the cab, and eased back onto the highway. Thirty seconds tops, real smooth. Half a mile down the road I pulled off and dumped the gas into the cab. Only five gallons, and probably had outboard motor oil in it but it should keep us going long enough to find a gas station. I put the empty gas tank in the trunk. Might come in handy. DeeDee still slumped against the door, useless.

Wasn't more than a few miles later that we came upon a combination Gas/General Store/Liquor/Equipment Rental/Bait Shop and Chuck's Towing, all packed into a hut about the size of my first wife's ass. Call it a size 18. After I pulled in I noticed the "Full Service" sign on the right side so I backed up and switched sides. I had to see this full service. Nobody came out, so I tapped the horn. A minute later the screen door opened three inches and somebody yelled "We're closed!" The door slammed shut again. Finger stub screaming. Helluva way to do business. Maybe I stumbled into a pack of devil worshipers, probably in there milking goat semen and chanting in bad Latin that translated into something like "Oh Dirty Underwear, show us the way to San Jose."

The Full Service pump was dead. I walked around the side of the building searching for evidence of depravity. I saw a switch labeled "Master Cutoff to Pumps" turned to the OFF position with a padlock hanging open on the hasp. I remedied that, returned to the cab and Self-Serviced the tank with premium unleaded. Then I stretched the hose to the limit and soaked the doorstep down with gas. I dug around in the glove box until I found some matches. I thought better of it and threw the matches back. No sense in drawing attention. I reached for the keys and a bottle caromed off the rear window and smashed against one of the pumps. The engine caught and I floored it but the outboard gas must have fouled the plugs or the carburetor, or maybe the goddam Chevy hated me because I hadn't voted in 2004 and look what happened. It coughed and died.

I heard somebody yelling something about a gun and the back of my head so I raised my hands and slowly reached for the door handle.

"You just stay in the car, mister."

A serious voice. Female, with a hard edge to it that implied "This puppy's got a three pound trigger pull and I've taken up two of it." What was it about this trip? Every babe I meet has a gun and wants to use it. I stayed in the car and checked the mirrors. The left mirror reflected a large redhead with a cannon handgun, maybe ten feet back. I was reading the "Objects In Mirror Are Closer Than They Appear" sticker as she smashed the passenger side window, spraying tempered safety glass across the front seat and raising everybody's insurance rates. I glanced at DeeDee. She was probably dreaming about her gun. She had a silvery sliver of drool hanging from her chin.

I caught the redhead's eye. Uh-oh. This was a pissed-off woman. You can tell by the lips. I have experience in this area. I guessed this woman had been through a couple of loggers and a poet before she'd discovered all men were pigs.

"Did the poet lie?" I asked.

She slowly and silently drifted the gun to the general area of my guts and looked into my eyes. I nodded towards the sign.

"Where's Chuck?"

She was kinda cute. Little ponytail, freckles, deep blue eyes and a gweat bwig pistol aimed at my belly. Pippi Longstockings playing pistol-packing mama.

She smiled. She smiled! There was hope! She centered the gun's muzzle on my chest and sighted down the barrel.

"I'm Chuck and you owe me—" she took a quick glance at the pump, "twenty-seven dollars."

I remembered the amount from when I pumped it.

"Seventeen," I said, jerking my thumb towards the pump. "See?"

"I have a gun," she replied calmly.

"I have a busted car window."

"My gun is loaded and aimed at your Jockey shorts."

This was a very good point. It's tough to argue with a lady so well trained in debating skills.

"Twenty-seven bucks sounds about right," I agreed.

There was a long silence.

"I can't give you any money if my hands are in the air."

"Okay, but don't try anything stupid."

I couldn't tell if she meant not to do anything stupid or if she was calling me stupid. Oh well, she did have the gun. I dug into my pocket and fished out a twenty and a ten. She took the bills with her free hand and stuck them into her shirt pocket, keeping the gun idly pointed in my general direction.

"What about my change?" I asked, blinking my innocent eyes at her.

She actually laughed aloud at that. "Change, sure, okay." She started back to the door and added over her shoulder, "Come on."

What the hell? Come on? This was one cool little lady. Too weird. I got out. She leaned over the front step.

"What did you do, spray gas all over my steps?"

I frowned. "Gas? No…. Had to be somebody else."

She didn't look too convinced, just said "Uh-huh" and held the door for me.

I stepped through and looked around.

"Where do you keep the goats?" I asked.

She walked behind the counter.

"Goats? No goats. Got just about everything else."

"I know, I saw your sign."

She pulled three bucks out of the till and handed it to me.

"So, what are you doing in a taxi way out here? Besides stealing gas from helpless women."

She set the gun down and put her elbows on the counter.

"Well, actually…." I hesitated. "I stole it."

She straightened and reached over her head.

"I know."

I heard a soft hiss of static and a clipped voice. Enough to get the gist. Police scanner.

"Bad TV reception out here," she said. *Her face was completely expressionless.*

I eased close to the gun. She picked it up again.

"They say you're a 'person of interest' in the murder of some punk drug dealer in Orlando."

She popped the clip free and set it in a drawer. She looked at me appraisingly and made a decision.

"State boys run a speed trap about ten miles farther down on a little downgrade. They'll spot that cab for sure." *She flipped off the scanner.* "You a drug dealer too?" *she asked as she walked towards the other side of the tiny room.*

"No, never." *I caught myself.* "Well, not any more. I was young once. How about you?"

Red pony tail. Jeans and cowboy boots. Freckles. Handled a weapon like a Marine.

"Me?" *She shrugged.* "I've got the annual cocaine binge, doesn't everybody? A little loco weed now and again."

She opened a cooler, pulled out a Bud long-neck, and twisted off the top. She brought it back and set it on the counter in front of me. That was a damn fine idea. I drained half of it.

"Actually, the bastards took my wallet. One of 'em still has it and I want it back."

She picked the gun up again and worked the action, neatly catching the cartridge as it flipped in the air. I could see things got a little slow out here in the middle nowhere. She set the gun in the drawer, locked it, slipped the key in her jeans.

"I can relate," *she said flatly.*

I emptied the beer and set the bottle down. A minute passed.

"I should be going now."

She took the empty bottle and dropped it in a waste bucket. I really wondered what was next.

"That will be a buck-fifty for the beer."

I didn't want to leave. I slowly dropped the three bucks on the counter.

"Keep it."

She left it there.

"Thanks."

She reached over and pulled a map from a counter display and tossed it to me. It hit me in the chest and dropped on the floor.

"There's a county road about three miles down on the left, it hooks up with the highway again a couple miles past Clewiston."

I picked up the map.

"Thanks."

I opened the door.

"That'll be two seventy five for the map."

I dug out a fifty and tossed it on the counter.

"Keep the change, babe."

She let it sit on the counter.

"Thanks. Don't call me babe."

I waved the map.

"Bye," I said over my shoulder.

She smiled and waggled her fingers.

I walked back to the cab and spent a few minutes clearing the shattered glass from the seat. I sat for a moment watching DeeDee slumber. Do these things only happen to me? The Chevy fired right up and I pulled onto the road, then stopped to look back at the little store. It was still there in its ramshackle elegance, reeking of gasoline. The last light inside went out. I almost expected it to be POOF, gone, like in one of those old Twilight Zone episodes. Gotta travel back this way someday, maybe. I found the county road and we bounced on it for an hour or so. DeeDee didn't even stir.

MURPHY

Murphy walked up the concrete stairs of the office building that housed the Florida Lottery headquarters. The receptionist pointed her toward the room where the drawing was taking place. An armed guard and a state trooper stood watch at the door. Murphy produced her identification. She knew the trooper by sight and nodded at him. Inside, the room was filled with folding chairs, and there was a small public gallery behind a glass panel. Murphy walked to the front of the room and pushed past a young man scribbling on a clipboard. She faced the lottery machine. It was smaller than it looked on television. An older man with silver hair and beard, dressed in a charcoal suit, motioned for her to sit. She looked back and saw the camera crew adjusting their equipment.

A row of flashing lights started and the stage director counted down from five with hand signals. The camera's red light glowed. Recorded music swelled. The silver-haired man walked into the spotlight with two young women. One was Miss Sanibel; she wore a long satin gown, a wide red ribbon, and a tiara. The other wore a short skirt, a loose blouse, and an incandescent smile. Skirt made a big show of presenting the package seals for the camera and unwrapping the three decks of oversize cards. The silver-haired man, with a grand flourish, fed the decks into the shuffling machine. The cards were a blur as the machine manipulated them. Twenty seconds later the first card spit out. Short skirt grandly pointed both hands at the card which could be viewed in a mirror. It was a 7. The number was duplicated on a numeric display. The numbers came up one by one. 37, 41, 19, 6, 38, and 22. Murphy had the numbers from Elke's ticket scribbled on a slip of paper in her purse. They matched. She felt weak and light-headed. Below the numbers the figure $150,000.00 flashed. The whole show was over in exactly 60 seconds. The lights went off and Skirt turned off her smile. Miss Sanibel took off her tiara and blond fall and tossed them into a make-up case. She lit a cigarette as she marched out of the room.

Murphy looked back at the public gallery. There were only a couple of people up there and she picked out Elke instantly. She wasn't at all surprised. She waved at Elke to come down. Then she caught the eye of the trooper and pointed at Elke. The trooper gave an OK sign. Murphy waved her badge at the gray man. His name tag said Milton Heilbronner. Heilbronner peered through glasses hanging around his neck by a silver chain. He looked at her identification very thoroughly, front and back.

"Nice to meet you, Captain Murphy, what can I do for you?"

"I'd like to get a closer look at your machinery and get an idea how it works."

"Great, I like showing the Octopus off. Sorry—we call the beast the Octopus, I guess because it's such a good shuffler. I think there was a cartoon dealer like that. And who is this young lady?"

Elke had appeared at Murphy's side. She blushed at being called young.

"Elke Rittenauer, pleased to meet you," she said.

"Charmed. Well, step up here, ladies. We get sealed and certified cards from the Bicycle Card company. It's our own design, you can see they are twice the size of regular cards. The machine shuffles them, just like the shufflers you might use at home, except industrial strength, you might say. In twenty seconds the cards are mixed several thousand times. The result is quite random. A rather beautiful system, I think. That's all there is to it."

"Have you ever had any problems with the machine getting altered or with the game being rigged?"

Heilbronner laughed. "Oh no, the process is very tight. The technicians are screened closer than CIA operatives and they never work alone." He pointed to the corners of the room. "You can see all the security cameras, they run twenty-four hours a day. The Octopus is checked eleven times between drawings to make sure it shuffles and randomizes properly. I can assure you, there is no possibility of cheating and we've never had a hint of scandal. No question about it. Our records are complete from the day this thing was first powered up."

"Does the thing operate by itself or is there some kind of computer connection or something?"

"We have a computer network just like they use in Vegas or on Wall Street. It has firewalls and seven different layers of security."

Elke drew the ticket from her purse and handed it to Heilbronner. He looked at it, then checked the numbers still flashing on the display. His cheerfulness and humor evaporated instantly.

"Watson, bring me a loupe." He pointed at Elke. "You stay right there," he said sternly.

The trooper from the door wandered over. Heilbronner pointed at him and jerked his head at Elke.

"If she moves, shoot her."

Murphy and the trooper raised their eyebrows at each other. Murphy shrugged.

One of the clipboard operators produced a jeweler's loupe. Heilbronner pointed at a bank of lights in the ceiling.

"Turn these lights on," he commanded.

He scratched off the ticket's security patch and read the numbers to his assistant who then rushed off. He placed the ticket on a small table and bent over it with the loupe. He examined it carefully then flipped it over and examined the opposite side. The assistant reappeared and nodded yes.

"Okay. This ticket looks authentic but I still think it is a fake. That means there should be a bundle of losing fakes around here some place."

"Heilbronner," Murphy said quietly. "You mean that Ms. Rittenauer has a couple of suitcases full of fake tickets that she selected from in about sixty seconds so she could hand you the winner?"

"We've had people try to pass off counterfeit tickets..."

"Sure, I've heard the stories. They pop up a week or two after the drawing. This gives them time to print the ticket and make sure that the real ticket won't turn up."

Heilbronner wilted like a snowman in Miami.

"I'll be damned." He turned to the assistant. "What are the odds that Ms. Rittenauer would win?"

"About one in two hundred thousand that she would win. Much higher odds that she would be here for the drawing with a winning ticket. That hasn't happened before."

"I'll be damned," he repeated. "An amazing coincidence, absolutely astounding."

His good cheer began to return.

Murphy shook her head. "Isn't it more likely that someone has jimmied your 'Octopus'?"

He exploded. "Not a chance. Impossible." He shook his finger in her face. "You can be arrested just for suggesting such a thing. Our security is flawless. We pay out more than twenty million dollars a week. In addition, we pull in several million for the state. We only make that money if people buy lottery tickets. People won't buy them if they think the game is rigged. To suggest such a thing is extremely irresponsible. With millions of dollars at stake the sanctity of the game must be preserved. If you breathe a word of your outrageous theory, you'll have the Governor, the Lieutenant Governor, the Police Commissioner, the Department of Revenue, and the Lottery Commission all screaming for a hunk of your hindquarters. There won't be enough left to feed a swamp rat."

Heilbronner's face was red. He was so agitated that spit flew from his mouth. He dabbed at his face with his handkerchief.

"Excuse me." Everyone turned to look at Elke. She picked the ticket off the table. "Can you tell me where I can cash this sucker in?"

CHAPTER 10

Late Wednesday Afternoon, May 21

GLEN

"DeeDee?" Glen poked her hard and she stirred slowly, stretched, and wiped her mouth. "We're getting close to Belle Glade."

It was early afternoon. The air roaring in the window was steamy and hot.

"Okay." She sat up, rubbed her eyes, and yawned. She rooted in her purse and found a little pill bottle. She washed down a couple of white pills with a pull from a warm bottle of Mountain Dew. She offered the pill bottle to Glen. He dismissed her with a wave of his hand. She lit a cigarette and slipped on her sunglasses.

"When we get to South Bay, follow Highway 80 to Belle Glade. We're going to turn toward the lake on 880 and we'll cross the canal. Manny's cousin has a place on the water on Torry Island. Turn left just after the bridge."

"What's his cousin's name?"

"Luis. He lives out there with his wife and a couple of kids. The oldest is one you have to watch. He's always trying to feel me up when Manny is not around. A good-looking boy, but a real mean son-of-a-bitch. A creep. Sick inside."

"What's his name?"

"Wesley. If Manny doesn't want to get his hands dirty, he'll let Wesley have you. Manny is tough, but he doesn't have a taste for blood."

"Try telling that to Pablo."

"That was just business to Manny. He doesn't the love wet work like Wesley does," she said.

"Does Wesley get a lot of practice?"

"Mainly feeding dogs ground glass or antifreeze, or drowning kittens. Torching a hobo. Kid stuff. He's going to have a lot of fun with you."

"He sounds like a real gentleman."

She turned toward Glen and ran her fingernail up the inseam of his slacks.

"It's not too late. We can go back to Orlando and get a condo. I could take real good care of you."

Glen's penis swelled under the heat of her hand.

"When I get my wallet back we'll talk, okay?" he said.

"You won't get your wallet back, you'll just get this thing chopped off and handed to you." She gently patted his crotch.

"Maybe."

The rest of the trip was made in silence. They located the house in a small development. The homes looked like vacation places. A Chevy Suburban and a Lexus LS430 were parked in the driveway. The LS430 was dirty and had Orange County plates. Luis had a neatly groomed green rock lawn. There were flowers growing around the front door. Glen knocked on the door. A dark-skinned and pleasant looking woman answered. She was wearing an apron and had a wooden spoon in her hand. The air from the house was rich with chili and spices. She spoke with a heavy Cuban accent.

"Allo?"

"I'm a friend of Manny Rodriguez."

"Yes, yes. They are out fishing. You can wait on the dock or inside if you want to cool off."

"The dock sounds fine."

"Okay, hold on, I'll give for you some beers."

She lugged out a five gallon bucket filled with ice and Miller High Life in bottles. She pointed them around the house. They crunched on the gravel walk around the house. White sheets hung limply on the clothesline. It was so hot the sheets were sweating too. There were some folding chairs on the dock. The water was shallow and green. Dike water flowed by lazily and an egret sailed by. Glen sat in a chair and opened a beer. He flipped the cap into the water.

DeeDee opened her mouth to complain about it but shut up when she noticed the cans and broken glass in the water.

"Pigs," she complained.

She dug in the ice and got a beer. She sailed her bottle top into the water too. Glen was hot in his jacket but he did not remove it. They watched the sun inch across the sky for 20 minutes before a jetboat roared up the canal. The driver reversed and neatly pulled up to the dock. Glen took a line and tied up. Manny jumped out of the boat, grabbed DeeDee, and bent her over for a big kiss. They went at it so hard Glen was surprised that Manny's tongue didn't protrude from DeeDee's butt. Glen sized up the other two. The driver was obviously Luis; black hair, deep tan, shirt open at the neck, and wearing a wispy mustache. About 50. That meant the other was Wesley. He was in his early twenties with long black hair pulled back into a ponytail. His upper arms crawled with tattoos: knives, hearts, bare-chested women. His features were perfect: clear olive skin and a hard flat stomach. His lips were full and red like a woman's. He looked sweet and innocent with doe-like brown eyes. He was pop-star pretty, Michael Bolton's Cuban brother.

Wesley watched Manny and DeeDee intently.

Manny came up for air, held DeeDee loosely around the waist, and turned to Glen.

"Okay, motherfucker. What is it you want?"

Glen kept his eyes on Wesley and did not answer.

"He says he wants his wallet back," DeeDee said. She touched her lips gingerly, they were swelling, bruised from Manny's kiss.

"Well, what the fuck. Let's go for a little ride." Manny jumped back in the boat and jerked DeeDee roughly in behind him. "Not you, Wesley, you bring his car around and meet us by Sand Cut."

Wesley didn't look too happy about missing any of the fun but he jumped onto the dock. He gave DeeDee a lingering look. Glen hopped in the boat and tossed Wesley the keys.

"Don't scratch up the paint."

Wesley flipped him the finger over his shoulder as he strode up the dock. Luis hit the key and the boat started with a roar. They screamed by the Slow, White Heron Nesting Area sign. Glen nursed his beer with his skin melting and welding to his shirt. He was baking but still did not remove his sport jacket. Riding on the lake was like boating in hot Won Ton soup. The dike around the lake looked like the rim of a soup bowl, the water was green with mossy leeks and floating waterchestnuts, and the low clouds looked steamy. Glen expected a giant spoon to descend from the sky and scoop them up. He shook his head to clear the ridiculous vision. Manny was standing with his head above the windshield. The wind roared through his hair. One hand held a Miller and the other was down DeeDee's shirt and massaging her roughly. She passively smoked a cigarette and stared at the horizon. Her eyes were hidden behind the sunglasses.

Luis cut the engine and the boat nosed into the bank where Wesley was waiting. Wesley caught the rope and tied the boat to a rotting pier post. The taxi was parked on a gravel parking area. It was a party and make-out site adorned with a couple of cold firepits and filthy with beer cans and other trash. Glen toed a soggy bright yellow condom with disgust. Luis tossed a large leather suitcase onto the shore. Manny opened it and sorted through the contents. Glen saw an Uzi, a 9mm Baretta, and some bags of dope. Manny took a small pair of bolt cutters out and laid them aside. He pulled out some handcuffs and a small metal detector. He scanned Glen by running the detector up his legs and over his back. He reached into Glen's pockets and tossed out his keys, change, and cellular phone. He found the wad of Raymond's cash and looked at it for a moment before stuffing it in his pocket. The metal detector bleeped at the stainless steel pins in Glen's knees but Manny patted him down and didn't comment. Manny took his arm and handcuffed him to the taxi door handle.

"Now we can get down to serious business," Manny said flatly.

Glen said nothing.

"Goddam it, Manny, we took his wallet and he wants it back. You don't need to make a big deal out of this," DeeDee said desperately.

"This is bullshit, get out of my face," Manny said, giving DeeDee a push.

He went to the suitcase, pulled out a rubber-banded bundle of credit cards and a large roll of greenbacks. Under all that lay a couple of dozen wallets.

Manny brought out a handful and scattered them on the ground.

Glen brightened. "That's it," Glen said, pointing. "The black leather one, there."

"Well, damn." Manny picked it up and examined it. "What's so special about this? Did you inherit it or something?"

"No, it's just a department store wallet. The only thing special about it is that it's mine and I'd like to have it back. Please."

"You must really think I'm stupid. You didn't track me across Florida for this cheap wallet." He opened it and took out a couple of photographs. "Was this what you're after?" he said, pointing at a picture of a woman.

"That's my first wife," Glen said.

"Kind of an ugly woman," Manny commented, looking closely at the photo.

Glen shrugged. "Only in the face. I liked the way her ass jiggled when she rode a bicycle. She caught my attention one sunny day when she rode by me around Green Lake in Seattle."

Manny and Luis exchanged baffled looks. Manny tossed the photo into the gravel. He looked at the next photograph.

"Who is this one?"

"That's my second wife."

"You only like ugly women?" Manny winked at DeeDee.

Glen shrugged again. "She could blow smoke out her mouth and suck it up her nose at the same time."

Manny discarded this photograph also. The last photograph was a picture of an old Harley Davidson.

"That's my old motorcycle. That was a beautiful old bike."

"Yeah, nice. What is it, a '68?" Manny handed the snapshot to Luis.

"No, '64," Glen said. "You can tell by the exhaust pipe." He stretched out to point. Manny slapped Glen's hand away. He took the photo back from Luis and slipped it into his pocket. The only contents left in the wallet were business cards, an airline mileage plus card, and some cash machine receipts. Manny scattered them on the gravel.

"I don't see your Swiss bank account number or the safe deposit key for your fortune," Manny said as he opened the wallet, held it upside down and shook out the last bits of paper. He waved the metal detector over it. Dead silence. He took a last look at the wallet before slipping it into his pants pocket.

"I don't get your trip, dude. I suggest you tell me what's on your mind. Now."

DeeDee sighed and walked over to an outcropping of limestone. She sat and buried her head in her hands. Tears streamed through her fingers. Wesley followed her and started rubbing her neck.

"Throw me a beer, will you, please?" Glen asked.

Manny hesitated, then nodded at Luis. Luis retrieved a couple of beers from the boat and tossed one to Glen, who caught it one-handed. He held the bottle against the car with his body and twisted off the cap.

"Come here, Wesley."

Wesley looked up from nuzzling DeeDee's neck.

"Show wallet-man some of your moves."

Wesley grinned and sauntered over. Glen drained his beer and broke the bottle on the car door. He held the jagged glass loosely in his free hand.

Manny, Luis and Wesley looked at each other and laughed.

"We have a sum bitch mother here, I think," Luis said.

Wesley stretched and rolled his shoulders, loosening up. He took a few practice jabs in the air. He was fast. Glen could tell he was well coached, a trained boxer. From his pretty face, clearly he wasn't hit very often. A dangerous boy. Glen leaned back against the car door as far as he could.

Manny hopped up to sit on the bow of the boat. "Wesley, you get this bad man to talk and I give you DeeDee. I know you want her. I'm sick of her fat face, you can love her to death."

Wesley grinned even bigger until his face nearly split in half.

"My pleasure." He stepped in and hammered Glen twice to the gut, rattlesnake fast. Glen lurched as far as he could to his right and swung with the jagged glass. Wesley was fast but Glen caught his chin. Wesley's face instantly turned dark, he cupped his jaw and a trickle of blood ran through his fingers. He slapped the glass out of Glen's hand and started hitting him in earnest. In thirty seconds Glen was hanging by his arm, collapsed on the ground.

Manny caught Wesley's arm. "Hang on." He tilted Wesley's head and examined his jaw. "That's going to scar up on you." He handed over a handkerchief.

Wesley knocked it away.

"Let's see if he will talk now." Manny bent down and lifted Glen's head.

"Hey, wallet-man? Are you still with us?"

Glen was silent. Manny pulled his straight razor out of his pocket. With a flick of his wrist the blade locked open. Wesley tapped Manny on the shoulder.

"No, Manny, look. Did you notice he's missing a finger? Maybe he'll talk if we chop him up some more?"

Manny looked up and nodded. He put the razor away. Wesley bent and picked up the boltcutters. Manny bent down and lifted Glen's head. From six inches away he stared into Glen's eyes. He clamped his hands on Glen's. Glen couldn't move much because of the handcuff anyway. Wesley positioned the cutters.

"Last chance, wallet-man," Manny said.

For 30 seconds they stared into each other's eyes. Then Manny nodded and Wesley put his weight into the cutters. Glen's hand exploded into a raging fire. A geyser of blood sprayed the taxi. Glen howled like a wolf caught in a bear trap.

"Oh, fuck it," Manny said with distaste while dabbing at a drop of blood on his polo shirt. Wesley was watching Glen with a crazy-crooked smile on his face. Glen pressed his hand against the door to try to stop the blood. The agony was intense but his body was in shock. He knew the pain was trivial compared to what was coming down the path. Pure misery was a black snorting monster coming to a theater in Glen's neighborhood real soon.

"Wesley, can you catch us a gator?" Manny asked.

Wesley nodded yes. From a paper bag he brought out a dead chicken reeking of rotten meat. He bound it with fishing line and cast it into the weeds near a culvert. Within a minute he drew it out and a twelve foot alligator swam lazily after it. Manny roughly led DeeDee into the boat.

"Wesley, you clean up here and meet us back home. Your woman will be waiting for you all heated up and in the mood. Right, DeeDee?" She stared out over the water. The boat fired up and they roared away. Manny waved as they receded.

Wesley tossed the chicken onto Glen's lap. Glen reached to the back of his jacket and tore his little ceramic knife out of the lining. It was a nasty little six inch number: serrated, razor sharp, the blade gleamed like bone. Ceramic, so it didn't set off metal detectors. Glen moved his hips and tossed off the chicken. When Wesley bent to pick it up, Glen lunged and buried the knife to the hilt in the center of his chest. The blade went through the bone easily. Wesley stood up and looked at the hilt. He could not register what had happened. Where did that funny looking knife come from? He fell over backward and for a moment his eyes searched the sky for answers, then gave up. The gator nosed at the chicken, glaring at Glen. Glen staggered to his feet and broke the taxi window with his free elbow. Pain, a hungry black beast with red eyes, breathing hard, was coming down the track. Fast. Glen didn't have much time. He stretched inside and pulled out the baseball bat with his fingertips. He got a good one-handed grip and smashed it between the gator's eyes. That was the end for Glen. He slid down the side of the car, embraced by dark waves of torment and swallowed by the black cloud of unspeakable agony.

Reality flashed in and out of Glen's head like a weak television station. He managed to get on his feet again. He reached in the broken window and found his travel kit. He choked down a handful of his Canadian 222's and washed them down with a drink of hot Mountain Dew. He didn't want to look at his hand, but something needed to be done. He flipped the latches of his suitcase and fumbled among the clothes. He found a clean T-shirt and wrapped his hand in it. The pain was so intense he knew he'd feel it in his next life, and all previous ones too. The gator was stirring. Glen was surprised, he thought he'd hit it hard enough to split its skull. He leaned over and worked the ceramic knife out of Wesley's chest and set it beside him on the car roof. The air filled with flies, probably attracted by the blood that was everywhere. Even the sky was bloodied by the setting sun. The gator rotated its snout in Glen's direction. The fucker seemed to get bigger by the minute. They looked at each other for a lifetime or two. *Come on, motherfucker, give it a try, I'll cut you from head to tail and make a suitcase out of you.* Glen knew he was losing it from the sun, the pain, and the pills. *Fuck you, what do you want?* He picked his finger out of the dirt and looked it over. The end was ragged and ugly. He tossed it to the gator and there was an instant snap; in a flash of yellow teeth it disappeared. After glaring at Glen for a moment the gator turned to Wesley and dragged him into the swampy lake. Fair enough, Glen thought. *If I can just sleep here for a year or two, I'll be okay.* He slumped in the shade and was carried into dreams of death by black wings of smoke.

PART THREE

Dreams relating to death or dying, unless they are due to spiritual causes, are misleading and very confusing to the novice in dream lore when he attempts to interpret them. A man who thinks intensely fills his aura with thought or subjective images active with the passions that gave them birth; by thinking and acting on other lines, he may supplant these images with others possessed of a different form and nature. In his dreams he may see these images dying, dead, or being buried, and mistake them for friends or enemies. In this way he may, while asleep, see himself or a relative die, when in reality he has been warned that some good thought or deed is to be supplanted by an evil one. To illustrate: If it is a dear friend or relative whom he sees in the agony of death, he is warned against immoral or other improper thought and action, but if it is an enemy or some repulsive object dismantled in death, he may overcome his evil ways and thus give himself or friends cause for joy. Often the end or beginning of suspense or trials is foretold by dreams of this nature. They also frequently occur when the dreamer is controlled by imaginary states of evil or good. A man in that state is not himself, but is what the dominating forces make him. He may be warned of approaching conditions or his extrication from the same. In our dreams we are closer to our real self than in waking life. The hideous or pleasing incidents seen and heard about us in our dreams are all of our own making; they reflect the true state of our soul and body, and we cannot flee from them unless we drive them out of our being by the use of good thoughts and deeds, by the power of the spirit within us.

- Gustavus Hindman Miller in 10,000 Dreams Interpreted

CHAPTER 11

A few moments on Wednesday Afternoon, May 21

GLEN

Haze. Before me, beneath me, and around me. A reddish, wispy haze that reached from behind to a horizon that... wasn't there. I tried to reach out but I couldn't. I simply couldn't. I couldn't move. I couldn't even TRY to move. My old snapshot of hell had returned, larger-than-life-size. Nothing but a hot, dry, dim, surreal fog. Was I going blind as well? Blind. I seemed to be blind. Couldn't tell. Can't think. Blind and paralyzed? Was I nothing more than a free meal lying helpless for the wolves? No. No wolves here, just gators. There be gators here. Bad ass hungry gators. I'd stolen a pencil from a gator once. No, a blind man. I'd stolen a yellow pencil from a blind man's cup once for no particular reason. Maybe the gators were coming to steal their pencils back. I'd stick 'em with my little white cane, I would! Poke! Poke! What a scene. "Bad gator! Bad! Sit! Roll over. Lie down!" I laughed and my head moved. I moved! I'm NOT blind! I can move! Somehow that was logical. Blind men can't move, can they? How would they know? Senses, they could be TRICKED. Give me 20/20 vision or give me death. If only I could see. Almost paralyzed, but with colors now, an explosion of colors! Shapes and forms. I'd never seen and never imagined such a swirling mayhem of figures. Figures that rushed towards me, near me, through me, and beyond. I could do nothing but close my eyes that stayed open or closed and how would I know, being deaf as I am.

Bad acid in 'Nam. Sgt. Stephens had warned me, but I'd been young, oh so young and smart. Then twelve hours in a closet, twelve hours in a closet. Was I still in the closet? Couldn't think. Was I still crouched, thinking so extremely hard in the cramped closet of an old Asian whorehouse while the walls melted and the crows sang love songs of hate? No, that was another life. Flashbacks are just an indicted Republican's dream. Or nightmare... Am I in hell?

"Funny you should ask," said a reedy voice from behind me.

I stood in the blood-red haze and considered turning around. I was frozen. Standing on solid ground. Dependable nonpartisan DIRT. Or rock. I bent to touch it. Whatever it was. I straightened, took a cleansing breath, and turned to face the voice. A shadowy form. Short and thin with details lost to the haze.

We stepped towards each other and the mysterious red fog seemed to part in our path. I stared. Male, middle-aged, balding, it looked like... No, it couldn't be.

"You look like Woody Allen."

He frowned and his forehead wrinkled. This made him look even more like Woody Allen. He had a dimestore notebook. He flipped it open and made a small mark. He crossed his arms and looked back at me rather smugly, I thought.

"Bet you got a tiny little limp dick."

I don't know why I said that but it seemed like a safe bet. He sighed and opened his notebook again. He made another mark and looked back at me.

"How am I doing?" I pointed to his notebook. "Does neatness count?"

Woody shook his head slowly. I glanced at his shoes. He had very nice shoes and the suit wasn't bad either. Italian. His lips twitched, probably his version of a smile. He crossed his arms again and puffed out his chest, looking very self-important.

"Hellbound, this is your moment. Your chance to plead your case. Petition well and seek some small forgiveness. Cite your father, your mother, society's entrapments, or the unavoidable needs of the flesh." *This sounded like a canned speech to me.* "Tell me how Fate steered you onto an unchosen Path and survival dictated your immoral deeds."

I studied his face.

"The devil made me do it?"

Page flip, pencil lick, black mark. *Shit, tough crowd.*

"You've got a thing on your nose." I said.

He raised an eyebrow.

I continued. "No, really. Right there." I pointed. "Looks a big zit."

I leaned closer.

"Wow, what a monster."

124

He reached up and felt his nose.

"No, the other side."

He found it and squeezed. He looked at the white ick before wiping his fingers on his pants.

"Three hundred years I've been doing this, nobody says a word," he sighed. "Where was I? Ah, cataloging your immoral deeds."

He popped the latches on his briefcase and pulled out a black book with gold-gilded pages. He riffled through a handful of pages, raised both his eyebrows, and peered at me. He turned a page, then another, and shook his head.

"Which are numerous," he added.

He flipped through a few more pages, then stopped.

"Oooh… what's this, a Special Note?"

He pulled a pair of glasses from out of the haze and settled them on his nose. He examined me through them.

"I don't really need these, it's just the bad light in here. Oh, never mind."

He ran a finger along as he read. Some passages he read twice.

"Did you really do this? Scratch that, of course you did. It's in the book."

He looked up into the mist and tapped a finger alongside his jaw. He started to take a step back and stopped. He shrugged.

"I'm supposed to finish with 'Convince me your soul is misguided not wanton, and perhaps some arrangements of penance will serve', but I think we can forego all that."

I digested for a while and came to the obvious conclusion.

"So, you're a lawyer."

His eyes narrowed. He opened his notebook and scribbled something, slashed through some stuff, and made several checkmarks. He was pressing so hard that the paper ripped. He looked up without a smile.

"Lawyer jokes aren't popular here," he stated primly.

"Imagine that. Look, I need to talk to your boss."

"That isn't done."

"I'll bet subchapter 17 of volume 88 has the appropriate paragraph. You know, the one you fell asleep while reading in your junior year of college."

"You are incorrect, sir," he sputtered.

Woody was lying, I could tell. Then again, we were in hell. They probably had competitions. Judges with scorecards critiquing technique—"Well, John, he nailed the compulsory, but showed us nothing new in the Freeform... Look at those scores! A 5.9 from the French judge!"

Woody scowled at me. "We can read your thoughts and that's not funny. It doesn't even make sense."

"Sure it does, Wood, lighten up."

"This is hell, we don't 'lighten up'."

"Give it a rest, Wood." I pointed at the notebook. "Look here, you guys need to upgrade. I can put you in touch with IBM and get you a good discount on some new equipment."

I pulled out my own notebook. Remarkable, it looked just like his. Someone around here is showing a noteworthy lack of imagination.

"I can get you guys an RF-linked LAN at cost, we're talking 40 gigabaud throughputs and real-time video messaging. Maybe give the minor demons voice-only to trim the peak load, but that's a tough call without knowing what kinda numbers we're looking at." I made several small checkmarks. Scribbled something. "Got a lot of demons here, Wood?"

Woody looked thoughtful. "Yes, if we include the imps and the junior partners." He looked in his notebook. "Actually, we're rather understaffed at the moment, but..."

He gasped, stiffened, and stared out into the haze. He shuddered and then seemed to snap out of it. He glared at me.

"We're virtually omnipotent, you idiot! We don't need your material hardware!"

He popped upright again and gazed intently over my shoulder.

"Please, not my job!" he said to someone who wasn't there.

He looked distraught.

"I love this job, and I've only... this is the first... yes, I understand. Of course you're right, you're always right... yes. Right away."

He relaxed again and looked around rather sadly.

"Trouble with the boss, Wood?"

"No. Yes. Shut up." He poked at me with a gaunt finger. "This is your fault!"

"Now look here, Wood..."

"Stop calling me that!" He poked again with that finger. Damn it! He was poking at me with one of my own fingers.

"Okay, sure. But listen."

I grabbed the finger. It dissolved into red sand and the red sand dissolved into red smoke. I held my hands in front of my face and wiggled them. I didn't know what was up with the finger, all mine were intact.

"I don't want your job, okay?" He looked hurt. "I mean, it looks like a real hoot," I added, "it's just that I've got other plans."

"You don't know what you're saying." He started to pace. "This is a great job compared to the others." He shivered. "This is, this was, so nice."

I surveyed the barren rock and the wispy trails of reddish fog. "Oh yeah. Quite the spread you've got here, Wood."

Our eyes met.

"We didn't invent this crap, Wilson. Red smoke? Gators? Stupid little notebooks? Amputated fingers? You don't think WE made up this stuff?"

"Sorry."

I did a 360 and checked out the site. Interior decorating isn't my gig. A whole lotta scarlet haze going on around here. Metaphysical bullshit.

"Purple would be better. Is Jimi playing his Strat around here somewhere?"

Woody looked something—groggy, confused? I assumed that drunk was out of the question.

"I thought you knew by now," Woody said sarcastically.

"Well I dunno, Wood, you've probably been here since Christ was a gleam and I've put in a solid five minutes." *And took your job*, I didn't add.

Woody jumped. "Don't say that!" He looked around.

"Don't say what?"

"The 'C' word! The boss hates that!"

"Okay, we're in hell, Wood. I'd have to expect that." Actually, I hadn't thought of it. Guess I have to start watching my language. Politically correct behavior in hell. Hell had swear words? When in Rome?

"Anything else I should know? Like the way to the bathroom? Where to put the empties? What time the maid turns down the sheets?" There was a thought. "Got many good looking babes here, Wood?"

Woody shook his head. "This is YOUR hell, Hellbound."

Oh. That would rule out the "naked babes on the throw pillows" scenario. Damn. Another dream shot to hell. Literally.

"Call me Glen." I paused. "Or 'Great Master of The Big Chunk of Rock With Haze That Should Be Purple.'" I paused again. "With a Really Big Dick."

Woody rolled his eyes at that one.

"Hell is what you expect of it, Glen."

I could see he was serious. "I'm very serious," he said.

Scary shit.

"Reading my mind? How come it's not purple like I expected?"

"Deep down, from somewhere, you conjured red." He rubbed his temples. "Frankly, you have a rather disturbing persona, aura, projection. It's difficult to describe." He threw me a curious little sideways glance as he turned and began to walk away. "Have you really so little fear?" He stopped, looked back, and waited for my response.

"Fear of what?" That was too flip, so I pondered his question a bit.

"That's an essay question, Wood, and I don't think we've got the time."

He didn't move and I didn't continue. It occurred to me that we probably had lots of time. Like ALL of it. Eternity on this damn rock?

"Well, Wood, I fear a lot of things, just not enough to let them slow me down." Damn, I needed a beer. "I've been homeless, pal, though I guess that's just another cliché these days."

Wood could read my thoughts? Fine. Read this, buddy.

Fear, Wood? Fuck you. Been there. No fear left. Woody still hadn't moved on. What was he waiting for? We all gotta die, what's to fear there? Billions of people have done that, how tough could it be? The way I see it, I was dead once and it didn't hurt a bit.

Woody spun to face me. "You really think it's that simple?" He waved an arm or two. I think it was two. "Been a bad boy, go to hell? Live like a saint and get satin pillows in the clouds? Saint Peter and I," he waved an arm or two again, I think it was one this time, "negotiate the borderline cases?" He laughed. "You'd learn it yourself, sooner or later <jerk>, but the fact is, heaven and hell are the same place, the only difference is point of view."

"Did you just call me a jerk?"

"Oh. You're picking it up faster than most."

"It's okay. I think you're a complete waste of time, and a dickhead."

"Well, I can see that you're going to fit right in. But if you screw it up, you're gonna do time as a..." He consulted his notebook again. "Oh. You're scheduled to be a... huh?"

He flipped a few pages. Flipped them back. Looked at me. "Forget I said anything. Anyway, you either advance to the next lifeform, or you don't. In some cases it's deemed best that you, um, fall back to relearn some lessons that may have been glossed over."

"Let's go back to that scheduling thing. What's that all about?"

"You sure you want to know?"

"Sure. Scare me to death."

"Well, okay. You're scheduled to be a wretch."

"A wretch? What in the hell is that? I don't think I want to be a wretch."

"Neither did the other wretches."

"Very funny, Wood. You're killing me. Now get outta here. I need to talk to the Man."

"It won't be what you're expecting..." Woody started to fade. He looked startled. The surroundings began to shimmer. He reached toward me and I felt a small tingle, though our hands didn't meet. Woody sent me a crooked little smile.

"Looks like you'll get your wish. I'm sorry..."

He was gone. And then so was I.

Blackness. Or less. There is a television engineering term: Blacker than black. Nothing. Less than nothing. Like silence. Only quieter.

"Hello?"

This couldn't be a good sign.

SILENCE!

That hurt. Okay, that hurt. I hurt now. Lots of hurt here. We won't be needing any more of that. Silence? I can do that, not a problem. Ol' Silent Wilson, that's what they'll call me. Not a peep. Nope. Quiet like a mouse.

"Would you shut up? That was just a tiny demonstration, you paltry and insignificant nothing."

The voice seemed to surround me and invade me. The inky blackness was growing impossibly blacker in front of me. It seemed to be developing form and substance. I had nothing to judge size, no references, but it seemed huge nonetheless. It projected power and strength. A small knot of terror grew within me and I couldn't hold it back.

"You're probably not the Good Humor Ice Cream Man, are you?"

The form shifted and grew closer or larger, I couldn't really tell. It didn't appear to have a discernible shape. A black hole of fear in my guts was clamoring for attention.

"Wait, I've got it. You're Alice. You played Alice on 'The Brady Bunch'."

The raw power emanating from the dark was awesome, horrifying in its intensity. Terror hammered at the door, screaming "Wilson! Shut the fuck up! Shut up! SHUT UP!"

After a moment the Voice rumbled again, this time more softly, which only made it more terrifying.

"You interest me, mortal. This happens occasionally, though rarely."

The black shape was becoming more solid, but still defying my attempts at discerning anything recognizable.

"You project a straight line. A directness of purpose that serves you well. Perhaps this could be useful to me. Somewhat. Bearing in mind your insignificance, of course. Bearing in mind your weakness and your inability to affect events in any but trivial ways."

"I'm flattered. So you're... the Devil, right? Satan? Beelzebub? The guy that made Ebony Cat trip on the stretch at the Stakes in '88? Cost me seventeen thousand and change? You're the guy?"

We had a horizon and ground. I was on Ebony Cat pounding down the homestretch feeling the big thoroughbred giving it all shedding flecks of foam flying from his exhausted muscles. The crowd was roaring. A divot of earth flung from the leader's hooves, rising to strike Cat squarely in the right eye. Cat stumbled and we went down. We hit the dirt hard and started rolling, sliding... and it faded to black again.

"Do you really think I'd meddle in such a mundane affair?"

"Pretty good effects, Spielberg know about this? DreamWorks may be willing to take on another partner."

My vision seemed to be improving. With a little imagination I could almost perceive enough edge to determine a shape. I couldn't focus precisely on it.

"Here's a clue, mortal. You haven't decided what I look like yet."

"I haven't decided?"

"And I thought you were a sharp one."

"I decide you look like Marilyn Monroe. Dress blown around your head and no underwear."

"Your failing organic subconscious is deciding differently."

"Sometimes I hate that damn thing." I hesitated. "What is it?"

"You're not here for a chemistry lesson, you're here to cut a deal."

Ah, finally something I can sink my teeth into.

"Is this where I sell my soul in exchange for a blues riff?"

The blackness upon the blackness began to look vaguely humanoid. Just a hint. That might be a head. Those may be arms.

"I already have your soul. You have nothing to trade. Nothing to deal with."

"Then why are we having this conversation?"

I was trying to 'decide' the shape into something a wee bit more aesthetic than a tenuous black blob with impossible appendages but I wasn't having much luck.

"You're here because I don't need you."

I had an ex-wife say something similar once. Or maybe I said it to her, I don't remember.

"I thought I was headed for remedial wretch training?"

"I think not. That can wait. Though close, you're not yet dead in the material world, and you've been doing such fine work there."

"Thanks. I think." Satan appreciated me. Somehow this didn't feel like a real kicker reference to use on my resume. Well now, let's review. You never held a job for more than a few years, never finished your degree, no major accomplishments to speak of... what's this? A letter of recommendation from Satan? Well well, that changes everything! Upper management material! I believe we have a vacant VP level position in Human Resources...

"Okay, wretch. I'll put it to you straight. The decision has not been made. We got a fax from the other place."

"You mean—?"

"Don't say it," he interrupted. "Don't even think it, piss-ant."

"Okay." Touchy, touchy.

"Frankly, I don't see it. But take the two muggers for example. You remember Tim and Willie? Tim ends up shot in the head by a Cambodian while robbing a doughnut shop. You'll run into him around here somewhere. But Willie, that's a different story. He takes your advice, goes to Junior college, then Florida State, and becomes a GP in the inner city." He wrinkled his nose in distaste. At least, I think it was his nose. "Goes on to lead a good life. Enough to turn your stomach, isn't it? Therefore, it's been decided that we will return you to your inconsequential life and let things play out a little longer. Return to your mortal coil, Hellbound. You will return to me later, so this means nothing. It's just the mad dying of a few billion of your brain cells."

I began to feel pain. And illness. And gravity. The scene grew brighter. The black blob was moving into the distance, still mostly shapeless. Pain began consuming me from the edges. It was better talking with the devil.

"Wait! We're not done. What do you really look like? What about those Bulls? I haven't had a chance to guess your name. We decided? Who's we? Can we set up a meeting? Let's not be too hasty."

"See you later, mortal." The rumbling voice was a faint and eerie echo.

"But what if I change my ways, reform?" I yelled.

"You are incapable." A barely heard reply. And laughter, did I hear laughter?

It was hot, hotter than hell, which I found ironic. The sun was a blast of heat and light that scorched my eyes. I was drenched with sweat. It looked like I'd managed to vomit greasy chunks down the front of my shirt. Waves of pain paced my plodding heartbeat, just to remind me of where I was, and why. Then the WHY dissolved like a daydream. I'd try to catch up with that thought later. Maybe I'd been a bit hasty turning down that wretch gig. I searched the sky for answers and found nothing but buzzing blowflies. I stretched and caught the handle of the boltcutters and dragged them over. Somehow I managed to get to my feet and worked the handcuff chain into the blades. Using my weight against the car door I cut the chain leaving just a fashionable steel wristband. I tossed the bat through the shattered window and got behind the wheel. The keys were still there. Thank God, or somebody. I coughed up some more vomit and spit into the lake. It's time to find a Doctor willing to share his stock of needles and Morphine.

The Chevy started right up. I floored it, spewed gravel, and roared away.

CHAPTER 12

Wednesday Afternoon, May 21

GLEN AND DEEDEE

Manny drained his beer and threw the bottle overboard. It arced and flashed in the bright sunlight. DeeDee pulled out a flotation seat cushion and held it to her chest. She wrapped her purse straps around her neck and poised on the edge of the boat. Her short hair whipped in the 30 mile-per-hour slipstream.

"What the hell?" Manny asked.

"Fuck you," DeeDee replied as she launched into the air.

"Why'd she do that?" Luis inquired.

"I guess she doesn't want to be Wesley's girl."

Manny pulled the Uzi out of the suitcase and pulled back the firing lever while Luis slowed the boat. Looking back, Luis started laughing. Manny looked puzzled. Then he looked back at DeeDee bobbing in the shallow water. She was at least four miles from shore. Manny joined the laughter and released the firing lever. He tossed the squat gun back in the suitcase.

"Let our little mermaid swim back. If Wesley wants her bad enough he can come back and rescue her."

DeeDee dog-paddled determinedly towards shore. Manny saluted her with a fresh beer. Luis opened the throttle and they raced home.

It took a year or two, but eventually DeeDee dragged herself onto the bank of the levy and collapsed in the marshy grass. She didn't want to move but didn't like the feeling of things crawling on her. She was sunburned, waterlogged, and covered in mud. She clawed her way to the top of the levy, climbed through the barbed-wire fence, and crumpled in the gravel at the edge of Highway 15. Every few minutes a car or pickup would stop but she waved them by. She saw the yellow cab approaching. It weaved between the left and right shoulders at a crawl.

She was not surprised to see Glen coming, but could never explain the feeling. She got up and found she was still gripping the flotation cushion. She tossed it into the weeds.

Glen could not focus. His hand was numb, so the codeine and aspirin pills were working, but he was completely spaced out. He had trouble keeping the car on his side of the highway center stripe and moving forward at the same time. He didn't believe he was on land, the road was rolling so much he thought he was piloting a ship on a stormy sea. *Chain me to the spanker, there's a bad storm brewing. Women and children overboard first.* He knew he was losing it when he saw one of the mud people standing on the shore. He stopped to say hello and recognized DeeDee. She had a sprig of swamp grass stuck in her collar.

"Glen, I'm so glad to see you, are you okay?" she said, peering in the driver's side window.

Glen was instantly angry. Beat to shit by Wesley, another finger hacked off, a face-down with an alligator, and dealing with the Devil in what he hoped was just a bizarre hallucination. *Oh yeah, I'm doing just perfectly, how about yourself, sweetie?*

Glen scooted his butt over on the seat and kicked the door open.

"Shut the fuck up and drive," he said before blacking out again.

When she got to Canal Point she realized she did not know where she was going. She pulled to the edge of the road and tried to wake Glen.

"Glen?" She stroked his face and pulled his ears. "Glen, where are we going? Should I cut over to Palm Beach?"

Glen did not stir. They were near a road sign, so she drove until she could read it. If she went straight they would pass through Belle Glade. That wouldn't do. She took Highway 98 East.

She saw a sign for a Days Inn on Okeechobee Boulevard. The sun was low and casting long shadows before her. All she could think of was finding a hiding place to sleep. She pulled into the parking lot. Her purse was filled with brown water that she poured onto the asphalt. She found a Mastercard and wiped off the muck. She adjusted the mirror to look at herself. She still had swamp grass in her collar: it looked as if it was growing out of her head. She pulled it out and tossed it out the window. She was a mess; her hair was caked into muddy barbs and her Keds oozed brown water. She smelled like a dead muskrat. The clerk barely spoke English and after a quick glance would not look directly at her. His eyes flicked left and right from his racing form. She filled out the room card and the clerk imprinted her credit card.

"You like second floor?" the clerk asked.

"No!" she said sharply. "I'm sorry. Ground floor, please."

"Smoking?"

"No. Yes. I don't know. Anything."

The clerk pushed the key across the counter.

She stopped the car in front of their room. She got the room door open and pulled Glen out of the car. He fell limply onto the parking lot. She called his name and tapped harder and harder on the T-shirt wrapped on his hand until he roused.

"What the fuck?" he said thickly.

His tongue wouldn't move properly. It felt like a dead toad in his mouth. The pills were wearing off. He made the scientific discovery that the shortest distance between two points was the distance between his hand and his brain where the pain traveled in hyperspace waves. He struggled to his feet and DeeDee supported as much of his weight as she could.

"We gotta get to the room," she said, pointing at the door ten feet away.

Glen focused, pointed his nose in the right direction, lowered his head, and made the journey. He flopped face down on the bed with his injured hand lifted in the air. As he lost awareness his hand floated softly down to the bed.

MANNY

Manny sucked the last morsel of meat from a pork rib. He leaned back in his chair and drained his beer. He watched Luis's kids slurping up their Jello.

"Luis, your wife sure can cook. I've gotta have the recipe for these ribs." He winked at Luis's wife, Maria.

"Just ribs boiled in beer with some chiles," she said with her face flushing.

"Well, it's just great. But now, I really must be going. I'd like to be in Fort Myers before it gets too late."

Maria started clearing the table. Luis followed Manny out the front door.

"Wesley is taking his time with that guy."

"He gets carried away sometimes," Luis said wearily. "He's still young and has some growing up to do. I'm sure he's okay."

I'm not so sure, Manny thought.

Manny gathered Luis in for a hug and they patted each other on the back.

"Nos vemos, hermano," Manny said. We'll see each other, brother.

"Si," Luis replied.

LEONARD

Leonard was cramming bills into a one-gallon pickle jar. The jar was so full he had trouble screwing on the lid. He needed to figure out something to do with the money, there was too much of it. It didn't seem like a great idea, but he considered just giving gas away for free.

"Help me out, Dog."

Dog lay on his burlap and did not respond.

"Worthless mutt," Leonard commented.

He pushed the jar under the desk as far as he could. When he stood up he saw a rusty old Dodge pickup pull up to the pump. The truck was raised a yard in the air. It rattled and spewed black smoke. It had a 6.2L Cummins Diesel under the hood. The driver was Jack Sterner, jr., the son of the infamous competition fisherman. The son was to serious fishermen what Bob Vila was to serious building contractors.

Leonard walked up to the cab and looked up at the driver.

"Sorry, Mister, don't got diesel. I can sell you some number two fuel oil if you're desperate."

Sterner wore a floppy hat with fishing lures stabbed in it. He opened the door and swung out of the cab. His thin red hair cascaded limply from under his hat. He had about a million freckles.

"Don't need no fuel, I filled up back at Andytown. What's the name of this place," he said gruffly.

"This used to be called Clem's place but now it's mine and I call it Leonard's Lunch-N-Lube."

"Well, it ain't much to look at, is it?" the visitor said as he spit a black stream of chaw into the gravel. "Do you know who I am?" he asked.

Leonard looked at him carefully.

"Nope."

"Don't you watch TV?"

"No, the reception on Channel Seven is okay but my TV broke ten or twelve years ago. Clem had a little black and white Zenith so I could watch reruns with him now and then, but he got sick of the OJ trial and smashed it with a golf club."

"Good. My name is Smith, okay? John Q. Smith."

"What does the 'Q' stand for?"

"Shut up. Now listen, my dad had a special place where he went for bait. Got these red worms about yay big," he said, holding his fingers about three inches apart. "You got worms here?"

"Yeah," Leonard said. "Got a tub around back. I don't remember Clem ever selling any, I thought they were pets."

They walked around the building. Smith became excited when he saw the worm tub. He lifted the wet burlap and dug his hand in the dirt. He came up with a handful of damp mud and wriggling red worms.

"I can't believe it, these are the ones."

"They're great worms, ain't they?" Leonard said.

"You know anything about competition fishing?" Smith asked.

Leonard shook his head no.

"How about largemouth bass?"

"Nope," Leonard said.

"Perfect," Smith said. "I'll back my truck around. You got a motor lift or something to get this tub in the back of my truck?"

"You want the whole tub?"

"Yes, I'll give you a check for a thousand dollars."

"I can't sell Clem's worms," Leonard said.

"Okay, Gump. I'll make the check out for five thousand. Let's get this thing hooked up and I'll get out of here."

This scared Leonard. What am I going to do with five thousand dollars! I don't have enough pickle jars, he thought in panic.

"Look," Leonard said while hopping from foot to foot like he needed to pee. "I can't sell Clem's pet worms. I gotta think. I don't know what to do. You need some seashells? I can sell you some seashells. How about some black rocks, Red Vines, a Grape Crush?"

"No, I want these worms and I'll make it worth your while. You're a sharp negotiator. Name your price, I gotta have these worms."

"No," Leonard said. "'Scuse me, I gotta go bad." He walked toward the bathroom as fast as he could.

"Idiot," Sterner muttered under his breath.

Dog, watching from his burlap bed, agreed.

Sterner looked for a hunk of chain. I'll chain this fucker to the bumper. As he approached the tub, Dog snapped to his feet. He narrowed his eyes and bared his teeth. He growled menacingly and stalked Sterner. Sterner cussed and walked quickly to the cab.

"You ain't seen the end of me, you fleabag mongrel," he shouted through the cab window.

Dog One, Idiot Human Race Zero, Dog thought as the truck lurched onto the pavement and disappeared in a cloud of dust. Dog padded proudly back to his bed.

MURPHY

Murphy stirred Cremora into her coffee with a plastic stirring stick. The sun was low on the horizon. She closed her office blinds to reduce the glare. She had just explained the events at lottery headquarters to Webster who was not paying attention as he was playing with his laptop computer.

"I don't know what we are doing. Are we going to follow Glen south? Are we going to arrest him? For what? Questioning? We don't really have any evidence to hold him. I don't understand this AES stuff."

Webster closed the lid of his computer and unplugged the modem cable.

"There. I booked us on a redeye flight to Seattle."

"Seattle! I don't have jurisdiction outside Florida. Why am I going?"

"We're going to interview Glen's family and his boss. I want to get inside his head and see what makes him tick. Then we'll pounce."

"Pounce? What do you mean pounce? Arrest him? Sneak up behind him and say boo? What is the point of all this? He was at the scene at Pablo's, but he didn't kill him. He shot a motel room television set. A bunch of drunks woke up with headaches and missing wallets at a party. Where's the federal crime?"

"My boss gave me freedom to run this case my way. Your boss gave the okay for you to assist me in Seattle. We're going. Pack some pantyhose and pick me up at my hotel in ninety minutes. We're getting close to breaking this thing wide open, I can feel it."

"I'm not asking you to reveal any secrets. Please, just tell me what federal crime we are trying to solve."

Webster sighed and wore a pained expression on his face.

"It's about the AES security algorithm. The algorithm has a back door. If we get a Judge to sign a petition, we can monitor the contents of all encrypted messages. One of Glen's crimes is that he's been sending messages that we can't monitor."

"Privacy is illegal?"

"Yes, of course it is. I don't have time to explain all this technical stuff. We're wasting time." He looked at his watch. "The plane to Seattle leaves in eighty-three minutes."

Murphy stood in her office doorway and looked around before she flipped off the lights.

"Let's get our fannies in gear," Webster said, making a motion like he was going to swat her on the butt.

"You'll draw back a stub if you touch me," Murphy said in a low and serious tone.

Webster raised both hands innocently.

"Don't get modern on me, Murphy." He pointed at his watch. "Let's get rolling."

LEONARD

Jack Sterner Jr. pulled into The Glades parking lot. The bar was a squat cinder block building adorned with flickering Lone Star and Pearl beer signs. The lamp segments that worked actually said "one Star" and "Pea". The paint was losing a battle with the heat and humidity, sloughing off the walls like shedding skin. The parking lot was filled with muddy trucks. One had a fly-bitten little deer hanging on the grill. Probably roadkill. It had been there a few days. Sterner gave it wide berth as he approached the front door. The proud hunter was probably celebrating inside with a three day bender. On entering the building, Sterner's eyes slowly adjusted to the dim light. A couple of locals with leathery skin, cowboy boots worn down at the heels, sweat-stained hats, and hard round bellies were shooting pool. Their custom-made cue sticks gleamed in the light emitted by dusty bulbs hanging in their sooty fixtures. While Sterner watched, the one with Buddy stitched on his bait shop jacket flubbed an easy shot. A hundred and one degrees outside and the guy wore a jacket.

"Shoot ya?" Buddy said.

"Quarter a ball?" his partner added.

"Dad told me to never play pool for money with a guy named Buddy," Sterner said politely. "I'll buy you guys a beer and shoot with you for fun if you like."

"Fun, yeah, right," Buddy said, dismissing Jack. Then he casually banked in an impossible shot from across the table.

Sterner took an open stool three away from a large damp woman who was communing with the spirits in an oily looking glass. The bartender, dressed in a stained T-shirt and apron, wandered over. Sterner ordered three Dos Equis with lime and waved for two to be delivered to the pool table. He had a chance to take one cool drink before the fat lady slid over and knocked over his glass. Sterner was drinking from the bottle so he didn't care. "Oh! Excuse me," exclaimed Sarah. "I'm such an airhead since my husband passed away." She instinctively searched for a ring on Jack's hand. No ring, no blemish in the tan. A clear field. She grabbed his arm.

"I just lurve a man that wears—" she hesitated, "—is that Old Spice?"

Jack blinked at her and tried unsuccessfully to pull his arm away.

"No," he replied, disconcerted at Sarah's onslaught. "It's skeeter lotion, my own making."

He tugged at his arm, but Sarah tightened the clamp. Her eyes, reddened and puffy from the previous night's gin, locked onto Sterner's. "That's simply fascinating, homemade insect repellent. My goodness, such a clever man." She moved closer. "Unlike my dear Clem, rest his soul," she added.

She looked both ways and then back to Sterner.

Her eyes narrowed.

"You have a market, of course," she whispered conspiratorially.

Jack frowned.

"Huh," he said.

Sarah frowned at his truant question mark.

"A market. You know, a place to sell it."

"Sell what?"

Sarah nodded wisely.

"Exactly, that's what you need. A market for your bug spray. We could make a lot of money."

"We," said Jack with much irony, lifting his beer left-handed.

Sarah looked hurt. She released his arm and eased off the stool.

"Fine." She raised her chin. "I have a store, you have a product, I thought maybe we could help each other."

She sniffed and turned to leave, rather slowly. Jack suddenly had second thoughts.

"Wait! What kind of store?"

Sarah stopped and turned around. She flashed Jack her most becoming smile.

Jack flinched. Three hundred pounds of grinning ugly, wrapped in snakeskin, he thought, trying his best to grin back.

"Well, it's not mine yet," Sarah qualified as she returned, "but when the papers are signed, it will be." Her smile morphed into a sneer. "And that idiot, the shit-eating mutt, and his damn worm tub can hit the road."

She stopped in front of Jack.

"So, are you buying me a drink, sailor?"

"Worm tub?" Jack asked.

"Oh, don't worry about that, it's history. I'm planning a display of tulips there," she made a square with her fingers and sighted on a distant wall, "to highlight a rack of windchimes overhead." She dropped her hands, tilted her head at Jack, and continued. "Does this bug spray of yours really work and do you have child support payments?"

Jack was offended.

"Course it works! I'm a pharmacist," he said, rubbing his bristly jaw. "And this store has a worm tub, you say." He peered at her. "Big worms, fat, red, about this long." He held his fingers up. Sarah shrugged.

"Sure," she agreed, "exactly." She eased closer. Jack instinctively backed away until he struck a store display. He was trapped. He could smell the stale gin on her breath. "The biggest, fattest, reddest worms you ever saw," Sarah promised.

Jack looked down at her, suddenly unsure if any tournament trophy was worth it. Sarah had an idea. She smiled up at him.

"You can have the whole damn tub!"

Jack couldn't help himself.

"I'd pay five," he said.

"Bullshit. You'll pay ten and stop taking me for a fool."

"I've got five thousand, I'll pay another thou when I hit the big one. That's all I can do."

Five thousand! She would have gone down to four to swing a deal—and that was dollars.

"Okay, you help me out and it's a done deal."

Sarah leaned back to give him some air, and grinned. She held out her hand to shake. Jack reluctantly took it. It occurred to him that he wasn't precisely sure of what kind of deal he'd just agreed to.

"What is it I'm helping you with?" he asked.

Sarah replied without looking at him.

"Well, first, you're helping me buy a drink."

It was close to midnight before Jack could convince Sarah that any more drinking would come out of her five thousand and that they should leave. Sarah was miffed at first, but brightened considerably when Jack pulled the bottle of Jim Beam from beneath the seat. She held the bottle in her lap like a baby as they swung onto the road.

"Oops! This isn't the way to my house, sugar," she said, peering out the window. "I don't think, anyway," she added.

She looked at Jack.

"Your store and that tub full of worms is out this way and that's where we're going," Jack informed her.

Sarah concentrated for a moment.

"Oh, yeah. Those goddam beautiful worms."

She took a long pull from the bottle and passed it to Jack. He wiped the top off before taking a drink and returning it to her. They drove in silence for a while, then Sarah giggled. Jack ignored her. She giggled again. Jack glanced over.

"What?"

"I wish I could see that idiot's face when he tries to figure out what happened to his damned old worm tub," said Sarah. "We'll tell him the Martians came down and took it. He'll believe it."

Jack tried to picture the scene and started giggling too. Before long, Sarah had tears streaming from her eyes and Jack was pounding the steering wheel and swerving all over the road.

Deputy Rawlins, parked by the last convenience store on the way out of town, saw them go by and instinctively reached for the ignition. He stopped with his hand on the key. That had been Sarah Bremmer in the passenger seat, he was sure of it. He settled back. He wasn't up to dealing with Sarah tonight. He went back to browsing his Guns and Ammo magazine.

At the old house behind the Lunch-n-Lube, Dog dreamed. He was lying in a field enjoying the shade of a large tree. Out in the field, in bright sunlight, he watched hopelessly fat bunnies romp though the clover. They were slow, they smelled of chocolate, and they kept coming closer to where he lay in wait. It looked as if he wouldn't even be forced to move from the shade to snap up one or two of them. Suddenly he was awake.

It was dark and something was wrong. His ears perked and his nose sifted through reams of data from the air. The visions of bunnies faded as he rose to his feet and eased his way to the back door. On sultry nights like this it was left open for whatever cooling breeze might choose to enter. Don't laugh, sometimes it happened.

Dog stopped in the doorway. There were muffled voices. He held himself very still and sampled the night air. Traces of liquor, tobacco, perfume, and human body odor drifted through the air. Dog's olfactory processing geared up for battle intel, deciphering the myriad of scents. Two people; one a male with hints of fish discernible under the beer. The other... The other... An image of Sarah Bremmer flashed into Dog's mind accompanied by her shrill voice and a twinge in the ribcage from a well-remembered kick. The fur rose along Dog's spine and his ears flattened to his head. He instinctively crouched lower and slunk through the door, seeking the shadows, becoming the deadly hunter he was born to be, preparing to battle to the death, to kill or be killed, to rip and slash and ignore the pain his enemies may inflict, to die if need be, in order to protect, to defend....

To defend Leonard? The idiot with the pressure washer? Dog straightened, padded back inside, and lapped Leonard's face to wake him. Dog would let the idiot fight his own damn battles.

Leonard woke up and pulled on his overalls. He looked through the closet seeking the right weapon. There was a broom with the bristles worn to nubs, a rubber mallet, and a rifle he'd inherited from his dad. It was a turn-of-the-century lever action .32 Winchester Special. Unfortunately, a bad reload had expanded a casing and the retractor had pulled off the cartridge rim, so the gun was useless. However, the rubber mallet looked plain silly, so Leonard grabbed the Winchester anyway. He ran across the field and hid behind a pile of rusty 55 gallon drums. Sarah and the Fisherman, John Q. Smith, were trying to hoist the worm tub into the back of the pickup. Dog nudged Leonard and twitched his head toward the scene.

"I'm going, I'm going," Leonard whispered to Dog. He gathered his courage and stood up straight. Dog trailed at his heels.

"Scuse me," Leonard said.

Smith started and dropped his end of the tub. One of the claw feet landed square on his boot.

"Goddam, goddam," he screamed, "get this thing off me."

Leonard leaned the rifle against the wall and grabbed the rim of the tub. All three lifted and Smith pulled out his foot. He collapsed and rubbed the boot. There was a large crease across the toe. Sarah, reeling from alcohol and exertion, walked over and picked up the rifle.

"This is it, idiot," she said through gritted teeth.

She worked the action and aimed at Leonard's head. He looked at her with puzzlement.

"I would have given you the hundred bucks he was giving me. This place is mine. I'm tired of you standing in the way of my plans. Say good-night."

She pulled the rifle tight against her shoulder and braced for the kick.

She pulled the trigger. Click. She tried levering in another cartridge. Click.

Leonard walked up to her and slugged her in the jaw. Her feet evaporated and she keeled over. Smith struggled to his feet and tried to limp to his truck.

Leonard grabbed his collar and pulled him to where Sarah lay.

"You're not leaving this thing here," he said, pointing at Sarah.

They clasped the sides of her muumuu and heaved her into the back of the pickup. Leonard scooped some dirt and worms into a coffee can. He handed it to Smith through the truck window.

"I don't care to see you around here no more," Leonard said.

Smith pulled out without a word. Leonard watched until his running lights disappeared. He looked at his fist with wonder.

"Pow. Did you see that, Dog? Pow, one shot, instant KO. Somebody call that black guy with the wild hair, I'm the champ."

Dog scowled a dog scowl, did his best to project his telepathic request, and looked at Leonard expectantly.

Think you could knock out a can of dog food, champ? Saving your ass makes me hungry.

After a minute of watching Leonard try to muscle the worm tub back into position, the loyal and heroic Dog gave up on the idiot and looked around for a ripe garbage can to knock over.

CHAPTER 13

Thursday Morning, May 22

GLEN

Glen rose slowly from sleep. His hand felt like it was being stung by ten million fire ants. No, more like it was being dipped in boiling acid. He was still dressed, though DeeDee must have pulled off his shoes. DeeDee slumbered. She didn't look comfortable stretched longways across the bed, nude, and wrapped in a sheet up to her waist. Glen admired her breasts. The sight almost distracted him from the roaring pain in his hand. The air-conditioner was off and the room was stifling. He spent a few minutes watching a drop of sweat inch toward her nipple.

He could see her damp clothes hanging on the shower curtain in the bathroom. The contents of her purse were spread on the dresser to dry: random pieces of paper and some greenbacks. He took a quick count: she had sixty-six dollars. Glen didn't remember where he was or how he got there. He carefully moved his head and looked around. It was a cheaply furnished room, it could be anywhere in the United States. He saw a cockroach scurry across the bathroom floor, so he assumed he was still in Florida. He had to piss but did not want to move. Eventually he turned over and sat up. This is going to be bad, he thought. It was.

He pissed and tried to look at his hand. The T-shirt bandage was crusted with blood and dirt. Something had to be done, and soon. Glen wrinkled his nose at the tub clotted with mud and grass from DeeDee's bath. When he was done pissing he sat on the bed and rubbed DeeDee's back. She groaned and tried to push his hand away. He moved his hand down and massaged her ass. She had firm buttocks and a small tattoo of a butterfly on her hip.

"I'd love to feel your butt all day, but we gotta get some medicine for my hand. I need you to go find some Peroxide and some bandages."

"Let me sleep."

Glen swatted her hard and raised his hand to do it again.

"All right, damn you. I'm up," she growled.

"I need some hydrogen peroxide and big bandages."

"Where am I going to find that stuff?"

"There's got to be a Wal-Mart around here someplace. Look in the goddam phone book."

She found the address and location on a map in the phone book. She put on her damp clothes and ran a wet comb through her hair. Glen had her bring in his laptop computer from the car and guided her to plug in the modem.

"Get some food, some Pop Tarts or something. And some milk, whole milk, not the low fat stuff."

"Sure Glen," she said sarcastically, "I'll pick up some health food. Shall I get you some Twinkies too?"

"Yeah sure, that would be okay."

"Asshole," she said as she slammed the door.

"Bitch," he replied.

Glen logged into a hypertext database and racked his brain for keywords. From a Veterans Administration file server in Atlanta he got some names of medics who served in the Vietnam era. He crossed those with 305 area codes.

This left 47 names. He scrolled through them. A name popped out of the screen and screamed through nearly 30 years and into his brain.

PFC Glen Wilson was only 20 years old but he looked older due to being hung over and strung out on diet pills and beer. Jack "Chopper" Reynolds pounded his fists on the counter. Chopper had Captain's bars on his hospital jersey and his sleeves were stained with blood.

"God damn it! Somebody get out here!" Chopper yelled.

Glen rolled his eyes and threw down his pinochle hand. He walked through the maze of stacked crates and faced the captain.

"Shit," he growled. "What the hell do you want? We're off-duty. Come back tomorrow."

"You dipshits have a box of scalpel blades for me."

"We do not."

"Check your fucking manifest, the damn things arrived the day before yesterday and I need them."

"You want frozen chicken, we got frozen chicken. Jungle boots, size 8? No problem. We don't have your slicers."

"*Look here, Wilson. You guys can steal all the Baby Ruths and cigarettes in Saigon, but don't screw with my medical supplies. Find yourself in my hospital and you might wake up unable to count to 21 anymore. Got me, asshole?*"

Steve Stephens came out of the can hiking up his pants. He rolled up his magazine and stuck it in the front pocket of his cammies.

"*Glen, don't dick with the Captain. His stuff is over on D-7.*"

Steve grabbed Glen's arm as he brushed by.

"*You never know when you're going to need one of these guys,*" Steve said.

Glen jerked his arm away.

"*I don't like doctors.*"

"*That's your problem. You got a bigger problem if they don't like you.*"

Glen spit on the floor and walked into the warehouse.

"*Bullshit,*" he said.

They watched him disappear behind the crates.

"*Hey, Steve.*"

"*Hey, Chopper. Don't mind Wilson, he's a pinger. How goes the battle?*"

Chopper Reynolds. Who would have thought? Glen found a classified ad on one of the commercial on-line services. Chopper had a veterinary clinic just outside of Delray Beach. When DeeDee came back Glen was standing in the parking lot. She rolled down the window.

"What's up?"

Glen walked around the cab and jumped in.

"Go back to Highway 91 and head south. I've got an old friend who'll sew me up."

The sign hanging on a chain outside said Morikami Pet Center, Jackie Reynolds, DVM. Glen grunted. Jackie? He pushed the door open with his shoulder. A bell tinkled. A tall fiftyish woman dressed in a crisp and blinding white dress moved briskly down the hall. Her eyes were drawn immediately to the dirty T-shirt on Glen's hand. The woman looked familiar, like she was Chopper's sister. Glen held out his hand.

"You gotta help me. Please call the doctor."

She looked concerned. She ushered Glen and DeeDee into a small examining room and started cutting away the cloth with stainless steel scissors.

"Gosh, what a mess," she said huskily. She had a soft voice which Glen found sexy. He focused on a corner of the ceiling and tried not to faint.

"Oh my. Did you save the finger?"

"No, it was too screwed up."

She waved a long finger at him. Her nails were painted with pale pink enamel.

"Always bring them in, we can usually save something. You always were an asshole," she said gruffly as she carefully filled a syringe.

"Do you know what you're doing? Where's Chopper?"

She froze.

"It's been a long time since anyone called me that," she said dreamily.

Glen had a sinking feeling. He looked at her carefully. Her short grey hair was pulled back in a neat bun. She wore light make-up and delicate wire-rim glasses. She looked back at him calmly. Chopper.

"Jesus Christ on a fucking crutch." Glen stumbled over his words. "I can't... you didn't?"

DeeDee looked back and forth between them. She hadn't quite caught up yet.

"I did," Doctor Jackie Reynolds said, waving the syringe slowly in front of his face. "Look, Wilson, do you want the damn morphine or not?"

Glen didn't reply. He looked at his hand, then the door, and then back at his hand. He flopped down on the examining table and held his hand out.

"Will you quit fucking around and patch me up?"

DeeDee sat down on the guest chair. She pulled a Twinkie out of her purse and started eating it.

MANNY

Manny's body felt achy and leaden. The motel room was dim from the heavy curtains and hot because the air conditioner had not been turned on yet. He had been ignoring the telephone, but it was still ringing insistently. The girl—he couldn't remember her name—was sleeping on his arm and it was numb. He poked a hard finger in her breast. She groaned and rolled over. He ran his fingers through his hair and peered at his face in the mirror as he pissed in the bathroom sink. He was hung over and the sheets had left imprints on his skin. He scratched his hairy chest and shook a few yellow drops from his penis. He walked naked to the phone. It had been ringing at least ten minutes.

"Yeah," he grunted.

It was Luis.

"Manny, the cops found Wesley in the swamp by the landing. Dead. Stabbed in the chest. The gator had been at him. No sign of the guy except someone in Belle Glade said they saw him heading toward Miami."

"Well shit, Luis. I'm sorry. You sit tight and I'll take care of this."

"No, Manny. You find him, then I take over. This guy's got to pay. This is blood."

"Okay, Luis. I'll find the guy if I can. Then he's yours, brother."

"I want the girl, too."

"No problem. I'll take care of it."

Manny put the phone down. He lit a cigarette, grabbed a beer from the minibar, and walked to the window. He pulled the curtains open and stood blinking in the bright morning sunshine.

"Is this really about a stupid drugstore wallet?" he mumbled to himself.

A girl of about eight sat on the edge of the pool outside and stared intently at him. She tapped the shoulder of another little girl who was swimming and pointed up at Manny. They giggled and looked around for someone else who might be interested in the large nude man standing in the window.

MURPHY

Murphy was talking on a public phone. Webster stood nearby shifting from foot to foot like he needed to pee.

"I made it to Seattle fine. I'm tired but in one piece," Webster listened-in on Murphy's side of the conversation. "I don't know if you're feeling anything like I'm feeling..."

"I don't want to go too fast either, I just think..."

"Yes, okay. Look, you take care, all right?"

"Good-bye."

"I didn't know you had a beau," Webster said.

"Just leave me alone," Murphy said, sounding depressed.

"Murphy, I got a convertible for the same price as a sedan, isn't that cool?"

"What did you do that for?"

"What do you mean?"

She grabbed his sleeve and pulled him over to one of the terminal windows.

"What do you see?" she asked.

"Well, it's raining."

"Why do we want a convertible if it's raining?" Murphy asked patiently.

"Maybe it will stop."

"You've never been to Seattle before, have you?"

"No, so what?"

"Shut up. Let's get out of here."

LEONARD

Mr. Benford was Everglades City's Most Valuable Player. He'd earned this title the old-fashioned way: he'd inherited it. Granddaddy Benford had been The First Banker of Everglades City back when there was a Model 73 Winchester repeater set inside the vault door in case some uncivilized yahoo tried to make off with the hard-earned wealth of Lincoln County's prominent citizens. Today, things are much more civilized and advanced and the Winchester has been replaced with a fully automatic Colt AR-15.

Business was simple and the bank flourished. Granddaddy Benford's oldest son, Daddy Benford, had done a fine job of keeping the bank afloat during the Great Depression with short-term, high-interest loans the more adventurous locals needed to purchase hardware and supplies. The hardware was used to convert their cash-poor crops into more profitable commodities. The hardware included mash boiling pots and copper tubing. The supplies included corn. The product was profitable commodities like quart jars of Uncle Chester's Elixir ("It'll cure what ails ya!") and Martha Wilson's Snake Bite Medicine, popular in the homes and barrooms of Miami.

Business in the 'Glades was slow following Prohibition, but Daddy Benford made a real killing after WWII selling off the farms and businesses of war-widows who could not keep up their payments or work the acreage. Patriotism rung like a bell in the Glades.

The extended Benford family had a reunion each year on Independence Day, renting the local high school cafeteria for the event. This year no less than seven of the eldest attendees had served in The Big War. The war that demonstrated how true power was based on industrial and economic strength. The incredible technological advancements made possible and necessary during the short years of the war strengthened the nation's already blossoming fascination and belief in the Miracles of Science. (Insert images of thin black ties and white short-sleeve shirts, black horn-rimmed glasses on earnest young white men with short black hair, shown in grainy black and white on a big screen in the darkness of the local movie theater. All scratching complex formulas on a blackboard with raspy white chalk. Some things will always be black and white.)

The Wheels of Progress are lubricated with money, and Leonard had none.

The current Mr. Benford's air-conditioned office was appointed in pseudo-luxury. Persian (rayon) rug. Walnut (veneer) desk. Classic (print) paintings adorned the mahogany (stained pine) walls. The banker read in silence while Leonard bobbed his head and shifted his hat around in his hands. Benford sat behind his more-or-less walnut desk occasionally looking down his nose at Leonard. There were several reasons he looked down on Leonard: because he'd had his desk and chair placed on a three-inch platform; because he'd had three inches sawed off the legs of the only other chair in the room; but really because he was simply a pompous ass.

Benford's bank held notes on every major business and farm, legal or otherwise, for a thirty-mile radius. Leonard didn't know or care about that. He only knew that he needed money to build his dream, and Benford was the only real money in town. So, he'd donned his Sunday clothes, scraped a little at a stubborn chili stain on the wide lapel of his polyester sport jacket, and cleaned his boots with a broom to get the worst of the mud off. It would just have to do. He slicked up his hair with Brylcreem and took his battle plan to the Great Man Himself.

The current Mr. Benford had Leonard's sheets of Big Chief notebook paper in his hands and rimless glasses on the end of his narrow nose.

"Do all this yourself?" he asked with some disdain.

Leonard beamed. Benford scratched at some of the letters.

"Is this crayon?" Benford asked.

Leonard stood and leaned over the desk to see.

"Oh. No sir, that there's just something got spilt." He grinned with pride. "It's all done up proper, with a pencil."

Leonard pulled a two inch stub of a pencil from his shirt pocket. The eraser was worn down to a nub.

"That's nice, Leonard. Sit back down."

Benford leaned back in his chair as if fearing something might 'get spilt' on his new paisley power tie. He leaned forward again.

"Do you know how much of a capital outlay you're looking at here, Leonard?"

"No sir, I'm not going to the Capital, I'm staying right here."

Benford shifted to the second page, shaking his head.

"No, I mean, you want a full garage? Hydraulic lift? Mini-mart, deli..."

He turned back to the first page. "And what's this about a 'gator pond'? Are you sure that's legal?" He pushed his glasses onto his forehead and continued.

"Clem was barely breaking even out there, Leonard." He set the papers down and clasped his hands. "And frankly, if he and Willie-Joe weren't drinking buddies, he wouldn't have passed the county inspection the last time around." Banker Benford looked out his bay window into the parking lot and thought important thoughts. "The place is not worth bringing up to code, but the land is worth a little something." He made a command decision. "You think about it, Leonard. If you decide to sell, the bank will be more than fair, I'm sure. We can pay a couple of thousand." He smiled tightly and held out his hand.

Leonard leaned over the desk, shook his hand and said, "Oh, I wouldn't sell the place, uh-uh!" He gestured at his papers. "So, when do I get the money?"

Mr. Benford hung his head for a moment. He stood up, walked to the door, and called his assistant.

"Mary! Could you come in here, please?"

Benford met her outside the door, whispered a few words to her, waved her through, and left for an early lunch. Leonard thought Mary was a goddess. Mary thought Leonard was a few apples shy of making a turnover. Mary's clinging red dress exhibited a lot of ex-cheerleader thigh and gym-enhanced chest development. They shook hands. Leonard found it nearly impossible to raise his eyes above her neckline. She asked him to sit again, pried his hands off hers, and bent down to explain.

"Leonard, you have done a fine job here," she said, waving at his business plan, "but the bank simply is not going to give you any money."

"I know, Mary, but I need the money to put in one of those sandwich cases and to dig the Gator Pool. You see? Leonard's Lunch-N-Lube, Gator Petting Zoo, and Gator Rodeo. There won't be any trouble paying back the money and I'll pay some extra for your trouble. I'll pay some interest too, if you want."

"Leonard, how can I put this gently? You're an idiot. We can't give money—stop looking down my dress!--to people with shit for brains. You see what I'm saying?"

Leonard was unconscious, still working out the details in his mind. "Will I get the money in cash?" He was half out of his chair.

"Leonard..." She crossed her arms and obscured Leonard's view. Leonard sat back down. "You're not getting any money, Leonard! You're not getting any money! We're not giving you, renting you, selling you, letting you smell, or letting you anywhere near any money! You're just NOT GETTING any money! I'm sorry but that's the way it is. Okay?"

Leonard stared at the floor, then stood slowly. He placed his hat on his head. She sighed and walked over to him.

"Oh Leonard... I'm sorry." She gave him a small hug.

Leonard looked up with a dazed and baffled look in his eyes. "I know you're not GIVING me money. I know all about that. You don't have to treat me like I'm stupid." He paused. "I know it's a loan and I have to pay it back." He put his hat on. "Can I have my loan money now?"

Leonard stood in the bright midmorning sun outside the bank not exactly sure what he'd done to deserve his treatment. You didn't need to be a genius to know that beating customers with a file folder was hardly a good business practice. Leonard would not beat his gas station customers, not unless they really deserved it. He'd talk to Mr. Benford about Mary next time he went to the bank.

It was a truly gorgeous day and already too warm and sticky to be wearing a sport coat. He tossed it in the back of his truck and slapped the hood. Good old Truck. As he walked around the front he noticed he'd left the lights on again. They gleamed feebly. No problem, he was parked on a little hill. He opened a package of Red vines, they were soft and spongy from the heat. He shoved a wad in his mouth. He released the parking brake and the old Dodge started groaning down the slope backwards. When he figured he had enough speed built up he ground the gearshift into reverse and popped the clutch. The old truck bucked and roared to life in a cloud of blue smoke. He slammed on the brakes and skidded to a lurching halt in the middle of the street. A baby blue Acura

Legend swerved to miss him, clipped a parking meter and newspaper stand, and strewed papers across the sidewalk. Leonard didn't notice; he was planning his improvements and what he would do first when he got the loan money.

He was in gear and headed out to his place with his elbow firmly planted outside the window and eager to flip the Lunch-N-Lube CLOSED sign back to OPEN. He didn't see the red light at Main and Oak. Three cars slid to a screeching stop in his wake. He had a good head of steam up now with the fenders flapping in the breeze and rust-tinted dirt swirling behind him from the bed of the truck.

He did not notice the jacket fly out of the bed.

He swung onto the county blacktop, Highway 29, pushing the envelope at a blistering 40 miles an hour. Truck was running good today. Good Truck. By the time he hit milepost 13 he had seven exasperated drivers stacked behind him, weaving in and out of oncoming traffic and searching for an opportunity to pass the goddamned pinhead weaving down the highway in the piece of shit truck.

Truck. Dog. Lunch-N-Lube. Red Vines. Big Plans. It was truly a wonderful day.

CHAPTER 14

Thursday, Around Noon, May 22

MURPHY

"Wilson's an asshole."

Murphy and Webster were at ICC Corporate Headquarters in Redmond, Washington. They drove up I-405 in blinding rain, bumper to bumper from Southcenter to the I-90 interchange. Their average speed was a maddening 25 miles per hour. They found the ICC building surrounded by evergreens in a business park. The company president, Lance Parker, led them through a maze of office cubicles and introduced them to a portly man, Dean Grayson. He had thinning black hair and thick glasses. He wore a neatly trimmed beard that ran over his double chins. Dean's office was a generic ten foot square of carpeted pressboard linked to dozens of other ten foot cubicles of carpeted pressboard.

It was a soothing lavender maze for the rodentia of the Info Age rat race. The air was filled with the sounds of clattering keyboards and people yammering on telephones.

"We already know he's an asshole, Mr. Grayson," Murphy said patiently. "We're looking for some additional background."

Murphy gave a stern look at Webster to stop him before he could add anything. Too late.

"Mr. Grayson—may I call you Dean? Thanks," Webster said in one breath.

Webster turned to meet Murphy's gaze. She raised her eyebrows assertively.

"Shut up," she mouthed silently.

"You shut up," he mouthed back.

He snapped his attention back to Grayson.

"Dean-o," Webster continued, "we suspect Wilson is involved in a highly sensitive situation." He paused for effect. "Extremely sensitive. That's why I'm here. High profile cases are, well, rather my specialty."

Grayson toyed with a gold plated mechanical pencil and glanced at his Macintosh e-mail icon. No new mail. He picked up his phone. No messages waiting. He looked at his Franklin scheduler. Meeting in twenty minutes. Born to middle management. Born to be mild.

"Again, what flavor of Feds are you?"

"Mr. Grayson," Murphy explained patiently, "I believe we've gone over all that. Special Agent Webster is with the FBI and I'm from the Florida State Police Investigative Division."

"But you're really some kind of federal spooks, right?"

Webster raised a hand to silence Murphy, then stood. Grayson stuck his pencil in his pocket and rolled his chair back. Webster approached the desk and tossed his identification in front of Grayson for the second time.

"Look, Dean-bo, this is an ongoing investigation within the geopolitical boundaries of the United States of America. The CIA, the NSA, and the Girl Scouts do not have jurisdiction in this matter. Your wife doesn't have jurisdiction in this. I do. The EFF—BEE—EYE." He snatched his identification off the desk and stalked back to his seat. Murphy rolled her eyes. Webster caught her.

He leaned over and whispered "What?"

"Fly. Your fly is wide open."

She stood and smiled at Grayson while Webster checked himself.

"Mr. Grayson, we—"

"You, little lady, can call me Dean," he interrupted, smirking. Murphy's black wool skirt had shrunk in the last wash. She'd packed in a hurry and hadn't noticed. Now she was stuck, wishing she'd worn something less revealing. Like an old potato sack. Murphy sighed inwardly. She hated to use her sex, but it might get them out of here more quickly.

"Dean. Thank you. Call me Murphy." She hesitated and smoothed her skirt around her thighs. "We're not exactly sure what Wilson's up to. We know very little about the man. What motivates him. What he may be trying to accomplish, if anything. We're hoping you can fill in some of those blanks for us." She sat on the corner of his desk and dangled a leg. She wore glossy white hose. "For me."

Grayson stared at her leg. "Well." He licked his thin lips. "Wilson's been with us for a while now." His eyes flicked up. Murphy shifted her weight a little. "We've had some complaints, but nothing that would warrant action, not when weighed against his results. He's nailed us some big accounts."

Murphy stretched her leg out and idly scratched her kneecap. Dean and Webster were hypnotized.

"What kind of complaints? From clients? Co-workers? What kind of results? What exactly does Wilson do? What's your personal relationship with the man? Help me out here, Dean." Grayson didn't respond. "Dean?"

"Oh. There's been some ethical questions, like some of his deals were a bit more involved than what was in the contracts."

"Is that uncommon?"

Grayson looked up. "Of course it is. Everything we do here is completely above board! We're a Fortune 1000 company with a fine legal department. Integrity is vital to our corporate image." He looked nervous. "You're really just after Glen Wilson, nobody else?"

"Cross my heart, Dean." Murphy slowly traced an X across her left breast. She wore a cream colored blouse with a flowery embroidered pattern. Dean's eyes followed her finger, then darted toward a desktop photograph of a smiling middle-aged woman and two kids wearing braces.

"He doesn't socialize much with the crowd around here. That's been a bit of a problem. He blows off meetings and doesn't show up at work for weeks sometimes. Some of our customers love the guy, but others won't do business with him at all."

"He's really just a salesman?"

"Yes." Grayson frowned. "Like I said, he's landed some major deals for me. For us, I mean. For the company."

"He seems knowledgeable about computers. Like he's a programmer or hacker or something," Murphy said, peeking at the papers on Grayson's desk.

"Yeah, right. He doesn't know jack-shit, pardon my French. He talks big, but he doesn't even have a degree. Not even a two year one. Me, I graduated from UC Davis, Masters, 1980. Technical, not liberal arts."

"That's fine," Murphy said. She pointed to a framed picture. "Your wife?"

"Oh, that. No. Well, yes, technically. But we're, she's out of... We're separated. More or less. Not legally. Yet. But we're seeing other people all the time. Constantly, it's an open marriage. Well, not me. I don't do that. I mean I do, I would, of course." He tugged at his tie.

"Warm in here. Damn Facilities people. You folks okay? Can I take your jacket?" The question was directed at Murphy, but Webster piped up.

"Thank you! But no, I need to keep my jacket on." He lifted a lapel to show his shoulder holster. "Glock 19, no less. Ever seen one? Excellent weapon. Fires a supersonic 32 grain round at…"

Murphy broke in.

"Are you and Wilson close, personally?"

"Close? With Wilson?" Grayson looked surprised. "Nobody's close with Wilson. He's in a world of his own. Nut case, if you ask me." He glanced at his watch. "I really don't know what more I can tell you. I have a meeting in ten minutes. It's my meeting, so I have to be there." He lifted his schedule book as evidence. "Maybe we could continue this conversation over wine at dinner?"

Webster stood and extended his hand.

"We understand, Deanovich. We don't want to keep you. We have just about all we need. Thank you for your time, you've been most helpful."

They shook hands. Dean's eyes were glued to Murphy's thighs. Murphy poked Webster in the side.

"Could you wait for me in the lobby? I just have one more question for Dean, a little thing I need to clear up."

"Pardon me?" Webster stared at her. He looked at Grayson, then back at her.

"Please, it'll just take a minute."

"Whatever." Webster waved a hand. "Do what you want."

He turned and walked out. He was grumbling as he left. Dean smiled at Murphy and Murphy smiled back. She stood and smoothed her skirt. She leaned over the desk.

"You're holding out on me," she whispered. "This is a federal investigation and we're not fucking around. Talk to me now or you'll be wearing this skirt in a federal pen, is that clear?"

Their eyes were six inches apart. Murphy's were narrow slits.

"I, uh, what? You, I don't, what? I thought…"

"You think with your dick, that's what. Wilson's pulled a lot of shit. You're his boss and you're in on it. Talk to me now or your next stop is McNeil Island."

Grayson paled. He stood up and looked over the top of the cubes. The room was strangely silent.

"Not here," he whispered. "Follow me."

He grabbed his scheduler and led her down a hallway until they reached a darkened conference room. "In here."

Grayson flipped a light switch and closed the door. He motioned Murphy toward a chair.

Murphy slipped her hand in her purse.

"You sit. I'll stand," she said.

He sat and ran a hand over his face.

"I'm not sure what you expect. Should I have an attorney present?"

"I don't know. Should you?"

"You said you were just after Wilson."

"That's correct, that's what I said."

Murphy didn't offer more. Grayson stared at the table, then spoke without looking up.

"Glen doesn't hang out with any of the employees. The only person he's friendly with is the janitor. An old guy named Tyler. I have no idea why, the guy stinks like a cesspool, and hasn't bathed since the seventies as far as anyone can tell. Perry Tyler, lives down by Seward Park in the Central District."

"What else," Murphy said, scribbling in her notebook.

"Okay." Grayson exhaled wearily. "We've done a few kickback deals. Christ, everybody does that. Just chump change, nothing big. I don't know half of what that guy does! No one does. He's probably got dirt on most the execs in this company." He blinked a few times, raised his eyes. "Maybe that's why he let me in on those deals?"

"Gee, think so? Maybe he helps you because deep inside he's such a nice man."

Murphy picked up Grayson's scheduler and started paging through it.

"Are you really separated from your wife?"

"This is harassment."

"Precisely. This looks like your wife's pager number. Do you have an ironclad prenuptial? Maybe I could give her a call?"

"You bitch."

"You, Mister Grayson, run the inadvisable risk of pissing me off."

She dropped the scheduler and pulled the stainless .357 from her handbag. She carefully pointed it at the floor. Dean's eyes widened and he sat very still. Murphy studied the gun, flipped out the chamber, and checked the loads. She flipped it back closed.

"When was the last time you heard from Glen?"

"I got some e-mail a couple of days ago. He says he's tracking a major deal. Probably bullshit. Working some major deal with the girls at the pari-mutuel or something. He said he'd be a little late getting back. The usual crap from Glen."

"Did he say where he was or where he was headed?"

"No."

"I'll need to see that mail."

"I deleted it."

"Where was it from?"

"I don't know. He can dial up his account from anywhere."

"I'm aware of that. Answer the question, please."

"I don't remember."

"You don't remember." Murphy made it a statement. She slid into a chair and placed the gun on the table in front of her. Grayson relaxed a little.

"I didn't need to! I just send messages to his account here at work and he can have them forwarded or access his account remotely. You'll never find him that way."

"I don't know." Murphy smiled. "For one thing, you're going to help. You're going to forward a copy of all future correspondences to this address."

She ripped a page from his scheduler and plucked his mechanical pencil from his shirt pocket. She scribbled down a number.

"You really think that's going to work?"

"I'll tell you what I think, Dean-baby. I think most of the secretaries in this building would just love for you to get your balls shot off." Murphy smiled and picked up the gun. "But that would be too messy." She put the .357 back, snapped her purse shut, and leaned over the table.

"I think you're dirty," she whispered. "I think this whole company is dirty. Maybe I'll recommend that the Justice Department launch a full investigation into this shitty little pigpen. Then you'll cooperate, one hundred percent." She clipped his pencil to the sheet of paper and slid it across the table. "Don't lose that, okay?"

She stood by the door with her hand on the handle. "Your meeting is in two minutes, Mister Grayson. You better go splash some water on your face."

Grayson was flushed and sweaty. He wiped his bald head with a handkerchief as she left the room.

She was humming softly as she made her way to the lobby. Webster was pacing in the reception area. He stopped as she approached. He faced her with his hands on his hips.

"Interesting technique," he complained.

"Don't start with me."

"Why didn't you just unbutton your blouse and wave your tits in his face?"

"The man's a pig. I used that. Now shut up."

They signed out of the guest log and headed for the exit. They stood watching rain pour down on the parking lot. It didn't look like there would be any break in the next month or so. The cloud cover was a low solid mass.

"Grayson gave me a name of someone Wilson hangs with." Murphy looked at her notes. "A guy named Tyler, a janitor."

"Wilson is friends with a janitor? Does that make sense?"

"Yes, actually it does," Murphy replied.

"Murphy?" Webster said hesitantly after they stood silently for a moment.

"Yes?"

"Are you involved with anyone?"

"Forget it, Number Three. N-O-Y-F-B. That means none of your business. Don't let this train of thought even enter your mind." She hesitated. She stared dreamily across the parking lot. She drew an unrecognizable shape on the steamy glass, then wiped away the image with the back of her hand. "I'm sorry," she said. "I shouldn't be so rude."

She smiled. Webster had not seen her smile before. The world seemed brighter and gravity eased its hold by a fraction.

"Tell me something, Webster. Would you do something for me?" Murphy asked.

"Yes, sure, anything," Webster replied eagerly.

"Okay. Would you pull the car around so I don't get wet?"

She smiled sweetly and waved her eyelashes.

"Sure, Murphy," Webster replied, rolling his eyes.

LEONARD

Leonard was intently painting a sign as the Paulson Fuel truck rumbled in. The driver, Horace Paulson, swung out of the cab and walked over to Leonard. "Leonard!" he hollered. Leonard jumped up. His brush and black paint flew through the air.

"Gosh, you scared me," Leonard said accusingly.

"Sorry, Leonard. Didn't you hear the truck?"

"No. How do you like my sign?"

They stood side by side and looked at it.

Undor New MA\an Owner
No Mor Water in the Gas
Git Red Vines Here

"Very nice, Leonard," Horace commented. "Don't you have a dictionary?"

"What for?" Leonard asked.

"Forget it."

"Come on, look." Leonard grabbed Horace's hand. "I'm going to put a real lift in the garage, I'm going to have a 'gator pond out back… This place is going to be better than Disney World. People from France are going to visit."

"I need to talk to you, Leonard," Horace said.

Leonard turned. His eyes were shining with ambition.

"Did you come to fill the tanks? I've sold a lot of unleaded the last few days."

"No, Leonard. I can't give you any gas. Clem hasn't paid for the last delivery."

"Wait a minute. I need gas. How can I sell gas if you won't leave me any?" Leonard sensed his dream fading away. "I can't run no gas station with no gas."

Leonard's eyes got misty. Dog raised his head and growled at Horace.

"Come on, Leonard. I can't give the stuff away. Clem didn't pay the bill."

Leonard's eyes narrowed. He chewed his cheeks. A look came over his face similar to the one his dad had when negotiating the sale of a quart to a preacher.

"I have money, I can pay."

"Send a check to the office. When that clears, I'll come back and fix you up," Horace said.

"No. Come with me now." Leonard led the way to the office. "How much do I owe you?"

Horace pulled a notebook out of the bib of his overalls. He leafed through it.

"A hundred and six dollars and forty-four cents."

Leonard crawled under the desk and pulled out a pickle jar. It had a tape on it that read $134.72. He handed it to Horace.

"Okay. Now we can have gas?"

Horace lifted the jar to look inside. It was packed with bills and coins.

"Geez, Leonard, can't you just send us a check?"

"There's nothing wrong with this money. You take it and pump me some unleaded."

"Okay, Leonard, okay. We'll credit the extra to your account," Horace sighed. He threw the jar into the cab of his truck and started hooking up his hoses.

Leonard jumped on Dog and gave him a big hug.

"We got gas, Dog! Nothing can stop us... Nothing can stop Leonard Allen Mullins."

He jumped up, whirled, and kicked his boots in the air in an impromptu dance.

"All right!"

Horace watched the scene with wonder as he filled the tank.

GLEN

Jackie tore a last piece of tape and applied it to the bandages on Glen's hand. Glen's arm looked like a giant cotton swab. Jackie sat back in her chair and rubbed her forehead with a paper towel.

"That's better," she said.

She turned to DeeDee and put out her hand.

"We haven't been properly introduced. I'm Jackie Reynolds."

"I'm DeeDee."

She shook Jackie's hand. Jackie's hand was large and soft. Warm. "Well, DeeDee No-Last-Name, you can call me Chopper if you like, I guess."

"I've never met a... uh?"

"Transsexual?"

"Yeah, I've never met a transsexual person before. Did you?" She made a scissor mime with her hand.

"Yeah, all the way. Look, let's get some tea. You like Earl Grey?"

"I've never met him, but some tea sounds fine," DeeDee grinned.

"Ha ha. Okay. Come this way. Glen will be out for a few hours if we're lucky."

Jackie led the way down the hall. DeeDee dawdled and looked at the prints and photographs hanging on the wall. A blurry picture showed eight or nine muddy guys standing by an old truck. DeeDee studied the faces and located one with a vague resemblance to Jackie. Jackie with three days' beard and a cigar.

Jackie walked back to look at the picture.

"You?" DeeDee asked.

"A long time ago. In another life," Jackie said.

"Do you have any old pictures of Glen?"

"No, why would I?"

Jackie waved DeeDee to follow.

They walked through swinging doors into a small kitchen. It was color coordinated and spotless. Jackie poured some bottled water into a teapot and adjusted a gas flame under it. She brought out some delicate china cups with a bluebell design.

"Aren't you and Glen old friends?" DeeDee asked.

"No. Lemon and honey in your tea?"

DeeDee nodded yes. She sat at the dinette table.

"What happened to Glen's hand?" Jackie asked.

"His finger was chopped off with bolt cutters. He's been messing with some people he should leave alone. They—well actually, I stole his wallet. Glen is determined to get it back. I don't know what we'll do now."

"Did Glen get his wallet?" Jackie asked as she poured steaming water into the cups.

DeeDee shook her head no.

"Then Glen will keep trying to get his wallet back." Jackie pushed a jar shaped like a honeycomb across the table. She squirted lemon extract from a lemon-shaped bottle into her cup.

"You must be kidding," DeeDee said, raising her eyebrows. "That would be suicide. He was lucky they just chopped off his finger. Next time they kill him."

"Glen won't care as long as he gets buried with his wallet."

"He has a fetish about wallets?"

"No. He's just an asshole. Let's talk about something else."

They sipped their tea for a minute.

"So... you were a man and now you are a woman?"

"That about covers it."

"That must be strange for you."

"Well, life's a bitch and now I am one." Jackie said.

"Very funny," DeeDee said.

"Let's not talk about that, either," Jackie said.
They sat, sipped their tea, and said nothing.

CHAPTER 15

Thursday Afternoon, May 22

MURPHY

Webster was driving and Murphy was navigating. They were on Highway 99, north of Seattle almost to Lynnwood. The scenery was an endless landscape of car dealers, Burger Kings, and topless dancing joints. They were looking for Glen's mother's house. They were close but the area did not look promising.

"There!" Murphy called out. She pointed a rolled-up map at a house across the cement lane divider. They had to drive another quarter mile before they could turn around and go back. The house was huddled between a Costco parking lot and a huge discount furniture store. Webster parked the car on the shoulder of the highway. The yard was filled with trash: aluminum cans, soggy newspapers, and a dead cat. Paint peeled from the siding and the roof was a bright emerald green from the moss. Some depressed daffodils were growing limply in a planter in front. A hand-painted sign stood on a tilted pole. It said:

Real Estate Agents Fuck Off

"I've seen places like this before," Murphy commented. "People refuse to sell even after the neighborhood has been zoned commercial. A ratty little place like this could sell for a half zillion or so, but they still won't sell."

The clouds had lifted but a misty drizzle oozed from the sky. They got out of the car and walked up to the front door. Webster pressed the doorbell and knocked. An old crone with a few missing teeth threw open the door and waved a pistol between them as if she couldn't decide whom to shoot first. Webster stepped into the lilac bush beside the door. Murphy took a step back, then made a realization.

"It's a squirt gun, Number Three."

"Damn right, babe," the old woman said. She turned the barrel around and shot a stream into her mouth. "Smirnoff," she cackled.

Webster brushed water from his soaked slacks. His mouth was compressed to a tight line. The old woman returned a hand-rolled cigarette to her mouth where it waved beneath her mustache. Her squinting eyes glittered through the smoke.

"Get your ass off my goddam porch," she growled.

"Mrs. Wilson, take it easy, we're from the FBI." Webster waved his identification.

"I don't give a rusty rat's rectum if you are from God, you assholes. Fuck off."

"We're here about your son," Murphy said, trying to peek around the woman into the darkened house.

"Did that cocksucker finally kick the bucket? Tits up? Bite the dust? Boot Hill? Is he buzzard bait?" She paused to catch her breath. "Did he pass on and exit this veil of freaking tears?"

"No, Missus Wilson."

"Well, if it's about the bodies rotting out back of his place, you'd think you shitheads would learn a damned lesson. Wetlands, National Historic Registry Site, Indian Burial Grounds, Endangered Species Act, et-fucking-cetera. You can't dig back there. Now leave me alone!"

Murphy exchanged a glance with Webster.

"If we can just ask a couple of questions we'll be happy to leave you alone."

"Where's your warrant? Besides, you'll leave me alone if I blow your bloody moron pin-heads off, won't you?" She reached behind the doorway and tilted the barrel of a rusty side-by-side shotgun out so it could be seen.

"But the mess, the noise," Murphy said patiently. "Might be less fuss if we just sit down and chat a minute. Off the record."

Webster elbowed Murphy. "Off the record?" he hissed. "What do you mean off the record?"

"Off the record," Murphy said firmly.

Mrs. Wilson lowered the pistol.

"If it's off the record then you got 10 minutes."

She waved them in. Mrs. Wilson plopped herself onto a threadbare old Lazyboy. It was surrounded by untidy heaps of romance novels. A small Japanese TV perched on a flimsy stand a few feet in front of her nose. Murphy gathered a stack of TV Guides from the couch and stacked them on the floor to make room. Webster leaned against a fireplace that clearly had not been used in many years.

"Have you heard from Glen in the last few days?" Webster asked.

"I ain't talking to you, sonny. I'm talking to the lady."

She picked up a novel that was splayed open on the arm of her chair. "Have you read this one? This is a good one."

Murphy shook her head no. Mrs. Wilson peered closely at the cover.

"No, it wasn't this one. Here it is."

She found another one and passed it over. Murphy looked at it and shrugged her shoulders.

"I'll send it to you when I'm done."

Webster cleared his throat to get Murphy's attention and pointed at his watch. Murphy waved him off.

"Mrs. Wilson?" Murphy asked gently, "have you heard from Glen in the last few days?"

"You're a pretty one. This isn't one of those paternity things is it?"

"No," Murphy chuckled, "this is one of those computer things."

"Well, I hope this computer thing don't take long, Montel's on at one. Do you want to watch it with me?"

"No ma'am. Can you tell me the last time you saw or heard from Glen?"

"Glen doesn't come by much. He sends a check when I need money, that's about it. Unless he needs money, then I see him. I think Montel's talking about one of those computer things. We should watch it."

Webster was upset.

"This is going in circles. Back off, Murphy, let me handle this one for a change." He crouched beside the old woman's chair. "Look, you shriveled up old bitch. I'm with the FBI. You answer the questions or we're going to have some trouble. Serious trouble." He grabbed her arm and squeezed.

"I think that was a threat." She craned her neck to make eye contact with Murphy. "Is this limp dick threatening me?"

Murphy stood resignedly and reached for Webster. The old woman waved her off. "It's okay," she said.

"Hans!" she shouted.

A muffled answer came from a room down the hall.

"I'm on the Nautilus, damn you, leave me alone."

"Hans! Come here a minute. Hans!"

"Goddam it."

A door in the hallway opened and a blond monster came out. He was wearing Speedo trunks, a weight lifter's belt, and a torn Madonna tee-shirt. His body was glistening with sweat.

"What's the problem, you old bag of shit."

He spoke with a Danish accent. His eyes were deep blue and he had at least a size 24 neck.

"Shut up, Hans. This guy is flipping me some hassle. Would you rip his arms off for me please?"

"Can't you handle this little punk by yourself?" Hans nodded politely at Murphy.

"I'm a tired old woman."

"Bullshit." Hans carefully draped his towel across the back of a chair and stalked toward Webster. Webster stumbled backwards until his back was against the fireplace. He fumbled his Glock and it fell to the floor. He grabbed a poker from a rack by the fireplace and waved it threateningly. Hans laughed with a deep rumble.

"I'm working out now. If you want to play later, that's fine. Until then," he said, waving a sausage-like finger in Webster's face, "you be nice to the old shrew. Okay?"

Webster's face was paper white. He nodded slowly. Hans turned and grabbed his towel. Murphy admired his wide back. Hans was no less than a 300 pound slab of muscle.

"You'll make me some soup, Hans?" Mrs. Wilson said petulantly.

"After Montel, just like always."

He lifted her liver-spotted hand and gave it a gentle kiss, then rambled back down the hall. The house shook when he slammed the door closed. Webster's knees gave way and he slid down the fireplace until he was seated on the hearth.

"Some bodyguard," Murphy commented as she sat back down on the couch.

"That's no bodyguard, that's my boyfriend," the old woman said, winking and leering.

MANNY

Manny leaned against a pillar at the front of the hotel and looked at his watch. The men he was waiting for were late. He saw the van pull around the corner. It was a Ford Aerostar, all tricked out; a low-rider with chrome wheels and dark tinted windows.

Manny crushed his cigarette out on the pillar, flicked it into the shrubbery, and walked down the stairs to the van's passenger door. He pulled it open and jerked his thumb at the rear seat. Caesar grumbled but got out and jumped in the back while Manny swiveled into the front seat. Manny exchanged gang sign and handshake with James, the driver. James was one of Manny's oldest employees. He turned and shook hands with the guys in the back. They were Hector 'Heck' Pedrigo Jimenez, a former cop from Nicaragua. Heck looked bored. After shaking Manny's hand he returned to cleaning his fingernails with a large Navajo Skinner knife. Leon, who never used a last name, held a boxy looking Cobray M-12 machine pistol on his lap. He'd worked with Manny almost as long as James had. Leon had a bad eye and his head constantly rotated on his shoulders like a snake to make up for it. The last guy, Caesar, didn't know his original last name, but went by Chavez because he thought it was funny. He had a scar across his neck and part of his ear was missing. He looked like a junkyard dog with his three days' growth of beard, hanging jowls, and stumpy lump of nose. He was the new guy, recently thrown out of the US Marine Corps for a heroin habit. He wore a cammy jacket that still had the Chavez name tag attached.

"Whose idea was it to do this in the middle of the fucking afternoon?" Chavez said. "I don't think this is smart."

Manny glanced over his shoulder at Chavez. He twisted around, grabbed the name tag, and ripped it off, then turned back around. He threw the name tag out the window.

"Nobody asked what you think," Manny said. He poked James in the ribs.

"What do you think?"

James crushed his cigarette butt in the ashtray.

"I'm paid to drive. You want me to think, I get a fucking raise."

He chuckled over his joke, then reached between his legs and pulled out a map. "What's the cross street again?"

Manny grabbed the map from his hand.

"You nuts or something?" He opened the glove compartment and tossed the map inside. "The downtown bangers see a map, they'll think we're tourists or just fell off the boat." He checked the next street sign. "Besides, I know this area. We want the third street up, hang a left."

The guys in the back were arguing about the movie Pulp Fiction.

"The briefcase must have been filled with gold, man," Heck said.

"Bullshit, it would have weighed hundreds of pounds," Leon replied. "It had to be some radioactive shit, the way it glowed."

James looked in the rearview mirror.

"What are you guys talking about?" he said.

"That John Travolta movie, the one with Samuel Jackson, you know?" Manny said. "That's a great-ass movie. You never saw it?"

James shook his head.

"Naw, I don't watch TV. Too busy."

"Not TV, a movie. Busy doing what?" asked Manny.

James shrugged.

"I got the garden, the wife, two kids." He snorted. "I'm in the fucking PTA!"

The car burst into laughter.

Manny pointed.

"That's our street."

He pulled a stainless steel Sig-Sauer 9mm from the open glove compartment and looked over at James.

"This thing's clean?" he asked.

James glanced at him and nodded slightly. He eased a sawed-off shotgun from beneath the seat. He flipped his blinker and swung into the left turn lane. Manny screwed a silencer on the Sig's threaded barrel.

"You still use steel shot in that hog's leg?"

"Yeah," James replied. "Lead's bad for the environment, man. Don't you read the papers?"

Heck stuck his head between the seats.

"Don't you lose penetrating power?" he asked.

Manny pushed Heck back.

"You guys ready?" he said.

There was commotion from the rear.

"You're sitting on my clip."

"Is this yours?"

"Aw, man! There's chocolate on my heat."

Manny rubbed his temple for a moment, then spun around in his seat.

"Goddammit! If I'd wanted Girl Scouts, I would've RENTED Girl Scouts."

"I don't think you can do that," Caesar said from the back seat. "Can you do that?" he asked Leon.

"No, I don't think so. If you have a worthy cause they might volunteer. You know, maybe mop up the blood. I can get you a number to call. They don't make as much money off the cookies anymore."

Manny and James exchanged irritated looks. James checked the mirrors.

"Bunch of goddam comedians. Looks clean, we going in?" he asked.

Manny scowled and jerked a thumb at the back seat.

"Park down the street and we'll see if these clowns have their shit in a pile."

Manny turned and addressed the men in the back.

"Gentlemen, quit joking around, we have our business to take care of. Let's get serious," Manny lectured. He noticed Chavez struggling with his clip.

Fucking junkie, he thought. "Chavez, you stay with the car."

James frowned as he backed the car into an alley.

"Uh, pardon me." He turned to look at Manny and scratched his stubble of beard. "But if the loser's staying with the car…"

"Then you're coming in with us," Manny snapped back. They stared at each other. The car became silent. James' eyes narrowed and Manny's eyes widened.

Caesar broke the silence.

"Who you calling a loser, homeboy?" he demanded.

James swiveled in his seat, grasped the knife in Heck's hand, and jammed it into Caesar's chest. Caesar said, "Huh, huh, huh" and slumped forward. He came to rest with his head on the back of James' seat with his eyes wide open.

Heck pushed the body over and wrenched out the knife. He looked at James with disgust as he started cleaning the knife and his hand with a napkin. James turned to Manny.

"Guess I'll be staying with the car?" he said, half question and half statement.

Manny slowly lowered his weapon to the floor. James' shotgun tracked all the way. Manny spread his hands and showed them to James, palms up, a gesture perhaps older than bipedal locomotion.

"Sure, James, you stay with the car."

James relaxed. Manny twisted in his seat and grabbed a handful of Caesar's hair. He looked into his eyes. Nothing.

"It's okay, James," Manny said, "the fucker was pissing me off too." He dropped Caesar's head back to the seat. "But, we're a man short now. You are one crazy motherfucker, you know that?"

"I simply prefer to stay with the car, okay?"

"Fine," Manny said, shaking his head. "This damn job. You know, it's not about the money, the drugs, or the babes. It's about power."

"It's been a few years now, Manny," James said. "When does this power thing kick in for me?"

Manny scanned the street with some field glasses.

"Soon," he said.

Leon poked his head between the front seats again. "Chavez is bleeding on me. What we gonna do with him?" he asked.

Manny spoke without lowering the binoculars.

"James made the mess, so he'll take care of it." He shoved the binoculars into the glove compartment and picked up the Sig. "Right, James?"

"Sure. We gonna do this, or what?" James said as he checked his watch. "Let's move it, I gotta take my youngest to the dentist."

"Okay, it looks good, swing around the back." Manny looked over. "You should've said something earlier, family always comes first," he reproached him.

James pulled out of the alley and swung the car onto the side street.

Manny tensed as they approached the apartments. He looked in the back.

"You Girl Scouts ready?" he asked.

Hector nodded and Leon raised his machine pistol. Manny spun back around as James braked to a stop in front of the complex. The car doors opened and the three men, minus James, strode to the front door casually with their weapons held down at their sides. An old man slouched on the steps with a paper bag between his legs. He shook his head as they approached.

"I told 'em," he muttered, "I told 'em not to be messin' with you, Manny."

Hector raised his pistol. Manny stopped the barrel as it rose.

"How's your eyesight today, old man?" Manny asked.

The old man shook his head again.

"Oh, it ain't so good today, can't see a thing, Manny."

He offered Manny the bottle. Manny declined by raising a hand. The old man nodded and pulled the bottle back.

"You was always a good boy, Manny."

Manny started for the door with Hector right behind him. Leon grabbed the old man's bottle as he passed and took a long pull before handing it back and following the other two into the building. The old man peered into his bottle.

"And you was always a piece of shit, Leon."

Manny led the way down the hall not bothering to check the numbers on the doors. The building was strangely silent and the hallway empty. They came to an emergency stairwell and Manny pointed to Hector. "Open it," he commanded.

Hector grimaced.

"Why me?" he asked as he put his hand on the bar. He opened the door and stepped through, not bothering to hold it for Manny and Leon. Manny caught the door before it struck him in the face. He held it for Leon and glared at Hector's back. Manny elbowed past and led the way up the stairs.

"You know, I met Al Pacino once, and he said..." Manny started.

"I'd kill my mother for a face like yours," finished Leon.

Manny stopped at the landing.

"Who's telling this story?"

"Nobody," said Leon, "because I ain't listening to it again."

Manny stared at Leon. He waved his gun at Hector.

"Heck hasn't heard it," Manny pointed out.

"I've heard it," Hector said. He pointed at the door. "We gonna do this, or what?"

Manny took a step closer to Hector.

"What did you hear?" Manny said as he poked his 9mm into Hector's chest.

Hector looked down to the barrel and back up to Manny's eyes.

"Hey, that story's all over town, man. People think you're the next Scarface."

He gently pushed the barrel of Manny's 9mm to the side.

"And the next time I see that in my chest I'm gonna shove it up your ass and squeeze off a few rounds, understood?"

Manny and Hector stared at each other. A bead of sweat formed on Hector's brow.

"How about those Buccaneers?" offered Leon, nervously.

"Yeah, how about 'em," Manny muttered, looking at Hector.

"Dolphins are the better team," Hector said.

Manny smiled.

"You got some big cojones, Heck. I like that." Manny turned to face the door. "Sometimes."

He checked his weapon and spoke without turning around.

"Okay. It's the third door on the left. We're a man short, so no screwing around. No shooting unless you have to. We just grab the stuff and leave, got it?"

He didn't wait for an answer. He stepped forward and tried the door handle. He hesitated, released the doorknob, and stepped back. He nodded to Hector.

"You open it."

Hector rolled his eyes.

"Sure, boss," he said as he stepped past and through the door.

Leon followed Hector with a carefully blank expression on his face. The three of them grouped outside the door to the apartment. Hector took a deep breath and tried the doorknob. It was locked. He stepped back and raised his eyebrows at Manny. Manny nodded at Leon. Leon stepped up and raised his silenced machine pistol. He firmed up his grip. Manny and Hector backed away and Leon fired several short bursts into the hinges with the skill of a surgeon. He moved to the side and raised the barrel of his gun towards the ceiling. Hector pushed the door with the flat of his hand and it fell over. Manny gestured for Leon to watch the hallway. The two men moved into the room.

Inside, two girls were sitting on a ragged couch peering with fear over their shoulders. They had a big bowl of popcorn between them. Oprah was ranting and raving on the television. Heck darted in and out of the other rooms checking for other occupants. The place was empty. He nodded at Manny. Manny walked to the couch and looked at the girls. They were young, around sixteen.

"Hi, girls," he said.

"Hi," the bleach-blond managed to say in a high pitched voice. She had short hair that stood straight in the air as if she was being electrocuted.

"My name is Manny, the handsome fellow with me is Hector and you can call him Heck. The guy outside is Leon." He looked at them expectantly.

They looked at each other, then back at Manny.

"I'm Holly and this is Tanya," the blond said hesitantly.

"Okay, Holly and Tanya. I think you know why I'm here."

Holly nodded yes and Tanya nodded no.

"So, where is it?" Manny asked Holly, running the pistol along the part in her hair.

She flicked her eyes toward the kitchen.

"Let's get it, then."

He gestured with the pistol. Holly got up slowly and walked to the kitchen on shaky legs. She moved a toaster and pried a piece of paneling off the wall.

Manny held out his hand and she handed the paneling to him. It had magnets epoxied to it to hold it in place.

"Clever," he said. He showed it to Heck. "Ever see anything like this?"

Heck shrugged his shoulders. He went back to the living room to keep an eye on Tanya. Holly pulled out a cigar box and put it on the counter. Manny flicked the lid open with the barrel of the pistol. The box was crammed with plastic packets filled with powder that looked like brown sugar. Manny got to admire the stuff for about ten seconds before hell broke out. Leon did not notice the silenced 22 that poked around the corner near the floor. His body hitting the floor made more noise than the gun. Looking over his shoulder, Manny saw Heck turn his back on Tanya. Tanya lunged, spilling popcorn everywhere. Heck stiffened as her thin knife entered his heart from behind. He tried to turn but collapsed, dead before he hit the floor. Tanya turned toward Manny. He took careful aim and placed a slug in her left eye. Holly ducked and tried to get away but Manny grabbed her by the collar and dragged her around the breakfast bar.

He whispered to her with white-hot intensity with the 9mm stuck under her chin.

"You've heard of me and you know what I can do for you and you know what I can do to you. You help me or you die. Make up your mind now!"

She closed her eyes for a moment, then nodded yes. Manny took a Navy Arms TT-Olympia 22 from the back of his belt and worked it under her shirt.

"How many are there?"

She held up two fingers.

"Go tell them I'm dead."

She took a deep breath and nodded. She got up and walked to the kitchen door.

"Guys, it's me. We got them all."

The pair looked into the room suspiciously. She walked into the living room and kicked Hector hard. He didn't stir. She knelt by Tanya and stroked her hair. Her hand came away sticky with blood. The guys came in and took a quick look at Hector. They walked slowly into the kitchen. Holly stood up and pulled out the 22. She took a couple of steps forward and fired into the tall guy's head from about two feet away. The other turned to find the gun pointed at him.

"What the hell, Holly?" he said.

"Sorry, Jimmy," she replied as she pulled the trigger.

Manny popped around the breakfast bar and scooped up the cigar box. He grabbed Holly's arm. He idly looked over the bodies.

"Come on, Holly. We gotta get the fuck out," he said.

She nodded and grabbed a suitcase from the bedroom. They ran down the stairway and flew out into the alley. The van was still running but James' head was hanging out and dripping blood down the door.

"Shit. We need wheels," Manny said. "You got keys?"

Holly nodded yes and pointed at a big Chevy Custom/10 pickup. She tossed Manny the keys over the hood and swung into the cab. The V-8 roared to life and Manny hit the throttle. They could hear the sirens approaching as they pulled into traffic.

"That was intense. Shit," she said. She patted her chest. "Man, I thought my little heart was gonna burst."

Manny relaxed a little as they pulled onto Pine Island Road.

"My mouth is as dry as the Mojave," she said. "There's a Mickey D's up ahead. Pull in the drivethrough so I can get a soda, will you?"

Sounded good to Manny. They ordered happy meals and large drinks.

CHAPTER 16

Thursday Afternoon, May 22

LEONARD

Leonard pointed a dirty finger at Dog.
"Sit."
Dog sat.
"Good Dog. Here, have another Red Vine."
Dog took the licorice around the corner and dropped it behind the worm tub. He returned wagging his tail. Dog thought it was best keep to the idiot amused, at least until he finished chewing through the pressure washer hose.

The humugity kept the tourists at bay, or at least in check. Maybe the lack of attractions contributed. Leonard wasn't sure. He'd spent the afternoon clearing sawgrass behind the station. He staked off areas for the "Gator Rodeo" and "Gator Petting Zoo", but other than a few handmade signs there wasn't much to see. From the middle of the road his signs looked small and... drifty. His mother's word, used to describe any manner of things. Things like Leonard's attention span. He stood in the middle of the baking asphalt contemplating his drifty signs as an 18-wheeler swung into the lot in a cloud of choking dust and the pounding of aged jake brakes.

Leonard stared. He'd never had a big rig in the station before. He wondered how much gasoline they'd want. He might have to tell them to move along to another station and hope they wouldn't get mad. As he approached he noticed the unusual paint and insignia. A huge 'DOCTOR ZALOOQ' emblazoned the side of the trailer in letters seven feet four inches tall. Leonard had a gift for such things. Everybody had at least one gift, or so said Billy-Joe-Esther in the morning's Sunday meeting. Nobody asked about the 'Esther' part of his name since the incident.

The passenger door opened while Leonard was cautiously approaching . A burly man with long red hair and a matching Viking beard jumped to the ground.

"Diesel?"

Leonard hesitated. "Well, I sell all kinds of stuff, got a special on seashells this week, month." He pointed to a drifty sign.

The man removed his sunglasses and wiped his forehead with a shop towel. His sleeveless khaki shirt revealed faded tattoos on his beefy arms. He looked at Leonard's signs. He looked at Leonard. He looked at Leonard's signs.

"Gator Petting Zoo?" His boots kicked up dust as he walked over to the cleared area. "Where's your gators?"

"Don't have the gators yet, gotta get a permit. I'm low on unleaded, how about premium, no extra charge?" Leonard trailed along like an anxious puppy.

(Can we, Spike, huh, huh? Whaddya say, Spike?)

"Gator Rodeo? That'd be something to see."

The truck's horn blared. The Viking raised his arm and stuck out his middle finger. He started back to the truck with Leonard in tow.

"So, you got diesel here or what, pal?"

"Diesel?" Leonard caught on. "Diesel?"

"Yeah, you know. Diesel. Makes truck go vroom vroom."

"I can mix a little premium with #2 heating oil, that makes a good diesel."

Red Burly Man replaced his sunglasses and clapped Leonard on the shoulder.

"Great idea. You wait here and I'll talk this over with my partner."

He left Leonard standing in the dust and climbed on the driver's side running board.

"Got some odd kind of idiot here but no diesel."

The driver looked a lot like Red Burly Man, except he was a Blond Burly Man.

"Well shit, Red." He tapped a gauge on the dash. "Maybe we should turn around. We might make it back to that last station." Red checked his watch.

"Then you'd better drive like you know what you're doing." He stepped down, then reached up and opened the door. "Screw that noise." He pulled himself back up. "Get over, I'm driving."

Leonard watched in dismay as the truck used all of the available space to swing a one-eighty. It narrowly missed several of Leonard's signs before pulling back onto the road. Red tooted the horn and raised an arm as he vroom-vroomed past. Leonard sighed. Dog came over slowly swishing his tail.

"Nice guy, huh, Dog?" Leonard dropped to one knee and scratched behind his ears. Then he scratched behind Dog's ears.

The afternoon sun baked the Lunch-N-Lube from a different angle from the noonday sun. Other than that there was little difference. Business was slow and Leonard spent most of the day clearing weeds and brush until about 3:30, when the group of potheads and their VW bus rattled in again. An ancient motorhome pulled in behind them. By the time Leonard could walk over from his clearing, both vehicles had emptied and the station swarmed with '60's throwbacks.

"Look here, dude."

"Check this out."

"Too cool."

"Told ya."

"Man, this place is too weird."

"Hey, catch the inside!"

"I'm 'zoning."

"Anybody got a quarter?"

"Heavy."

"Hey! Get a picture!"

"What's this?"

"Shoulda brought the chicks."

"We did."

"Oh."

"Where's the camera?"

"Is it open?"

"We should get a place like this."

"This is a nexus of power."

"No, it's an axis of power."

"I have an anus of power."

"Where's the crazy dude?"

Leonard and Dog lurked behind the corner. They poked their heads around at the same time. Dog whined and backed up with his tail between his legs. Leonard felt like doing the same, but this was his place, his station. Besides, they'd seemed friendly enough the last time. They even bought some Red Vines. He took a deep breath (what was that smell?) and came out from behind the building.

"Uh, hi, guys!"

The entire group stopped and stared. The silence broke with a scrambling from inside the station as another half-dozen burst onto the porch to stare. Leonard decided to try a grin.

"Dude!" One that Leonard recognized spread his arms wide and laughed.

"Hah ha!" He was spun in a circle. "What's up with you, man?"

Leonard didn't know what to say.

"Well." He tried another grin. "Not too much. Uh, yourself?"

Another that Leonard remembered rushed forward and embraced him in a crushing hug.

"Brother! You're real! No one believed us when we got back to Tampa."

This one wore a loose cotton serape and dreadlocks pulled back into a braid. The strange odor was very strong. A sweet cloying smell, rather pleasant. He swept Leonard around with an arm around his shoulders while he waved at the group of hippies.

"Friends all! Brothers and sisters, come to share the vibes and absorb the dude's karma. I haven't felt this righteous since Captain Trips passed on to the next dimension."

He gave Leonard another hug before stepping back. He kept both hands on Leonard's shoulders.

"We had the most amazing trip, dude," he continued, "after we left here the last time. Like beautiful. All of us. Just beautiful. Your soul, man. It's incredible. Beautiful."

He beamed the biggest smile Leonard had ever seen. Leonard began to grow embarrassed at the flattery, though he had no clue as to what any of it meant. At least they seemed to like him.

"Well, thanks. I like you too. And you uh—" he searched for something nice to say, "—smell good."

As the afternoon waned, the amazing Leonard found himself the object of respectful adulation. His overalls exposed a few patches of skin where his guests had covertly snipped a piece. He was poking a questioning finger through one of the holes when Braids appeared.

"Brother! We have a union that requires your blessing."

Braids stood in front of a small group gathered by the gas pumps. He spread his arms. A couple of skinny teenagers held hands nervously. The girl wore a garland of dandelion flowers and kudzu. They were both barefoot. Their feet were filthy.

With the crowd clapping and chanting the couple walked slowly until they were facing Leonard. Leonard didn't understand what was happening and looked for some escape. The crowd was silent and they looked at Leonard expectantly. Leonard's eyes flicked between the young couple. He racked his brain for something to say. Someone sneezed.

"Bless you," Leonard said on reflex.

"Well said, brother," Braids cried.

The couple embraced while the crowd clapped their approval.

Leonard's new friends parked on the edge of the clearing and were busily setting up tents and tables and tarps and chairs. They took care to avoid the staked off areas. One of them worked on Leonard's drifty signs. The colorful new Gothic letters were easily visible from the road.

Leonard watched uneasily. They seemed so friendly that he hadn't been able to say no to anything they asked. A willowy girl in jeans and poncho threw a stuffed animal for Dog to chase. Dog seemed delighted at the attention. His tail wagged furiously as he barked for more.

As evening fell it began to get cool. The breeze made things almost pleasant. Leonard was thinking of closing up when the same 18-wheeler from earlier in the day braked to a shuddering halt on the far side of the road. Red leaned out the window.

"Hey!" Leonard jogged closer. "You seen a car painted like this truck go by here?" Red asked.

Leonard thought back carefully.

"Nope."

Red pulled his head in and looked at his partner who was fussing with the controls of a cellular phone.

"Well?"

"It's still toast, man. I can't raise anybody. Nothing, not even static."

He slammed the phone into the console. "We're hosed. Totally screwed."

"Aw, shut up. We got until tomorrow night." Red leaned out the window again. "How do we get to Clearwater from here?"

Leonard thought for moment.

"I don't think you can."

Red blinked a few times. *Okay*, he thought.

"You got any maps in there?" He nodded towards the station.

"Sure! I just bought all kinds of maps!"

Leonard was elated. He had yet to sell a map. Red swung the truck into the side of the clearing opposite the campers and left it running as he climbed down. The hippies came running. They walked around the truck, leaving hand prints on the dusty sides. Red followed Leonard over to the shiny new map display. Red searched through them.

"Kentucky, Tennessee, Texas." He frowned at Leonard. "You got any Florida maps in here?" Leonard frowned back.

"No. We're *in* Florida. Why would you need a map of Florida?" Red blinked a few more times.

"Of course. What was I thinking?" Red said. He looked around. "How about a telephone?" Leonard pointed. "Great."

Red lifted the handset and punched a few numbers while Leonard looked over his shoulder. Red listened to a recorded message and looked questioningly at Leonard. Leonard gave him a sheepish grin.

"No long distance, Clem didn't pay the bill. Sorry."

Red slammed the handset down. He tilted his head back and closed his eyes.

"How far to the next town?"

Leonard had to think.

"About fifty miles, but they're closed after five o'clock."

Behind his shades, Red's blinkers showed signs of wearing out.

"The whole town is closed?"

Leonard nodded. Red brushed past without a word, walked across the parking lot, pushed through the crowd, and climbed into the truck. Blond Burly Man looked hopeful.

"Well?"

"We sleep here tonight."

The late afternoon sun kept things warm. A thin cloud cover moved in and a light breeze kept the campers comfortable and the mosquitoes down. Red and Blondie abandoned the truck to take advantage of a tarp's shade. They regaled a few of the girls with strange tales of life on the road with the Doctor Zalooq show.

Leonard finally gave up for the day and flipped his sign to "CLOSED". He loaded a wheelbarrow with ice, pop, tea, and junk food. He trundled it over to the clearing with Dog playfully nipping at his heels. The head with the braided dreads met him with open arms.

"Join us, Brother!"

Leonard kept his distance.

"I brought some food," he said.

Red grabbed a bag of peanuts.

"Got any beer in there, pinhe—, I mean, uh, Brother?"

Leonard thought for a few seconds. This might be a good way to get rid of the last of the stuff. He'd already canceled future orders. Leonard did not like beer.

"Sure! Wanna give me a hand?" Red and Blondie exchanged looks.

"I think we can do that."

An old Lincoln limousine swayed on the bumpy road. The driver was nervous. He hadn't heard from the equipment truck in a while and they didn't answer the phone. The step-van and the tour bus, all painted with the Doctor Zalooq logo, made for an odd caravan. The driver tried to figure out a way to break the bad news to the Doctor. The glass panel slid down. Doctor Zalooq stuck his head through the window.

"We lost or what?" the Doctor asked.

The driver glanced over his shoulder to try to gauge the Doctor's mood.

"Sorry, Walter, but I think we are."

Zalooq's real name was Walter Crawley. The crew was docked fifty dollars if they called him Walter in public. The Doctor pointed to the side of the road.

"Hold it! There's the truck! What the hell?" He pressed his face to the glass and looked back. The driver hit the brakes. "Back up. Something's weird here. The damn equipment truck's sitting on the side of the road back there!"

He poked Angela, who had been dozing. She seemed dazed and confused.

"Goddam that Red. He's always pulling some kinda shit," Walter complained.

The driver whipped the limo around and slipped it in neatly beside the truck. The campers gazed in awe at the sight of the truck and the limousine with the matching paint. They cupped their hands and tried to peer into the tinted windows. Braids faced the group.

"Brothers and sisters! I believe it is evident that we have entered an arena of power." He thrust a finger at Leonard. "This man—" Leonard looked behind himself to see who he meant. "—is apparently a Mecca point. Let us honor him."

The hippies lowered their heads in unison. Several mumbled mantras were offered. Red tossed a Bud to Blondie and chortled.

"Looks like they found us. Come on, let's go see what's what."

Inside the limo, Walter made a decision.

"We'll try out our new material here," he said.

He grabbed the bottle of Chivas from between Angela's legs and took a hit.

"Let's get into our costumes."

"We're supposed to be off today," Angela whined, but she did start pulling her gown out of a steamer trunk in the back. She passed Zalooq his cape, cane, and boots.

Walter addressed the driver as he raised the privacy glass.

"Tell the boys to set up the small stage."

"Okay, boss."

The driver weaved through the mingling hippies and found Red.

"The boss says set up the small stage."

"What the fuck, man?"

"What's the big deal?"

"The deal is, you ain't gotta carry the equipment. This is unscheduled. We got a union, you know."

"You tell Walter." The driver looked around. "Ooops, I meant you tell the Doctor."

"Fuck you. This is gonna be overtime."

Red stomped off to get another Bud. Blondie shrugged and followed. Doctor Zalooq waved his hands toward the crowd and smiled.

"This is wild. Look at them. Reminds me of the hippie fairs and craft shows I used to do with Wavy Gravy." He slowly looked around, taking in the setting sun and the backdrop of trees and undergrowth. "Not exactly Madison Square Garden, but I have a feeling about this one. Let's do the works, okay?" He exited stage left, toward his limo. Red lit a cigarette and tossed the lighter to one of the new workers.

"Smoke 'em if you got 'em now, he's in a mood and this could be an all-nighter, know what I mean?"

The roadie threw the lighter back. Red flinched, but he caught the lighter before it reached the ground.

"I don't do that shit, man," said the roadie as he pulled a carrot from a plastic bag he kept in his fanny pack. "My body's a temple." He smiled. "Trade this for that filthy cigarette?" He offered the raw carrot to Red. Red stared at the carrot for a moment, then extended his left hand to the side wiggling his fingers. The roadie's eyes followed. His brow creased in a puzzled frown.

Red slapped him hard with a right hand, knocking him to the ground. Red stepped over the dazed roadie and waved the rest of the crew closer. They moved swiftly, none of them so much as glancing at their fallen comrade who was sitting on his butt wiping dust off his carrot.

"Okay, grunts. We'll be doing the full nine yards tonight, so you'd better get humping, and I don't want to hear any bitching." Red emphasized the last point by waving his cigarette towards the worker he'd slapped, who was up to all fours and about to go for the big one, a full-fledged wobbly two-legged stance. The work crew broke huddle and started for the trucks without a word being said. Blondie, Red's driving partner, stopped at Red's shoulder and handed him a beer. Red pressed the cold brew on his tender hand.

"You gonna deck somebody before every show now?"

"Hell, no." Red switched his beer to the other hand. "Look at this, it's going to bruise up."

Blondie peered closely at Red's hand.

"Yep, it gonna swell. You should wear gloves. Look." Blondie pulled a heavy work glove from his hand. "See? Smooth, no scaly calluses. Women don't like rough hands." Red hesitated, then placed his hand next to Blondie's and compared them. He shook his head.

"Just wearing gloves makes that much difference?"

"Oh, no. I use a good moisturizing hand lotion too. That's very important for healthy skin. Get something with aloe in it," Blondie said.

Red looked up. Their eyes met. Blondie flushed and pulled his hand away.

"Hey, I'm not gay. I used to shack it with a chick that sold Avon, okay?"

He put his glove back on and hitched his shoulders. "We gonna get to work here, or what?" His voice was rough. Red clapped him on the shoulder with his sore hand and winced. They started towards the stage.

The hippies had been joined by some friends and their friend's friends. The occasional lost tourist pulled in to see what was going on and a fair number of the Doctor's crew mingled amongst the crowd selling tickets. Leonard and Dog had retreated to the porch. The crew members were linked with ear pieces and wireless mikes; it was odd to see them silently talking to themselves. The stage was decorated with Arabic symbols: partially dressed dancing ladies, stars, moons, and daggers.

"Hey, Dog. Lot of people, huh?" Dog glanced up at Leonard and swished his tail twice. Dog had never seen so many people and had never imagined so many people even existed.

The crew had set up the stage in record time and the sun still brightened the western sky from beyond the horizon when the speakers came to life bathing the crowd in soothing tones. The carefully composed music would approach something familiar, close enough to touch a memory, then drift away, interspersed with staccato percussion and barely audible effects, sometimes bouncing from speaker to speaker, each swelling its volume in turn, creating an eerie sensation of physical motion. Buried within were subliminal sounds too faint for the conscious mind to decipher, sounds aimed straight at the brain stem, no words for the frontal lobe to decode, but frequencies and rhythms geared to resonate the precise synapses the good doctor wished to resonate.

Doctor Zalooq considered himself an artist and the human psyche was his medium of choice.

The audience quieted. Conversations ended with sentences unfinished and thought trains were lost. The stage lights began to brighten, so dim as to be unnoticed at first as they played over the assembly. The whir of the servo motors was timed precisely to blend with the doctor's music and became part of the effect. The lamp colors flashed at rates calculated to further stimulate specific responses. Hormones flowed, glands secreted, and an underlying theta rhythm began to develop from the confusing array of melodies. From the control room in the trailer, Doctor Zalooq watched the crowd closely. Many of his techniques were empirically derived from continual experimentation. Tonight the theta rhythm would be more pronounced. Later, a video record would be analyzed at length to determine the effect. The crowd seemed ready. The doctor was ready. The equipment was in place. Showtime.

A pair of spotlights illuminated the back door of the van. A recorded drum roll echoed across the parking lot. The door was opened by a crew member dressed in a black tuxedo with clawhammer tails. Doctor Zalooq and Angela appeared. The lights reflected from holographic reflectors made faint iridescent haloes a few inches above their heads. The effect was barely noticeable but it was one of the Doctor's favorite and most expensive tricks. The crew cleared a path through the crowd and Doctor Zalooq bounded onto the stage.

GLEN

DeeDee was watching television while Jackie did some surgery on a pet ferret. She eased the little animal into a wire cage. Jackie checked on Glen and went back to speak with DeeDee.

"Glen is awake if you want to talk to him."

DeeDee shrugged and put the remote control down. She followed Jackie back to the examining room. Glen's face was pale and the dark bands under his eyes made him look like a raccoon. He had a couple days' growth of beard. He looked more dead than alive.

"Am I okay? I feel like roadkill."

"You'll be fine. You need to stay here for a week or so until you heal a bit."

"How long is it going to take for my hand to heal?"

"That depends on what you mean by healing."

Glen closed his eyes and thought about it.

"My idea of healing is when I hit someone in the face, I expect it to hurt them more than it hurts me."

"That's cute, Glen. I don't know. Maybe six months, maybe never. How long did it take to heal the other finger? This will take longer because you're older now."

"That's too long, dammit."

"Glen," Jackie said hesitantly, "maybe there is something we can do. I've been assisting with some animal testing for the University of Miami. It's some new genetic engineering stuff. When you get better we can talk about it."

She prepared another dose of morphine.

"You have some stuff that will heal me quick?"

Jackie swabbed a patch of flesh and inserted the needle.

"It will heal you if it doesn't kill you."

Glen nodded thoughtfully, sailing into the narcotic fog.

"Perfect," he said absently, as sleep claimed him.

CHAPTER 17

Late Thursday Afternoon, May 22

MANNY

Manny stuck the security card in the hotel room door. When the light in the lock turned green he pushed the door open. Holly stood behind him carrying a bucket of Boston Fried Chicken and a case of Miller Highlife. He looked back at her questioningly.

"Aren't you going to carry me over the threshold?" she asked petulantly.

"Okay," he said.

He picked her up easily and carried her. She weighed about eighty pounds. She set down the beer and food and walked around the room peeking through the curtains, picking up stuff like ashtrays and postcards, looking at them and putting them back. At each stop she pulled off some of her clothes. First, her T-shirt and shorts, then her red bra and panties. Manny watched her with disbelief. In thirty seconds she was nude except for her high-top sneakers. She was silhouetted by the bright light pouring through the curtains. She was thin, with bony knees and downy pubic hair. Her breasts were small and bulged straight out, like lemon halves with dark little nipples.

"What?" Manny said.

"I always hated that shit—will she, won't she, the teasing, the stupid sexual guessing games. Let's just fuck, get it over with, then we can eat some chicken. Okay?"

"Okay," Manny said with perplexed wonder.

Manny was at least three times her size and well hung to match. He thought he might hurt her but she was moistened and ready. They fit together just fine.

LEONARD

The music and lights stopped abruptly. The audience jerked. The Doctor smiled, he always liked that part. A murmur of disappointment began to rise from the crowd, fading away in hushed expectation as the stage lights slowly brightened, then flared intensely bright. In unison, the crowd gasped and stepped back. Doctor Zalooq stood at center stage, resplendent in his shimmering cape. Dead silence filled the clearing. Doctor Zalooq smiled. The crowd regarded him with induced fascination, completely quiet. Dog barked. The Doctor's smile froze. There was always something. He mentally sighed. He raised his arms and two young ladies dressed in one-piece bathing suits and high heels appeared from the wings and removed his cape. They smiled at the crowd with their expensive smiles. The Doctor had paid top dollar for their dental work. One leaned close.

"The bugs are eating us up, Doc," she hissed through her smile.

The Doctor nodded and narrowed his eyes, motioning her to get off the stage. He raised his arms higher, palm to palm over his head, then spread them out over the motley crowd.

"Good people! Welcome! Welcome to my humble offering!" His voice boomed from the speakers, shattering the silence and prompting a great cheer from the crowd. One of the technicians flipped a single switch. The music and lights returned to their hypnotic task. The crowd stilled and the Doctor stepped aside as his lovely assistants wheeled a large table to the front of the stage. The table held a single black box about one foot square. The girls retreated to opposite wings, taking the opportunity to give the Doctor dirty looks as they passed by with their backs to the audience.

Doctor Zalooq solemnly regarded the box and silently cursed the mosquitoes and black flies. He'd hear no end of the bitching after the show. He stepped behind the table and raised the lid of the box with exaggerated care, handing it with a flourish to a smiling assistant with murder in her eyes. The mesmerized audience watched closely, frozen in anticipation.

"And just what, could be, in here," intoned the showman.

"A bunny rabbit?" asked someone from the crowd. This was one of Doctor Zalooq's planted employees, right on cue. The Doctor liked to keep the mood lighthearted. The audience tittered and the Doctor smiled condescendingly. That employee and others would also be scanning the crowd for any signs of possible trouble. One could never be too careful, as evidenced by a fiasco long ago on the outskirts of a small Midwestern town. The Doctor had accidentally stimulated an area of the brain related to sexual activity. The resulting orgy had practically ended the Doctor's career. It might have been a rousing success in California, but in the Bible Belt the stunt had almost resulted in a lynching when the people woke and found themselves in random naked arrangements with their neighbors. Doctor Zalooq refrained from that particular combination of stimuli these days, although he kept painstaking records of the cause and effect of his work. It might come in handy later. In Amsterdam, for example: a place on the Doctor's short "must visit" list.

Doctor Zalooq reached both arms into the box and looked up at the crowd. He pretended to be trying to lift something very heavy. The stage lights dimmed and a small spotlight trained upon the box. The Doctor smiled at the audience, removed his hands from the box, and held out his palms.

"No, I think not," he said.

He spread his arms wide to encompass the crowd. "I, Doctor Zalooq, shall raise your level of consciousness, to where you, good people, will tell me what is in this box." He stepped away from the table and the girls arrived to place it at the back of the stage. The audience always thought this part was a scam. It was actually the only part of the Doctor's magic act that was untainted by technology, and it had launched his career. The music had slowly been entwining middle eastern accents into the passages. The lights playing over the crowd slowed their tempo and softened to pastel colors. Atop the speakers, small fans spooled up. A technician in one of the trucks flipped the safety cover from a switch and grinned at his partner.

"Here we go again, filling prescriptions without a license."

He pushed a button and two chemicals met in a fine mist behind the fans. The combination of chemicals formed a thin haze that blew over the crowd, drifting slowly in the still air of the evening.

Leonard watched the show from the safety of the porch, but Dog roamed freely through the crowd, getting his ears scratched and scoring the occasional handout. Leonard figured Dog could take care of himself. In fact, Leonard wasn't worried about anything at the moment. He felt very relaxed and didn't really feel like doing much of anything. Sitting here on the old porch and watching the people and the lights and listening to the music and the words of the fellow on stage was a pleasant way to end the day. Maybe he could talk this gentleman into doing the show more often. Make it a weekly addition to his other planned attractions? He was wondering how much money the show made, when

Deputy Rawlins braked to a stop in front of the porch. Rawlins stepped out and leaned on the open car door, staring at the crowded field in disbelief.

"Jesus Christ, I heard the report on the radio and couldn't believe it. What the hell do you think you're doing here?"

He slammed the car door shut and walked to the bottom step of the porch. The deputy waved a hand in front of Leonard's face.

"Hello? M-B? Anybody home?"

Leonard chuckled softly.

"That's funny, Deputy Rawlins," he said. Leonard reached back and pulled up another chair. "Here, have a seat. Care for some ice tea and a fruit pie?"

Rawlins stared at Leonard.

"No, I don't want a fruit pie, you idiot," he snarled. "I want to know why there's a hundred people standing in a field," he frowned, "a field that wasn't even there the last time I was here, and I want to know how you're involved, and I'd like to see some sort of event license." He paused for breath. "I see no sanitation facilities, no provision for security, and the parking situation's a mess. It's down to one lane out there!" He jabbed a finger at the road. Leonard hadn't noticed that. Maybe the deputy had a point or two.

"Wasn't me, Deputy Rawlins. I didn't plan any of this." He pointed towards the stage with his chin. "You need to talk to him," said Leonard.

Rawlins hitched up his belt and pulled his hat brim lower, glaring at the stage. "Okay, M-B. I'll start with him, but you and I have some unfinished business…"

He started towards the clearing. Doctor Zalooq saw him coming.

The Doctor held a dove in each hand, which he had just materialized from the "spiritual ether" or his sleeves. He was a competent magician in the classical sense, but it was a tough field these days. The big budget performers ruined things with their vanishing jets, statues, and bridges on national television, but the simple tricks were still useful for the Doctor's purposes. Though most people even knew the actual mechanisms involved, it was still a craft, a performance art, and the crowd responded appreciatively. Besides, by now they were in such good humor they'd have cheered at dime-store card tricks.

Doctor Zalooq often dealt with local officials. Each situation required a different approach, and he had become a master at determining the proper course of action. A single small town officer with an attitude could be far more trouble than one would expect. But he had no intention of letting this show go sour. He smiled and bowed with the doves in hand, the bow being an indicator to his assistants that this particular part of the set would be cut short. He held the doves at arm's length and the girls glided to his side with smiles a trifle forced. They didn't bother asking questions. The Doctor was a fair ventriloquist, and spoke though his smile.

"Fuzz. Just one. Ten o'clock." The girls each took a dove and left without a word. They met behind the stage, minus the doves, and began working their way around the edge of the crowd, receiving a barrage of lewd propositions and an occasional marriage proposal. They made a brief stop at one of the trucks to warn the tech controlling the lights, then managed to meet Deputy Rawlins as he reached the outer rim of speakers.

"Good evening, Deputy," said one.

"Come to watch the show?" asked the other.

They each took an arm.

"No," said Rawlins, shaking himself free. "I've come to close it down. This is illegal as hell." He pointed to Doctor Zalooq, who now stood at the front of the stage with his hair on fire and a puzzled look on his face.

"What?" the Doctor asked the audience. "What's wrong?"

The crowd was eating it up, laughing and pointing to his flaming hair.

Rawlins' eyes grew wide.

"How does he do that?" he asked, amazed.

"It's all smoke and mirrors, officer," said one of the girls. She took his arm again and led him beneath one of the speakers. The alpha rhythm pulsed strongly, the lights shifted to concentrate on the deputy's location, and the small fan above the speaker increased its output. Even the girls, who were treated to counteract the drugs, began to relax. They were happier now that the fans were on and the mosquitoes had disappeared. One of them tugged on Rawlins' sleeve.

"Officer? Is this what you're concerned about?" She waited for the deputy to shift his gaze and slowly reached towards her barely covered, surgically improved breasts. The deputy's eyes grew wider still. She removed a slip of paper that would never have fit in typical cleavage and held it out to Rawlins.

"It's a little damp, I'm afraid," she continued. She smiled apologetically. Rawlins took the paper numbly, no longer exactly sure why he'd objected so strongly to the show. He shook it open and peered closely at it in the flashing lights.

"The ink is smeared. What is it, anyway?" He returned his attention to the stage where Doctor Zalooq now levitated three bowling balls overhead and passed a large metal hoop over and around them. Rawlins laughed and handed the paper back.

"I've seen that one before, but he's pretty good. I guess you guys are okay." He smiled at the second girl. "Unless you've got more ink-smeared papers for me to try and read in this light?" The other girl grinned sheepishly.

"We're just a small show, officer. Just trying to make a living, you know?" She nodded towards the audience. "And we make people happy, should that be illegal?" She took the deputy's hands and placed them on her hips as she turned around. They were very shapely hips. "Hang on, I'll get you to the front row," she laughed. Rawlins hung on.

Doctor Zalooq's repertoire of standard tricks lasted about an hour. Tonight he'd pulled out a few old standbys and the show was running a little long. Most of the audience was now sitting or lying prone in the grass. Deputy Rawlins had reached his front row seat, and one of the girls stayed alongside, occasionally pressing herself against him to explain the inner workings of one trick or another. The deputy had worn the same vacant smile for some time now.

The Doctor judged the mood of the crowd, and decided to get to the fun part. He'd noticed some restless stirring in the rear. Couldn't afford to lose anyone with an audience this small. He flashed a hand signal to the truck and the stage lights dimmed. The music gradually shifted from the vaguely middle eastern passages to a complex, hypnotic rhythm pattern, overlaid with softly keening voices and low frequency pulses that went unheard by the audience, save one. Dog heard them, and trembled. He trotted for the safety of the porch. The people in the field came from differing backgrounds. There were the new age hippies, there were Japanese tourists with cameras, retired couples, bikers, teenagers from town, and a compliant deputy sheriff. Some considered themselves worldly and some were not so foolish. All were in for a surprise or two.

Doctor Zalooq waved his remaining assistant from the stage. He disappeared behind the backdrop and returned with a small wooden case adorned with odd carvings. He placed it with reverence on the table. He turned to face the audience.

"What you are about to experience will remain with you for the rest of your lives," he recited. He opened the wooden case and removed several objects, placing them on the table in a precise order. "Throughout the evening, I have sensed that someone among us is in pain, in great need." He placed his hands on his temples and closed his eyes. "Such despair, so much anguish," he intoned.

He snapped his hands wide and his eyes open. "Will that person come to me now," he ordered. He turned his back to the audience and waited. One of Doctor Zalooq's paid flunkies stood up and began working his way to the stage, but Deputy Sheriff Bill Rawlins was much closer, and beat him to it.

The deputy stood and the Doctor's assistant promptly snagged his pant leg.

"What are you doing? Sit down!" She tugged at his leg. He gently pried her fingers free.

"I've got a bad back," he said grinning wickedly. "Let's see if that Doc of yours can fix me up."

He made his way to the stairs at the side of the stage and met the intended "patient" at the bottom. Rawlins placed a hand firmly in the other man's chest. "You can be next," he said as he pushed past. Doctor Zalooq heard the hard heels of cowboy boots as they crossed the stage and smiled to himself.

Many of his own people harbored doubts about the Doctor, not realizing the planted patients were a safety net, nothing more. It was working without a net that kept things interesting. He composed himself and turned to meet his subject. A mental alarm went off when he saw the uniform, but he pushed it to the back of his mind. He greeted the deputy with a warm smile and shook his hand.

"Okay, guys, get to work now. What's the story?" he whispered through his throat microphone to the crew in the van.

"Oh, shit." The more experienced technician snapped upright.

"What? We miss something?" the second asked.

"I wish. Keep an eye on things for a second," the first replied.

He lifted a key ring from his belt and opened a drawer. From inside the drawer he removed another key, then rose from his chair and crossed the width of the trailer to a small panel set into the wall. He opened it with the second key and stared inside for a moment, then toggled a switch and slammed the panel shut. He flipped out a computer keyboard, quickly typed some codes, and a satellite link was established.

"Okay, that's that," he said.

He stopped at the cooler on the way back to his chair and pulled out a bottle of Sprite.

One of the girls reported in. She had lifted the Deputy's wallet.

"Deputy William Rawlins." She read off his social security number.

"Okay. Three minutes, outside."

The Doctor paraded the Deputy around the stage and asked some questions that the Deputy answered with monosyllables.

"What exactly is your problem that you seek Doctor Zalooq's help, Deputy Rawlins?"

"You're the Doc. You tell me."

The Doctor had an idea from watching the Deputy walk. He listed slightly to the left and the movements of his right leg were stiff and slightly wooden. The Doctor could feel some imbalance in his back muscles as he steered him around the stage. He got a report from the van.

"Age thirty-six. Not married. Birthday April Seven. Back injury in a car wreck in 1977. Sees an osteopath in Fort Myers, last visit six weeks ago. Takes Carisoprodol for muscle spasms. An injection of 1147-5 from the U of M with infrared heating will probably work."

The Doctor's crew prepared the treatment. He smiled, thinking of Arthur C. Clarke's words. Something to the effect of: "Any sufficiently advanced technology is indistinguishable from magic". No shit, he thought.

Doctor Zalooq combined his unlicensed medicine with a trade from the oldest world known to humanity. Some years before, after the Doctor graduated from Harvard Medical School (even his crew did not know the Doctor's background), he blew off internship and found himself passing through a small West African nation. With no intention of remaining any longer than it took to find passage elsewhere, he ended up staying for three years. The country is known as Togo and its people call themselves Ewe. It is from there that the roots of some of the Doctor's magic branched, merged with his classical Western medical training, and infiltrated into his connections to the underground medical community.

The Doctor moved to the table. He lifted two objects from the table and turned to face Rawlins.

"Remove your shirt," the Doctor said with authority. Rawlins looked at the objects in the Doctor's hands. The left held what appeared to be a primitive whisk broom of animal hair. The right held a long and crudely shaped black knife. An aluminum flight case was opened. He could see glittering surgical instruments and racks of chemicals. A chill crawled up the deputy's spine.

"I don't think so, Doc."

Rawlins backed away. Doctor Zalooq moved closer. The fans above the speakers and stage had ceased all pretenses of subtlety. They now emitted a heavy white smoke that flowed over and through the audience, over the stage, and over Deputy Rawlins. The Doctor approached to within inches of the deputy. They stood, face to face. The Doctor's eyes glittered.

"You will remove your shirt." His voice held gravel and it rasped through Rawlins' mind. The deputy felt hands working at the buttons of his uniform. He looked down. They were his hands.

Braids, the unofficial leader of the New Age hippies, squinted at the stage through the mind-numbing fog. There was a lot of activity on the stage but he couldn't make out what was going on. He glanced at the person next to him, who happened to be an aluminum siding salesman from Tampa. Braids tapped him on the shoulder.

"Is it just me, or are there some seriously weird vibes going on here?" he asked. The salesman looked over, his eyes glazed. He frowned at Braids.

"Did you say something?"

He sounded drunk, slurring his words as he turned back to the stage where Doctor Zalooq was now imploring the audience to concentrate and join with him in collective homage to the healing spirits. The Doctor's words were monotonous, rhythmic, musical in their inflection and timing. He droned along.

Rawlins felt himself sliding to his knees with the Doctor firmly guiding him to face the audience. Beyond the glare of the footlights Rawlins could see the front few rows of the crowd. Most had now risen to their feet with their eyes closed, swaying gently in time to the music and the Doctor's chant. The deputy saw the Doctor's broom of animal hair swishing through the air. Over a shoulder, over his head, and over the other shoulder. It scratched its way down his back. Doctor Zalooq's chanting increased in intensity. The music and the lights picked up the tempo. The audience swayed faster, Rawlins could see their faces, could see their brows begin to furrow, and could see the sweat begin to bead and stream. He wanted to rise and run but knew he would stay where he was. His vision narrowed, the audience dimmed, muffled, and he felt faint and nauseous. He began to feel a throbbing hum through the floor of the stage and realized it had been there for some time, perhaps all along. Only now could he see the people in the crowd were swaying in a pattern that mated to it in some complex fashion. He watched, fascinated. He could almost comprehend the pattern; it was primitive, primal, and he should recognize it, he should know it, he had seen it, felt it before sometime, he had lived it. He drifted, colors played at the edge of his vision, and they were helping, the voices were helping, and the many hands that caressed him were helping, and he drifted and met some of the people who were helping, and he knew without turning when the Doctor left his side and went to the table, he knew when the magic man returned, and he was ready when the stillness fell over the people and the energy built in a great crescendo that Doctor Zalooq's screams focused into a burst that exploded within him and shattered the tenuous grip he had held. The deputy felt himself falling, slipping into a spiraling, downward plunge to a place best left alone, where urges gather to negotiate needs, where instinct is law and hunger is king, primordial schemes, primeval frenzy, the fire of life a raging inferno that blinded his mind in the dark summer night. Rawlins fainted.

The Doctor finished the procedure under bright portable lighting. He tickled Angela with the hair brush as she was putting the gear away.

"Stop it," she said, pushing him away.

The Doctor stood at the edge of the stage and watched his crew fleecing the crowd. Well trained, they always left some bills in everyone's wallet. If a wallet was empty, they would insert a few dollars. He was always amazed how easy it was, rarely did anyone complain. In ninety minutes the last of the gear was packed and the trucks pulled out. Doctor Zalooq scratched behind Dog's ears. He took a last look over the scene, then slid into the limousine. He uncapped the bottle and took a small drink. Angela shrugged out of her gown and stuck a leg into her jeans. The Doctor pulled the pants out of her hands. He lifted her by her rear and pulled her onto his lap.

"Walter, come on, I'm tired. Not tonight."

The Doctor ran his hands under her shirt and over her back. He gently scratched her bug-bites. He opened a tube and rubbed some aloe cream on the welts. She relaxed and took a sip from the bottle.

"That feels so good," she crooned, burying her head in his neck.

He worked her panties off and threw them in the back. He unzipped his pants. She wriggled on his lap.

"The Doctor is in, baby," he breathed.

CHAPTER 18

Late Thursday Afternoon, Pacific Standard Time, May 22

MURPHY

Webster took an exit off I-90 onto southbound Rainier Avenue. The neighborhood was endless tire shops, used clothing stores, and furniture rental joints. Most of the people on the street were black with the kids dressed in saggy jeans, flannel shirts, and the silver athletic shoe-boots that were the street fashion this season. With Murphy calling out directions, Webster found the left turn just past Gennesee. They idled along slowly, swerving to miss the worst of the potholes. Webster brightened as they drew closer to a freshly painted house with a low cedar fence and a neatly trimmed lawn. His face fell when he realized the house they were looking for was the one next door and its yard was decorated by a refrigerator with the doors torn off, a trampled chain link fence, and a half dozen twisted bicycle rims. Three little girls, standing side-by-side behind a weather-beaten picket fence, watched the car from across the street. All three had hair braided into corn rows, pierced ears, and dirty feet.

"Thank God," Webster said, looking over the weedy yard. "This isn't the place."

Murphy looked at the house. The numbers on the splayed garage door were 626. She rechecked her notes, they were looking for 629.

"This is the right place, the nine has spun on its nail," she said.

"Shucks," Webster said bitterly.

"Come on."

"This is a waste of time. We aren't going to learn anything in this neighborhood. It doesn't look like anyone is home. I'll stay, watch the car, and make sure no one steals the hubcaps."

"This rental car doesn't have any hubcaps, Number Three."

"I'll stay here," Webster said. He sat staring straight ahead with his hands clenched on the steering wheel. "You can't make me go in."

"Like the doctor said," Murphy said as she got out. She poked her head back in the car. "Suture self."

Webster turned to look at her.

"What?" he said.

"Nothing," she replied.

She waved at the girls across the street. They watched impassively, motionless. She adjusted the strap of her purse on her shoulder as she made her way up the shattered concrete walkway. She skipped across some muddy puddles. All the windows were protected with thick iron bars. A gang tag was scrawled on the garage door. The house looked deserted. She waited a few moments before knocking, listening for any signs of life from inside. Everything was still except for the rumble of a jet high overhead. She opened the ragged screen door and knocked. She glanced back at Webster; he was sitting in with his hands on the steering wheel and staring straight ahead. The girls had moved closer but they still stood inanimately, like little porcelain dolls.

The door opened a crack.

"If you're the Avon lady you might as well try down the street, 'cause I ain't buying nuthin."

The man had a deep and rumbling voice and his tone was grave. He sounded like a Baptist preacher from Murphy's childhood in Iowa. She proffered her identification.

"I'm with the Florida State Patrol and I'd like to visit with you a few moments."

"My nephew Willie is not causing trouble again, is he?"

"No, I don't know Willie, I'd like to chat with you about Glen Wilson."

"Chat means off the record, right?"

"Sure."

"Well, come in then."

The door swung open silently. Murphy stepped into the dim room and examined Tyler. He wore a satin smoking jacket and he reeked of cigar smoke. He was black, well over six feet tall, of indeterminate age somewhere between 35 and 60, thin, and wore a short-cropped beard laced with gray hairs. He held a huge coffee cup and had a newspaper rolled under his arm. She automatically expected to find him reading the sports page or the funnies, but when he laid the paper down she saw it was the Wall Street Journal. He flipped on a light switch and the room came alive. The floors were six-inch-wide oak planks polished to a warm golden glow. All the trim was wood and the walls were covered with a sedate blue wallpaper. Tyler chucked.

"Not what you expected from this neighborhood?"

"Not exactly."

Tyler led the way to the kitchen. A teapot was just starting to whistle. Light streamed through garden windows. Herbs were growing in little planter boxes. Stainless steel utensils were hanging neatly on the wall. A cast iron pot bubbled on the stove.

"I was just making some coffee, an Arabica blend. Would you care for a cup?"

Murphy nodded. Tyler opened a cupboard and brought out a pair of tall mugs. He poured coffee into paper filters and then spilled the steaming water through. Outside the window Murphy could see a small patio. The back yard was fenced and enclosed by large rhododendron bushes. Tyler poured heavy cream into the coffee and offered sugar cubes. Murphy took two lumps and stirred her coffee with a heavy silver spoon.

"This is sure a beautiful house," she said, glancing around the room. "On the inside. I never would have guessed..."

"That's the point. Nobody bothers me here."

Tyler sat on a stool across the breakfast bar from Murphy. He was older than Murphy first thought; deep wrinkles spread from his brown eyes.

"I'm sorry," Murphy said slowly, taking a sip of her coffee. "I don't mean to be insulting."

"No, not at all. I cultivate the image carefully. Come look at this."

He gestured for her to follow him. The garage held a rusted-out old Pinto, a wreck with cracked windows except for the ones replaced with plastic. Tyler opened a utility door and pulled out some grimy overalls.

"You were at ICC?"

Murphy nodded.

"Then they told you how bad I smell?"

Murphy nodded again. The odor coming from the clothes was so strong it made her eyes water. Tyler grinned and put the dirty overalls back. He led her back into the house.

"It's not so hard to be left alone if you want to be. I'm just the old drunken janitor at ICC. Part of the furniture. No one even notices me."

Murphy shook her head.

"I'm impressed," she said. They returned to the kitchen. "How long have you known Glen?"

"He's been working at ICC for 5 years or so. It took him about five minutes to see through my act. We've been friends ever since. Why do you ask?"

"The FBI is on a fishing expedition, I think. They are paranoid that Glen has cracked some computer codes or something. Skipjack? Clipper? AES? I really don't know."

"I don't know anything about that stuff. I know Glen talks with people around the world. Computer people. There are smart people out there who work cheap. Contractors. He does some interesting things. For example, when I first met him, he gave me five-thousand dollars for gathering some yellow sticky notes from some computers at a computer company I used to clean. Not all of them, he was very specific, just a few."

"Any idea why?"

"I think that he was gathering network passwords. A lot of people leave themselves these notes so they won't forget them."

"I see. In your opinion, is Glen a crook?"

"Oh yeah, he's crooked as a bowl of spaghetti. He runs on an alternate set of ethical rules. Hell, I think he operates on alternate laws of physics, but that is a different story."

"Is he dangerous?"

"That depends on whether you cross him or not. He surprises me sometimes. He preys on predators and usually leaves the sheep alone. I wouldn't try to fool him. Is there a warrant for his arrest?"

"No. No warrant. I'm not sure what we are doing. Just trying to figure out this guy and see what he might be up to, I suppose."

"You might just talk to him. Ask a straight question, you might be surprised, he might tell you what's what. He won't lie to you unless there's a buck in it. Especially a pretty girl like you."

Murphy blushed and pushed a stray strand of hair back from her face. She liked Tyler and his words surprised her.

"Let me tell you a little story," Tyler continued. "Remember the Black River Killer?"

Murphy nodded.

"One of those girls was friend of Glen's. In fact, they were married for a while, but that was years before. She had problems with the needle, if you get my drift. Anyway, after her body was found Glen pulled one of his disappearing acts. Didn't show up for work for almost three weeks. Came back banged up and had a deep cut on his chest. He wouldn't say what he was up to, just gave a few hints now and again. For example, two months later, Grayson was mouthing off about the Black

River Killer, and Glen told him to shut up. He said something like 'That sick fuck ain't killing no more girls'." Tyler looked embarrassed. "Sorry about the language," he said.

Murphy shook her head and gestured for him to continue.

"Not much left to tell. I watched the news and there were no more girls killed after that. So, what does it mean? Probably nothing, but still. Glen doesn't think like you and I. He gets himself in trouble and doesn't seem to care if he lives or dies. I really think that if he sets his mind to something, you'll have to kill him to stop him."

They sipped coffee in silence for a few minutes.

"It sure would help if I knew what we're after," Murphy said mostly to herself. "I feel like I'm blind."

"That reminds me of one of Wilson's stupid quips. 'There are none so blind as those who cannot see'."

"What the hell does that mean?" Murphy asked.

"Don't ask me," Tyler replied, shrugging.

"Any suggestions on what I can do to unravel the famous mystery of Glen Wilson?"

Tyler looked at Murphy appraisingly. He got up and walked to a cupboard and pulled out a tin of Nestlé's Quik. He pried the cover off with a spoon, reached in, pulled something out, and then tossed it to Murphy. She snatched it out of the air and looked at it in a perplexed manner.

"Why don't you just go out to Glen's place and have a look around?" Tyler said, laughing at her confusion.

Murphy opened her hand and stared at a silver key. She turned it in her hand, doing a careful inspection in the bright kitchen lights.

MANNY

Holly still wore her sneakers but nothing else. They sat on the carpet in the middle of the living room area. Manny handed her the box of chicken and she took her fourth piece. For such a little girl, she could really put the food away. They were looking at Manny's guns. The floor was littered with the Sig, the Navy Arms 22, and others.

"The AR-15 is kind of hard to find these days."

Manny took it out of the case and handed it to her.

"223 caliber. Kind of a workhorse for our business, but too expensive these days. Since the assault weapons ban the price has gone through the roof."

She pulled the bolt and checked for loading. She sighted at the lamp and clicked the trigger.

"Cool," she said, setting it aside.

She took a swig of beer and tossed the bottle over the couch, where it rolled noisily into the kitchenette. Manny pulled a Mosberg twelve gauge from its case. The barrel was shortened to a very illegal fourteen inches. She ratcheted the pump expertly.

"I love that sound," she said.

Manny beamed at her, proud like a father.

"Yeah, me too," he said.

"What's in the case?"

Manny leaned over and pulled the transit case over. He popped the latches and pulled out a Feather Industries 22. It was a nasty looking number with long clip and silencer. It looked like a prop from a seventies' espionage movie, The Parallax Factor or something.

"I get silencers from a machine shop in Miami, they're the best."

"Are they so quiet that we can we shoot here?"

Manny expressed surprise.

"What? Are you nuts?"

"You said the silencers are the best," she pouted. Her eyes grew misty.

"Come on, baby. I'll think of something."

He picked up the phone and called room service.

"I'm in room three-sixty-six. Send up every newspaper you can find. Go clean out all the machines. Bring them all up." He listened. "Yes, all of them. Now."

"Tell them to bring some scissors," Holly said, biting her lip with excitement.

"And bring some scissors," he said into the phone.

He hung up. He tipped the coffee table over and slid it against the wall. He gathered the guns and hid them under the comforter on the bed. He put on some boxer shorts. Holly was loading a clip with 22 long rifles.

"Ain't you going to put anything on?" Manny asked.

She shrugged and shook her head no.

"Fuck 'em if they ain't seen pussy before," she said.

There was a knock at the door. Manny grabbed the clip and the box she was loading from and stuck them under a cushion on the couch.

He answered the door. Four bellhops clustered around the door. All were loaded down with newspapers.

"Stack them there," Manny said, pointing.

The guys stole glances at Holly, who sat on the floor leaning back against the couch with her arms spread and her eyes closed. Manny opened a paper to the comic section and tossed it to her. She opened it and was mostly hidden from view while she read Robotman. As they were leaving, a maid pushed a cart up the hall weighed down with more newspapers. She handed Manny a ticket that he signed without looking. He stacked the papers against the table. Holly grabbed the scissors and started cutting pictures out of the papers. She made targets out of the president, Prince Charles, Saddam Hussein, Jesse Jackson, and a prison photograph of Hillary Rodham. Manny put out the Do Not Disturb sign and locked the door. By sitting with their backs against the bed they were able to get a range of about 25 feet. Manny jumped and Holly laughed every time a hot casing landed on his lap.

An hour later the air was thick with cordite smoke. Manny had to smash the smoke detector with his shoe. They had fired approximately two thousand rounds. Manny could tell by a quick count of the empty shell boxes. The newspapers were shredded, but only one slug had hit the wall. Manny took a peek into the hall, but the bullet did not go through.

Holly pawed through the chicken and found one last leg. She wrapped her arms around Manny's neck and gnawed the chicken.

"I can't remember ever having so much fun," she said.

"You gonna wear those shoes all the time," Manny asked.

She took a last bite of the leg and threw it into the kitchenette. She did a little dance as she slowly unlaced her shoes and kicked them off, scattering shell casings. She'd been nude all afternoon but Manny had never seen anything so sexy as that little show.

"Come here," he said.

She flopped down beside him and wrapped her arms around his neck.

"I love you, Manny. What's your last name?"

"Rodriguez. What's yours?"

"If we get married it will be Rodriguez. Holly Rodriguez. I love you so much, I wish I could show you. I know!"

She picked up the 22 and grabbed his foot. She placed the barrel on his little toe.

"We could shoot off each other's little toe. That would be like exchanging rings or something. We'll be bound by blood."

Manny eased the pistol out of her hand. "Surely we can figure out some other way to show our love?" he said.

He gave her a deep kiss. She wrapped her legs around his thigh and gripped him tightly. She raised off him and pointed at his groin. "Don't point that thing at anyone unless you intend to shoot them with it," she said, rubbing his throbbing penis.

She grabbed it, tugged him to his feet, and led him into the bedroom.

And there they stayed until morning.

MURPHY

Outside Tyler's little house, the three little girls were standing at the fence directly across from Webster. They were giggling and whispering among themselves. When Murphy approached the car she saw a huge man bent over talking intensely to Webster who stared straight ahead with his white knuckles clamped on the steering wheel.

"What seems to be the problem?" Murphy called out.

"This fuck is messing with my girls, now I'm going to mess with him." The man had a shaved head and piercing brown eyes. Veins were leaping like eels on his forehead.

"There must be some misunderstanding, that's just Number Three, he's not going to bother anyone."

The man walked around the car and stood before Murphy with his muscular arms akimbo.

"I'm going to rip his dick off and feed it to the cat. What's this Number Three stuff?"

"He likes to brag that he was number three in his FBI class." She stuck her hand out to shake. "I'm Captain Margaret Murphy, on loan from the Florida State Patrol. Everyone calls me Murphy."

He looked at her hand for a moment, then shook it.

"We're leaving now, no harm done?" Murphy asked.

"Okay, good enough. I better not see this Number Three hanging around here any more. Got me?"

"Deal," Murphy replied. She opened the car door and swung into her seat.

The large man tapped on the window. Murphy rolled it down.

"You'll probably need these." He tossed the car key onto her lap. He reached behind his back and drew out Webster's Glock. He popped the clip out and checked to make sure the chamber was clear before tossing both to Murphy.

"Thanks," she said.

Webster grabbed the key and started the car. He spun the tires as he pulled away from the curb. Murphy rolled the window partly up, then wrinkled her nose at an acrid odor. She looked at Webster. He'd spread open a map on his lap. She left the window rolled down.

"You spilled coffee on your pants?" she asked.

"Yeah, coffee." He changed the subject. "I just offered those girls some gum. I wasn't doing anything. Can I have my gun back?"

"Later. Let's get some food, I'm hungry. Tyler says they have good pizza at the Northlake Tavern. See if you can find it, it's under the Montlake bridge."

"Did Glen Wilson enter the conversation while you were talking to the janitor about pizza? I knew that would be a waste of time. Pizza," he snorted. "You fly across the country to talk to a janitor about pizza."

After they stuffed themselves on pizza, Murphy drained her beer and smacked her lips. The table was littered with the skeletal remnants of a huge pepperoni pizza. She told Webster everything that Tyler had said. Webster wiped his face and sat back in the seat.

"I wish I'd been there to kick the truth out of that guy. Black River killer. Bullsnot. Horse apples."

"Webster, I've had it with you," she whispered with quiet intensity. "You are the most incompetent, wrong-headed fuck-up I've ever seen." She tossed his gun onto the table. "I'm sick of this so-called case and putting up with your rookie bullshit. I'm not baby-sitting you any more." She stood and tossed a pair of twenties on the table. "Good-bye, Number Three, you asshole."

"Murphy? Hey, I'm sorry," he called out.

She turned and walked toward the door. Webster grabbed her arm.

"Look Murphy, I'm sorry. Come back a minute. I need to talk to you."

Murphy jerked her arm away and continued toward the door.

"Give me two minutes. Please, Murphy."

She stopped, shook her head, and sighed. "Two minutes and I'm out of here, okay?"

Webster nodded eagerly. They returned to the table and Webster gestured to the waitress for two more beers, a draft for Murphy and another Thomas Kemper root beer for himself. He took a long drink, then began to speak.

"You're right, Murphy, I'm a screw-up. Back in the car, I thought that guy was going to kill me. I almost peed in my pants."

"Almost?" Murphy said. She looked at her watch. "You have one more minute."

"I'm a jerk. I can't do anything right. I wasn't even third in my class, I was one hundred and thirty-third." A single tear rolled down his cheek. "You can help me Murphy. I want to be like you."

"No."

"I'll do anything. Come on, Murphy. You're a great cop, please train me."

Murphy closed her eyes and let her head droop over the table. *Don't do this,* Murphy, she thought. *Don't.* She took a deep breath and looked at Webster.

Damn.

"You'll do anything I say?"

"I swear to God, Murphy."

He crossed his heart.

"I can't believe I'm buying this shit," she said as she swigged the rest of her beer. "Okay, to start, we need some sign language. When I raise my index finger, that means you need to shut up. Immediately. When I wave my hand at you, that means you need to shut up. When I make the football time-out sign, that also means you need to shut up. In fact, whatever gesture I make, that means shut your goddam mouth. Is that okay with you?"

He opened his mouth. Murphy raised her index finger and gave him a stern look. He closed his mouth with a snap and nodded his head vigorously.

"We do things my way," she continued. "Then later, if I have time, I'll tell you what I'm doing and why. Got it?"

Webster nodded. He stuck his hand across the table to shake. Murphy hesitated, then took his hand.

If I'm so smart, why did I agree to this hopeless situation? she asked herself.

Webster pressed his lips together tightly and shrugged his shoulders. He looked like a very happy puppy.

Because I've always had a soft spot for dumb animals, Murphy reflected.

CHAPTER 19

Early Friday Morning, May 23

LEONARD

Leonard woke slowly. The sun reflected brightly off some empty bottles on the porch. He was confused. He looked around and saw Dog sleeping next to his chair snoring softly. He realized he must have fallen asleep during the magic show. He rubbed the sleep from his eyes and noticed a lot of other people had done the same. The field was covered with sleeping bodies. He got up and stretched. He headed for the field to check things out. As he stepped off the porch he suddenly realized the trucks were missing. Also missing were the limo, the stage, and lights, and speakers. As if they had never been. He walked over to where the stage was located and recognized Deputy Rawlins lying in the grass with his shirt tossed over him like a blanket. Dog padded over and sniffed at the deputy. He raised a leg. Leonard grabbed him by the collar and pulled him away.

"No, Dog!"

That had been close. Deputy Rawlins twitched, made a moaning sound, and lifted up on one elbow. He focused on Leonard, then sagged back to the ground. He spoke into the grass.

"Damn, M-B. What did those freaks do to me?"

"I don't know, Deputy Rawlins," replied Leonard. "I guess I fell asleep."

He fidgeted, wondering how angry the deputy was and if he would blame Leonard for what had happened. He bent over the miserable deputy.

"Are you okay? Can I get you anything?" he asked.

Rawlins sat up slowly, wincing at the bright sunlight. He slipped his shirt on and looked around the field at the sprawl of bodies.

"Jesus, M-B. Anybody alive out here?"

He struggled to his feet, feeling to make sure his gun was in place. As he tucked in his shirt he wedged a foot under the nearest body and flipped it. The aluminum siding salesman groaned.

"Nothing," he muttered.

Rawlins grunted and turned away.

"Nothing," repeated the salesman. "There is nothing in the box."

Rawlins headed towards the gas station and his patrol car, waving Leonard to accompany him.

"Look here, M-B. I'm not exactly sure what transpired here last night." He avoided looking at Leonard. "But I don't think I like it."

They stopped at the side of the car. Rawlins studied the front grill.

"I don't want to see anything like this going on out here again, you understand me?"

Leonard nodded.

"You hear me, M-B?"

"Yes, sir. I understand. No more magic shows," promised Leonard.

"Okay, then." Rawlins rounded the front of the car and opened the door. He stopped and stared at the field, knowing he should probably do something, but he was strangely reluctant to be involved. He sighed. "You get those people awake and out of here, and we'll just say this never happened." He hesitated, then stepped away from the car and closer to Leonard, looking into his eyes for the first time. "You got that, M-B? This never happened, understand?" Leonard couldn't tear his eyes away.

"Sure, never happened." Leonard swallowed. He didn't understand at all, but he knew Rawlins was acting strangely. Rawlins nodded, satisfied.

"All right, I'm out of here."

He turned and bent to get into his car. He stopped halfway, then straightened, placed his hands in the small of his back, and bent again. He leaned over and touched his toes. He stood up straight and wiggled his shoulders.

"You sure you're okay, Deputy Rawlins?" asked Leonard.

Rawlins got into his car before replying.

"Yeah. My back feels pretty good today."

GLEN

Glen drifted toward consciousness. He had dreamed of animals howling and hissing through the night. As he awoke, he determined most of the noises in his head were real. They came from a kennel out back somewhere. His body was leaden and a deep pain had taken root on the end of his left hand. The pain was as much a part of his body as his legs or his heart. He was lying on a small cot. A poster of a pregnant horse was on the wall showing a cutaway drawing that showed a pony ready to be born. He raised his left hand and held it before his eyes. Born with ten fingers, now down to eight. He realized that the morphine was still with him, bending his thinking and drawing a gauzy curtain across the real world. He was stoned but his body cried for another shot. He resisted for a few heroic seconds, then called out.

"Hey! Medic! It's time for more dope."

He choked down a few sips of stale water from a cup by the bedside table, then threw the cup at the door. It was plastic, so it just bounced off and rattled on the floor. He was trying to reach something heavier and more fragile when the door opened.

"Good morning, Glen," Jackie said cheerfully.

She had a syringe and bottle. She prepared the shot while Glen watched eagerly. She sat beside the bed and smoothed her cotton skirt absently.

"Do you really want to heal in a big hurry and get your wallet back?"

Glen nodded, watching the needle intently.

"Do you remember what I said about some experimental drugs?"

"I think so. Something that might make me heal quickly?"

"I also mentioned some other drugs. I might be able to make your finger grow back. I'm part of a network of animal experimenters working with some genetic research. Some mutagens based on amphibian DNA. You know how a snake can grow a new tail? I really think we're onto something. Our trials with rabbits look very interesting."

Glen looked at her sharply. "I don't like the word 'interesting' in the way doctors, lawyers, and women in general use it."

DeeDee appeared in the doorway. She wore an Edison-Ford Complex T-shirt that looked as if it had been washed several thousand times. The thin material hardly hid her bare nipples. She cradled a black and white floppy-eared rabbit.

She scratched its head idly. The rabbit had one brown leg.

"Bring Bugsy over, please," Jackie said.

DeeDee gently put the rabbit on Glen's chest. Jackie put the needle on the bedside table. She stuck the brown leg directly in Glen's face.

"Look. This rabbit grew a new leg in a couple of weeks."

"You mean it accepted a transplant?" Glen asked suspiciously.

"No. It grew a new one."

"It doesn't look right. Why isn't the new leg black and white? This rabbit looks fucked up to me. What's the catch? What happened to the old leg?"

Jackie picked up the rabbit and kissed its nose. She handed it back to DeeDee.

"I don't know why the new leg is brown. The rabbit is fine. The old leg was surgically removed."

"You chopped its leg off so you could try to grow a new one." He addressed DeeDee. "Did she tell you why everyone calls her Chopper?"

DeeDee shook her head no.

"I didn't think so. I know there's a catch somewhere." He thought for a few seconds. "How many rabbits did you kill before you had a success?"

Jackie looked embarrassed. "Over a hundred laboratory animals were consumed in my research."

"How many?" Glen insisted.

"Okay, damn you. One thousand and eighty or so. I'm not trying to minimize the risk. I thought you might like to have your finger back, that's all."

"You said there is something else, something that will help me heal without all that genetic stuff. I want you to give me that."

"Yes. That one is approved for livestock. You'll heal in a week or so. It's not exactly legal, but you'll probably live."

"I don't care about my fingers. My hand is going to look funny, but that's better than growing two heads."

He could see that Jackie's feelings were hurt. She picked up the needle.

"Roll over on your belly," she said grumpily.

"Look, I'll buy you a couple thousand more rabbits to play with," he said as he rolled over.

"I'm tired of playing with rabbits," she said as she roughly jabbed the needle into his ass.

JACK

The early morning light, or lack of it, made it difficult to see what Jack Sterner was doing. He liked it that way. His father had once won this fishing tournament and he intended to repeat the feat in much the same way, come hell, hurricane, or ten-foot dog-eating gators.

Jack had inherited a sixteen-foot Ranger, a solid old bass boat with a 200 horse Mercury crotch-rocket C-clamped to the transom. That boat was good for a quick start off the line, important in this particular event since every contestant fired off the line at the same time, heading for the favored spots that nobody knew about, which everybody knew about, which were blatantly marked on the map in the resort store. If you could call it a store. Jack was still a bit miffed about that. Without a liquor license the little shack should be disqualified from being called a store, in his opinion. Jack happened to have disqualification on his mind.

The sturdy Ranger was long gone. There were witnesses who affirmed that the stranger held three Aces to Jack's double pairs of Kings and twos. Proof in Jack's mind that God really doesn't love a drunk. Now Jack was stuck with a patched-together 1958 kit-built cabin cruiser. Wood with a rough fiberglass overlay. The main structural supports had a bit of dry rot, none of the amenities functioned, and the trailer was a jigsaw puzzle of rust and latex house paint. None of that had anything to do with winning a bass tournament.

What mattered to Jack was the powerplant. He and a friend had spent the last two weeks rebuilding the boat to accommodate an "acquired" Ford drive train. The rebuilding consisted of many hours jig sawing, working through a gallon of silicon sealant, and consuming several cases of Old Milwaukee. Time being of the essence, they'd been forced to leave the drive train complete.

This meant Jack had the only boat this side of Bangkok with a four speed manual transmission complete with clutch and shift lever. Then some son of a bitch stole the gas tank for his trolling motor. That was okay, Jack would win the damn tournament without trolling.

Since the store didn't carry beer, it was a damn good thing for all concerned that Jack happened to have an emergency cache of beer and chaser on block ice in the livewell. Only two cases, but if he nursed them they might last the day. Hot in Florida, you know. Things could've gotten ugly... Even uglier than the ancient bitch minding the "store", who seemed to find Jack less than attractive as well. Jack thought back to the encounter.

"Where's your beer," he said as he tossed a couple of packs of Marlboros on the counter.

Jack rarely used question marks.

"Don't have no liquor license, need ID for the smokes."

"I'm forty fucking two years old, and you need ID for smokes."

"Yep, watch your language."

A staredown ensued. Jack lost.

"The State has my license."

"Thank you Mister Trebeck. What is a drunk?"

"Pardon me?"

Jack spared a question mark.

"You're trying to buy beer at four thirty in the morning, which ain't legal, you know it, and you're a drunk."

She took a luxuriant drag off her Benson and Hedges.

"You've got no ID 'cause the State took it, there's an empty fifth of Jim Beam on the console of your boat, if that's what you call that thing. It's illegally parked, by the way, and what happened to your father, another drunk, who won every damn tournament for miles around a few years back, as long as he was fishing alone, which means he was probably using live bait on the sly." She started to snuff her smoke and hesitated. "You want the last hit offa this?"

Jack stood back.

"You insulted my father."

"Yep, and I insulted you and your boat too."

"People have died for less," he said as he took the smoke from her fingers and drew the last drag out of it.

"Don't see how and don't give a flying fig either," she said as she took the butt back and stubbed it out.

"What do you mean by that?"

Jack grudgingly allowed another question mark.

"Got a sawed-off four-ten under the counter and my hubby is a tournament judge."

"Oh."

Jack decided to leave, not while he was ahead, but while he was still somewhat in the game. None of that really mattered; what was important was Jack's Secret Weapon, the worms he'd finally found, the worms he'd gotten from that idiot near Carnestown. Jack's father, rest his besotted soul, had sworn by those worms, had won more than a few events with those worms, and Jack Junior figured to do the same. To this very day, Jack remembered the wise words of his father: "Boy, forget them girls, they ain't worth the troubles... Use these here worms for tournament fishing, rules are for tourists and fools... And stop picking your nose in public, it's dis-fucking-gusting."

Those worms were different. Different in appearance, and apparently different in smell or taste or the wriggly vibrations they emanated. Hell, maybe they screamed, "Eat me! I'm so damn delicious I'll melt in your fishy little mouth! Once you've had a bite of me you won't care if you got a barbed hook stabbed through your face." Jack didn't know or care why they worked. They worked, 'nuff said, pass me a beer.

MURPHY

"I really think this will unravel Glen Wilson's secrets," Webster said while rotating the Yale key in the morning sunlight and examining it closely. "This is going to break the case wide open."

Murphy winced at the word "case". It still seemed as if they were chasing randomly around the country for no particular reason. There was no case.

"Well, it can't hurt to look around a little bit. You understand that we won't be able to use anything we find? Just a friendly visit out of curiosity."

Webster grinned. "The door was open, we thought we heard someone call, we went in to investigate."

"Yes, something like that, sure."

They pulled in front of a duplex just south of Marysville. The neighborhood was semi-rural and slightly better than Perry Tyler's Central district community. They sat looking at the weather-beaten old house. It had been remodeled as a duplex with one residence accessible via a long stairway up the side. Glen was in the A section, downstairs. The place looked deserted with dark curtains pulled tight. A Honda Goldwing motorcycle was parked under the carport with a few parts strewn around. As they walked up the sidewalk, a thirty-ish girl in a torn flannel shirt and cutoffs walked from around the back. She was scrubbing part of the bike's carburetor with a gas-soaked rag.

She wore open-toed sandals, had a bandanna wrapped around her head and a small screwdriver stuck over her ear like a pencil. She was listening to classic rock on a boom box: "Don't Fear the Reaper." She seemed startled by Webster and Murphy approaching, but she received them with a grin.

"You must be here to see Glen. He's not around."

She had a slight accent. Murphy placed her as originally from West Virginia or North Carolina. She stuck out her hand but withdrew it when she noticed how grimy they were. The girl reeked of gasoline.

"We got a key from one of Glen's friends, we thought we'd look in and make sure everything is okay?" Murphy made it a question.

Webster brandished the key.

"We're with the…" he began, but stopped when Murphy gave him a stern look.

"Hey, no problem, the door probably isn't locked. Glen's a sweetheart, he won't mind if you look around a bit. Best landlord I ever had."

Both Webster and Murphy looked puzzled at the "sweetheart" description.

"Well, go on, I got to get this bike running."

She turned back to the carport and hunched down. They walked onto the porch and tried the door. The girl was right; it was not locked.

"I expected barbed wire and Rottweilers. Security cameras, alarm systems. Not a cute babe working on a motorbike."

"Yeah, she is cute, isn't she," Murphy said, looking back at the girl over her shoulder. "Here we go."

She slowly opened the door and they entered the darkened room.

GLEN

Glen worked on an instant message to Elke.

Elke:
Sorry I've been out of touch, I've been injured, but don't worry. I need the lottery money, please deposit it in my Peoples Bank account 7001 4457 82.
Thanks. See you.

Elke replied back right away.

Glen:
What do you mean injured? Are you okay? I have so much to tell you. There are some people asking many questions about you. Orrin Webster from the FBI and Captain Margaret Murphy of the

Florida State Patrol. Webster is useless, but I like Captain Murphy. We've talked a couple of times. I hope that is all right with you. They say you had something to do with the murder of a drug dealer.

Please explain this.

I've deposited $62,367.12 into your account. How did you know that your lottery ticket would win?

I'd like to be with you. Where are you? Can I come see you? Please tell me what is going on?

Elke:

I'm fine, a doctor is treating a little wound I got.

I don't have any problems with the law. Tell them whatever you like. I'm the only innocent man left in the world. I didn't kill the drug dealer. Let me know if the cab driver wants to make any charges, I'll take care of that in a big hurry. This should not be a problem.

I didn't know that the lottery ticket was a winner. Do you know of a way to assure a ticket is a winner? Please tell me.

I can't receive any visitors right now. Sorry.

Regards.

Glen:

You sent me a lottery ticket and told me I should collect the money and split it with you. I understand the odds of the ticket being a winner and me being present at the lottery are astronomical. How did you do this?

PS: I hope you get better soon.

Elke:

Sorry, I thought you knew of a way to ensure that a ticket is a winner. I would like to know how to do this. The best my consultants have been able to do is get the odds up to 94.38%. They claim that is the best we can do with the equipment and software we have now. The goddam programmers are always holding me up for more money for equipment.

Regards.

"Quit screwing around with your computer for a minute, I want to start your treatment."

Jackie backed into the room with a tray full of chemicals and surgical tools. Glen looked up from the bed. He unplugged the laptop computer and set it aside.

"Great. I'm glad to see you. My hand is starting to hurt. I need another shot."

"No more morphine. It might interfere with the priantilate treatment."

"You're just pissed because I don't want to be one of your dead rabbits."

"If you don't want to make medical history, that's fine. You like typing with one hand, that's okay too."

"Don't rag on me. I just want to heal and get out of here. How about nitrous oxide or something to take the edge off?"

"Don't be such a baby."

She started cutting off the bandage.

"Not even a beer?"

"Nothing. Now quit whining."

"Shit," Glen muttered.

CHAPTER 20

Friday Morning, May 23

LEONARD

Dog lay in the dust and considered biting Leonard. Dog had never bitten anyone and Leonard seemed like an obvious place to start. The idiot didn't move very fast and he was available. Dog's eyes followed Leonard as he puttered around the station, polishing this and straightening that. Dog rose to his feet when Leonard bent over to inspect the trash can, but the canine crusader dropped back down to rest his head on his paws. After all, the idiot fed him well and didn't spit on him or kick him out of the doorway. Except for the pressure washer incident he had proved to be a vast improvement over the fat guy. Dog figured the fat guy was dead. Dog understood dead. The food chain was a primal concept. Something had eaten the fat guy. The idiot had somehow escaped. A puzzle.

Leonard finished cleaning the front window and stood back to admire the view. Dog performed mental calculus. Half a jump to reach the ankle, a quick snap, and two jumps out the front door. Around the corner and into the brush before the idiot could react. A new life on the road. Travel, see the world. Live on roadkill and whatever he could steal from trash cans. Maybe meet a poodle or two. Roadkill wasn't bad if you got to it soon enough.

Leonard started sweeping the front porch. Some of the dust drifted into Dog's eyes. Dog moved to the shade of the gas pumps, snapped at a fly, and stretched out on the warm concrete. He wondered what it felt like, to bite someone. Just a quick nip, no blood. Well, maybe a little blood, but not much.

He drooled into the dust, daydreaming of ankles.

A red Mercedes 500SL convertible pulled to the far side of the pumps. Leonard wiped his hands on a rag as he approached. The driver, a lone brunette wearing dark glasses and a scarf, opened the door and stepped out.

"See the sign?" she said, pointing.

"Yeah," Leonard replied, puzzled.

"Self Service. That means I pump the gas and you don't touch the car."

"Fine. I won't touch the car. Got a special on premium today," Leonard offered.

"That'll be fine, just don't touch the car. I'll get it."

"Sure, okay." Leonard winked at Dog. Dog dropped his head back to his paws and stretched his hind legs. Maybe if he only bit the customers a little, the idiot wouldn't notice. He rolled over to check the customer's ankles. Uh oh, high heels. Those looked painful. A new data point; some customers are armed.

He rolled over to await easier game.

"I don't think this pump is working."

The brunette, dressed too warmly for the day, pumped the handle in exasperation.

"Sometimes it sticks. Here, let me get that."

"Don't…"

"I know, don't touch the car." Leonard wasn't stupid.

She pulled the dispenser free of the tank just as the pump made a clicking sound and Leonard's premium unleaded gushed over the rear of the car.

"Shit!" she cried.

Leonard rushed forward to help and tripped over Dog. He fell into the brunette at high speed and knocked her off her feet. They sprawled in the dust entangled like lovesick Crane flies. Leonard struggled to free himself, mortified.

The brunette made a few choking sounds, then started to giggle. She pushed Leonard away with her hair awry, and started patting the ground for her sunglasses, evidently prescription from the amount of squinting going on.

"If my car explodes and we survive, you're a dead man."

Leonard found the sunglasses and handed them to her. Only one lens was cracked.

"I'm really sorry…"

"What are we going to do about the gas all over my car?"

It was 45 minutes before she was convinced Leonard had removed every trace of the gasoline from her car. Most of it simply evaporated leaving Leonard an oily sheen to carefully polish off with an old cotton T-shirt. The job was done carefully, under close supervision, and with much unneeded advice and direction. He ended up washing the entire car. Then she allowed him to fill the tank. In the meantime she'd lost the high heels, let her hair down, and shed a significant portion of her business suit.

"The fill-up's free, considering," said Leonard, as he nervously watched her regard his work. She kneeled to sight along a fender, wiped a finger across the hood, and stooped to sniff at the trunk seam. Her nose wrinkled.

"Don't worry about it. Pre-menstrual. Sometimes I get... Never mind."

She looked around the station. She noticed her bare feet and the pile of clothes in the back seat. The humor of the situation struck her. She reached over and took Leonard's hand.

"How do you feel about meaningless, gratuitous sex?"

Leonard started.

"Well." He looked at Dog. "I... Wow."

He shook her hand.

"I'm sure it's, just fine, really. The Reverend and my mother told me about girls..." He stopped. "I mean..."

"Forget it," she sighed. "It was a bad idea anyway."

She hopped over the door and into the driver's seat.

"It's this trip, it's starting to wear me down."

Leonard stood with his hands in his pockets and watched as she screeched onto the road without checking for traffic. She waggled her fingers as she receded and Leonard waved back.

"Dog, maybe I could have handled that differently."

Leonard beat the midday heat by poking about in the garage. He arranged the crescent wrenches and the screwdriver on the tool racks. He was clearing floor space with a worn-out pushbroom. Visions of his new power lift made the job less tedious. The garage was looking tidy for the first time in years. Outside, a mud-splattered pickup rumbled to a stop.

"Yo, Leonard! How you doing?" Bucktoothed, sunburned, and grinning, Leonard's cousin Eddie stumbled from the truck, beer in hand. Eddie didn't come by much, mostly because he still owed Leonard from several years back.

Something to do with a bachelor party. They were both fuzzy on the particulars.

"Hi, Eddie," Leonard said, frowning at the beer. Eddie noticed and tossed the half-full can in the back of his truck. One of his yellow dogs yelped in surprise.

"First one today, Lenny. Honest Injun."

He tripped over the washer hose and caught himself on the garage wall.

"Sure, Eddie," Leonard said. "What do you want?"

"Moving that damn washer hose would be a good start, man could kill himself." Dog nodded in agreement. Eddie pushed away from the wall and followed Leonard around.

"Whatcha doing there?"

"Making room. Gonna put in a power lift."

"No shit? You got that kinda money now?" Eddie said, swaying a bit in the still air. "Breezy in here." He leaned back against the wall. "Ol' Clem must have left you a fortune, eh? Brown paper bags full of sawbucks, or what?" He pulled a pouch of Red Man from a shirt pocket and bit off a huge chaw. Dog, watching from the shade of the pumps, tucked his tail between his legs and moved underneath the porch.

"No, just the Lunch-N-Lube."

Leonard stared at the compressor pump jutting two feet into his newly cleared area. He sighed, knelt down, and with one smooth motion lifted the 150 pound pump onto the nearest workbench. He stood back. The floor jack was still in the way. He removed the four-foot steel handle and carried it towards the corner that Eddie occupied. Eddie's eyes widened. Leonard set the jack handle in the corner and plucked a hammer from the rack.

"Guess I'll have to start hanging stuff from the walls now. You feel like helping?" Leonard asked, knowing the answer. Eddie swallowed, gagged a little, coughed, and spit.

"Uh, no. Sorry, gotta get down to the bank and cash my disability check."

He slapped his hip. "Remember?"

Leonard frowned. "Well, no," he said.

"Neither do I, but I think it happened at that damn bachelor party." He grinned. "What the state don't know—"

"Could get you in big trouble," Leonard finished.

"Aw, lighten up, Lenny. Ain't but three people in the world know about that and two of 'em are making money off it. Damn child support."

"Eddie, you know my name is Leonard. Leonard!"

Eddie made his way back to the truck remembering to limp this time.

"Okay, Len, okay. Don't get your pecker in a twist," Eddie said, pouting as he got back in his truck.

222

A county sheriff's car pulled in as Eddie pulled out. Deputy Rawlins leaned out the window.

"Is Eddie sober, or should I go pull him over to protect the innocent?"

He didn't wait for an answer, opened the car door, stretched, and looked around.

"The place is really looking up, Monkey Boy. I see you ran off the hippies and the tourists. Good job." He removed his mirrored sunglasses as he stepped into the garage.

"Have you caught Clem's killer yet?" Leonard asked.

"Well no, M-B. That's why I'm here." He leaned against the wall. "State guys seem to think we're looking for a couple of psycho killers." Rawlins crossed his arms and looked skyward as if full of important and secret information that Leonard wouldn't understand. "In my experience as a law enforcement officer in this county," he said grandly as he strolled around the garage, picking up items and setting them down, "the answer is usually a lot closer to home." He stopped, turning a wrench in his hands. "So the station is yours now, is that right, M-B? Making money hand over fist, are you, M-B?"

Leonard could see where Rawlins was heading.

"I didn't kill Clem. I was in the bathroom. I heard a…"

"Big American V-8, I know," Rawlins interrupted.

"You can't think that I did it." Leonard was scared.

"Who else had anything to gain?" Rawlins asked.

"I didn't know I'd get the station!"

"Yes sir, old M-B sure cleaned up on this deal," said Rawlins, setting the wrench back down.

"I'd give it all up to bring Clem back!" Leonard was upset.

"Sure you would, M-B. Sure you would." Rawlins opened a cupboard, then another. "Don't have any handguns registered, M-B. I checked. Pretty unusual around these parts, for a man not to have a gun or three, don't you think?" He moved to another cupboard.

"You got a warrant for that?" Leonard surprised them both. Rawlins closed the cupboard and stood very still.

"What do you know about warrants, M-B? You don't even have a TV. Besides, this ain't no search, just a friendly visit, making sure you're doing okay out here." He turned around, smiling. He put his glasses on and headed outside.

"You're not my friend. You're just a big dumb bully." Leonard's face flushed with anger. "And next time you want to look through my stuff, you bring a warrant and you call me Leonard." Leonard walked stiffly towards the deputy with the hammer still in his hand. "Or sir. I've heard you call the banker Benford that, and now I'm a businessman just like him. You call me sir next time, Deputy Rawlins."

Deputy Rawlins stood beside his car in the midday Florida sun with a look of wonder on his face.

"Okay, Len-o. No problem. You know, M-B, I don't think you're quite as stupid as you want everyone to believe. You've made out pretty well on this deal." He hesitated, started to say something else, stopped, then opened the cruiser door. "From now on, I'll be watching you. You make a single wrong move—and sooner or later you will—and I'm going to get you."

He had one foot in the car when Dog darted from around the corner and clipped him firmly on the ankle. The canine crusader raced away and disappeared behind the garage with Deputy Rawlin's screams of outrage echoing behind him.

JACK

"You call that thing a boat?" Some of the other contestants were grinning and trying to refrain from outright laughter. Some were not successful. It's an odd tradition, but you never insulted another man's boat. Unless it was better than your own, of course. The onlookers on the dock, however, were under few constraints. Jack flushed and ignored the catcalls as he backed down the ramp.

"Hey, Junior, find that washed up on the shore, did you?"

"What's that registered as, flotsam or jetsam?"

"Somebody call the Coast Guard, put 'em on alert!"

"Hey, look! It's got a propeller!"

"Let's hope it's got one helluva bilge pump."

Jack stopped backing up when he heard the exhaust pipes on his truck begin to gurgle. He slammed the door, pulled the brim of his Copenhagen hat lower, and stalked to the trailer. The dock grew silent. The boat floated freely and listed only slightly to port when he released the catch. He threw the rope to the dock without looking. A startled bystander caught it, and after a moment's indecision, decided to pull Jack's boat in, carefully. When Jack returned from parking the truck his boat was neatly tied up at the end of the dock, rocking gently in the wakes of boats already maneuvering for position. The crowd parted to let him through. Jack stared straight ahead and silently vowed that the next person to say anything would be going for an early morning swim. Since this was clearly written on his face, a wave of silence followed Jack down the dock, until he reached his boat.

A young boy stood at the end of the dock, all sunburn and freckles. He wore a baggy University of Minnesota sweat shirt with the sleeves ripped off. Excitement was written on his face. He looked up at Jack.

"Wow, mister! Cool boat." He looked back at the boat. "Can I maybe go for a ride later? After the tournament?"

"No." Jack freed the stern line and timed the swells. He stepped down into the boat. He moved forward to the console.

"I wouldn't be any trouble, honest," the boy pleaded.

"No." Jack turned the key and the engine caught immediately, settling into a steady rumble. A few heads turned and the more experienced onlookers nodded sagely at the evident power. Jack allowed himself a little smile.

"What the hell you got in that thing?"

Jack didn't bother replying to the shouted question. He pointed to the bowline.

"Boy, get that."

The youngster hurried to comply. Jack pushed away from the dock with one hand, worked the clutch, and engaged the transmission. He idled toward the starting position. On impulse he picked up his Dad's old white cowboy hat, beat it against his thigh, and sailed it to the dock. It landed at the boy's feet.

"It was my Dad's," Jack said.

"Thanks, mister," the youth said as he settled the old Stet on his head.

As Jack drifted toward the starting line he spun his hat backwards.

"Flip that hat backwards, boy, 'cause I ain't buying you another one," he whispered, as his father had told him so many times before.

Jack's beater boat caught everyone by surprise, blasting off the line with the power of 300 horses of big block Ford. Shaking, rattling, and slamming through the wakes until he pulled ahead and reached the glassy undisturbed water of the main lake. He stood up and the rush of air almost took his hat anyway. He checked the shoreline, got his bearings, and headed for a little cove on the far side. A quick glance at the rearview mirror reassured him that he'd have plenty of time before the others arrived.

He pulled back on the throttle dangerously close to shore and slammed the transmission in reverse while still on a plane. The wake boiled over the transom spilling in a fair amount of water. Jack didn't care. He leapt to the bow and threw his coffee-can-filled-with-concrete anchor into the water, and drifted in closer to a bank of weeds. He grabbed one his three casting rods, and after a quick check of the shoreline and surrounding waters, opened the small compartment he'd built into the boat. The compartment destroyed the boat's watertight integrity but Jack didn't care about that either. The can of worms lay nestled in a small Styrofoam cooler, just as he'd left it. With an evil grin he threaded one of the fat wigglies onto his treble hook and used an expert flick of the wrist to place it precisely at the edge of the line of reeds. Within seconds Jack Sterner had his first catch of the day, netting a three-pounder with one hand, and only losing half the worm. That was good, as he only had a few dozen of Leonard's crawlers.

In the minutes it took the next fisherman to reach the cove, Jack landed three large bass, and had time to switch poles while the other boat was still a hundred yards away. He exchanged a friendly wave with his competitor, who maintained a polite distance. Jack reeled in his standard top water plug and traded the pole for a set of field glasses. In the dim morning light it was difficult to be sure, but it looked like Spot Number Two was still open. He raised his anchor and headed back to the console. The stern drive roiled up mud and weeds when he opened the throttle and hammered out of the cove at reckless speed, smashing over and through the increasingly choppy water.

His luck held at the second location and Jack managed another two respectably sized fish before being forced to swap poles again. He tried fishing the plug for a few minutes without a strike, so he moved to pre-selected Spot Number Three. This produced a magnificent eight-pounder, sure to be in the running for catch of the day. The battle with the monster bass lasted over five minutes. Two other boats arrived before Jack could safely net the fish.

"Nice fish!" one of the boats yelled over. Jack waved.

"Whatcha use for bait, kittens?" asked the other.

Jack shrugged and raised his anchor.

"I'll leave you guys the little ones," he yelled back.

As he dropped down from the bow he noticed the deck was now awash in several inches of oily water. He rudely gunned his engine as he left, earning cries of outrage as he headed for favorite spot number four. Spot four was occupied, so he veered away and moved down the shoreline to a less favorable location. It didn't seem to matter. Leonard's magic worms seemed to call fish from across the lake, and Jack's livewell became so crowded that he was forced to move his beer into the heat. The sun being well over the horizon, Jack figured it was time to start on that beer anyway. He guzzled the beer, sat on the bow, and drifted on an unpopular section of the lake. He hauled in some small to average size bass, all of which would count at the final weigh-in.

When the morning bite seemed to be over and the beer supply grew dangerously low, he ceremoniously clipped the treble hook from his line and watched it sink into the dark waters of the lake. He checked for anyone watching, then opened the little styrofoam cooler and threw the can with the few remaining worms into the brown water. A free lunch for the bass. He secured his poles and gear and hopped to the deck. He landed in water up to his knees. He'd thought the boat had been riding a bit low. With his brain fuzzy with beer and baking sunlight and his outlook rosy, he'd sat on the bow and damn near let his boat sink. A hell of a note. His cheek stung with an imaginary slap. Whatcha thinkin about, boy, his dad said. He checked his watch. He'd be limping back, but there was still plenty of time to make the deadline. If the engine started.

The old Ford motor caught instantly and Jack offered a prayer of thanks to whoever watched over fools and drunks. The extra weight of the water made the craft sluggish to respond and Jack didn't have even a rudimentary manual pump to remove the excess baggage. He couldn't manage to bring the boat up to a plane, overpowered or not. He checked his watch again, calculated the time it would take to plow all the way across the lake, and started to sweat. His boat continued to ship water from some unknown leak and Jack watched with disbelief as the waters of the lake grew ever closer to the edge of his boat. This couldn't be happening. He realized that a single rogue wave might be enough to swamp him. He suddenly regretted the hole he'd cut in the watertight compartment. Then he recalled a trick heard of somewhere, sometime, somehow. He used the bowline to fix the wheel and sloshed his way to the stern of the boat.

By leaning well over the rear he could just reach the drainplug. As long as the boat remained moving forward, water would actually flow from inside the boat out the open plug—or so he'd heard. Seemed like a reasonable theory at this point.

He got the stem of the plug lifted, but it stubbornly refused to budge. He shifted position to improve his leverage and the plug slid free without warning and Jack promptly fell out the back. In desperation he grabbed for the transom and managed to catch it with one hand. He was now being dragged through the water behind his own boat, the treasure boat, filled with a trophy catch of status redemption. Not to mention a cash prize.

With an effort never to be repeated in this lifetime, he swung his other hand up and grasped the transom, lifted himself free of the propeller wash, and splashed into the bottom of the boat. He lay for a long moment with his head barely above water and blinked up at the sky. A can of beer bobbed against his head.

"Don't mind if I do," he said to the sky and he popped the top.

The tournament judges held court by the weigh-in scales surrounded by a crowd that oohed and aahed as each master fisherman's catch was measured for length and added to the scale. The absolute final deadline approached. Most had wisely returned with ten to twenty minutes to spare. A few, knowing they had no chance, hadn't bothered, and watched from their boats. One of the judges checked the official clock for the hundredth time as one of the onlookers gave a shout.

"Look what's coming in!"

All turned to stare at the lake.

Jack, with water within inches of the gunwales, plowed along with his engine screaming. He rocketed straight for the shore and the judging stand. The people along the shore backed away as it became apparent he had no intention or capability of slowing. As the old boat crunched into the bank Jack watched the edge of a particularly nasty rock thrust through the floorboards. He shut the engine off and the stern settled to rest on the bottom. He sloshed forward to the livewell and grasped one side. The crowd had closed in again, staring at the wreckage with awe.

"Somebody get that other side," Jack commanded. A man stepped forward and grabbed the other handle. Together they heaved the box over the side and set it on the beach. Jack stumbled over the side and the two of them strained the livewell to the judging stand. One of the judges reached out and shook Jack's hand with a grin.

"Congrats Junior, you just made it." He reached over and struck the bell with a ball peen hammer. "Time!"

Some time later the crowd had migrated toward the nearest bar to lie about how close they'd come to winning. Jack sat in the shade with the trophy in one hand and the check in the other.

"You going to fix her up?"

Jack looked up. It was the kid. He was wearing Jack Senior's too big hat tilted far back on his head.

"My dad died thinking I wasn't worth shit. He wanted a baseball player, a diesel mechanic, a fisherman, whatever. I'm a pharmacist."

"Geez, mister." The kid pointed at the trophy. "Today you're the champ."

"You're right about that. Today I'm the champ."

Jack stood and handed the trophy to the kid. He fished in his damp jeans and dug out the keys for the boat. He handed those to the kid also.

"The boat's a wreck but the gear is worth a couple hundred bucks. You—"

"Yes, mister?" the kid asked.

"—are going to be just fine," Jack said.

He straightened the kid's hat, nodded, and walked to his truck without looking back.

CHAPTER 21

Friday Afternoon, May 23

GLEN

"Something's wrong here! Goddam it, Chopper. Chopper!"

Jackie stuck her head in the door.

"Quit whining, I said you'd feel a little discomfort."

"Discomfort! I'm fucking dying in here."

"You're such a baby. Just ride it out and you'll be fine. Now shut up before I gag and restrain you. Play with your computer," she said as she slammed the door.

She and DeeDee played two-handed Pinochle and listened to classical music on the public radio station.

"You seem to be comfortable here. Are you happy?" DeeDee asked.

"Well, as happy as you can expect. I have the animals and my research. I do wish I had a man to share it with, sometimes. You can imagine the problems. The men I've met that are willing to forget I used to be a man.... You can imagine. Men are assholes, you know that. Still, you dream of a man out there somewhere who is decent and kind, strong but gentle, secure, and ready for a long-term commitment. You know, walks on the beach, quiet evenings at home in front of the fire, someone who will massage my feet."

"I used to be impressed with the nice cars and the silk suits, the coke, the parties. The smart guys and their money. Now, I don't know. I just wish I could find a simple man, some one I don't have to worry about disappearing when some other short skirt walks by, someone to grow old with."

"Wow, you just described our Glen perfectly."

DeeDee looked up from her cards in horror. Jackie was trying not to chuckle. They both broke out laughing. They held on to each other and giggled helplessly. When they were done, Jackie found a box of Kleenex and they wiped their eyes.

"If you want to get out of here, you can cut out, I'll get Glen back on his feet," Jackie said.

"I feel like I owe him something. If he's really going try to get his wallet back I think I should help him. Besides, I don't really have anywhere else to go."

"Well, that can be a problem sometimes," Jackie sighed. She piled the cards in the middle of the table. "Whose deal is it?"

MANNY

Manny looked in on Holly. She was sitting on the toilet reading a piece of bullet-tattered newspaper. She grinned at him as he pulled the door closed. When she came out of the bathroom he was getting dressed. She stood on her tiptoes and gave him a kiss.

"I feel good, baby," she said. "How are you doing?"

Manny was achy. The room was strewn with chicken bones, shell casings, beer bottles, and ripped up newspaper. Manny sighed and stuck two hundred-dollar bills under his pillow for the maid. He looked around, sighed, and stuck another bill under the pillow.

"You good under pressure, baby?" he asked.

"Sure. If it's gonna be real bad, just give me a 'lude, I can maintain."

"My guys are all dead and I don't have time to put another local crew together. I need to make a pickup and it'll probably get ugly."

"Good," she said.

She opened the transit case and looked through the contents. She found a Mitchell AP9M semi-auto 9mm. She looked inquiringly at Manny and he nodded his head okay. She found a box of Black Talon cartridges and nimbly loaded the 20 round magazine. She put the Mitchell in a large paper sack. She found a tiny Grendel P-12 380 that she stuck down the front of her jeans. Manny loaded the Mosberg and put a Smith and Wesson 639 into his shoulder holster. The Mosberg hung on a clip in his overcoat. He filled his jacket pockets with shotgun shells. He closed the transit case and dragged it into the closet. As they left the room he flipped the Do Not Disturb sign so it displayed the maid service request.

The Chevy started right up. Manny pulled through the drive-up window at McDonalds a mile or so down Pine Island Road.

"Hi Patty," Holly said, leaning over so she could read the counter-person's name tag. "I'd like two sausage muffins with egg and coffee," she said sweetly.

"Sorry ma'am, it's after eleven and we aren't serving breakfast anymore," Patty replied.

"It's 'leven-oh-five. I can still have breakfast."

"No, sorry, you order off the lunch menu after eleven," Patty said firmly.

"Goddam it," Holly said, fumbling with the gun in the paper sack.

Manny put his hand on her arm.

"Let's get some Big Macs and I'll buy you a cone," Manny said. "Okay?"

"A cone? Make it a large one," she said as she reluctantly lowered the paper sack back to the floor.

Manny paid. As they drove off, Holly offered Manny the first lick on the cone.

They crossed the Matlacha Island Bridge, Little Pine Island, and took Stringfellow Road north on Pine Island. For the whole trip, Holly munched her burgers and stared out the window. They pulled up to a warehouse a few blocks from the Bokeelia Pier. They shared a long kiss before leaving the truck. Manny smiled into a security camera as he pressed a button by a door just off the loading dock.

Rafael Banderas pulled the door open and gave Manny a big hug. He pretended not to notice the shotgun under Manny's coat.

"Manny, brother, how nice to see you."

They went in. Holly pushed the heavy door shut and leaned against it.

"How cute, you brought your daughter," Rafael said brightly.

"I'm his woman, you asshole," she said, as she shot him in the face through the paper sack.

Manny whipped out the Mosberg and fired into the two stunned dark-skinned guys who were frozen at the sight of their boss suddenly face-down on the floor. Holly ripped the Mitchell out of the bag and ran upstairs. She killed a fat lady who was screaming into a phone. She took the phone from the woman's limp hand and checked. It was a dial tone. She cradled it up and checked. There was no one else around.

"Damn it, Holly," Manny said, "you're on a hair-trigger."

"Life is too short to spend it fucking around with assholes," she said, kicking at Rafael's body. "We gonna duke it out or do we have some business here?"

"All right, we're looking for a couple of suitcases about so big," he said holding his hands two feet apart.

Outside, Doctor Zalooq's Lincoln eased to a stop in front of the run-down warehouse. The Doctor checked the address again. It was correct.

"I don't see why you still do these readings," Audrey said, miffed. "It's not like you need the money."

"I get tired of the big show and these readings keep me sharp. Besides, ten thousand is nothing to sneeze at."

He gave her a peck on the cheek, grabbed his case, and got out of the car. He knocked on the metal warehouse door. The place looked like a chop shop. Scrap car parts filled several 55-gallon drums. He could hear some muffled banging through the door. No one came, so he picked up an old rocker arm and pounded on the door. Inside, everything became quiet. The door opened a sliver and a gruff voice said: "We're busy so fuck off."

"I'm Doctor Zalooq and I have an appointment with Rafael Banderas." The Doctor waved his paper. The door slammed shut and there was disagreement inside. Thirty seconds later the door flew open and a burly man dragged the Doctor in. Instantly, all the Doctor's senses were alert. Several men were clearly dead, thrown around in dark puddles of blood. A young girl with blond spiky hair walked over from where she was tearing through a file cabinet. With the back of his hand, the ape checked to make sure the paint on a dark green Jaguar was dry, then leaned against it.

"What's your business here, asshole?" Manny asked.

The Doctor took a deep breath and tried not to look at the dead men.

"A reading. For Mister Banderas. I have an appointment."

Manny waved at one of the bodies. The girl lifted the head. Manny waved a ham fist casually.

"You can see that Senor Banderas is out of service."

He pulled a Smith and Wesson 9mm from a shoulder holster and pointed it at the center of Doctor Zalooq's forehead.

"You have five seconds to speak your last words."

The Doctor wondered for an instant, then his body relaxed.

"Today is not my day to die," he said tonelessly.

"If I pull the trigger, you will die."

"No, you won't pull the trigger. If you do pull the trigger, the gun will be empty. If the gun is not empty, the shell will misfire. Today is not my day, I know this."

"Do you believe this mystical hocus-pocus bullshit?" Manny asked Holly.

Manny did not fire. He considered the situation for a moment, then put his gun away.

"Since you're here, maybe you can do a reading. What do you say, Holly, shall we see what the Doctor has to offer?"

The Doctor put his briefcase down and pulled out a little painted box. He handed the box to Manny.

"Shake the box, remove the lid, and pour it out here," he said, waving at the desk.

Manny grinned and shook the box slowly. He removed the top and poured it. The box was filled with twisted little ivory pieces that looked like rodent bones. He looked at the Doctor questioningly. The Doctor caught his eye and said, "Bats."

Manny shrugged. The Doctor bent over and examined the pile carefully. He picked a few bones out of the mound and gently placed them back in the box.

"Interesting," he mumbled, lost in thought.

"You're a fake. I don't buy any of this crap," Manny said.

The Doctor took offense. "Just because I'm a fake does not mean I don't get a real reading now and again. If you're quiet, I can concentrate better."

"Let me shoot him, Manny," Holly said.

Manny waved her away.

"Go find the money," he said sternly.

The Doctor absently whistled through his teeth. He got down to eye level. His head was only a couple of inches away from the little pile.

"Interesting," he said.

"What?" Manny asked. "What do you see?"

"OW!" The Doctor jumped back as if burned. Manny and Holly reached for their guns.

"Holy shit."

"Can the dramatics, Doctor Bazooka."

"Zalooq. ZAH-LOW-KAH."

He put the bones back into the box with shaking hands.

"What is going on?"

The Doctor put the box back in his briefcase and closed the latches. He was pale and sweating. His voice quavered.

"I saw you running across a field. I saw a huge black bird swoop down and snatch your soul. I saw you rotting in Hell. All very soon."

He pointed at Manny with a quivering finger.

"You have a black shadow that you will not escape."

"Nice work, Doc. Now say nighty-night."

The Doctor picked up his case and walked to the door.

"My life does not end on this day."

"Can I?" Holly asked eagerly, waving her silenced Mitchell.

Manny shook his head no.

"Nah, let the dipshit go. What can I do?" he called out after the Doctor.

"You can try running," the Doctor replied as he walked out of the door.

"It won't work, but you can try," Zalooq whispered to himself.

On shaking legs, he walked to the big Lincoln. He flopped in the seat and held out his hand. Audrey passed him the bottle. He took a drink.

"You look like you saw a ghost," she said.

"I did," he replied.

"Did you get the money?"

"This one was a freebie," he replied. "Let's get out of here," he said to the driver.

MURPHY

Murphy stuck her head in the door and flipped on the light. Her heart was pounding. After all that had happened she did not know what to expect from Glen's house. Trap doors, a shotgun trip-wired to the door, who knows? Instead, the room was almost barren, with green shag carpets and walnut veneer paneling. There was one piece of furniture in the room, a Naugahyde love seat. Very 70's. She took a deep breath and walked in. The kitchen had vinyl flooring worn through to the plywood around the stove and the sink. The faucet dripped loudly every few seconds. A bowl, a spoon, and a coffee cup stood alone in the dish rack. The cheap dinette had two chairs and a neat pile of Journal American newspapers. Murphy checked the dates. The latest was from the previous Saturday. Webster stood in the doorway and watched. Murphy looked at him and shrugged.

"Go ahead, look around," she said. "And try not to break anything."

They walked through the bathroom and bedroom. There wasn't much to see. The bed was made. There were a half-dozen identical gray suits hanging in the closet. Webster dragged an old leather suitcase from under the bed.

"Heavy," he said. "Shall I open it?"

Murphy frowned and shook her head no.

Their inspection took ten minutes before they were looking at the same things over again. There was one door that would not open. It looked like a closet door but it had a new-looking Yale lock. Webster wiggled the handle and looked at Murphy with the question in his eyes. She nodded okay and Webster tried the key in the lock. It slid in smoothly. He turned it and they heard a muted click. He eased the door open. A stairway led into a dark basement. Webster could make out the hot water heater and furnace. He pulled the string for a hanging light and flooded the stairway with light. He could hear a fan running and the hum of a transformer. They walked down the wooden stairs and found a dull metal door. It had a latch like a walk-in freezer. Murphy put her ear against the door. All she could hear was a faint 60 cycle hum. She pulled the door open and the lights inside came on automatically. They walked in the room. It was much larger than they expected, as if it had been excavated beyond the foundation of the house. They looked around in amazement at the seven computer screens all displaying lines of ratcheting text and graphics. The center of the room was filled with a large circular object that almost looked like a round couch with a fabric cone rising in the center.

"Oh," Murphy said, "I've seen one of these before. This is a Cray computer."

"Wow," Webster said. "I've been wondering if I should buy a Ultra Mac and this guy has a Cray."

Some information on one of the color screens caught Murphy's eye. She saw her name scroll by, followed by her social security number, and some other numbers including her bank and 401k retirement account balances. She recognized her credit card numbers and account balances. There were a lot of numbers she did not recognize. Some medical charts and dental records, including X-Rays of her teeth, scrolled by silently. Her high school yearbook photograph flashed by along with a picture of her graduating class at the State Patrol Academy. She felt sick to her stomach. She recognized the biopsy results from a test of a lump in her breast. Her knees felt weak, so she sat in a high-backed chair. It rolled a few inches on silent wheels. She found it hard to catch her breath. It was as if she'd been hit by a truck.

Webster turned. "Murphy, roll over here and check this out," he said.

Murphy's legs felt spongy, but she managed to roll the chair to the screen that Webster was watching. The pictures of two large pushbuttons were displayed. One said Orrin Webster, press here and the other said Margaret Murphy, press here. Murphy moved the mouse over her button, looked into Webster's eyes, and clicked the left mouse button. A message box opened on the screen. It said: Hang on Murphy, I'm paging Mr. Wilson... The number of dots at the end of the message increased every second or so. The computer beeped. Another message box opened.

Hi Murphy. I hope you're enjoying the comfort of my home. There is some Pepsi in the ice box if you like.

No, I'm fine. Is this Glen Wilson?

Yes, I'm glad to finally meet you. I assume your partner Orrin Webster is with you? The one you call Number Three?

Yes. I hope you don't mind us looking around a little.

No, not at all. I always try to support and cooperate with law enforcement. My house is your house. If you use the toilet, make sure to wiggle the handle or it won't stop running.

Well, this is odd. I'm not sure what to say.

Okay, I'll help a little bit. I did not kill Pablo Estevez. I had a little disagreement with the cab driver but I'm positive he will not testify or press any charges. Elke won the lottery, we cheated a little but there is nothing traceable to me. I'm currently recovering from an accidental injury near Miami and I don't expect to be available for questioning for another two weeks or so. Anything else?

This is Orrin. What about the AES crypto algorithm?

What about it?

Are you in violation of any articles of security? Have you or any of your associates hacked this algorithm?

Yes. It's pathetic and no one who is serious about security uses it.

That is an act of treason. You can get the death penalty.

Ho hum. You're dull, Number Three. Or should I say one-hundred and thirty-three? Bring Murphy back.

Yes, Glen.

I'm scrolling some stuff on the screen behind you labeled Frodo. Take a quick look and let me know when you are back.

Okay.

Murphy rolled across the room. She tried not to look at the screen that was still scrolling her information. Nonetheless, she saw her birth certificate flash by with ink prints of her tiny feet. A handwritten card that said Frodo sat on top of a twentyfour-inch flat panel monitor. A hypertext list of names in blue lettering filled the screen. The names on the list were all 100 members of the United States Senate. With the mouse, she selected her Senator from Florida. A list of items appeared. The headings included love letters, indictments, illegal campaign contributions, tax returns, investments, nasty rumors, and miscellaneous. She almost selected love letters but decided she did not want to know. She closed her eyes and took a deep breath then she rolled back to the screen with Glen's messages.

Okay, Glen, I'm back.

That was just a tiny sample. From what you saw, what do you think are the chances that I'll ever be prosecuted for any crime?

Zero?

Very good, Murphy. If you want to tangle, we can do that. Otherwise, I'm more than willing to be polite and helpful.

I get the message. Out of curiosity, what if we zero-toleranced this house, including all the files and equipment?

Now you're getting dull, Murphy. I could hardly care less. Anything else?

Can I talk to you again?

No problem, just make a note of the e-mail address in the upper right corner of the screen. I usually check that address a couple of times a day. Get yourself wired, Murphy. Without access to the net you're quite obsolete.

Thanks, I think. Good-bye for now?

Yes, good-bye for now.

Murphy took a last look around the room. She felt like an atom bomb had exploded in her stomach. Webster had a smug grin on his face.

"What a cocky bastard. I can't wait to put the long arm of the law on his ass."

Murphy made a slashing motion with her hand. Webster almost spoke again but thought better of it. As she was pulling the metal door closed, a beeping and flashing started on the computer they were using. It was flashing <MURPHY!> in large red letters. She jerked open the door and ran back to the screen.

Yes, Glen?

I almost forgot. Would you do me a big favor please?

She looked at Webster, who made a sour face. "What now?" he asked rhetorically.

If I can, I will, she typed.

Great. I didn't get e-mail to my milkman quick enough and there is probably milk in the box on the porch getting warm. Please stick it in the fridge.

Sure, Glen. Good-bye again?

Thanks, Murphy. Out.

After they put the milk away and locked the house up they sat in the car. Murphy sat behind the wheel and dabbed at the perspiration on her forehead with a handkerchief. She rested her head on her forearms wrapped over the steering wheel. Every muscle twitched as if she'd been hit with lightning. The pizza churned in her stomach.

"I don't see what the big deal is. This guy is a blowhard. I'll just pick him up by the scruff of his neck and boot him across the room like my girlfriend's house cat."

Murphy shook her head. She held her hands before her face and tried to steady them. She was mostly successful.

"Shut up, Webster. Just shut the hell up."

"Geez, Murphy. No need to get mental. What's our next step?"

Murphy started the car.

"I think we should go talk to your boss and see if we can find out what the goal is. You can't win a game if you don't know where the goalposts are. I feel we don't know where the field is or which players are on our side. I'm going to see if Elke can join us too. She may be able to contribute something. I need to either learn the rules or drop out of the game."

"So, we're going to Saint Louis?"

"Yes."

"What are we going to do when we get there?"

Murphy looked at him crossly. She held up one finger.

"When I do this, what does it mean?"

"It means you want me to shut up?"

"Very good."

They drove in silence for a few minutes.

"Do you want to stay at my place? I've got a nice condo downtown and some rib steaks in the freezer."

"I'd rather jam red-hot railroad spikes into my head. I'd rather pluck my eyeballs out with pliers and feed them to the crows. I'd rather fall face-first onto a chain saw running flat out. I'd rather…"

"I get the idea, Murphy. I'm not stupid, you know."

"No, I don't know. I'm still looking for some sign of intelligent life between your ears. Now, zip it and leave me alone."

They made the remainder of the trip to Sea-Tac in what Murphy considered to be a blessed silence.

MANNY

Manny answered the door in his boxer shorts. He paid the pizza deliverer, who tried to peer around Manny into the room. Manny slammed the door in his face. The kid'd either caught a glimpse of Holly or word was spreading around the hotel about the girl who only wore sneakers. Like she was wearing now. She was sitting between the suitcases, which were open and displaying the bundled one hundred dollar bills. The Mitchell was in front of her. They were arguing about whether they liked money, guns, pizza, or sex the best. It boiled down to money: with money you buy plenty of the other stuff.

"Isn't this enough money?" Holly asked.

"It's enough unless you can use it to get more. I'm a business man. I'm going to invest this money in commodities, then resell the commodity. This dough, almost two million, is not bad, but if you can turn it into twenty million in two weeks, then that's really something. That's real fuck-you money."

"Twenty million," Holly said with wonder. "A week ago I was trying to hock some shit for fifty bucks and now we have a shot at twenty million."

"Cash, cold cash. No capital gains tax, no B and O tax, no inventory tax, no income tax. Oh yeah."

"Twenty million."

Holly leaned over and took two pieces of pizza from the box. She straddled Manny and worked his cock free of his shorts. She fed him both pieces of pizza as she worked his sex into her.

"Twenty million," she repeated.

"Hmmmm," Manny replied.

CHAPTER 22

Saturday Afternoon, May 24

GLEN

"I've been trying to decide if I'm in love with Glen," DeeDee said.

Jackie used the remote control to turn off the sound on the television. Geraldo's IQ seemed to increase by twenty percent when they could not hear what he was spouting off about. Jackie looked at DeeDee with a puzzled expression.

"Well, he's an okay lover. He seems to have money. He has grit. A girl could do worse."

"You don't know what you are saying."

"You knew Glen a long time ago. What was he like? What made him the way he is now? You said he wouldn't stop until he's killed or gets his wallet back. Why? It's insane. I don't understand it."

Jackie rubbed her eyes.

"I don't know either," she said. "I'll tell you about Glen in Vietnam. That was a seriously fucked-up place. Now we have electronics assembled in Ho Chi Minh City and Love Boat cruises along the Vietnamese coast. I was clinically depressed and insane during the sixteen months I was there. I started as a gung-ho medic and ended as a burned-out heroin addict."

She took a sip of tea.

"The hospital was run by a Major, Major Bradley. Bradley had graduated from one of the Ivy League schools and was a racist. He'd hold up medicine for the blacks and send them back to the field before they were ready, refuse to send them home, he had a million tricks. I had a fixation on the guy. A pure hatred. I'd been drinking heavy and following him, he had an apartment near the center of the city with a couple of teenage girls he was fucking. I had a crazy plan to jump in his jeep with a grenade and blow us both to hell. I must have told Glen about it in a bar or something; somehow he heard about it. I was really going to do it and I often wish I'd succeeded. Glen literally took the grenade out of my hand and talked me into doing something else. Bradley was drugged and put in the hospital, where I amputated both of his legs."

"My god," DeeDee said. "That's where the 'Chopper' came from?"

"No, they called me that before, but it was more of a joke. Chopper Reynolds, the junkie medic. Glen took care of my habit and I took care of the limbs of his enemies. None as bad as Bradley, just some toes, a foot now and then. As the war wound down and it was clear we were pulling out, Glen locked me in a hooch and fed me rice and beer for a week. After the week, Glen put a forty-five to my head and said I'd stay clean or die right there. Some fucking cure. The Glen Wilson Intervention and Drug Abuse program. It worked, though. Does this sound like a man to fall in love with?"

"Sometimes I wonder if there isn't a decent man anywhere in the world," DeeDee said.

"You and me both, sweetie," Jackie replied.

"What about the sex change? Was this something you were born with, trapped in a man's body or something?"

"No. I just hated myself so much that I needed to become someone else."

"Wow," DeeDee said.

MURPHY

Murphy and Orrin Webster walked up the concrete stairs of the FBI building. Being Saturday, there was not much foot traffic and the place was nearly deserted. When they reached the top, Webster tugged at Murphy's sleeve. She turned to face him.

"I've got to warn you about the receiving clerk."

"What about him?"

"I detest that donkey's ass. His name is Art Nishimoto. He's a very hateful man. He's going to give you some trouble. The best way to handle him is to keep your mouth shut, sign your name everywhere he tells you to, and get out of there. I've reported his rudeness a couple of times but everyone is scared of him and nobody does anything. He must be sixty-five. I wish the old goat would retire or die or something."

"Okay, Number Three. Thanks for the advice."

They pushed through the revolving doors. Security camera servos whined as the camera heads tracked them across the lobby. They signed in with the guard at the reception desk and pressed their thumbs on an electronic scanner. They entered a small room. A husky Japanese sat behind a battered metal desk reading USA Today. He ignored them for a few seconds, then sighed, folded his paper carefully, and put it in a desk drawer.

"What is it," he said gruffly.

"Signing our weapons in. Got a meeting with Tom Baker. This is Captain Murphy."

"I don't give a shit if it's Nefer-titty, the Queen of the goddam Nile. Let's see some ID."

Murphy had hers ready and she laid her pocketbook open on the desk while Webster fumbled with his wallet. Nishimoto adjusted his reading glasses and scrawled some information on a form on a clipboard. The clipboard was ancient and worn but a touchscreen under the paper was WLAN-linked to a host computer.

Murphy could see a form on a computer screen being filled out while Art worked.

"Humph." Art cleared his throat. "I knew a Florida State Patrol Murphy once, a useless prick named Carter Murphy?" His tone made this a question.

"That was my dad. You're right, he was a prick. A goddam good cop, though."

"You're fucking right about that. They don't make genuine assholes like that any more," he said as he tossed her pocketbook down. "That cocksucker had a hand in the Albertson case, blew that little shit out of his loafers, am I right?"

"Yeah. Wounded in the right shoulder, he plugged Albertson left-handed with four of six from his Colt 44."

"That's son-of-a-bitch'n good shooting. And here you are, a quota-queen, sucking the government nipple while real men roll in their soggy graves."

"Yeah, you and me both, Equal Opportunity piss-ant parasites."

Nishimoto carefully examined Webster's ID and compared his face to the picture as if he hadn't seen him before. He tossed the wallet back. He attached another form to the clipboard.

"You packing, Queenie?"

Murphy pulled out her little Rossi and a quick-loader.

"Here you go, dickwad," she said as she slid the gun across the desk.

Webster was horrified. He placed his Glock on the desk with a shaking hand. He tried to catch Murphy's eye to tell her to back off, but she ignored him.

"Thanks, bitch," Art replied. He slipped the gun and shells in an envelope, rolled across the room, and put them in a cabinet. He repeated the procedure for Webster's Glock.

"Now get your fucking ass out of here, tough guy," Art said, looking Murphy directly in the eye. His eyes glittered in the fluorescent light.

"See you fucking later," she replied.

As Webster escaped through the door in a hurry, Murphy nodded curtly at Nishimoto. He winked at her, then put his feet on the desk and unfurled his newspaper between them.

"What was that all about," Webster asked when the door was safely closed.

"You're right, he's an asshole," Murphy replied.

In a large conference room, Murphy buttered a croissant and stood looking over the river. Tom Baker bustled into the room escorting Elke. Murphy set her coffee down and shared a firm handshake with Baker. He was about 50, with a shaved head and bushy mustache. Murphy hugged Elke.

"Captain Murphy, what a pleasure," Baker said heartily. "I've talked a few times with your boss, Major Smythe, and he speaks quite highly of you."

He drew a cup of coffee from a stainless steel urn and sat at the table. When all were seated, Baker used a remote control to close the curtains and lift a walnut panel. A large computer screen appeared behind the panel. The FBI logo faded onto the screen as it warmed up.

"I know you are losing patience with us, Captain Murphy," Baker continued, "and I don't blame you. If you'll bear with us, I'd like some folks to come in and give some presentations. Afterwards, we'll debrief and plot our next move. Does that sound okay, Captain?"

Murphy nodded.

There was a knock and a slight man poked his head in the door. Baker waved him in. The man placed an untidy stack of folders and loose papers on the table. He shook hands with everyone as Baker introduced him.

"This is Doctor Clayton Thomas, one of our resident Ph.D.'s. He specializes in communications."

Clay Thomas wore a pink shirt with a lime green tie and polyester slacks. He wore one sock under his dirty Nike running shoes, his dirty ankle showed between cuff and shoe on the other foot. He peered around the room nearsightedly. He walked absently around the room as he spoke; it was clear that he had been, at one time, a college professor. He spoke clearly but quickly, hardly stopping to catch a breath. He tapped a pencil on his teeth when he was thinking.

"For many years we've had a search going, SETI, the Search for Extraterrestrial Intelligence," Dr. Thomas said, looking around the room to see if this meant anything to the people around the table. He shrugged, sipped his tea, and continued. "We scan radio frequencies and use digital signal processing to try to separate meaningful patterns from the background noise of space. Our methodical search of the nearest and most promising star systems produces oceans of data. Far too much data for humans to analyze. Computers monitor the incoming data and use pattern recognition algorithms to sift the chaff from signals of possibly intelligent origin. In the last 18 months of continuous operation the computers identified three sources of repeatable signals. All three had been pulsars. Interesting objects but definitely not intelligent," he said, gesturing with his pencil. He seemed to forget where he was for an instant, but then he picked up the thread.

"A single SETI site can't determine the source of a signal, only the direction from which it came. Other radio telescope sites around the globe assist by providing triangulation. Using precise timing of the signal's arrival an accurate distance can be calculated. Cesium clocks help align the coherence of the signals. The measurable difference could be in milliseconds or microseconds, depending on the orientation of the earth with respect to the incoming signal. Eight months ago, SETI's computers logged some signals from a Sol-like yellow star approximately 227 light years away. We received a two-minute series of pulses. Every eighteen minutes the pulses repeated three more times. This was very special. It really looked to be humanity's First Contact. You can imagine the excitement. For several weeks, around the world, researchers studied these signals. They were definitely not random and therefore were of intelligent origin. A graduate student at Cal Tech, named David Albright, noticed something about the signals that the billions of computer processing cycles had missed. You may have heard of him?"

Everyone at the table looked baffled.

"No? All right. He's one of those boy geniuses. I think he graduated from high school at thirteen and immediately started at Cal Tech. Anyway, looking at the pattern on an oscilloscope, he noticed amplitude modulation on what looked like a carrier wave. A series of long and short pulses of a frequency of little interest to the SETI community as it was in a band used extensively for our own communications. The great minds had expected any extraterrestrial signal to be in the 'Water Hole' bandwidth. This band is good for interstellar signals because of its lower attenuation by the great clouds of interstellar dust and gas. The frequency band was so named due to its relationship to the natural resonant frequency of water. Mr. Albright knew within minutes that he was looking at the simple amplitude modulation of a carrier wave. Very crude, but effective. This was a puzzling discovery. A series of pulses that differed only in duration. For no particular reason, Albright called in one of the old technicians, a Ham radio operator who knew Morse code. It took them about thirty minutes to decode it by hand."

"Spam is the practice of sending unsolicited sales pitches indiscriminately across the net. It's a rude and tasteless thing to do. It wastes bandwidth and generally just pisses everyone off. Oops, sorry, I should watch my language. To get to the point, our first coherent message from deep space was a spam."

He passed out photocopies around the room.

"Are there any questions?"

There was no response.

"Very well, then. I can be reached by Mister Baker if anything comes up."

Elke held up her hand.

"Excuse me, Doctor Thomas. Did you ever figure out how this was done?"

"The best we can figure is a virus in a deepspace probe computer caused it to transmit the message back to us. We never found out how it was done and never will, since the probe won't be back in this part of the galaxy for another twelve million years. Anything else?"

"Yes. What exactly was illegal about what was done?"

Tom Baker answered.

"Technically, I don't think we've identified any laws that were broken."

"Do you know how much money was spent trying to decipher this phony message?" Dr. Thomas said as he placed his teacup on the table. "In the United States alone, we spent about three hundred million dollars in research and supercomputer time. This does not include the Australians, the French, and so on."

"I understand this was expensive..." Elke began.

"And embarrassing," Dr. Thomas interjected.

"Sure, and embarrassing," Elke continued, "but what laws were broken?"

"I understand your point," Baker said, "but we just can't allow hacking of our expensive systems. The law hasn't caught up with certain new types of computer crime, that's true. But we still need to put an end to this type of vandalism."

No one said anything.

"Okay. Have a good day," Thomas said. He nodded at Tom Baker and left the room. In his trail a single sheet of paper drifted to the floor. Tom picked it up absently and ran it through a portable shredder.

Murphy took another look at the photocopy of the deep space message that Doctor Thomas had handed out. She wadded it into a ball.

2225 Megahertz P75 processors. Thirty-five percent off Intel's list price. Going fast! Contact Glen Wilson.

Murphy lobbed the paper ball at a wastebasket, three points, nothing but net. The door opened and a middle-aged woman entered. She wore a wool suit, white stockings, and clunky black shoes. She wore her gray hair in a pageboy style and had a long thin nose. Dark circles around her eyes indicated she didn't sleep much. She dropped a canvas bag on the table and shrugged off her jacket. Baker stood, shook her hand, and introduced her.

"This is Doctor Pia Sanduski. Doctor Sanduski has studied cryptography and computer security for thirty years. She's been working for us since she defected from Russia in the early seventies. Doctor Sanduski will brief us on AES technology."

"Please call me Pia." She spoke with a thick accent. Her clothes and breath reeked of cigarette smoke. She placed a flat screen terminal on the table. "I've spent my whole career studying public key cryptography. The best way to explain this will be via example. Suppose I want to send a private message, perhaps a message that includes credit card numbers or confidential information, maybe even a love letter. Yes, let's say I want to send a secret message to my lover, say he's married and he doesn't want his potato wife to read this message. Perhaps she has all the money and just gives my lover a small allowance, hardly enough to pay the hotel bills or buy me dinner. For the purposes of our example, we'll assume she is a cheap cow, and it is vital that she not see our sensitive admissions of love or the arrangements for our trysts."

Baker twisted his face sourly and made eye contact with Murphy. Murphy shrugged and turned her attention back to Pia who was speaking intensely with her eyes closed.

"So, we have this message, which includes the time and place we will meet, whether I should bring the wine and the flavored lubricants, and so on. We'll call it M, which I will encode with my lover's public key which we'll call P. This key, P, everyone knows. The original message is converted to a new message, a message encoded with key P."

She wrote on the terminal with a stylus. In her handwriting, the equation P(M) appeared on the computer monitor.

"This version of the message is meaningless. If the old cow looks at it, she will just see junk; happy faces and other crap. When my lover applies his private key, which we will call R, voila, the original message pops out."

She wrote R(P(M)) = M on the screen.

"With proper encoding and long key strings, it is virtually impossible to decode a message without knowing the private key. Recently, a French researcher cracked an encoded message that used a 40 bit key. It took about 64 MIP/years of processing power to do it at a cost of about twenty-five thousand dollars.

Of course, we usually use 1024-bit keys and the processing power required to break the code doubles with each additional bit. That means the pig can process for the rest of her life and still be a million miles from reading our sexy little message."

The Doctor pulled a stick of nicotine gum from her canvas bag. Unconsciously she unwrapped the stick, stuck it in her mouth, and dropped the foil wrapper on the floor. Webster rolled his eyes and leaned over to retrieve it.

"Now we get to AES. AES implements the Skipjack public key algorithm in hardware. This implementation has a 'back door'. At the same time a message is encrypted and sent on its way by the Clipper chip, another version is created and encoded with the government's 80-bit key. This new message is called the LEAF, or the Law Enforcement Access Field. The government key to the LEAF is held in two escrows. With a court order, we can take the key halves out of the escrow accounts and decode the LEAF."

The Doctor pulled the gum out of her mouth and looked at it with distaste.

"This stuff tastes like dung," she said as she stuck it under the lip of the table. "Where was I? Yes, this system works very well and helps us track drug deals and money laundering. Unless... unless some clever man encrypts the message before sending it through the security processor chip. Then, when we decode the message there is another layer of security that we have to break. Frankly, it's quite irritating to go to the trouble of getting a court order, going to both the escrow agencies, getting the keys, then finding that the message is still, how do you say— gobbledygook, yes? Now, about this Glen Wilson. He's a real stone in our sandals. Last year he sent over seventeen hundred privately encoded messages."

She leafed through some papers in her bag. "Fourteen months ago we decided to get Mister Wilson. We had a message that our intel determined was about the illegal export of encryption technology. This technology is classified as munitions for export purposes. We arrested him and took him to court."

"Why isn't he in jail?" Elke asked.

"It turns out that the message was not double-encrypted after all, it was just a bit-mapped graphics file. An easy mistake to make as the files look completely random."

"What was the picture of?"

The Doctor frowned. "That's what the judge wanted to know. That information is classified and held secret under court order."

"Is it illegal to use private encryption?" Elke asked.

"Yes, quite."

"Even if the message is innocent?"

"If it is innocent, then there is no need to encode it, is there?"

"Fine," Elke continued, "but how many convictions have held up in court for encrypting private messages?"

"The fokking judges and juries don't know anything about cryptography. They just don't understand."

"How many?" Elke insisted.

"We brought a case against Phil Zimmermann, the inventor of PGP, which stands for Pretty Good Protection, an implementation of Public-Key technology."

"You dropped that case! What else? I don't follow your example, you need privacy for your love letters, but it's okay if the government wants to snoop?"

"You ask too many questions," the Doctor said as she gathered her stuff. "I don't like you," she added as she walked out of the room.

"I think these are fair questions," Murphy said, addressing Baker. "And what was Glen's graphic file a picture of?"

"I don't see how that is relevant."

"The reason we're here is to find out why this case is being handled so oddly. We know where Glen is, but we just follow him. Weird things happen but we have nothing to charge him with. We ask many stupid questions. I haven't seen a warrant for his arrest. It seems like an expensive fishing expedition. Now I find you want to arrest him for some computer picture. I think it's fair to know what the picture was."

Elke nodded and looked expectantly at Baker. He sighed and took a red folder from his briefcase. He popped a wax seal and passed the picture around the room. The picture was a close-cropped close-up of Glen's face. His eyebrows were arched and he had an annoyingly smug look on his face.

"A face like that really should be illegal," Baker said dryly.

"But it isn't, is it?" Elke said, looking over the top of the picture at Baker.

GLEN

Glen looked at his hand wrapped in the bandage. It throbbed and hurt worse than ever.

"Damn it," he shouted as he started tearing off the bandage. He almost had it off before Jackie and DeeDee stuck their heads in the door.

"Stop it, Glen! I brought your shot, now hang on and you'll feel better in a minute."

"Something's wrong, I'm telling you."

He pulled the last piece of gauze off and looked at his finger. The missing finger was a bright pink stub about a quarter inch in length.

"What?" he said.

Then he realized what had happened.

"Goddam it all to hell, Chopper. I told you I didn't want your fucking frog juice. Fuck!"

"You're doing well, a couple more shots and you'll be whole. I'm sorry about going against your wish, but I had to do my best to take care of you."

"Bullshit. You just wanted to try that shit on a human guinea pig."

"Hold still and I'll give you the shot. You can sleep. I'll give you more morphine."

"You'll get that needle away from me or I'll stick it up your ass, maybe you can grow another bunghole."

Glen threw his clothes into his suitcase. He slipped his shoes on his bare feet. He pointed at DeeDee.

"You coming or staying here with this whacked-out bitch?"

DeeDee looked at the floor.

"I'm coming," she said in a small voice.

They threw their stuff into the old taxi. Jackie was crying on the front step of her clinic.

"I'm so sorry. I was just trying to help you. If you don't finish the treatment you'll be stuck with that little stub."

Glen walked up to face her.

"If you weren't a woman, I'd punch your lights out."

He turned back to the car and took a couple of steps.

"What am I thinking…?"

He turned back to her.

"You'll always be Chopper to me," he said as he punched her hard in the face. She collapsed in the doorway. He climbed in the passenger seat of the taxi. DeeDee floored it and they disappeared in a cloud of blue smoke.

"Don't you fucking say a word," Glen warned DeeDee as he examined his little pink stubs with a bitter expression.

MURPHY

"This is Doctor Victor Chu," Baker said. "Doctor Chu is an AI software expert."

Victor was a five-foot Korean. He was thin and childlike except for his wispy mustache and beard. His eyes floated behind thick glasses like grapes in a fish bowl. He was neatly dressed in a suit and tie. His dainty wingtips shone like polished brass. A back door to the conference room opened and a large black man entered. He sat at the end of the table without speaking. He gestured for Chu to begin his presentation.

"Good afternoon," Doctor Chu said. He nodded politely at all in the room. He pointed the remote control at the screen and selected a new image. "Mister Baker is incorrect, for no one is an AI, or Artificial Intelligence, expert. This technology is in its infancy and we are merely blind men and women tripping over random objects in a dark room."

The television monitor displayed some mathematical functions.

"AI is my vocation, but chaos is my avocation. Everyone here is familiar with the work of Kurt Godel? Werner Heisenberg? Elton Wang? Doctor Pepper? No? Excuse me, Doctor No? You've never heard of Doctor No? From Ian Fleming? Many pardons for my little joke. But this illustrates a small point. Humans are pattern seeking animals: when exposed to a set of elements we try to group them and this leads us astray sometimes. Computers do not go astray. If a link exists they accept it and operate on it no matter how illogical it seems."

Noticing the blank looks, Doctor Chu switched off the television.

"I'm going to skip all the math and tell you what I know. If you don't believe my conclusions we can meet later and work through the derivations. We've gone beyond programming computers in a deterministic manner. We literally set some basic rules and let the computers process data and learn. My area is allowing computers to make associations in raw data. As an example, I have a computer that trades in the commodities market. It's the first software program that owns a billion dollars. All on paper of course, not real cash. I'll skip all that too. You're interested in Glen Wilson. So am I. He's a strange attractor, a sort of catalyst for events. This means the computers have identified some odd connections which have only Mister Wilson as a connecting thread."

"Anything illegal?" Elke asked.

"Sure, yes, of course," Doctor Chu replied.

"Excellent. Let's process the charges, get a warrant, and put Wilson in jail. Finally we have something," Murphy said with relief.

"Illegal, of course. But nothing we can prove in court. Just probabilities ranging from high to near certainty of crimes Mister Wilson has been involved with."

"Can we cut out the crap?" Murphy cried out in frustration. "I don't want to get an engineering degree. I'm a cop. Point me at a bad guy, I'll run him down and slap on the cuffs. I don't need this metaphysical techno-babble."

The black man rapped his knuckles on the table.

"Excuse me," he said. "I know what you want and we don't have it. All we can do is watch Wilson with certainty that nasty things will be happen'n."

"I should introduce you," Baker said. "This is Robert Stephens of the DEA, the Drug Enforcement Agency."

"Both my friends and all my enemies call me Steve."

Elke stared at him with a dawning realization that Steve was Glen's boss from Vietnam. Doctor Chu held up a thin finger.

"Before I go, can I tell them what I found most interesting?"

"If you insist," Steve said resignedly.

"Very good. We've been running calculations on the probabilities of various people running for public office. For example, the former Governor from Texas has a forty-two percent chance of being re-elected. The other contenders are the usual suspects, no surprises. It's when we let the computer pick the long odds that things get interesting. For example, the computer thinks that Bobby Kennedy is still alive and has a small chance of becoming president."

"Why?" Elke asked. "Bobby died over thirty years ago."

"We don't know. As I've said, the computer is allowed to draw its own conclusions based on whatever data it can collect across the net. Interfacing can be frustrating. It's like talking to a combination con man and prophet. A four trillion instruction cycles per second Delphic Oracle. I ran calculations on everyone in the room. None of us has more than ten to the minus eighth chance of being president in the next election. It's more likely that, in the next hour, we'll die from being hit by blue ice falling from a commercial airliner. Extremely unlikely, one would hope. In contrast, the computer says that there is a zero-point-seven percent chance, assuming Glen Wilson survives the next six months, that he will be the President of the United States."

"It probably means that Glen has polluted some database or something. Probably doesn't mean anything," Murphy commented.

"You could be right. Maybe the computer is smart enough to take that into account, maybe not. We've run some experiments trying to fool the computer and it always detects and ignores the bad data. An interesting possibility is that the skill involved in manipulating data on the net is an asset in a presidential campaign. Who knows?"

The Doctor gathered his papers.

"If there are no more questions?" he said.

All were still and deep in thought except Orrin Webster, who reached across the table for a blueberry muffin. Doctor Chu nodded politely at them and walked out.

CHAPTER 23

Later Saturday Afternoon, May 24

GLEN

"Where are we going?" DeeDee asked.

"According to credit card records, Manny has been doing some business in the Fort Myers area."

"Where's that?"

"Do they still teach geography in school?"

"You gonna give me a lecture about how great things were back in ought-six or are you going to tell me where we're going?"

"Head west on Highway 98 to 80."

"Won't that take us through Luis's area? He'll be watching for us. Haven't we had enough of that guy yet?"

"He can kiss my ass."

"I have a bad feeling about this. Can't we take another route farther south or something?"

"You drive and I'll navigate, all right?"

My hand hurt, so I wasn't my usual patient and supportive self. We made it through Clewiston without any problem. Seemed as if every eighteen-wheeler pilot we passed was yammering on his or her CB radio. I didn't much like it but there was nothing I could do short of killing them all, which would be illegal, except maybe in Texas. Not to mention the noise and bother. We picked up a local motorcycle trooper by the Airglades Airport. The road is flat and straight and the speed limit is thirty-five. A revenue enhancement zone. He didn't turn on his blue lights until he was close enough to see our out-of-county plates. Prick. I speed dialed on the cell phone and caught Anderson at his desk. He wanted five hundred bucks but I talked him down to three because he owed me a couple of favors. DeeDee was about to freak. Her hands shook violently when the trooper asked for her license and registration. Anderson took his sweet time but came through. The speaker on the bike squawked and emitted an emergency tone. A 10-18 call followed by a terse 187 by a 918 Adam. If I remember my codes properly, this was something like a homicide by deranged mental patient. Whatever the translation, it got Trooper Stanley's attention. He gave us a stern warning and roared off to the East.

"What luck," DeeDee said with relief.

Right, luck, and I'm out three hundred bucks. Our good luck that most of the dispatch centers are computerized these days.

DeeDee pulled out. I had to raise my voice at her to keep the speedometer at eighty most of the way. The Chevy engine hammered like a blender full of nuts and bolts. The horizon turned black and ominous.

We hit a thunderstorm by Lake Hicpochee. The mad and random lightning speared the land in nearly vertical bolts. The dense rain made it seem as if we were under water. DeeDee slowed to seventy while I tried to remember if the tires had any tread. The sky was dark as the Chevy's motor oil.

"Someone's coming up fast," DeeDee said.

"Turn your lights on."

"They are on."

"Well then, turn them off."

She scorched me with an evil look as she hit the lamp switch. I twisted in my seat and watched the headlights approach rapidly. They had to be doing at least ninety. Running lights above the cab, it surely looked like a Chevy Suburban. Like the one parked in Luis's driveway. I reached over DeeDee, fastened her seat belt, and cinched it up tight. Then I fastened my own. "Lay off the gas and maybe they'll pass," I said in the instant before the Suburban smashed into us. *Okay, maybe driving through this area was a bad call.* The taxi fishtailed but DeeDee kept it on the road. Either the girl could drive or she's damn lucky. Hard to tell the difference sometimes.

"Good girl," I yelled. "Now punch it."

I got the distinct impression she'd rather punch me. The Suburban did a 360 and stopped with a headlight shining over the field beside the highway.

DeeDee gunned it and we roared through the rain, with no headlights, the road a dark blur, and the wipers working hard but losing to the rain. DeeDee's knuckles were white as she leaned over the steering wheel. If she'd asked, at that moment I would have married her. Apparently she had other matters on her mind. I lit a cigarette and stuck it between her lips.

"Thanks," she said, squinting into the heart of the storm.

I looked for something to throw out the window to slow the Suburban. An anvil or a barrel of TNT would be nice. All I found were a couple of two liter bottles of soda and the gas can I lifted from that boat many months ago. Maybe it wasn't months, maybe it was only a couple of days and a finger ago. I lobbed them out the window just for the hell of it. The Suburban regained the road missing a headlight and rolled over the debris. Those damn Suburbans are built like Bradley assault vehicles. Luis turned on his brights. Still just one eye. I looked at the map. The highway crossed the Seaboard Coast Rail Line a few miles ahead.

"There's a rail crossing at Goodno. Try to stay ahead as much as possible."

"What are we going to do there?"

DeeDee was losing it. She sucked the cigarette down to the last eighth inch and spit it out. I pitched the map out the window. Maybe I was losing it too.

"I don't know, I'll think of something."

She gave me a quick look that said: "You're stupid and out of your mind, we're gonna die, and I hate you, your wallet, your family tree, and any world that would stand to have you in it." Or something to that effect.

She held the taxi at eighty-five and the Suburban didn't gain any ground.

"Pull off after the rail crossing. Use the emergency brake and transmission, don't touch the brake!"

She looked at me as if I were crazy but, praise be, she did it. We skidded to a shuddering halt, mostly sideways and hanging on the lip of the road. I ran back and looked for anything. The place was all grass and fence posts. I found nothing so I stood in the road and waved my arms. The single headlight speared me like a crossbow. It bore down hard and fast. "Fuck you, fuck you, fuck you," I muttered, then cried one last "FUCK YOU" as I dived into the weeds at the last possible instant. The Suburban was pointed at the railroad crossing signal that I'd been in front of. The wide-eyed look on Luis's face indicated that he thought this was a rather nasty trick. He tried to recover but the wheels lost their grip. The big truck slid sideways on the slick pavement.

The Suburban slammed into the signal post. The irresistible force of five thousand pounds of Detroit heavy iron meeting the immovable object of the stainless steel railroad crossing signal made an ungodly noise. The Suburban buckled around the post before tearing it free with a crunch that was more felt than heard. Both flipped end for end. Truly amazing. The Suburban sprayed water like an absurd fountain as it came to rest on its side. The signal post flew by the taxi with a shower of sparks and cart-wheeled into the weeds.

I got up out of the ditch slowly. As I approached the wreck I grabbed one of the cross-members of a shattered sign, the side that said RailRoad. I flashed on playing Monopoly as a kid and always buying up the railroads. Two hundred bucks a pop if your opponents landed on the suckers. I figured this means Luis owes me two hundred bucks.

I was fifty feet from the smoking wreckage when the driver's door flipped open. Luis popped his head up and our eyes locked. I got the distinct impression that I could try and try, yet Luis and I would never be friends.

There is an old saying that a full life contains equal numbers of good friends and dead enemies. Actually, I contributed the dead part. I started running when Luis tumbled out onto the pavement. He struggled up and raised a shotgun. With a one right-handed shake, he pumped a round into the chamber, convenient because most of his left hand appeared to be a red smear on the roadway. He fired a wild round in my direction. I thought about ducking, but that would give him time to fire again. Only a couple of the pellets hit me. I smashed him in the head with the railroad sign, then again, and once again. He dropped the gun and tilted over a little bridge and I hit him one last time. The sign shattered in my hands. I inspected the broken end. Yellow pine and dry rot, no wonder. I dropped the useless sign, gathered a handful of Luis's shirt with my right hand, and bashed in his nose with my left. I felt pain all the way down to my toes. Still, gathering my resolve, I hit him again and again. I lost my grip and he collapsed on the guardrail. He hung on for a second then slipped over. I was pissed because I wasn't done hitting him.

After the excitement the pain kicked in. When it receded to intermittent waves of pure misery I got up and peeked over the edge. Luis lay crumpled with his head at a very unnatural angle. When I got back to the taxi, DeeDee was sobbing into the steering wheel.

"Let's hit it," I said, sagging into the seat.

"I'm so tired," DeeDee wailed.

"Just hit it, will ya? We'll feel sorry for ourselves later."

We pulled into Tice an hour later just as the sun broke through the clouds. It didn't make either of us feel any better.

CHAPTER 24

GLEN

Glen woke up when DeeDee came back to the room with bear claws and paper cups of coffee from the free continental breakfast. He hunched over his computer in the nude. He munched and sipped as he tapped email into his computer.

We met at the Orlando computer trade show. I've changed my mind and need some heavy hardware after all. Please e-mail a list of stuff deliverable quickly to the Fort Myers area and a price in dollars. I'll trade for RAMBUS-X modules. Many regards. GW.

"Glen, we need to talk," DeeDee said.

"Hang on, I want to get a status on the agent I've got checking Manny out."

He pulled up his account and read off some information.

"Can you really find out about someone with these computers?" DeeDee asked while stirring some artificial creamer into her coffee.

"I've got his social security number, his bank account numbers, his credit card records, his school records, his mother's social security numbers, his medical records, a lot of stuff. I have his beeper and his cell phone number. He's been using a Texaco card in the area and has a room charged on his Mastercard at the Pink Shell resort. He's charged some food. On Thursday he charged a bunch of newspapers. Seventy bucks worth of newspapers. I wonder why he wanted them? He's paying for double occupancy. Does he have a girlfriend down here?"

"Not that I know of, it's probably some babe he picked up at an all-ages club or something. Glen, where do you see our relationship going?"

"Is that what we have? A relationship? Now hang on, I want to call Manny."

Glen dialed Manny's number.

"Hello, who am I speaking to? Well, Holly, is Mister Rodriguez available? Tell him it's Glen Wilson."

Glen could hear Holly yelling at Manny. Manny didn't seem to know the name. DeeDee could only hear half the conversation.

"Hi Manny, it's me, Glen Wilson, the wallet-man. That's right."

"My hand is healing nicely, thank you for asking. The last I saw Wesley he was dancing with that big gator. I'm wondering if I might stop by the Pink Shell this afternoon and pick up my wallet? Would that be convenient for you?"

"Well, that's not very nice. Fuck you too, asshole."

Glen turned off the phone and tossed it on the bed.

"He sure seems attached to that shitty wallet," Glen said to DeeDee.

"You're the one that's obsessed. I don't get this wallet thing. You're willing to die to get it back. There must be something special about it. Why can't we just forget the whole thing and get out of here?"

"I'll die before I let some slime-bag drug dealer rip me off. It simply can't be allowed."

"Is this a death wish? I could save you a lot of trouble if you just want to check out."

"I don't give a shit about dying. I'm going to do what I do until the lights go out. That's the way it is."

"What about us?"

Glen's computer chimed.

"Hang on, I've got an e-mail," he said while tapping on his keyboard.

"Damn, that's fast, it's the guy with the hardware."

Glen scrolled through a list and placed an order.

"Yeah," he said. "What were we talking about?"

"Can I just go when you get your wallet back?"

"You can go now. Want me to call you a cab?"

"I don't have any money and I don't have anywhere to go."

"Whatever," Glen said absently. Another message came through on the computer. "Okay, that's that. Somebody named the Captain is going to deliver the stuff tomorrow morning. Now, go sit by the pool or something while I see if I can find out why Manny is down here. Work on your tan."

DeeDee watched him concentrate on his computer screen for a few minutes, then walked out of the dim room into the bright sun outside.

MURPHY

Elke got up and walked over to Stephens. She shook his hand.

"Wilson mentioned your name when we were talking the other day," she said.

"A bunch of damn lies, I'm sure."

Stephens had a deep voice and slight accent which Murphy placed from Arkansas or Mississippi. He had a close-cropped mustache that was peppered with gray. He was in his mid-fifties and radiated a physical power which made Elke's knees feel loose and wobbly.

"Your boss has been forwarding your reports and I'm quite impressed," Stephens said, addressing his comment to Murphy. "You'll call me when you're ready to move up to the major league? We can always use good men."

"I'll keep you in mind," Murphy said wryly, "I know a good man is hard to find."

"Please, everyone be seated and I'll provide a very overdue explanation," Stephens announced to the room. "You're quite right, Murphy, this project has been a fishing expedition. We worked out this trip to Orlando for Glen and sent Agent Webster to follow on a whim, not knowing what to expect. It's the computer, you see, it says there are things going on, so we send agents out to get some firsthand data. Let me tell you what we know, which ain't much."

He turned the computer screen on with the remote control. He selected a few screens and a topographical map of Florida appeared.

"Since I'm with the DEA, you can guess that I'm mainly interested in drugs. This histogram shows the path of drugs from South America. As time passes you can see a nexus appearing in southern Florida." A mug shot appeared on the screen. "Murphy, you may recognize this dude."

The photograph was of Pablo Estevez, whom Murphy had last seen duct-taped to a chair with his throat cut.

"Estevez, a drug broker, recently deceased," Murphy said.

"Murdered by Richard Nixon, if I recall correctly?" Stephens said.

Webster flushed red and stared straight down at the table. Another photograph popped up on the screen.

"This is Manuel Rodriguez, AKA Manny, formerly Pablo's muscle-boy. We think he killed Pablo and is taking over the operation. Recently, he's been implicated in some mayhem in the Fort Myers area.

The computer tells us that there is a big dope transaction taking place in the Everglades somewhere. The drug supply has been drying up along the East Coast and we expect Manny to start filling the pipeline with this shipment. Of course, we have informants and agents at work in the area, but there are hundreds of square miles and it's impossible to be everywhere at once. We can only play the odds. That brings us to Glen Wilson."

The computer screen displayed something that looked like a weather map over the outline of Florida.

"This is a locus of Manny's influence and travel in Florida. Billions of scenarios have been calculated. This is the result."

A green wave spread across the state starting with Orlando, sweeping down across the west shore of Lake Okeechobee, to North Miami, then across the southern end of the panhandle.

"The green is Glen Wilson's sphere of influence. The correlation to the predicted drug activity is quite striking. Now you can see why we're so interested in him."

"He is retired from the drug trade," Elke said.

"So he says. The computer says there is some connection," Stephens replied.

"Glen told me that Manny stole his wallet," Elke said.

Stephens stared at her intently, mulling it over.

"Christ on a walker," he said absently, "is that it? Can it be something that stupid? Wilson, you son-of-a-bitch. You're going to get in the middle of the biggest drug deal in ten years because this ape stole your wallet?"

A soft rumble emerged from his chest and grew stronger. Soon he was laughing uncontrollably and slapping the table. The laughter was contagious and all at the table joined in except Webster, who, with crumbs of muffin on his lips, looked around the table sure that all had gone mad.

The meeting had progressed. Empty pizza boxes overflowed the garbage cans; everyone was bleary-eyed and suffering from information overload. They were looking through raw data, software listings, and charts to try to figure out some other reason for Glen's linkage to drug activity in Florida. They'd called back Doctor Chu to assist.

Murphy had long since kicked her shoes off. Her jacket was thrown across a chair and her hair was in disarray. She threw down her pencil.

"I give up. I don't think we'll ever figure this out. Why don't we just call and ask him?"

"Ask a crook why he's a crook and what crooked schemes he has up his sleeve?" Baker asked.

"What do we have to lose?" Murphy asked.

Elke nodded in assent. Doctor Chu logged his laptop into a WLAN. Murphy read off the e-mail address. The computer said 'PAGING'.

It took about thirty minutes to get Glen connected.

Hi Glen, Murphy here.

I can see that you are calling from FBI HQ in Saint Louis. Who is there with you? he replied.

Orrin Webster, Elke Rittenauer, Tom Baker, Doctor Victor Chu.

Stephens whispered to Murphy, Don't tell him I'm here. Murphy frowned but did not type his name.

Fine. Hi Elke. Miz Murphy, what's on your mind?

They have some AI computers that link you with a large drug transaction down in southern Florida somewhere.

Interesting. There is some cool hardware there. Sometimes we link up and siphon off processor cycles.

What about this drug deal?

Not my affair. I'm retired from the drug business. I'm not buying and I'm not selling. I'm clean.

Can I ask where you are and what you're doing?

Yes.

Well?

Well what?

Where are you?

Fort Myers area.

Why are you there?

To take care of some personal business.

Drug business?

I'll logoff if you get dull, Murphy. I've had a tough day.

Glen, this is Elke. Is your business regarding your wallet?

That is correct.

Baker took over the keyboard.

Does Manuel Rodriguez have your wallet?

Yes.

You are aware that Mister Rodriguez is implicated in some murders and is probably making a move up the dope distribution food chain?

Yes.

You are aware that Mister Rodriguez is a very dangerous person?

Yes. Is that all? I need to get some sleep.

If you hear anything about a drug deal, will you let us know?

When I get my wallet back, it's all yours.

IF you get your wallet back?

WHEN. Logging off.

Glen? Glen?

There was no response to the queries.

"Well, that was informative," Webster said.

"I tend to believe it," Murphy said.

Elke nodded in agreement. Stephens grudgingly nodded in assent also. Doctor Chu gathered up his notes and optical disks. He excused himself and left the room.

Murphy slipped on her shoes and ran her fingers through her hair.

"I've had it," she said. "I'm going to have a drink somewhere. Tomorrow, I'll fly home and get on with my work."

"Okay, fair enough," Stephens said, frowning. "Can you be on standby for a week or so to help us coordinate if something does pop up down there?"

"If my boss will stand for it," she replied.

"He will," Stephens said.

"Grab a drink?" Murphy said to Elke.

Elke nodded yes.

"Sounds great," Webster said. Both Murphy and Elke scowled at him.

"I'm sure you're very tired," Murphy said pointedly.

"No, no. I'm good for a couple of hours. Come on, I know a great fern bar."

"You remind me of my little brother," Elke said. "Mom always made me take him with me whenever I wanted to go somewhere."

"Cool," Webster said with enthusiasm. "What's his name."

"Shit-for-Brains. I hated him then and still do now."

"Cool. Let's go to the bar, you can tell me all about it."

Elke and Murphy rolled their eyes at each other.

"If he says "cool" one more time—" Murphy said.

"I'll hold him while you do it," Elke said, laughing.

The bar was called "The Old Muddy." It was in an old brick building across a busy street from the Mississippi river. It was early afternoon and the place was nearly empty. Both Murphy and Elke had been biting lemons, drinking tequila shooters, and building rows of tipped-over shot glasses. Webster was drinking Perrier water with twists of lime. He tried to keep the conversation going.

"Did you know Murphy has a boyfriend?" he asked Elke.

Murphy raised an index finger to shut him up but he ignored her.

"I think things are a bit rocky between the lovebirds," he said tauntingly.

Murphy sat up straight. Her words were slightly slurred.

"It's never easy," she said.

"Why don't you tell us about it," Webster said.

Murphy slumped down again. She spoke into the table top.

"Love. I feel. So. Much. I've been shot. I've fallen off a horse. I've been hit square in the head with a line-drive baseball. Take all that pain, roll it up, multiply it by the square of all the hurt in the world, it still won't ache as bad. As. I. Feel. Right here." Murphy pointed at her chest.

"Come on, tough guy," Webster laughed nervously. "It can't be that bad."

Murphy looked up. She had a mad look and her eyes refused to focus.

"You don't have a fucking clue," she said. She cast her eyes around looking for something. Her glance fell on the silverware. She picked up a fork and stood it up on the table.

"I'm going to stab this thing into my hand until the pain matches what I feel in my heart," she said.

Webster stood up and tipped his chair over.

"My god," he said. "I'm going to be sick."

Murphy closed her eyes tightly and placed her right hand on the fork. The muscles of her forearm bunched and writhed.

"Murphy," Elke said softly. "Murphy," she repeated.

She slowly removed the fork from Murphy's grasp.

"Things are going to work out fine," she said gently.

"Do you promise?" Murphy said.

Elke poured some tequila on the four pinpricks of blood welling from Murphy's palm and clenched her fist around a napkin.

"I promise," she said quietly.

"I hope so," Murphy said as her eyes rolled up into her head and she passed out with her head lying among the shot glasses on the table.

LEONARD

"It's hot, Leonard. You need to stock beer or you're going to have some unhappy customers."

Leonard shook his head stubbornly.

"I don't like beer and I won't sell it."

Andy, the vending machine guy, opened the candy machine.

"Ha! Look, I told you. You only sold two packs of Red Vines and you're out of Snickers bars. I'll bet you ate the Red Vines yourself and didn't sell any at all. Now will you listen to me?"

The bell outside chimed.

"Got a customer," Leonard said as he walked out.

The customer parked his pickup by Leonard's. He wore rubber boots and bright red suspenders.

"Don't need gas, I just stopped for cold beer and ice."

"Don't sell beer no more," Leonard said defiantly.

"Ha, very funny," the man said as he entered the building. He pulled open the door to the cooler and poked around inside.

"Hey."

"Try some Barq's root beer."

"I've been buying beer here for twenty years."

"I don't sell beer no more, I don't like it."

The man swept bottles of soda onto the floor and rooted around. Only his legs stuck out of the cooler. Andy and Leonard exchanged looks. The man emerged with dusty bottles of Grolsch in each hand.

"I guess this imported shit will just have to do. Now son," he said, waving the green bottles in Leonard's face, "let me explain thermodynamics to you. When it's hot, a man needs beer. It's a natural law. Got it?"

Leonard scowled sourly but nodded his head in assent.

GLEN

DeeDee threw the motel door open. She grabbed the voice recorder out of Glen's hand.

"Damn it, you're going to quit talking to this recorder and talk to me."

She smashed the recorder on the floor and ground it into rubble with the heel of her tennis shoe.

"Hey!"

She pulled the Sigma out of her purse and pointed it at Glen's head. Glen rolled his eyes.

"Haven't we already done this?" he said with a bored tone.

She slowly moved the barrel of the gun until it was pointed at the laptop computer.

"All right, DeeDee. All right. I give up. We can talk. Put the damn gun away."

"So start talking."

Glen reached down and pulled a Corona out of the minibar. He slid back on the bed until he was resting his back on the headboard.

"The wallet doesn't mean anything in itself. You girls doped me and took it. I don't deserve to live if I'm the kind of man that lets stuff like that go by."

DeeDee dropped the gun on the floor and sat on the foot of the bed. Glen leaned forward and handed her the beer. She took a sip and handed it back.

"Is that supposed to make sense?" she said.

"I'm not a sheep. If you steal from a sheep, he reports it to the cops, fills out insurance papers, replaces his traveler's checks, and carries on."

"Bullshit. No one is going to risk death for a stupid wallet."

"You're right, it's not the wallet. It's getting old and losing your edge. It's wanting to stay home and watch football on TV. It's realizing that the game is lost while you're marking time at some factory job."

"That's it? Just macho hormone bullshit? The big man is scared of getting old and dying? That's so pathetic."

"I don't care about dying. I just think you need to live while you're alive. There's no reward in the great beyond. This is it."

"Okay. Now shut up."

"I don't want my tombstone to say Glen Wilson did a fine job washing his car."

"I think I've got it."

"Glen Wilson let some jerk steal his wallet and walked away."

"Shut up!"

"Glen Wilson…"

He stopped when she put both hands over his mouth.

"I've heard enough," she said through clenched teeth. "Are you going to stop it?"

Glen nodded. She lifted her hands off his face slowly.

"Glen Wilson lived—" he said quickly with a smile before she shut him up again. She could feel him grin under her hands. He wiggled his eyebrows at her.

"What can I do to get you to shut your goddam face?"

Glen beamed, reached around, and unhooked her bra.

"Okay," she said with resignation. "But not a word or I'm leaving."

Glen nodded solemnly.

CHAPTER 25

Monday Morning, May 26

MURPHY

"Murphy?" Major Smythe called as he knocked on the door and stuck in his head. Murphy was resting her head on her desk. The blinds were pulled and the room was dark.

"You'll have my report by noon," she said listlessly. "Now go away, I'm hung over and I have the world's worst fucking headache."

"You got a fax."

He floated the thin paper onto the stacks of paper on her desk. He watched as she read it. She winced as she jumped to her feet and grabbed her purse.

"Call Stephens of the DEA and Baker at the FBI."

"I already called them."

"What?" Murphy said, puzzled.

Smythe was embarrassed.

"Stephens wanted to be called first thing. His chopper will be landing in a few minutes, he was already at the airport."

"Stephens was here in Orlando?"

"Yes, and that FBI guy, Webster. They should be on the roof any time now."

Murphy sat back in her chair and read the fax again.

Captain Margaret Murphy
Florida State Patrol
Orlando Station.

Good morning, Murphy. I found out where the deal's going down. There is a cemetery between Carnestown and Ochopee. I'm not exactly sure where and the satellite photos aren't much use in

this area. I expect a little fireworks show there around noon. It might be worth your while to check it out.
Regards, Glen Wilson.

"I'm real tired of being jerked around," she said wearily.

"I can send someone else, I guess."

"Oh, bullshit. I'll go. I need some stuff, body armor and a bigger gun."

"Stephens said the chopper will be fully equipped."

The windows vibrated and they could hear the characteristic whomp-whomp of one of the big birds landing on the rooftop helipad.

"Okay," Murphy said as she strolled out of the office rubbing the back of her neck, "I'm on the case."

GLEN AND LEONARD

Glen pulled into Jungle Larry's Zoological Park. He was a few minutes early. He drove the cab around the parking lot looking for anything out of the ordinary. The parking lot was filled with rental cars and a few fools slapping at themselves because they didn't have bug repellent. A white Chevy van was idling in the back corner by a chain link fence. A bald cypress tree hovered listlessly over the fence. Glen parked a few places away, took a quick hit off the bottle between his legs, and got out of the car warily. DeeDee wasn't speaking and her eyes were focused at infinity. She'd been at the pills again. The driver of the van opened his door and stepped out. He was coal black and his damp skin was traced with tricklets of sweat. Glen held out his hand to shake.

"The Captain don't like to touch strangers," he said.

"Who?" Glen asked, looking for someone else in the van.

"The Captain," the black repeated. "I'm Captain Kirk of the starship Enterprise and we don't touch strangers."

"Gotcha," Glen said.

"You requested some old shit. Projectile weapons. Your obsolete technology makes me laugh."

And he did, with a deep rumbling. For a few seconds his shoulders shook, then he turned and slid open the cargo door. The cargo was in Anvil flight cases like the rock musicians use. The Captain popped the latches of one. An AK-47, several spare clips, three RPG-2 launchers, and their grenades rested in foam nests. Glen nodded and the

Captain put the lid back. Glen opened the trunk of the cab. They heaved the heavy case in and the cab rocked on its shocks. The Captain opened the latch of a long case and gestured at the contents.

"It took the techs all night to get the mods installed that you asked for. Very nasty and very clever."

"Thanks," Glen replied.

"Given your primitive twentieth-century technology," the Captain continued.

"Of course."

The Captain explained quickly how the Dragon missile launcher was assembled and how the homing device operated. Glen had him go over it twice and asked a few questions that the Captain answered patiently. They worked the case into the trunk and Glen lashed the lid down with a metal clothes hanger.

"Thanks, man," Glen said.

The Captain stood in front of the cab door.

"Isn't it customary to tip?"

"I wouldn't want to insult the Captain," Glen said, grinning.

A few seconds stretched while the Captain gravely thought about that.

"The Captain wouldn't be upset if you gave him a couple hundred bucks," he said, finally.

"Shit," Glen said, as he pulled some bills from his pocket.

"Be long-lived and get wealthy," the Captain said.

"Not at this rate," Glen muttered darkly as he drove toward the parking lot exit. DeeDee finally spoke.

"Since we're here, can't we take a few minutes and go see Jungle Larry's talking parrots?"

"Hell no," Glen replied as he pulled onto Highway 851 and drove south.

DeeDee had been silent for the last hour of the drive. She stared out into the endless sea of grass and swamp. The Chevy had picked up a bad knock and the oil light had been flickering for the last fifteen miles. Glen was in a foul mood and his hand still hurt from bashing Luis. The drugs hardly took the edge off the pain. Bourbon sloshed like boiling battery acid in his stomach.

He pulled into the full service lane at a run-down gas station. He made sure the Sigma's safety was off and stuck it in his belt under his shirt.

He popped the hood latch and climbed out of the car. He walked out on the road and checked both ways for traffic. It was dead quiet. A hand-painted sign said Leonard's Lunch-N-Lube. A tall blond man in dirty overalls and run-down boots came out from behind the building. He was followed by a large white dog. The dog stopped about twenty feet away and stiffened. He stared at Glen, frozen like a plaster of Paris statue.

"Are you Lenny?" Glen asked.

"Yes, but I'd rather you called me Leonard."

Glen's guts churned and his trigger finger clenched instinctively. He stared at Leonard for a few seconds, then nodded.

"Fine, Leonard. Fill it. Add a couple of quarts of oil."

"Thirty weight okay?" Leonard asked.

"Whatever you got," Glen replied.

Leonard worked the gas nozzle into the filler tube. When the gas was flowing he lifted the hood and poured in two quarts of bulk oil. He leaned down and peered through the gap under the hood at DeeDee. She stared out the window without moving. Glen paced impatiently between the road and the car. Leonard slammed the hood closed. Glen jumped and reached around for the gun. He was a bundle of raw and angry nerves.

"Is the pretty girl okay?" Leonard asked.

"She's fine."

Leonard noticed how the back of the car was loaded down. It was nearly on the springs.

"Whatcha carrying in there, a ton of lead?" he asked.

Glen proffered a twenty. When Leonard reached for it Glen pulled it out of reach.

"There's a graveyard around here somewhere?"

"Yeah, it's three miles down, watch for the sign on the left." Leonard pointed down the road. Leonard noticed Glen's disfigured hand.

"Wow, that must have hurt. What'd you do to your hand?"

"Nothing." Glen handed over the twenty. He climbed back in the car.

"Hey, you got a couple dollars in change coming," Leonard called out.

Glen ignored him and started the engine. Leaning forward, he pulled the gun out of his belt. He snapped the safety on and tossed it on the seat. He pulled out and pointed the car toward the cemetery.

Dog did not move until the car was out of sight. Leonard slipped the twenty into the pocket of his overalls and crouched beside him.

"What's with you? That guy seemed all right."

Leonard could not read the expression in Dog's eyes. Dog turned and padded off to his burlap bag in the shade by the porch.

MANNY

Manny held out some ties for Holly's inspection. She grabbed the whole bunch and threw them on the floor.

"You can't leave me here."

"Now Holly," Manny said quietly, "we've been all over this. I can't take you because I need to take my boys. I can't take any chances that my little sugarplum will get hurt."

"If you really loved me, you'd take me."

"It's because I love you that I need you to stay here."

Manny finished tying the knot in his tie. He tossed his MAC-10 into a sports bag. He threw the strap over his shoulder and hefted the suitcases with the money.

"Can't you leave some of the money?"

"No, baby. We need all the money so I can make more money and spend it all on you. We'll go to Saint Thomas, the Greek Islands, wherever you want."

"Disneyworld?"

"Sure, honey," Manny sighed. "I'll take you to Disneyworld. Now give Manny a kiss."

Holly wrapped her legs around his waist and gave him a deep kiss. Manny pulled away sharply. Holly hopped down and flopped on the couch.

"Dammit, Holly. You bit my tongue."

"I'll be bored if you leave me here alone."

"I'll be back in a couple of hours. Order a pizza or something. Bye, babe," he said as he eased the door closed.

Holly picked up the Feather and drew a bead on the wall. She wore her hightops, a pair of g-string panties, and one of Manny's huge shirts that flew about her like a cape. None of the buttons were fastened. She leaned over and grabbed the phone book and the cordless phone. She ordered a couple of pizzas. When the pizza boy knocked on the door she grabbed some stray bills and answered the door. The delivery boy was a pimply seventeen or so with thick glasses. He was about fifty pounds overweight. His eyes looked like full moons.

She glanced down to see what he was looking at and saw that her breasts were fully exposed. She read his name from his name tag.

"Hi, Eric. What are you looking at? Never seen a naked girl before?"

"Well, sure, lots of times. Not alive, though."

"You have a thing for dead girls?"

"No, I mean movies and, you know, magazines," he sputtered.

She stuck some bills in his hand, grabbed the pizza boxes, and threw them on the floor.

"I'll bet you'd like to touch me?" she said.

"Uh," he replied.

"Come here, kid," she said, pulling him into the room.

She could tell by the way his slacks tented that he was interested.

She pulled down her panties and kicked them aside. She took his hand and placed it on her breast. Eric looked as if he would faint. She lay back on the couch and pulled him down on top. He was breathing fast and his eyes were glazing over.

"Here's the deal," she said as she pulled the Feather from under the seat cushion. She placed the gun barrel to his head.

"You can screw me. But, if you go soft or come before I do I put a bullet in your head. What do you say, lover-boy?"

He glanced from the gun to her chest and back. He wanted it bad. She smiled at him dreamily.

"Oh, man," he said.

His head hovered over her breast. He stuck out his tongue and came so close. She pulled back the hammer of the gun.

"You promise you won't shoot me anyway?

"No."

He closed his eyes.

"Argh, shit. I better go."

He pulled up his pants and clutched them tight so they'd stay up. His face twisted in torture.

"Oh, man," he said as he ran out the door. Holly's laughter echoed down the hall behind him.

Holly opened the curtains and flooded the room with light. She danced around the room waving the Feather and tossing it from hand to hand. She felt young and free. She counted the money in her purse again. She still had over three thousand from the hock shop money and Manny had given her a couple of thousand more for shopping while he was gone. She was rich. The words from one of her Dad's old Tommy Bolin records drifted through her head. *Had money, just not to spend*, she sang.

Forget that noise, she thought, I got money and I'm gonna spend it all as quick as I can.

She waved at the kids in the pool, then collapsed on the couch panting from the exertion of her dance. She opened the top of one of the pizza boxes: the pizza was cold and the cheese congealed.

"Yuck," she said.

She lit up a joint and breathed smoke at the ceiling. Reflections from the pool made wavy patterns on the ceiling. She tossed the Feather on the coffee table and arranged the throw pillow under her head. Her mind drifted randomly as she drowsed. She leaned over, tore off a piece of pizza, and stuffed it in her mouth. She dreamed of a shelf covered with black rocks. The shelf was across from a dilapidated cash register that sat on an oily plywood desk. A fat guy grinned, then toppled like a melting snowman into the gravel. Her hand relaxed, the greasy pizza fell into the thick carpet, and she slept.

All of the above are part of a pattern gradually being formed by two trends.

The first is the growing, exquisite fragility of our technological culture. The machinery of commerce, industry and—increasingly— survival has grown so vulnerable that we all live by common consent and good luck.

The second trend is the growing destructive power of individuals. In tribal times, a dangerously disturbed person would be embedded in a family and community that limited his scope of action, and the weapons at his disposal were no more formidable than those of his neighbors.

In early industrial times, disturbed individuals were often free to roam, but they were limited in the amount of damage they could do. Now things are entirely different.

- Ron Wilson
Tech Tightrope Editorial
Electronic Engineering Times
July 17, 1995

CHAPTER 26

Monday Noon, May 26

GLEN

Glen drove by the cemetery slowly. Two hundred yards past the driveway a chain link fence prevented access to the canal levee. Glen used bolt cutters on the gate chain, opened the gate, and pulled the taxi through. He drove down the bank until it was out of sight. He stomped a few square feet of weeds flat. With DeeDee's help he hauled the Anvil cases from the trunk. He flipped the latches, took the tops off, and started assembling the equipment. Every few minutes he would scan the cemetery with field glasses.

"What is all this stuff?" DeeDee asked.

Glen wiped sweat from his forehead and gestured at the gear.

"These three are RPG-2 rocket launchers. RPG means Rocket Propelled Grenade. This is an AK-47 with a 10X scope. And this," Glen said, stroking a metal tube pointing into the sky that he had screwed together, "is a homemade Dragon missile launcher."

"What are we going to do now?"

"We're going to eat our sandwiches and wait."

Glen unwrapped a pastrami sandwich and offered it to her. She pushed it away. Glen munched and watched through his field glasses as Manny drove his Lexus into the cemetery parking lot. A van that was following pulled in and Manny waved it around. He waited for his boys to scout the area before he got out. Two new-looking Lincoln Towncars pulled in and spread out in the parking lot. DeeDee crept up beside him and looked at the ugly weapons.

"I don't believe you can actually shoot these guys in cold blood."

Glen inclined his head a fraction.

"Do you know the last words of the Turkish assassin Hassan Sabbah?"

"What? No."

"Everything is permitted."

Glen returned to the field glasses and watched the men transact their business. The money was inspected and the dope was tested and weighed. When everyone seemed comfortable with the deal, he aimed a rocket launcher, fired, and tossed the useless launcher aside. He repeated the procedure two more times. One of the Towncars roared to life and raced onto the road. The van and the other Towncar had taken direct hits. Glen sighted the AK-47 on the escaping Lincoln but let it go. He picked off the dazed guards standing near Manny with head shots. Glen scanned the area. Everyone was down except Manny. Glen waved a white rag and walked across the field. He approached Manny with his hands spread. With a remote control hidden in his hand he launched the Dragon. It streaked into the air behind him, leaving a trail of white smoke that dissipated in the light breeze.

"The fucking Wallet-man," Manny said, shaking his head. "You're a persistent son-of-a-bitch."

Manny leaned back on a tall concrete cross. He held a MAC-10 machine pistol loosely in his hand. Glen kicked a dried-up bouquet of flowers off a grave and collapsed in its place. The grave looked freshly dug. Glen traced the lettering. What kind of name is Clemson, he thought.

"I can't believe the trouble you've caused me. Wesley. Luis. The Feds are up my ass. All because you're too damn stubborn to cut your losses and go buy another cheap wallet. Look at this shit." Manny waved the gun at the scene. "This is going to cost me a bundle."

One of the aluminum suitcases had broken open and money was blowing out in loose handfuls. The wind plucked at the suits of the dead. Manny's green Lexus was burning. A small grass fire had started but died out. Glen wiped at sweat running down his forehead. He held out his left hand. It looked absurd with the thumb, index finger, and pink finger stub. It was healing okay, though.

Manny took the wallet out of his jacket pocket. "There's nothing here, man."

He threw it in the gravel in front of Glen. Glen didn't make a move toward it.

"Don't you want your wallet before I blow your brains out?" Manny asked.

Glen shrugged. The Casio watch he took from Raymond at the hotel was smashed. He took it off and threw it over his shoulder.

"What time you got?" Glen asked.

"What difference does it make? You're a dead man. Don't you get it? It's the end of the line, pal. Your butt stops here. You've had a lot of fun but this is it. Your next stop is hell."

"Just tell me what time it is. To the second, please."

"Sure, asshole. Rolex time is twelve-thirty-seven and ten seconds, eleven, twelve, et cetera. Check-out time for you."

"Good. We made it. That missile I fired?"

Glen pointed into the sky.

"Yeah, nice try."

"That was a modified Dragon surface-to-air missile. It has drifted down to about 1500 feet or so by now. We may be able to see it." Glen peered into the sky, shadowing his eyes with his hand. "See? There."

He pointed at a small object drifting below a small white parachute.

Manny didn't look.

"So what."

"It's had some modifications I should warn you about. You carry a pager, right? Five Five Five Eleven Twenty-seven?"

Manny's hand darted into his jacket. He stood up, pulled out the pager, and threw it as far as he could.

"Nice try," Glen said. "Unfortunately, at twelve-thirty-seven its thermal imager locked on the warm body nearest the pager. Unless I'm mistaken, that would be you."

Manny stood over Glen and dug its barrel into his head.

"You can shut it off," Manny said, looking into the sky.

"Yes, but I'm not going to."

"Then we both die, shit-bird."

"Yeah, that seems to be about it," Glen said calmly. A hundred dollar bill skittered by. Glen snagged it and stuck it in his pocket. DeeDee approached, walking slowly as if in a trance.

"What if I shoot the girl?"

"You'd save me the trouble. I told her to stay put."

Manny had a stricken look. He pointed his MAC 10 at the drifting parachute. He fired several bursts with no apparent effect. He threw the gun down and kneeled before Glen.

"Look, man, I'm sorry. If I'd known, I would have given you that damn wallet. Back at the lake, you asked me politely, didn't you?"

"Yes, I did."

"I came close to giving it to you, I swear to God. I'm sorry. What can I do?"

Glen shrugged, shielded his eyes from the sun with his injured hand, and stared up at the missile, which was several hundred feet away now.

"Well," he said, "you could try running."

Manny looked up. He turned and sprinted toward a stand of trees a hundred yards away. There was a flash from the missile and a small puff of white smoke.

"It won't work, but you can try," Glen whispered as he cowered behind the gravestone and covered his head.

Manny was very fast for a big man. He got halfway to the trees before the missile caught him. He disappeared and his limbs flew out in red streaks. An unidentifiable hunk of flesh wrapped in burning fabric landed in front of Glen. He rotated a cigarette in the little flame, then stuck it in his mouth. He struggled to his feet, bent over, and picked up his wallet. He dusted it off and stuck it in his pants pocket without looking at it. He walked to the highway which was flat and straight. He could see DeeDee a hundred yards away struggling with one of the heavy suitcases. He walked back to the levee and patted the old taxi on the hood. "One more time, old girl," he said.

The taxi started with a huge cloud of blue smoke. There was a horrendous knocking from under the hood. He backed it down the access road and eased it onto the highway. For an instant he thought about picking up DeeDee, but he turned the other way instead. He wasn't sure why.

MURPHY

Murphy's skin itched under the bulletproof vest. She checked the black enamel Uzi carbine for the third time. She watched the endless checkerboard fields stream by under the chopper and refused to talk to either Stephens or Webster. It was difficult to hear over the rotors and the screaming turbine engine anyway. She refused an intercom headset. She saw a large limousine race by on the highway below. It caught her attention because it weaved and passed an eighteen-wheeler at a high rate of speed. She spun her finger in the air and pointed at the ground. Stephens looked puzzled but rattled off some commands into his microphone. The chopper banked sharply and roared along the highway. They came up behind the car. The sunroof slid open and a guy popped out with a large bore rifle. It kicked fiercely as he fired a semiautomatic burst. The chopper took a nasty lurch and pitched sideways as they flew over. Murphy could hear some audible warning tones. Red lights began flashing on the control panel.

"Hang on, we're going down," the copilot yelled back.

The engine clattered, seized, then exploded with a bang and a roar. Webster held his nylon crash strap and moved his lips in silent prayer. The pilot nosed into the air and they stalled. The earth spun giddily as they autorotated to the ground. The aircraft slewed and the main rotor hit the highway first. The chopper lurched onto its side with a soul-rending shriek. Murphy lay on her back with Webster hanging from his restraints over her. Stephens pushed open the door. Murphy got out of the way and released Webster. Stephens looked at her with a question in his eyes. She nodded that she was okay. Very pissed off, but okay. A trickle of blood traced down her face from an abrasion on her forehead. Stephens heaved himself up through the door and leaned in to help her and Webster. They jumped to the ground.

The Lincoln approached rapidly and showed no sign of slowing down. The man protruding through the sunroof fired at them. He was so intent on his aim that he did not notice that there was no room on the road to go around the wreckage. The shattered tail span ripped the top half of his body off as the Lincoln raced by in a shower of sparks. The limo almost held the road but fishtailed and slid sideways into a pineapple field about 50 meters up the road. The tires spun out and they could not regain the road.

Murphy and Stephens sprayed the car with their Uzis but the car was armored. They scarred up the paint but could not penetrate the car. Webster fired his Glock blindly and uselessly around the helicopter. Murphy grabbed his arm and motioned for him to stop. He popped his empty clip. His hands were shaking so badly that he dropped his spare clips. He picked one up and reloaded. Murphy noticed some odd-looking gray bullets in one of the other clips. She picked it up and looked at the shells. Webster shrugged his shoulders, not remembering where he got them. She popped the cartridges out one-by-one and loaded them into an Uzi clip. She lay on the ground, eased around the body of the chopper, aimed carefully, and fired a round. The rear window blasted in and someone in the car started screaming. Two guns appeared in the shattered window and blasted the helicopter. It shivered with the incoming shells. Murphy calmly blasted out the front window. The guns disappeared and a tall guy in a black suit jumped out of the far door and ran for the field while firing a pistol over his shoulder. Stephens walked toward the limo with his gun held at his side. Intense flames poured out the limo windows. Murphy stood and steadied the gun on the side of the chopper. Stephens turned and waved his arms for her to hold fire. She steadied her aim and fired over Stephens' head. Stephens ducked with an incredulous look. The running guy's arm separated from his shoulder in a red explosion. He took two more steps and then fell onto his face. Stephens walked back and kicked in the chopper windshield. He hauled out the dazed pilot and copilot, stealing glances at Murphy's impassive face. From the Naples direction came the sound of multiple sirens. Traffic began to pile up a safe distance on either side of the wreckage. Murphy slid down the side of the chopper and stared into the fields with the Uzi held loosely on her lap.

Stephens crouched in front of her.

"Did you see that?" Webster said, stunned by the scene. "That guy wasn't going anywhere. That wasn't necessary. I'm going to be sick."

"Yeah, her boss told me how she is when the shit comes down," Stephens said, looking into Murphy's face. "Excessive and unnecessary force. Simply beautiful. That's why I asked for her," he said to Webster proudly.

Another helicopter hovered and set down on highway. The wind from the rotors kicked up a dust storm.

"Come on, Murphy, let's go," Stephens said, blinking and extending his hand to help her up. "We can let the local boys clean up here. Murphy?"

She slowly took his hand and pulled herself to her feet.

"Don't stand between me and a perp ever again," she said coldly. She was a foot shorter than Stephens. She held his eyes until she could see he got the message.

"Okay, Murphy," he said. "Come on." He led the way to the helicopter that just landed.

Webster wiped his mouth, shielded his eyes, and watched the chopper spool up, lift off, and race away to the south. A small part of him was disappointed to be left behind. The rest of him had had enough and was happy to stay.

DeeDee and Leonard

DeeDee's shirt was soaked through with sweat. She dropped the suitcase on the pavement and sat on it, panting and flicking sweat from her eyes.

The thought of throwing out some of the money to lighten the load entered her mind for a moment. She evaluated the blisters on her hands and decided she could walk a couple of hundred more miles before that would be necessary. The road was paved and in good shape. A car would appear sooner or later. She felt-heard a dull thump from the direction of the cemetery. A dirty brown cloud mushroomed into the air. She got up and walked as fast as she could. She thought she could see something in the distance. A sign or something. The sign was hand-painted. Leonard's LNL. At least there should be a phone, she thought.

The LNL, Lunch-N-Lube, cute. The place was run-down and looked deserted. She didn't see a phone. A tall sweaty man dressed in overalls with odd patches missing came out to greet her. He looked around, walked to the roadway and looked left and right.

"Hi, lady. Where did you come from?"

"I'm just passing through. Can I use your phone?"

"You can use it, but I'm sorry, it still ain't working."

He tried to keep his eyes on her face but her figure under the damp T-shirt was distracting. Leonard was sure she was the most beautiful woman he had ever seen. "Where's your car? I'll bet you could use a soda, couldn't you?"

"Oh, nothing sweet, a mineral water or something would be great."

"I have some imported water you'll like. It's imported all the way from Tampa," he said with pride.

He reached for her suitcase and she swung it away from him. He looked puzzled but ran inside to get her water. When he came out she was not in sight. His face fell. Then he saw her kneeling in the shade by the worm tub petting Dog. He ran up to her and handed her the water.

"Thanks," she said. "Nice doggy. What's in the tub?"

"This is my worm farm. You probably don't like worms?"

"Look, mister," she said stubbornly, "I grew up on a pig farm up in Iowa with three older brothers." She lifted a flap of burlap and stuck her hand in the soggy dirt. She brought out a fat red wriggler. She held it before her face and examined it closely. "Your worms aren't going to bother me a bit. I'll even cook you up a batch with my Mom's recipe if you want," she said, looking at him defiantly.

It was at that instant that Leonard fell completely in love with this odd girl with the spiky dark hair and sopping wet T-shirt. He stood up tall and held his hand out to shake.

"I'm Leonard Allen Mullins and this is my place."

She dropped the worm back in the tub, wiped her hand on her jeans, and shook with her dirty fingers.

Within an hour several helicopters had flown over and a steady stream of squad cars sped by. DeeDee looked nervous every time a car raced by. She insisted on helping Leonard wash windows. She wrapped a bandana around her head and she looked right at home. Late in the afternoon a large black man and a tired-looking woman stopped in. The man fed some coins in the soda machine and bought a can of Doctor Pepper.

"What's going on up there?" Leonard asked him.

"Did you see anything unusual?" Stephens asked.

"Except for all the helicopters and cop cars, it's been pretty quiet all day."

"And you, ma'am?" Stephens asked.

"Nothing," DeeDee said.

Stephens brought out a picture of Glen.

"Seen this guy around here? Probably driving a taxicab?"

"Yeah, sure. He bought some gas this morning. He asked about the cemetery."

Murphy sagged to the porch and leaned back on her hands.

"Was he alone?" she asked.

DeeDee's eyes begged him. Murphy's eyes flicked between them. Leonard did not know what to say.

"Yes," DeeDee said, "the guy was by himself."

Stephens turned to her.

"Did he say anything else?"

"No, not a thing."

Stephens handed her a business card.

"If anything comes to you..."

"I'll call," DeeDee finished.

After they left, DeeDee sat on the porch and wiped her forehead.

"Thanks for that."

"No problem," Leonard replied, not exactly sure what she meant. "Can you at least tell me what your name is?"

"I'm DeeDee DeWard," she replied. "It's good to meet you, Lenny."

"I'd rather you called me... Lenny, sure, you can call me Lenny if you want."

CHAPTER 27

Tuesday Morning, May 27

HOLLY

Holly rolled off the couch and landed on the pizzas. Her neck was stiff and her mouth tasted furry and nasty. The clock said ten o'clock. The light outside was bright, so she must have slept all day and night. She went to the bathroom to urinate.

Manny was late. She'd expected that because he was male and males were only on time for happy hour and kickoff time. It was expected, and it was okay, because it was expected and she'd planned for it. Because she'd expected it and expected things were not surprises she was not surprised or upset. Yeah right, she expected the sonovacubanbitch to strand her in this rich man's pleasure palace all alone and all alone and all alone. She picked up the Feather and took aim at the television, then decided against shooting it. She tossed the Feather to the floor and pouted at the walls instead.

Someone occasionally banged on their ceiling at someone else, with something, for some reason. Holly turned down her music a hair to see if she could figure out what her neighbor was doing to upset the people on the lower floor. She crawled on the floor to figure out where the banging was coming from. She pointed the Feather at the floor, aiming in the general direction of the hammering. Her finger caressed the trigger for a moment, then she shrugged and tossed the gun to the floor again. The Feather employed a notoriously light trigger pull and striking the floor was enough to slip a mechanical widget and the tempered steel firing pin slammed into the rear of the already chambered rimfire cartridge. The Feather discharged with a modest pop, and the bullet passed through the cheap flooring and into the room below.

There was a startled screech followed by a stream of expletives. A door slammed. She hoped no one was injured too badly, but wasn't planning to lose any sleep over it.

There were loud footsteps down the hallway and a strident pounding on her door. She grabbed the Feather and pointed it at the door. Changing her mind, she stuffed it under a cushion on the couch and headed for the door, flipping her hair back and tying the tails of Manny's shirt around her waist. The door had a peep hole that she ignored. She threw the door wide and immediately wished she'd kept the Feather in her hand.

A large black man, a very large black man, actually the largest black man Holly had ever seen in person, stood before her holding a bloody upper left arm and wearing an unpleasant expression. He made Manny look slight. Holly smiled.

"Can I help you?" she asked most innocently.

The man glared.

"Somebody shot the Captain," he hissed, turning to show her his arm. Holly inspected it with interest. She'd expected the Feather to do more damage. The bullet must have been slowed down a lot by the floor and carpeting.

"People don't shoot the Captain and then live long and prosper, bitch."

He shoved past her simply walking by as if she were a turnstile. "You by yourself here, little girl? You the one that shot me?" He poked his head in the bedroom and bathroom. He kneeled and fingered a splintery hole in the bathroom floor. He returned, walked directly to the couch, and pulled the Feather from beneath the second cushion he looked beneath. He checked the clip.

"We don't know what it is, but you crazy white bitches is always hiding your little guns under the couch cushions." He cleared the chamber and removed the clip, then tossed the gun to the couch. He inspected his arm more closely.

"Huh. Just a flesh wound, Bones. Phasers set to stun," he muttered. He headed for the door and Holly pressed against the wall to let him pass, but he slammed the door shut with a hand the size of Cleveland, then grabbed her by the neck and dragged her into the bathroom. She resisted for the first few feet but he didn't seem to notice, so she gave up resistance to concentrate on breathing. He ran the sink full of hot water without loosening his grip. Black spots and sparkly things began dancing before her eyes. He handed her a clean towel.

"Okay, Bones, you made this mess, so you clean it up, got me?"

Gasping for air, she pushed up his T-shirt, soaked the towel, and swabbed his arm. He pawed through her junk on the counter and handed over her eyebrow tweezers.

"It didn't come through. Dig it out."

She gritted her teeth and fished around in his arm. He held out his wide palm and she dropped the deformed slug in it.

"Full metal jacket. Good, only one piece. Got some bandages?"

Holly pointed to one of the suitcases. He set her on the edge of the sink and waved a fat finger at her to make her stay put. He popped the latches of the case, pulled some guns out of the way, and found a first aid kit. He threw the guns back in the case. She wrapped and taped up his arm.

"Okay," he said.

He grabbed her by the collar of her shirt, lifted her up on her tiptoes, and lectured her.

"The Captain is taking a break. Then some dumb babe shoots him with a peashooter. The Captain is very disappointed."

She managed to wedge her hands under one massive finger but couldn't budge it from her neck. She caught just enough air to wheeze.

"I'll fuck your brains out," she whispered.

He shoved her head in the bloody water in the sink. She struggled, or tried to, laboring to kick her way free, but the man's hand was a fleshy vise around her neck. When her thrashing became feeble he jerked her free of the sink and watched her sputter and cough and drip. He leaned to look in her eyes.

"Did you say you'd fuck my brains out?" he asked.

Holly nodded her head in short and desperate bobs. He frowned.

"Maybe the Captain will be interested later," he said as he thrust her head back into the sink. She managed a tiny whimper on the way down and snapped her heel toward his crotch. He grasped her foot and used it to leverage her head deeper into the sink.

He pulled her out and waited for her to regain her composure.

"You ready to stop this crap?"

She nodded yes eagerly while blinking pink water out of her eyes.

"Then say, 'Beam me up, Scotty'."

"What?"

He pushed her head toward the sink.

"Wait. Beam me up, Scotty. Beam me up, Scotty."

"What did you say?" he asked fiercely, while holding her off the floor.

"I said, beam me up, Scotty," she gasped breathlessly.

"Then it shall be so, the Captain said."

"Don't you mean 'Make it so'?"

"The Captain wants to know what you mean."

"On the TV show, the Captain said 'Make it so'."

"Are you mocking the Captain?"

She vigorously shook her head no.

"That's the New Generation shit. The Captain don't watch the new shit. Understand?"

"Yes, yes, yes," she pleaded.

"Fine," he said as he set her on the floor. He walked into the living room and with a ham fist smashed her radio, which had been blasting out Top 40 hits. As he walked toward the front door Holly dived for the Feather, pulled back the hammer, aimed at the back of his head, and pulled the trigger. Click. She'd forgotten that he'd removed the bullet under the hammer. He pulled the clip from his pocket and waved it at her.

"Phasers set to tickle," he said, grinning.

He tossed the clip to her, ducked out quickly, and slammed the door. She reached over and grabbed the clip, rammed it home, and ratcheted a shell into the chamber. She slammed open the door and jumped into the hall. There was no one in sight. She cursed and went back into the room. She got down on the floor, rolled on her back, aimed the gun at the ceiling, and flipped the safety on and off.

"He loves me." Click. "He loves me not," she sang. Click. "He loves me."

She dropped the gun. Still lying on her back, she pulled a baggie over and poured some weed on her chest. She rolled a joint, fished around on the table, found a lighter, and lit up. This was all Manny's fault. If he was going to strand her like this, well, things were bound to happen. He'd have to learn to expect that. She took a drag off the joint.

At that instant, like a javelin arcing from the sky and piercing her brain, she remembered where she'd seen the shelf with the black rocks. An old gas station in the Glades. Not far from Everglades City. In her mind a great black X marked the spot on a mental map. Dusty black rocks, a couple dozen of them, all patiently waiting for Holly to scoop them up.

In a hurry, she pulled on her jeans but left the shirt unbuttoned. She tossed the Feather aside and picked up her old reliable Colt .45 and tucked it down the back of her pants. She puffed the joint to life and grabbed her purse. In the mood for music, she placed headphones on her head, and clipped a minidisk player on the waist of her jeans. She left the room without looking back and marched quickly through the hallway.

The only person that saw her leave was Wade Brown, a thirteen year old kid on vacation from Nebraska. She walked quickly with her bare breasts bobbing and Manny's huge shirt wafting behind her like giant linen wings. The sweet smoke from her funny-looking cigarette trailed and filled Wade's nose. Wade could tell instantly that she was a very dangerous angel. A scrap of paper drifted behind her like an autumn leaf. Wade took two steps and caught it in his hand as she pushed open the door to the fire stairs and skipped down the concrete steps to the parking garage. The paper said "Inspected by 17". The paper was Wade's only assurance that she really existed. Wade saved that scrap of paper for the rest of his life.

EPILOGUE

"I am not a crook."
- Richard Nixon

"Americans reelect the good crooks and impeach the bad ones."
- Glen Wilson

LATER

LEONARD

"LEONARD! Customer's waiting!"

Darn it, Leonard thought. She said Leonard and that means she's mad. He sighed and put his People magazine onto the stack. He could hear the customer's truck skid to a stop. It was a big American V-8. Some of the valves needed adjustment. There was something about the sound of that engine, something that curdled the grits in his stomach.

BLAM!

Oh no, Leonard thought. *Oh no.*

He pulled up his overalls and burst through the bathroom door.

GLEN

Glen strolled into the office a little after nine. His desk was covered with magazines and letters; he couldn't even see the chair or his computer. He started throwing the stuff into his wastebasket. When it was full he traded it for his neighbor's, and filled that one too. His boss, Dean Grayson, poked his head in.

"Hi, Glen, welcome back," Dean said sarcastically.

Grayson seemed tense and kept running his hand across his balding head.

"I'm in a bad mood. Bug off, will you?"

"Sure, Glen. Okay. Look, man, the cops were here. I didn't tell them nothing. Okay?"

"That's a double negative, Dean. A Freudian slip? Forget it. Get me a cup of coffee, some of that Emerald City blend. It sure was tough to find decent coffee in Florida."

"Parker wants to see you right away," Grayson said.

"I'll see him at ten. I need to work on my expense account."

"Glen, the CEO wants to see you right away. You know, President Parker, the owner of this company? He said he wants to see you when you get in. He's really pissed off."

"I'll see him at ten."

"He's got the company lawyer with him. I'm sure it's important."

"No sugar."

"No sugar? What?"

"In my coffee. No sugar."

Glen stapled a wad of receipts to his expense report. He was very proud because it was some of his most creative work. As he tossed it in the accounting IN basket the accounts payable girls poked their heads above the partitions.

"Hey Glen, what's with the finger?"

Glen waved his mutilated hand.

"I was meeting a client and got a flat on the rental car. When I was changing the tire the damn hydraulic jack failed and the brake drum smashed my hand."

"Come on, Glen, you can do better than that. Drug dealers? Rabid dogs?"

"How about an alligator, maybe an alligator bit your fingers off?"

"Don't be so melodramatic, girls. What's the insurance paying for dismemberment for on the job injuries? This baby's got to be worth forty thousand or so."

"I'll have to look it up."

"You do that," Glen said, waving as he walked toward the lobby.

Glen greeted his lawyer, Saul Kovacek, and signed him in the guest register.

"Long time, Saul. You're looking good."

Saul wore a baggy and wrinkled JC Penney's suit. He reeked of cigar smoke and peered through his wire rim glasses.

"What's the story, Glen? You didn't say much in your e-mail."

"Same old shit, Saul. Just play it by ear."

"Twenty percent."

Glen stopped and looked Saul in the face.

"Two thousand retainer and fifteen percent, same as always."

"I got mouths to feed, Glen. Cut me a break, will you?"

"Feeding your bookie's kid's mouths. If you weren't the best I'd kick your ass out of here."

The receptionist gave up pretending she was reading her Redbook and stared at them as if they were crazy.

"That's right, I'm the best. Eighteen percent, you keep the retainer. I'll walk, Glen," he threatened.

"Okay, done. Whose side are you on?"

"Yours, of course, as long as the checks don't bounce."

Glen rapped on Parker's door and walked in without waiting. Parker stood up and started to sputter.

"You're late, Wilson. This is the last straw. You're fired. Who is this?" he said, finally noticing Glen's guest.

Saul pushed into the room and shook hands with Parker and Parker's lawyer, Ronald Fishbein. Fishbein was dressed nattily in a tan double-breasted suit and his black wingtips gleamed like obsidian.

"Hello, Saul, good to see you," Fishbein said cordially.

"Good to see you too, Ron. How are Delores and the kids?"

"Just fine. Tory is playing first violin in the school symphony."

"That's just great."

Parker sat down with a disgusted look. He swiveled his chair and stared out the window into the evergreen trees. The lawyers settled in their chairs. Saul opened his cardboard valise and reviewed some papers.

"What's your opening offer?" Saul asked, looking over his glasses at Fishbein.

"Glen agrees to pack up and get out without any fuss. He gets a hundred K termination payment and he agrees not to work for a competitor for a year. He agrees not to disclose the terms of this agreement."

Glen shook his head and pointed at his ruined hand. Saul waved him off and stood up.

"Well, this is a complete waste of time."

He addressed Glen.

"I suggest a civil suit. Let's see, you're over forty?" Glen nodded. "So, we go for age discrimination. I think ICC has made no accommodation for this handicap, so we pull in the Feds for a blatant violation of the Americans with Disability Act."

"Sit down, Saul," Fishbein said. "We can work this out. Does your client wish to stay employed at ICC?"

Glen nodded yes.

"Is your client amenable to considering a promotion in recognition of his years of good service?"

"Screw the promotion, let's get some cash," Glen whispered to Saul.

"My client believes that a promotion would be a management ploy, a prelude to premature termination. Completely unacceptable. We will accept some small compensation for the suffering that he's endured while pursuing the company's business."

"Fine, ten thousand?"

"I was thinking of something more like a hundred."

"Bullshit!" Parker exhaled loudly.

Fishbein waved at him to be quiet.

"Seventy-five and a company car?" Fishbein offered.

Saul scratched his head and glanced at Glen. Glen nodded his head yes and stood up.

"You'll have Suzy messenger the papers over," Saul said, "say, by end of business day tomorrow?"

"What?" Parker yelled.

"Consider it done," Fishbein replied, waving at Parker to settle down.

Fishbein stood and shook Saul's hand.

"Oh Christ," Parker bellowed. He pointed a quivering finger at Glen.

"What's happening? I gotta pay seventy-five thousand and this son-of-a-bitch still works here? What kind of fucked-up deal is that?"

"Just business," Glen said as he sauntered out of the room. The lawyers followed, chatting comfortably.

"Wilson!" Parker shouted.

Glen stuck his head back in the door.

"What's up, boss?"

Parker pulled a bottle from his desk drawer. He poured bourbon into a crystal glass and slugged it down.

"Tell me you at least made a couple of good sales while you were down there?"

"Why, of course, boss," Glen said.

He gave a little salute and pulled the door shut gently behind him. Glen walked to Bonnie's cubicle. She was listening to a CD and typing code. Glen tapped her on the shoulder.

"Hi, Glen," she said. "I heard you were back."

"Hey, Bonnie. It's been pretty intense this morning," he said, grinning. "Let's take a break. Can you afford to buy me some coffee? I'll tell you how I blew away some drug dealers."

"Oh Glen, you're so full of it," she said with her eyes sparkling.

"Yeah, so what," he replied, taking her arm and leading her toward the lunchroom.

NUMBER THREE

Orrin Webster stood at attention in front of his boss's desk.

"Relax, Orrin, you're making me nervous," Baker said.

"I regret to inform you, sir, that—darn it, here's my resignation."

He handed an envelope to Baker.

"Don't be hasty, Webster."

"I've thought about it. This business with Murphy and Wilson—I'm not a cop and I never will be."

"Hang on. I've got a better idea. You know Art Nishimoto is finally going to retire?"

"Don't expect me to be disappointed..."

"I'll get to the point. He recommended you to take his place. It's a desk job, but it pays the same and it will keep you out of the field."

"Wow. That's great, I think..."

"A done deal. I'll just get rid of this." He tore the resignation letter in half and flipped it in the wastebasket.

"I spent all night writing that. Won't you at least read it before you throw it away?"

"Poor grammar depresses me. It's bad enough I have to read your reports. Now go see Art and he'll train you."

"Yes, sir," Webster said.

MURPHY

Murphy walked to the water's edge to examine some driftwood. She turned and admired her companion's silhouette outlined by the sun melting into the Gulf of Mexico. They were north of Blind Pass Beach on Manasota Key.

"Truly beautiful," she said. She wore a white one-piece bathing suit and her hair was loose around her shoulders. A floppy hat protected her face from the sun. Her legs were caked with salt and sand and her nose was pink with a minor sunburn. She held a net sack full of seashells.

"I feel so full, so complete," she said dreamily.

"What about your job? Have you decided?"

"Fuck the job," she said bitterly. "I need a change. Wilson intrigues me. He's a crook, but an honest one. I know that doesn't make much sense. Director of Security for a candidate for United States Congress. I like the sound of that."

"Did he talk money at all?"

Murphy nodded. "Sure. He offered a hundred thousand a year if I play it straight, two hundred if I'm willing to bend the rules a bit. I made a little joke. I told him I wouldn't kill anyone."

"What did he say?"

"He said he'd contract out the killing. He was just kidding, I think. You know his weird sense of humor."

"What about you and me?"

"I won't go without you. I love you, baby. We have plenty of time to work out the details. Let's just take our time and relax for a few months."

"I'm so worried. We come from different parts of the world, from different backgrounds, and I'm ten years older than you. How can we ever hope to make it?"

"I hate to sound like an AM radio song, but our love will find a way."

Murphy turned so they were face to face.

"Don't worry, baby," she continued, "we'll be fine. I didn't wait my whole life to find you just to let you go. All right?"

Murphy tilted her companion's head up gently and gave a lingering and tender kiss. She brushed away the tears with her fingertips.

"All right?"

Elke nodded slowly. Her eyes welled with tears.

"All right," she answered quietly.

HOLLY

Holly cruised at a steady sixty miles an hour, occasionally powering up during a particularly hot piece of music. The Custom/10 Chevy was too heavy to do much more than a hundred. Once she had the rest of the gold she might pick up one of those cute new James Bond Beamers with a CD player and a little pink Harley. Get rid of the damn old truck that Jimmy thought was some kind of amazing.

"Built out of Detroit steel, babe!"

Unlike the lead I put in your head, Jimmy.

"1972, the last year they built 'em solid."

Yeah, I know. The gas crunch blah blah blah.

"Twelve miles to the gallon ain't that bad, considering."

Not bad for you, Jimmy. I was the one scamming and sucking dick for gas money, deadboy.

She spotted something moving in the road ahead. She slapped the truck into third and floored it, trying to head off the whatever before it could reach the shoulder and safety. The whatever moved too fast and she had to veer at the last second from a maniacal plunge into the ditch. Dust and litter flew in her wake. An oncoming car passed with much pointing and round-shaped mouths.

There would be another opportunity. No need to take chances over a whatever with all that gold screaming her name at the dumpy little gas station, which should be coming up soon, if she remembered right. She wasn't sure. Dead Jimmy had always been the navigator, and boss, and part-time pimp, and the source of many bruises. At least Manny treated her like… well, like an airhead, but that was okay. Manny was going places, everybody knew that.

She'd straighten him out later.

She drove past the Lunch-N-Lube without recognizing it. When she reached the outskirts of Carnestown she realized she'd gone too far. She swung the truck into a parking lot to turn around. One fun thing about the Chevy was its light ass end. She cranked the wheel tight and slammed the gas pedal. The truck spun in its own length and spewed gravel into a row of cars. The off-duty Deputy Rawlins narrowed his eyes. He stood in the little store flirting with the checkout girl. He heard the gravel tick-tacking into the cars and headed for the door to see which one of the local hotrodders had just earned themselves a negligent driving ticket. He caught a glimpse of the truck as it slung back onto the street and mentally upgraded the ticket to speeding, DUI, and reckless driving, as it looked to be an out-of-towner. He trotted happily towards his patrol car.

Holly knew she was close to the little gas station and the excitement transferred itself to her right foot that held the gas pedal to the floor. Her head rocked forward on the downbeat, a joint smoldered between her lips, and the Army Colt pressed into her back. She saw the Lunch-N-Lube coming up fast and from this direction she recognized it immediately. It looked a little different, but it was definitely her target.

She downshifted and hit the brakes. The front drums locked and the back end slewed. She pumped the brake and turned into the skid, sliding into the other lane on the exhilarating edge of panic when it looked as if she'd caught it too late and would fly off the asphalt. She instinctively turned tighter and a little yelp of fear escaped as the front tires reached the roadside gravel and the rear end started to buck, threatening to catch and roll the truck. The front tires struck a stray patch of pavement and the extra weight of the four-wheel drive assembly gave them just enough traction to grab and jerk the truck around, jolting her hands painfully from the wheel. The truck was now pointing back across the road with the front end on the shoulder and the rear end slashing through the weeds. She wrestled the wheel, gasping from the pain in her sprained wrists, almost regaining control as the rear wheels struck a large rock and the truck slammed onto its side. This caught Holly completely by surprise and drove her head into the top of the cab. The Chevy slid on its side, backwards, slowly rotating and edging back onto the road. The wheels caught and the truck righted itself, banging onto all four wheels, pointed in the right direction, in the right lane, with the engine still running, fifty yards from the station. Holly stared through the cracked windshield at the Lunch-N-Lube, stunned by the experience, letting the truck roll on its own, still in gear, very aware that she had come close to losing it all, and totally unaware that Deputy Sheriff Bill Rawlins followed at high speed less than a mile behind. For his part, he was surprised that he had yet to catch up to her.

Inside the Lunch-n-Lube, DeeDee's eyes ran down the list of items 'to be ordered' and noticed that Leonard had penciled in a ridiculous amount of red licorice. She crossed through his figure and scribbled in a more reasonable number, shaking her head, but unable to suppress a wry smile. If she'd had to pick a vice for the man...

Over the radio she heard a commotion outside. A trashed four-wheel drive rolled in almost to the door. She placed a finger on the paper to mark her place and yelled for Leonard. She went back to her figures, looking up as Holly stepped through the door, her stomach tightening at the sight of the gun rising towards her chest.

A turmoil of thoughts roiled through her mind. *No. I'm through with all that. That was a different life. I don't deserve this... what would Glen do?*

She spun the clipboard like a Frisbee into Holly's face.

Holly had intended to simply shoot DeeDee dead, grab the gold, and leave.

The clipboard struck the bridge of her nose and she flinched with the flash of pain. A shot spasmed from the automatic and went wild into the ceiling. DeeDee dropped to the floor and scrambled for the door.

"Lenny!" DeeDee yelled as she tumbled off the edge of the porch, sprawling in the gravel momentarily before lurching around the corner.

Holly's eyes were watering fiercely from the blow to the nose, but she could see well enough to spot the painted gold nuggets exactly where she remembered them. She grabbed a dirty bucket from the floor and swept the gold from the shelf, grimacing from the pain in her wrists, smart enough to realize that DeeDee's yell meant there were at least two people present, and that she needed to get out fast. She fired a round at the phone, but flinched and missed as her wrist anticipated the pain from the recoil. She dropped the bucket, grasped the gun with both hands and squeezed off two more rounds, thoroughly destroying Leonard's telephone.

Leonard watched through the window in disbelief as his telephone exploded before his eyes. In shock, it popped into his mind that here stood Clem's killer. A cute young girl with spiky hair, holding his bucket and a huge handgun. He watched frozen and numb as she walked out the front door.

She's stealing my bucket, he thought.

He started to shuffle towards the door, not at all sure if that was a good idea, but unable to stop himself. Through the open doorway he saw Rawlins pull in and park behind the Chevy. He saw Holly standing on the porch with the gun held behind her leg. He saw Rawlins step from the car with his sunglasses glinting in the sunlight, ticket book in hand, and with a stern expression on his face.

He saw that expression change to something else when Holly swung the gun from behind her leg and sighted down the barrel. She saw a white flash from the corner of her eye as Dog darted around the side of the building. She flinched and only winged Rawlins, who collapsed like a bag of potatoes. Dog exhaled doggy breath in her face as he landed on her chest and bowled her over. The gun arced through the air. Dog stayed down, but Holly crawled towards her gun, dazed from the impacts with Dog and the ground, but determined. Her fingertips were two feet from her Colt when Leonard planted a heavy boot firmly between her shoulder blades and pinned her to the pavement.

Deputy Rawlin's report emphasized his own heroics and no one argued. His picture looked good in the newspaper. Holly hired a good lawyer and pleaded insanity. She was committed to the mental hospital in Tallahassee. She tried but was not able to escape for almost two years.

The black-painted rocks were dusted off and rearranged on their shelf.

POSTSCRIPT

"The attacks on your Social Security are an obscene travesty of justice. The government made a contract with the American people to provide help after retirement. The primary focus of my work in Congress will be to reverse the government's theft of your future."

- Glen Wilson in a speech addressing the Washington Chapter of the American Association of Retired People.

"Social Security has outlived its usefulness. Who among you believes they will ever see a penny of Social Security money after the government is through raiding and bankrupting the system? Is it right for you to pay and pay with no return? I promise to work in Congress to end this theft of your futures."

- Glen Wilson in a speech addressing a graduating class at the University of Washington.

MUCH LATER

LEONARD

Leonard kneeled before the newspaper dispenser and scratched his head. He tapped the glass and pointed at a picture on the front page. "Dee? Ain't this the guy that stopped in here a while back? Was his name Wilson? And that Doctor, Doctor Zalooka? Remember I was telling you about his show?" He looked over his shoulder. DeeDee was nowhere around.

A Honda station wagon stopped in front of the self service pumps. The kids piled out and stood around Leonard tugging at his overalls and talking all at once. He absently passed out some Red Vines. The father walked over.

"What's the deal with this Gator Petting Zoo?"

Leonard pointed to a sign beside a small doorway. The sign indicated that no one over three and a half feet tall would be allowed to enter.

The man's wife walked over, running her fingers through her wind-blown hair.

"I don't like the looks of this," she said.

"Ain't lost any kids yet," Leonard said.

"Don't let them go," the mother said.

The kids started yelling, disappointed.

"I don't see the harm," the dad said hesitantly.

The kids cheered and ran to the little door, opened it, and walked in. There was a muffled roaring from inside the little room.

The man started toward the door but realized the sound was tinny and obviously recorded. His wife held his arm tightly and looked at Leonard accusingly. Leonard started filling the Honda tank.

After a few minutes the kids ran out the back clutching their rubber alligators. Leonard handed out more Red Vines. The kids hugged him and ran back to the car. DeeDee appeared from around back. She wore a pair of black stretch pants and a loose-fitting cotton top. Her hair, which was growing out, was tied back in a ponytail.

"I guess you were right," Leonard told her as the Honda pulled onto the highway. "Stuffed alligators are better for kids than real ones."

"Of course," she replied. She turned and smoothed her shirt over her distended belly. "Look, I'm getting too fat," she said, "I look like a potato dumpling."

Leonard's mouth was dry and he couldn't speak. She got bigger and more beautiful every day. He turned so she wouldn't see the tears in his eyes.

Leonard handed Dog a Red Vine. Dog stared up at Leonard and concentrated with everything he had.

Milkbone, you idiot. Dogs don't like candy. Dogs like Milkbone. Or dried pig's ears, those are good.

"Here you go, fella."

Dog sighed and gave up. There was no hope for Mister and Missus Idiot. He took the Red Vine around the corner and dropped it on the moldering pile behind the worm tub. He walked back, flopped onto his burlap bed, and took a well-deserved nap.

THE END

www.ingramcontent.com/pod-product-compliance
Lightning Source LLC
Chambersburg PA
CBHW020340180626
46812CB00001B/282